# Brahms's Elegies

Nicole Grimes provides a compellingly fresh perspective on a series of Brahms's elegiac works by bringing together the disciplines of historical musicology, German studies, and cultural history. Her exploration of the expressive potential of *Schicksalslied*, *Nänie*, *Gesang der Parzen*, and the *Vier ernste Gesänge* reveals the philosophical weight of this music. She considers the German tradition of the poetics of loss that extends from the late eighteenth-century texts by Hölderlin, Schiller, and Goethe set by Brahms, and includes other philosophical and poetic works present in his library, to the mid-twentieth-century aesthetics of Adorno, who was preoccupied as much by Brahms as by their shared literary heritage. Her multifaceted focus on endings – the end of tonality, the end of the nineteenth century, and themes of loss in the music – illuminates our understanding of Brahms and lateness and the place of Brahms in the fabric of modernist culture.

Nicole Grimes is Assistant Professor of Music at the University of California, Irvine. She serves on the Editorial Board of *Music Analysis* and is a member of the Board of Directors of the American Brahms Society. Her previous works include *Mendelssohn Perspectives* (2012) and *Rethinking Hanslick: Music, Formalism, and Expression* (2013).

MUSIC IN CONTEXT

*Series editors*

J. P. E. Harper-Scott
*Royal Holloway, University of London*

Julian Rushton
*University of Leeds*

The aim of Music in Context is to illuminate specific musical works, repertoires, or practices in historical, critical, socio-economic, or other contexts; or to illuminate particular cultural and critical contexts in which music operates through the study of specific musical works, repertoires, or practices. A specific musical focus is essential, while avoiding the decontextualization of traditional aesthetics and music analysis. The series title invites engagement with both its main terms; the aim is to challenge notions of what contexts are appropriate or necessary in studies of music, and to extend the conceptual framework of musicology into other disciplines or into new theoretical directions.

*Books in the series*

# Brahms's Elegies

## The Poetics of Loss in Nineteenth-Century German Culture

NICOLE GRIMES

University of California, Irvine

CAMBRIDGE
UNIVERSITY PRESS

# CAMBRIDGE
## UNIVERSITY PRESS

University Printing House, Cambridge CB2 8BS, United Kingdom

One Liberty Plaza, 20th Floor, New York, NY 10006, USA

477 Williamstown Road, Port Melbourne, VIC 3207, Australia

314-321, 3rd Floor, Plot 3, Splendor Forum, Jasola District Centre, New Delhi - 110025, India

103 Penang Road, #05-06/07, Visioncrest Commercial, Singapore 238467

Cambridge University Press is part of the University of Cambridge.

It furthers the University's mission by disseminating knowledge in the pursuit of
education, learning and research at the highest international levels of excellence.

www.cambridge.org
Information on this title: www.cambridge.org/9781108464765
DOI: 10.1017/9781108589758

First published 2019
First paperback edition 2021

*A catalogue record for this publication is available from the British Library*

*Library of Congress Cataloging in Publication data*
Names: Grimes, Nicole, author.
Title: Brahms's Elegies : the poetics of loss in nineteenth-century German culture /
Nicole Grimes.
Description: Cambridge, United Kingdom ; New York, NY : Cambridge University Press,
[2019] | Series: Music in context | Includes bibliographical references and index.
Identifiers: LCCN 2018041957 | ISBN 9781108474498 (alk. paper)
Subjects: LCSH: Brahms, Johannes, 1833–1897 – Criticism and interpretation. |
Vocal music – Germany – 19th century – History and criticism. | Brahms, Johannes,
1833–1897. Schicksalslied. | Brahms, Johannes, 1833–1897. Nänie. | Brahms, Johannes,
1833–1897. Gesang der Parzen. | Brahms, Johannes, 1833–1897. Ernste Gesänge.
Classification: LCC ML410.B8 G68 2019 | DDC 782.0092–dc23
LC record available at https://lccn.loc.gov/2018041957

ISBN  978-1-108-47449-8  Hardback
ISBN  978-1-108-46476-5  Paperback

*For Dad*


*And in memory of my Mum (1946–2006)*

# Contents

# Figures

# Music Examples

# Tables

# Acknowledgements

This book has two homes – Dublin and California. The research for the project 'Brahms and the Fabric of Modernist Culture' was carried out under the auspices of an International Outgoing Marie Curie Fellowship under the 7th Framework Programme of the European Commission. During this fellowship from 2011 to 2014, I had the privilege and joy of working at two music departments, the School of Music at University College Dublin (UCD) and the Department of Music at the University of California, Irvine (UCI). My attachment to each department, however, reaches far beyond this time. Prior to taking up the fellowship, I enjoyed several very happy years working at UCD. Some years after the fellowship ended, I took up a tenure-track post at UCI. Situated in the vastly differing landscapes of the east coast of Ireland and the west coast of America, I found that what characterizes and connects these two departments is an extraordinary warmth and collegiality wherein musicological thought thrives and friendship abides. Colleagues past and present at both universities have been a continuous source of support and intellectual inspiration. At the UCD School of Music, I am especially grateful to Majella Boland, Ciarán Crilly, Melissa Devereux, Siobhán Donovan, Desmond Earley, Anne Hallinan, Jaime Jones, Frank Lawrence, Wolfgang Marx, Alan Street, and Harry White. At the UCD Research Office, I am thankful to Máire Coyle and Gillian Boyle. At the UCD Humanities Institute, my thanks are due to Gerardine Meaney and Valerie Norton. I thank all of my colleagues at the UCI Department of Music, and in particular Amy Bauer, David Brodbeck, Peter Chang, Michael Dessen, Margaret Erel, Stephan Hammel, Margaret Murata, Colleen Reardon, and Nina Scolnik, not only for providing a stimulating and fortifying intellectual environment but also for making California my home away from home. The writing process continued in the years between UCD and UCI, when I took up a number of shorter appointments. I express my gratitude to my colleagues at Royal Holloway, University of London and Keele University.

Throughout this fellowship, I had three extraordinary mentors. David Brodbeck's probing and thoughtful scholarship has been an inspiration to me for many years. With profound insight and the most generous spirit, he has allowed me to benefit from his rich expertise on Brahms's music and its intricate socio-political context. Julian Horton's fervent passion for music analysis, shared through his exemplary mentorship and code of kindness, has inspired and guided this book. His incisive insights on the aesthetic and philosophical issues surrounding Brahms's music leave a marked imprint on these pages. Through the example of his own beautifully conceived writing, and through wisdom generously imparted, Harry White has vitally enriched my thinking on poetry and music. In an age in which the humanities are under siege, his unflinching and uncompromising insistence on the importance of thinking about music as a humanistic inquiry continues to embolden my spirit.

I am immensely grateful for J. P. E. Harper-Scott's enthusiasm for this project from the outset, for his warm encouragement, for the many invigorating conversations on elegies, loss, and idealism, and for his patience and kindness as the book came to fruition. He and Julian Rushton, the editors of the Music in Context Series at Cambridge University Press, worked through every page of this manuscript with an incisive and insightful toothcomb. Their critical refinements have rendered the analyses more penetrating and the prose far more elegant than it might otherwise have been. They have been the most sensitive, supportive, and alert editors. At Cambridge University Press, I express my heartfelt thanks to the commissioning editor, Kate Brett, and to Eilidh Burrett Lisa Sinclair, Lesley Hay, and Mathivathini Mareesan for shepherding the book through publication with efficiency and good cheer. Profound thanks are due to Walter Frisch, who read the entire manuscript and provided perceptive feedback and warm encouragement of my work.

Along the way, I have enjoyed great intellectual camaraderie with friends and colleagues who have shaped my thinking. I thank Dillon Parmer for a Brahmsian friendship of rich and engaging conversations over many years. I am grateful to Mark Evan Bonds for his wise counsel at various stages as the project unfolded, for engrossing discussions, and for his encouragement of my work. I thank Kevin C. Karnes for his energizing positivity and for a number of stimulating conversations, which had an impact on the Nietzsche chapter in particular. For his encouragement of this project from its very earliest stages, and for reading and responding to drafts of chapters, I thank John Michael Cooper. I am grateful to Benjamin Korstvedt for having read and provided astute feedback on Chapter 4. For nourishing me intellectually and with gastronomic delights, I thank David Kasunic, whose warm friendship makes him feel like family here in California. I express my heartfelt thanks to Styra Avins for long discussions on Brahms and her advice on translations. I am grateful to Scott Burnham for sharing his unpublished work on Brahms's fate-related choral compositions, and for engaging in conversation on these works. To Nina Scolnik and Natasha Loges, both of whom possess the enviable combination of being accomplished pianists and sensitive scholars, I thank you for your insights on the words and music in Chapter 2. I am grateful to Benedict Taylor, who shares my fascination with the process of recollection, for his thoughtful engagement with Chapter 1. For advice on Chapter 1, I thank Meredith Lee. To Matthew Werley, thank you for the *Schnaderhüpfeln*! For stimulating my thinking on the material in the book at conferences and elsewhere, I am grateful to Leah Batstone, Lorraine Byrne Bodley, Angela Mace Christian, Kathy Fry, Katy Hamilton, Áine Heneghan, Anne Hyland, David Larkin, Hannah Millington, Roger Parker, Reuben Phillips, Lee Rothfarb, Leonora Saavedra, Emily X. X. Tan, and Aidan Thomson.

The financial support of the Marie Curie Fellowship enabled me to spend extended periods in Vienna and Lübeck between 2012 and 2014, where I undertook research that was of pivotal importance for this book. For access to invaluable archival material in Vienna, I am especially grateful to Professor Otto Biba, Ilse Kosz, Ingrid Leis, and Günther Faimann at the Archive of the Gesellschaft der Musikfreunde. I also thank the staff at the Handschriftensammlung of the Wienbibliothek im Rathaus. For their kindness and generosity during my time in Vienna, I thank Alexander Wilfing and Christoph Landerer. At the Brahms-Institut in Lübeck, I express my gratitude to Wolfgang Sandberger; I am grateful to Stefan Weymar and Andrea Hammes not only for helping me to navigate Brahms's library but also for their advice on deciphering the handwriting of Hermann Levi. For so graciously hosting me during my time in Lübeck, I owe my warmest thanks to Beate Carriere and Tom Carriere. For a publications subvention to offset illustration costs, I am grateful to the Lloyd Hibberd Endowment of the American Musicological Society, funded in part by the National Endowment for the Humanities and the Andrew W. Mellon Foundation.

An earlier version of Chapter 1 first appeared as 'Brahms's Ascending Circle: Hölderlin, *Schicksalslied*, and the Process of Recollection' in *Nineteenth-Century Music Review* (2014). Some of the material from Chapter 5 appeared as 'The Sense of an Ending: Adorno, Brahms, and Music's Return to the Land of Childhood' in *Irish Musical Analysis*, edited by Gareth Cox and Julian Horton (Dublin, Four Courts Press, 2014). I am grateful for the permission to rework this material. Unless otherwise noted, the translations are my own. It would be remiss not to acknowledge, however, with heartfelt thanks, the sage advice I have received from time to time on translation from Styra Avins, Siobhán Donovan, and Wolfgang Marx. Any mistakes or oversights that remain are entirely my own.

Throughout the years during which this book came into realization, I have been sustained and nourished by friends both inside and beyond the academy. To them I owe my lasting gratitude for their treasured friendship and the joy they bring to my life. My warmest and deepest thanks I reserve for my family, my sisters Tamasine, Alison, and Louise, and my parents, Marie Grimes (who lives on in my heart) and William Grimes. Dad, this book is for you, with all my love.

# Introduction

Throughout his life, Brahms was preoccupied with the question of how humanity could come to terms with the harshness of reality and human-kind's ultimate fate – death. During the period when he conducted the Hamburger Frauenchor for several years from 1859, the number of works that he programmed concerning death is notable, including the Bach cantatas *Christ lag in Todesbanden* and *Ich hatte viel Bekümmernis* and Schumann's *Requiem für Mignon*.[1] Brahms set both sacred and secular texts related to death from his earliest published works, including his setting of 'Come Away, Death' from Shakespeare's *Twelfth Night* as the second of the *Vier Gesänge*, Op. 17 and *Begräbnisgesang*, Op. 13 for chorus and orchestra. An anonymous reviewer of Brahms's setting of this old German song on a text by Michael Weisse wrote presciently that his elegiac œuvre 'transfigure[s] earthly sorrow into eternal joy and hope'.[2]

*Ein deutsches Requiem*, Op. 45 (1868) marked the first occasion on which Brahms used sacred texts in an overtly secular fashion. In so doing, what he intended was to provide comfort to the largely secularized audience for whom he wrote. Concerning the premiere of the *Requiem*, Brahms famously posited that 'with regard to the text, I would happily omit "German" and simply put "Human"'.[3] Replacing the 'German' with 'human' not only elevated the work from the particular to the universal.[4] It also indicated the degree to which Brahms was concerned with humanity in this composition. Unlike other Requiem masses that pray for the souls of

---

[1] Dennis Shrock, *Choral Monuments: Studies of Eleven Choral Masterworks* (Oxford: Oxford University Press, 2017), 284.

[2] Anonymous review of *Begräbnisgesang* cited in Kurt Hofmann, 'Brahms the Hamburg Musician 1833–1862', in *The Cambridge Companion to Brahms*, ed. Michael Musgrave (Cambridge: Cambridge University Press, 1999), 3–30 (25).

[3] 'Was den Text betrifft, will ich bekennen, daß ich recht gern auch das "deutsch" fortließe und einfach den "Menschen" setzte.' Johannes Brahms to Karl Reinthaler, 9 October 1867, in *Johannes Brahms im Briefwechsel mit Karl Reinthaler, Max Bruch, Hermann Deiters, Friedr. Heimsoth, Karl Reinecke, Ernst Rudorff, Bernhard und Luise Scholz*, ed. Wilhelm Altmann (Berlin: Deutsche Brahms-Gesellschaft, 1907, repr. Tutzing: Hans Schneider, 1974), 12.

[4] Daniel Beller-McKenna, 'How "deutsch" a Requiem? Absolute Music, Universality, and the Reception of Brahms's *Ein deutsches Requiem*, Op. 45', *19th-Century Music* 22/1 (1998): 3–19 (3).

the dead, this work was to provide comfort and solace for those who mourn, those who continue to live with their loss. It would form a 'consolatory meditation on the common destiny of the living and the dead'.[5] The words of the prophet Isaiah evoked in the fifth movement of the Requiem, 'Ich will euch trösten' ('Thee will I comfort'), elegantly capture what Brahms sought to achieve with this and similar works, that is, to provide spiritual composition through the experience of which his audience would be comforted, elevated, and edified.[6]

In the 1870s and 1880s, Brahms wrote a number of choral works based on the secular texts of a group of humanist writers who were active in Germany at the turn of the nineteenth century: Friedrich Schiller (1759–1805), Johann Wolfgang von Goethe (1749–1832), and Friedrich Hölderlin (1770–1843). These compositions, *Schicksalslied*, Op. 54, *Nänie*, Op. 82, and *Gesang der Parzen*, Op. 89, are at the heart of a group of works that espouse a common aesthetic outlook and which I refer to as 'Brahms's Elegies'. Whereas many of Brahms's instrumental compositions might be described as elegiac, these three one-movement works for choir and orchestra can be distinguished from the larger group on account of the nature of their poetic texts. All three are concerned with the legends of classical antiquity as mediated through turn-of-the-century German Idealist poetry; all three address the gulf that is perceived to exist between the divine and the earthly realms; and all three confront the subject of loss, expressed in a distinctive poetic form in each of these three poems.[7] These works deal with the transience of life and the inevitability of death. Common to each of them is the promise that there is comfort and joy to be found for the living in a stoical acceptance of fate and of death. Such a message was consistent with beliefs about what it means to be truly human in a modern age, that is, to live without the surety of appeal to higher powers.

Also elegiac in its nature is the last work Brahms published in his lifetime, the *Vier ernste Gesänge*, Op. 121 of 1896, a setting of texts from the Luther Bible on the subject of death. Brahms's choice of text consciously avoids any reference to God or to the notion of an afterlife. When viewed together, these choral and vocal works speak to the poetics of loss in

---

[5] Malcolm MacDonald, *Brahms* (New York, NY: Schirmer, 1990), 196.

[6] This English translation is by Michael Musgrave, *Brahms: A German Requiem* (Cambridge: Cambridge University Press, 1996), 17.

[7] Although the *Alto Rhapsody*, Op. 53 is also a one-movement work for choir and orchestra that sets a text by Goethe, it does not fit in this elegiac mode because it does not deal with death and the perceived disjunction between divinity and humankind and it does not deal with classical antiquity.

German culture, addressing themes including nostalgia, loss, and mourning, a thread that runs through German intellectual thought from before these Hellenic humanists up to figures such as Martin Heidegger and Theodor W. Adorno.[8] As is the case with *Ein deutsches Requiem*, these works provide a mechanism with which their audience can contemplate the human condition without relying on religious dogma. The sense of comfort and reconciliation that this aspect of Brahms's output continues to rouse in his audience is amongst the most widely commented upon facets of the reception of his works since the late nineteenth century.

Such consolatory readings of Brahms's Elegies are invariably bound up with reflection upon how each of these works ends. For, in each case, the sense of reconciliation that comes with the close of the composition is at odds with the bleak – at times despairing – poetry that precedes it. Scholars have attempted to account for such anomalous endings by exploring matters as diverse as the suitability of a particular text for musical setting, the incompatibility of such texts with Brahms's music, and tonal and formal ambiguities in Brahms's wider oeuvre.

Rarely, however, has anyone attempted to immerse themselves in the literature upon which Brahms based these works in their quest to account for these apparently anomalous endings. I neither refer here only to the poetic excerpts that Brahms set nor restrict my exploration to the literary works from which these excerpts are taken. Rather, I suggest that in order to fully appreciate the context in which these compositions were created, and to gain an insight into their rich poetic resonance, one must come to terms with the whole literary and philosophical movement that surrounds Brahms's Elegies and the aesthetic sensibility they espouse. This is bound up with the notion of *Bildung*, with its characteristic assimilation of philosophical thought, which applies equally to the individual human life and to the individual work of art.

*Bildung*, often rendered in English as 'formation through culture' is a self-motivated process based on the premise that understanding culture and history leads to a deeper and more profound understanding of the self.[9] The process of *Bildung* leads to well-considered judgements and actions through which one can arrive at truth, knowledge, and understanding. This

---

[8] A very useful source dealing with this aspect of German culture is found in Mary Cosgrove and Anna Richards, eds, *Sadness and Melancholy in German-Language Literature and Culture. Edinburgh German Yearbook* (Rochester, NY: Camden House, 2011).

[9] For a detailed exploration of the concept, see Kristin Gjesdal, 'Bildung', in *The Oxford Handbook of German Philosophy in the Nineteenth Century*, ed. Michael N. Forster and Kristin Gjesdal (Oxford: Oxford University Press, 2015), 695–719, on which the present discussion relies.

critical and reflective notion has its roots in the Enlightenment, with its characteristic emphasis on the formation of the self. The Enlightenment ethos is evident in the emphasis on individual responsibility, a belief in democracy, and an appeal to reflection and independent thought. *Bildung* is a concept that has its roots in philosophy, although its tentacles reach into the humanities at large. It also has a bearing on politics, having been conceived of as an intense reflection on the French Revolution. It embraces the notion of recovering an ideal nature from which humanity has been alienated. The humanist ethos of *Bildung*, as Kristin Gjesdal points out, goes hand in hand with a process of secularization, which in turn involves a new sense of freedom: human nature is not given, but instead it forms itself in an ongoing process of cultivation.[10] In literary studies, as will be shown, *Bildung* is manifest in the *Bildungsroman*, the novel of cultivation, a genre whose finest examples include Goethe's *Wilhelm Meister* (1795–6), and Hölderlin's *Hyperion* (1797–9).

The process of *Bildung* is beset by an essential homesickness or nostalgia that is concerned equally with the individual and with the collective. While it is a psychic process that relates back to the inner emotional life of the individual, it is also a quintessentially German phenomenon that remains intricately bound up with issues of German national identity. Following Kant, Schiller cast the education (*Erziehung*) required for self-formation as aesthetic, seeing the arts as central to the process of *Bildung*, which he considers to be bound up with a mediation between conceptual understanding and the imagination.[11] In this Schillerian sense, which is pivotal for the arguments in the present book, the aesthetic ideal of *Bildung* is intricately linked to the basic three-stage scheme of what Constantin Behler calls aesthetic humanism, a phenomenon that looks back to an earlier ideal unity of human nature and espouses its recovery as the goal of cultivation, morality, and history. This process is further described by Behler as 'nostalgic teleology' because of the manner in which it looks simultaneously to what has been lost in the past and to its future recovery.[12]

This intrinsically temporal concept therefore postulates a metaphor for renewal and a theme of reawakening. Assimilating philosophical thought with cultural, moral, and pedagogical imperatives, *Bildung* has been deeply influential since the turn of the nineteenth century. It is exemplified in the poetry and dramatic works of Goethe (particularly his short epic poem

---

[10] Gjesdal, 'Bildung', 697.     [11] Gjesdal, 'Bildung', 707.

[12] Constantin Behler, *Nostalgic Teleology: Friedrich Schiller and the Schemata of Aesthetic Humanism* (Bern and New York, NY: Peter Lang, 1995).

*Hermann und Dorothea* and the novels *Faust* and *Wilhelm Meister*); in Hölderlin's lyrics, hymns, odes, elegies, and his novel *Hyperion*; and in the philosophical writings of Hegel, particularly his *Phänomenologie des Geistes*. These writings bespeak a peaceful (as opposed to revolutionary) reform in the wake of the French Revolution. They laud the originality and naturalness of this living heritage as ideal qualities for the foundation of humane political and historical action. By way of a heightened sense of historical consciousness, these writers draw attention to the relationship between antiquity and modernity and the possibility of a philosophical vision that mediates both. They enhance cultural understanding of ancient literature and provide a theoretical understanding of their own poetic output by way of envisioning a more beautiful sense of the future. The ideal of humanity and of a society that stems from this aesthetic humanism has continued to shape intellectual and literary thinking from the late eighteenth century to the present. It informs the philosophy and critical theory of a host of figures from Nietzsche to Adorno, Husserl, Heidegger, Gadamer, and Marcuse to such a degree that René Wellek would refer to Schiller's Neoplatonic aesthetics in 1955 as 'the fountain-head of all later German critical theory'.[13]

There is much to be gained by viewing Brahms's Elegies as a group and exploring their shared aesthetic sensibility in the context of this broader cultural phenomenon. The single-movement choral works *Schicksalslied*, *Nänie*, and *Gesang der Parzen* have been thought of as Brahms's practice pieces on the path to the completion of the First and Second Symphonies.[14] Whether or not we can meaningfully understand them as such, they have far more to offer. As a distinctive genre, they allow us to explore the relationship between Brahms's music and the German intellectual tradition beyond the intimate confines of the Lied and to consider how these large-scale works for choir and orchestra confront weighty philosophical and existential issues.

Brahms was an avid reader, deeply engaged with the literature of his own time and that of the past. This is evident from the time of his youth in the notebooks now housed at the Wienbibliothek im Rathaus, *Des jungen Kreislers Schatzkästlein*, in which he recorded excerpts of poetry that were particularly dear to him.[15] The range and richness of Brahms's library

---

[13] René Wellek, *A History of Modern Criticism: 1750–1960. Vol. 1, The Later Eighteenth Century* (New Haven, CT: Yale University Press, 1955), 232.

[14] See, for instance, Walter Frisch, *Brahms: The Four Symphonies* (New Haven, CT and London: Yale University Press, 2003), 32–37.

[15] Johannes Brahms, *The Brahms Notebooks: The Little Treasure Chest of the Young Kreisler*, trans. Agnes Eisenberger (New York, NY: Pendragon Press, 2003).

further testifies to this.[16] His library also reveals an enduring interest in philosophical matters. Along with the volumes of Herder, Schopenhauer, and Nietzsche that he read and annotated were anthologies of philosophy such as Friederike Kempner's, the first of which (1883) contains excerpts of Kant, Locke, Cartesius, Friedrich the Great, Marcus Aurelius, and Rousseau, and the second (1886) includes passages from Plato, Leibniz, Cicero, and Saint-Pierre.[17] Brahms was deeply preoccupied with questions regarding the human condition, fate, and mortality. As Hanns Christian Stekel proposes, he sought out the same difficult questions on death and on the gulf between the divine and the human in his Biblical settings as he did in his secular choral orchestral works in order to 'legitimize' them.[18]

Literary figures often provide a much more complex and nuanced philosophy of the human condition than many of the ideologies and philosophies that dominated the nineteenth century. For instance, in the compositions explored in the first three chapters of this book, we find the philosophical ideologies of Kant and Hegel filtered through the writings of Hölderlin, Goethe, and Schiller. Brahms's choice of texts from the Bible also reflect a philosophical mindset. The texts he chose for the first two of the *Vier ernste Gesänge*, for instance, have frequently been associated with the writings of Schopenhauer.[19] As I argue in Chapter 4, his setting of the text in the last song may well be related to his reading of Nietzsche in the last years of his life. In Brahms's unique treatment of form in all of these pieces, we see the composer grappling with the weight of these philosophical issues in all of the literature he set, and responding to it through musical means.

Upon his death, Brahms bequeathed his personal library to the Gesellschaft der Musikfreunde (with whom he had a long-standing and close relationship from the time he was the Society's Artistic Director from 1872 to 1875) and to a private collection in Hamburg, now housed at the Brahms-Institut, Lübeck. In consulting the books in Brahms's library, one sees that he heavily annotated them, leaving his characteristic *Kratzspuren* (the term Kurt Hofmann has given to the scratches Brahms made with his

---

[16] See Kurt Hofmann, *Die Bibliothek von Johannes Brahms* (Hamburg: Wagner, 1974).

[17] Friederike Kempner, *Auszüge aus den berühmtesten Philosophen von Plato bis auf unsere Zeit in beliebiger Zeit und Reihenfolge* (Berlin: K. Siegismund, 1883–6).

[18] Hanns Christian Stekel, *Sehnsucht und Distanz: Theologische Aspekte in den wortgebundenen religiösen Kompositionen von Johannes Brahms* (Frankfurt am Main, et al.: Peter Lang, 1997), 67.

[19] See Daniel Beller-McKenna, 'Brahms on Schopenhauer: The *Vier ernste Gesänge*, Op. 121, and Late Nineteenth-Century Pessimism', in *Brahms Studies*, ed. David Brodbeck (Lincoln, NE: University of Nebraska Press, 1994), i, 170–90.

fingernails when he found a passage of particular interest),[20] and markings and marginalia. While being cautious of the risk of reading too much into such markings, there is much to be learnt from them if they are judiciously considered together with documentary evidence from Brahms's letters, the recollections and memoirs of those who knew him, and the hermeneutic analysis of the compositions related to this literature. The first four chapters of this book undertake this analytical task.

The conclusion of *Schicksalslied*, as we shall see in Chapter 1, has confounded scholars for two reasons: Brahms's setting of Hölderlin's ostensibly despairing poem ends with an orchestral section that evokes comfort and reconciliation, and the postlude transposes the material of the introduction down to C major, bringing the piece to a close in a key other than its E♭ major opening. Peter Petersen argues that this represents 'a rare instance of a composer not merely placing an arbitrary interpretation on words but explicitly contradicting a poet's statement'.[21] John Daverio and Christopher Reynolds hold similar views, seeing Hölderlin's poem as if divorced from the novel *Hyperion*.[22] Although the poem marks the chronological endpoint of the novella, it is intricately bound up with levels of time, and it serves to engender further events in the novel, a process that is apposite to M. H. Abrams's notion of 'the ascending circle, or spiral'.[23] The recollection of music in an altered key in Brahms's postlude is also apposite to Abrams's notion. Drawing variously on musical and hermeneutic analysis, on evidence from Brahms's personal library, and on newly discovered correspondence from Hermann Levi, I argue that Brahms's 'eccentric path' – like Hölderlin's – leads us away from the original unity of the work in order to restore it in a heightened manner. The postlude prompts reflection and realization on the part of Brahms's listener akin to that of Hölderlin's reader.

Brahms returned, four years after the premiere of Symphony No. 2 in 1877, to the writings of the Weimar Classicists in his settings of *Nänie* (1881) and *Gesang der Parzen* (1882). This was unfinished business for the composer, and our grasp of the richness of his creative process is severely

[20] Hofmann, *Die Bibliothek von Johannes Brahms*.

[21] Peter Petersen, 'Werke für Chor und Orchester', in *Johannes Brahms: Leben und Werke*, ed. Christiane Jacobsen (Wiesbaden: Breitkopf & Härtel, 1983).

[22] John Daverio, 'The "Wechsel der Töne" in Brahms's *Schicksalslied*', *Journal of the American Musicological Society* 46/1 (Spring 1993): 84–113; Christopher Reynolds, 'Brahms Rhapsodizing: The *Alto Rhapsody* and its Expressive Double', *Journal of Musicology* 29/2 (Spring 2012): 191–238.

[23] M. H. Abrams, *Natural Supernaturalism: Tradition and Revolution in Romantic Literature* (New York, NY and London: Norton, 1971).

diminished if we ignore the New Humanist aesthetic that pervades each of these works and the attendant poetic resonance that traverses decades of Brahms's output.

In Chapter 2, *Nänie* is explored in relation to Schiller's aesthetic theory of mourning, while Schiller's poem is considered in relation to matters of form in Brahms's setting. Situating *Nänie* in relation to the Schillerian 'idyll' opens up new perspectives on the intertextual nature of this composition and its frame of allusive reference. It is shown that the allusions in both the poem and the composition are bound up with particular moments in time. Schiller's literary allusions extend to Homer, just as Brahms's musical allusions go beyond self-allusion and extend to Beethoven and Schumann. This composition concerns not only the literary and the musical realms, however, but also the visual realm, a testament to the vital role that visual art played in Brahms's intellectual world as he composed his elegiac choral works in the 1870s and 1880s. In *Nänie*, this artistic element is directly related to the death of the artist Anselm Feuerbach (1829–1880). The visual, the literary, and the musical are intricately interwoven in Brahms's composition, being drawn together by their common German Idealism. *Nänie* is connected to the group of artists known as the *Deutsch-Römer* (German Romans, of whom Feuerbach was a key member), and they, in turn, are related to the new humanism of Schiller, Goethe, and Hölderlin. Brahms brings all three art forms together in *Nänie* in what I argue, with recourse to the theories of Reinhold Brinkmann, is a musical manifestation of a Schillerian 'idyll'. In setting Schiller's elegiac poem to music, Brahms created a lasting connection between composer, artist, and poet, all of whom, to varying degrees, may be understood as heirs to Johann Joachim Winckelmann's (1717–1768) neoclassicism in the literary, visual, and musical realms. Schiller, Feuerbach, and Brahms are further united around their varying relationships to German Idealism, with their focus being predominantly fixed on the reflective conception of ideas (*Begriffe*) rather than perception (*Anschauung*).

Attitudes toward German Idealism changed substantially throughout the nineteenth century. The power of its aesthetic force at the beginning of the century was matched only by the degree to which it then completely disappeared as an aesthetic category at the century's end. After the horrors of the Franco-Prussian war and the Paris Commune (1870–1), Idealism seemed like an implausible utopian project. Within the space of a year, in his elegiac choral output, Brahms could represent both the early and the late stages of this literary concept. Whereas *Nänie* is a paean to musical beauty that espouses the optimistic Idealism of the earlier part of the century, when Brahms turned to composing *Gesang der Parzen* in 1882, his position on musical beauty and his approach to tonality had altered considerably. At this point, Brahms was no longer attempting to seek Schillerian harmony in an ever less harmonious world, but was instead exploring the nature of dissonance, both tonal and existential.

In correspondence with his friend Theodor Billroth in 1882, Brahms explained that he wished to conceal any association with Goethe's *Iphigenie* on the title page of his composition *Gesang der Parzen*, Op. 89. Posterity has been slow to take the composer at his word on this matter, instead associating Op. 89 with Goethe's (and Euripides's) *Iphigenie* setting(s). Scholarship has also discounted the connection Brahms established between the *Parzenlied* and Goethe's Juno Ludovisi, disregarding the fact that the Head of Juno once belonged to a statue just as the poem Brahms set once belonged to Goethe's drama.

Aesthetic contemplation of the *Parzenlied* in and of itself when divorced from Goethe's play reveals this one-movement choral work to recount the tale of the fall of Tantalus in classical mythology, which is analogous to the notion of original sin in the Christian realm. This tale of divine justice and eternal punishment is retold in many of the books in Brahms's library, including Homer, Ovid, Aeschylus, and Sophocles. Due to Brahms's manipulation of formal functions and his vexing of cadential structures, this work, much like Tantalus, steadfastly refuses to allow the listener to 'touch' that which seems to be within their reach, from the sense of consolation the major modality offers in the fifth stanza to the ostensible tonality of the entire piece (D minor). *Gesang der Parzen*, whose 'remarkable harmonies already take it far away from tonality', as Anton Webern insisted, refrains from offering resolution.[24] Instead, this most desolate piece seems to offer only emptiness. Brahms persistently associated *Parzenlied* with the Book of Job, and the juxtaposition of Biblical and mythical tales of divine punishment in relation to this secular choral work provides a broad hermeneutic context for its interpretation. Whereas numerous commentators have understood Feuerbach's depictions of *Iphigenia* to form an artistic analogy to Brahms's *Gesang der Parzen*, owing to their common source material in Goethe's *Iphigenie auf Tauris*,[25] I propose that the beauty, savagery, and indifference with which

---

[24] Anton Webern, *The Path to the New Music*, ed. Willi Reich, trans. Leo Black (Bryn Mawr, PA: Universal Edition, 1975), 46.

[25] The dissonance and despondency that characterize *Gesang der Parzen* is difficult to perceive in these Feuerbach paintings. Instead, Feuerbach's *Iphigenia* settings have an affinity with the ennoblement of mourning found in Brahms's *Nänie*.

Brahms's composition is marked instead finds a kinship with the art of the Italian Renaissance, with which Brahms was deeply preoccupied at the time of writing this piece.

From a formal perspective, these choral works do not sit comfortably in sonata form.[26] As I argue in the chapters that follow, attempts to view these pieces within the closed forms of instrumental music hinder hermeneutic interpretation and limit our understanding of Brahms's subtle sense of form in these pieces. Each composition, however, can be understood to work against the formal processes of sonata form. The fact that a piece is not in sonata form, and does not rigidly follow its procedures, does not mean that we cannot profitably consider it in relation to sonata theory and glean important insights into how its form operates. The methodologies of sonata theory developed by James Hepokoski and Warren Darcy in recent years have explored how form and hermeneutics interact, and how form relates to narrative, drama, and expression.[27] The methodology put forward by Hepokoski, in particular, has allowed insights into formal processes in these single-movement Brahms elegies that might otherwise have remained obscure. These methodologies further enhance our understanding of how poetry and music interact in Brahms's output. These analytical findings, in turn, open up a wider debate on the subject of Brahms's relationship to literature, to philosophy, and to the German intellectual tradition more broadly.

The present book, therefore, is as concerned with Brahms's music as it is with the intellectual tradition upon which the composer drew, for it recognizes how deeply his fate-related compositions are indebted to this cultural heritage and, moreover, how much later strands of this same cultural heritage in the twentieth century are indebted to Brahms. It is the first study to investigate Brahms's place within the rich matrix of aesthetics and modernity that extends from German Idealist thinkers to the Frankfurt School.

Two important figures who appear along that continuum are Nietzsche and Schopenhauer with whom, I suggest in Chapter 4, Brahms engages in the *Vier ernste Gesänge*, Op. 121. In this work, the composer returned in the winter of his life to an intense contemplation of the Luther Bible, which

---

[26] Despite sonata form not being a vocal norm, various authors to whom we turn below consider Brahms's choral pieces through the lens of sonata form, including Margaret Notley and Timothy Jackson.

[27] James Hepokoski, 'Beyond the Sonata Principle', *Journal of the American Musicological Society* 55/1 (2002): 91–154; Hepokoski, 'Back and Forth from *Egmont*: Beethoven, Mozart, and the Non-Resolving Recapitulation', *19th-Century Music* 25/2–3 (2002): 127–54.

he treated in a self-confessed 'godless' manner. Op. 121 has much in common with *Schicksalslied*, *Nänie*, and *Gesang der Parzen* on account of its ending. The last of the four *Serious Songs*, a paean to love, is the only setting of a passage from the New Testament (the first letter of St Paul to the Corinthians). Its rousing and uplifting countenance is at odds with the air of Schopenhauerian pessimism that pervades the first two songs, 'Denn es gehet dem Menschen wie dem Vieh' ('For what happens to the children of man and what happens to the beasts is the same'), 'Ich wandte mich und sahe an' ('Again I saw all the oppressions that are done under the sun'), and the powerful utterance of the third, 'O Tod, wie bitter bist du' ('O death, how bitter is the thought of you').[28]

The 1895 edition of Nietzsche's writings housed at the Brahms Bibliothek at the Archive of the Gesellschaft der Musikfreunde in Vienna has escaped the attention of Brahms scholars.[29] This single volume containing *The Case of Wagner*, *Twilight of the Idols*, *Nietzsche contra Wagner*, *The Antichrist*, and a selection of poetry reveals Brahms's particular interest in Nietzsche's *The Antichrist* (1895). Here Brahms marked several passages not only with his usual *Kratzspuren* and marginalia but also with large exclamation marks. He was particularly drawn to Nietzsche's indictment of German Protestantism as articulated through the philosopher's attack on St Paul and Luther. Nietzsche's charge that Luther had robbed Europe of its last great cultural harvest, and his claim that 'If we never get rid of Christianity, the *Germans* will be to blame', seem to have struck at the heart of Brahms's German patriotism and his cultural Protestantism.

Brahms's late decision to set the first letter of St Paul to the Corinthians obtains great significance in this context. Furthermore, poetic texts included in a sketch for Op. 121, also housed at the Archive of the Gesellschaft der Musikfreunde, reveal the scale of conception he had in mind when composing this work. He engages not only with the German

---

[28] These translations are taken from *Die Bibel/The Holy Bible, Übersetzung nach Martin Luther, Altes und Neues Testament/English Standard Version Containing the Old and New Testament* (Stuttgart: Deutsche Bibelgesellschaft and Wheaton, IL: Crossway, 2009), with the exception of Ecclesiasticus 41:1–4.

[29] This is due to its absence from Kurt Hofmann's 1974 catalogue of Brahms's library, *Die Bibliothek von Johannes Brahms*. I became aware of Brahms's possession of this collected edition through Mark Peters, 'Introduction to, and Catalogue of Brahms's Library', unpublished Master's thesis, University of Pittsburgh (1999), and I am grateful to David Brodbeck for drawing this thesis to my attention. The volume in question is Friedrich Nietzsche, *Der Fall Wagner. Götzen-Dämmerung. Nietzsche contra Wagner. Der Antichrist. Gedichte* (Leipzig: Druck und Verlag von C. G. Naumann, 1895).

musical canon and the Lutheran Bible but also with German literary history and the German philosophical tradition from Schopenhauer to Nietzsche. When considered in this context, the *Vier ernste Gesänge*, with its closing paean to love, may be understood as Brahms's last great cultural harvest and perhaps a response to – or an act of defiance against – Nietzsche's pronouncements.

The quintessentially German nature of these works, with their shared secular humanist outlook, highlights the cultural dissonance that existed in late nineteenth-century Vienna between German Protestantism and Austrian Catholicism. At this time, the social and emotional structures of *Pietas Austriaca* – that is, the relationship of Catholic religious practices and symbols to the House of Habsburg – were still strong. Brahms and his circle of learned liberal friends in Vienna, including Max Kalbeck and Theodor Billroth, were German by birth and Protestant by identification if not by faith. This exploration of the *Vier ernste Gesänge* allows us to better come to terms with the subtle tensions that existed between secular humanism, German bourgeois culture, and Brahms's engagement with Viennese *fin-de-siècle* liberalism and modernism.

Following Brahms's death in 1897, I trace the reception history of Brahms and the persistence of all these ideas to the writings of Theodor W. Adorno. Despite having been born seventy years after Brahms, Adorno in his youth inhabited an intellectual world that, in many respects, resonates strongly with that of Brahms. In his early formative years, Adorno's musical world centred on the canon of German music of the bourgeois era from Bach to Brahms.[30] He was deeply preoccupied with the literary writings of Schiller, Goethe, and Hölderlin, whose works Brahms set in his one-movement choral works, and the philosophical writings that are filtered through these authors.[31] The writings, aesthetics, and philosophical outlook of this Marxist critic are heavily indebted to the poetics of loss in German culture stretching back to the German Idealism that is so important to Brahms's Elegies.

Adorno wrote relatively little on Brahms, yet what he did write is of great significance. In his 1934 essay, 'Brahms aktuell', Adorno argued that Brahms breathed new life into tonal music's late period by considering

---

[30]  See Richard Leppert, 'The Cultural Dialectics of Chamber Music: Adorno and the Visual-Acoustic Imaginary of *Bildung*', in *Brahms in the Home and the Concert Hall*, ed. Katy Hamilton and Natasha Loges (Cambridge: Cambridge University Press, 2014), 346–65.

[31]  See, for instance, Adorno, 'Parataxis: On Hölderlin's Late Poetry', and 'On the Classicism of Goethe's *Iphigenie*', in *Notes to Literature*, trans. Shierry Weber Nicholsen, (New York, NY: Columbia University Press, 1974), ii, 109–49 and 153–70, respectively.

harmonic structure anew as it relates to thematic motivic requirements. This judgement came at a crucial moment following tonality's late phase. Adorno acknowledged that sonata form had changed following the harmonic and expressive innovations of Schumann, but argued that Brahms was the only composer who knew how to work with these changes. 'Brahms aktuell' was written months after Arnold Schoenberg's 1933 radio address on Brahms in Frankfurt (where Adorno lived), the same radio address that was subsequently published in 1947 as 'Brahms the Progressive'.[32]

'Brahms aktuell' privileges the logic of Brahms's music at the expense of its tone. This must be understood against the backdrop of the reception of Brahms's music in Weimar Germany. The popular image of Brahms in the Weimar era, as Michael von der Linn points out, 'was deeply influenced by a belief that the composer had never truly been appreciated'. It was thought that through the neglect of his music something important had been lost to posterity, namely the musical ideals of the *Bildungsbürgertum*, that is, the educated upper-middle classes.[33] These ideals included a respect for tradition, the promotion of the concept of *Bildung*, and the notion that the arts should edify and inspire individuals to lofty goals. These *bürgerlich* ideals were considered to be under threat from a contemporary music that was intricately linked to modernism – that is, to a disenchanted world marked by industrial noise and speed. Modernism, in turn, was associated with degeneracy, as evidenced in the writings of the Hungarian-born physician, novelist, and public intellectual Max Nordau (1849–1923), who exerted a powerful influence on judgements of art at this time. The negative effects of modernity were considered to have 'infected' contemporary artists. Degenerate compositional techniques were characterized by 'an undue emphasis on tone colour and expressive intensity at the expense of traditional priorities such as motivic development and form'. Degenerate music was deemed to be 'overly sensual, narcotic in effect, and sometimes shockingly brutal to the listener's nervous system'.[34]

Weimar-era writers such as Felix Weingartner, Walter Niemann, and Karl Geiringer saw Brahms as an alternative to the musical degeneracy associated with modernity and attempted to reconnect his music with

---

[32] See Thomas McGeary, 'Schoenberg's Brahms Lecture', *Journal of the Arnold Schoenberg Institute* 15/2 (November 1992): 5–99.

[33] Michael von der Linn, 'Themes of Nostalgia and Critique in Weimar-Era Brahms Reception', in *Brahms Studies*, ed. David Brodbeck (Lincoln, NE: University of Nebraska Press, 2001), III, 231–48 (231).

[34] von der Linn, 'Themes of Nostalgia and Critique in Weimar-Era Brahms Reception', 236.

*bürgerlich* ideals.[35] In a similar vein, Heinrich Schenker considered Brahms to be 'the last master of German composition'.[36] Paul Bekker, meanwhile, asserted that 'Brahms is definitely the last of his line, and the more the temporal distance from him grows, the clearer this knowledge becomes'.[37]

Much like his contemporaries, Adorno also attempted to rescue Brahms from the neglect of his music in the 1930s. But he took a decidedly different approach. He was convinced that the *bürgerlich* ideals associated with Brahms were weighed down with their own cultural baggage. In casting Brahms's motivic, thematic work as this music's highly innovative development, Adorno attempted to unburden Brahms's music of its bourgeois weight. Having identified its innovative features, he located their historical significance not in relation to Brahms per se but instead in the manner in which Brahms's developments paved the way toward the 'new music'. In other words, for Adorno, Brahms serves as an integral cog in the wheel of music history as it advanced from Beethoven to Schoenberg.

The Second World War, Adorno's 'terminus of history',[38] brought an end to the faith in *Bildung* that had prevailed since the end of the eighteenth century. Figures such as Adorno and Thomas Mann raised questions regarding why the educational programme of *Bildung* had offered so little resistance to the machinations of the Third Reich and the rise of fascism.[39] It was criticized for inhabiting a lofty realm and for turning its back on reality. Andrew Bowie convincingly argues that similar remarks by Adorno, which seem as if they were rooted in the events of the Second World War, precede the Holocaust, as is also the case with 'Brahms aktuell'.[40] We might consider such utterances either to be prescient or to

---

[35] See Felix Weingartner, *The Symphony Since Beethoven*, trans. Maude Barrows Dutton (Boston, MA: Oliver Ditson, 1904); Walter Niemann, *Brahms* (Berlin: Schuster & Loeffler, 1920); and Karl Geiringer, *Johannes Brahms: Leben und Schaffen eines deutschen Meister* (Vienna: Rudolf M. R. Ohrer, 1935), 307.

[36] Heinrich Schenker, *Beethoven's Ninth Symphony: A Portrayal of Its Musical Content, with Running Commentary on Performance and Literature As Well*, trans. John Rothgeb (New Haven, CT: Yale University Press, 1992), dedication page.

[37] Paul Bekker, *Anbruch* 15 (1933), 57, as cited in Margaret Notley, *Lateness and Brahms: Music and Culture in the Twilight of Viennese Liberalism* (Oxford: Oxford University Press, 2007), 219.

[38] Robert Spencer, 'Lateness and Modernity in Theodor Adorno', in *Late Style and Its Discontents: Essays in Art, Literature, and Music*, ed. Gordon McMullan and Sam Smiles (Oxford: Oxford University Press, 2016), 220–34 (228).

[39] For a discussion of this issue, see Gjesdal, 'Bildung', and Behler, *Nostalgic Teleology*, particularly ch. 2, 'The Hidden Violence of *Bildung*'.

[40] Andrew Bowie, *Music, Philosophy, and Modernity* (Cambridge: Cambridge University Press, 2007), 343. Bowie cites Adorno's essay 'On the Social Situation of Music' (1932) and a 1929 essay on Hanns Eisler's songs *Zeitungsausschnitte* ('Newspaper Cuttings').

reflect the destruction of meaningful experience by the First World War. Despite Adorno's relentless criticism of the tradition of *Bildung* from this point onward, however, he was never entirely willing to abandon it as a philosophical ideal.[41] Nor was he willing to let go of his embrace of the music he associated with that aesthetic ideal. This is closely tied to his 'experience of historical dislocation',[42] a glimpse of which we are afforded in an important passage on Brahms in the unfinished manuscript on Beethoven, also written in 1934, which is coloured by the notion of lateness.[43] Chapter 5 therefore considers both Adorno's pieces on Brahms written in 1934 side by side.

If lateness, or late style, is to be divided into two categories, *Alterstil* or biographical lateness, on the one hand, and *Spätstil*, or historical lateness, on the other, then it is the latter category with which Adorno is concerned and which he conjures up in relation to Brahms.[44] As Robert Spencer contends, 'it is less the artist's age than the age in which the artist lives and creates that intrigues Adorno'.[45] Hence Adorno's preoccupation with a sense of lateness in Brahms's music, the composer's late position at the end of the period of tonal harmony, and his chronological positioning at the end of the nineteenth century. This pervades every aspect of Adorno's view of Brahms, from the general to the particular. In the passage in Adorno's unfinished Beethoven manuscript, it is Brahms's finales that he admires most and, moreover, he is preoccupied with the manner in which Brahms ends these finales. The integrity of these endings, as Adorno sees it, lies in their 'splendid resignation'. For here, he argues, it is 'as if music were returning to the land of childhood'.[46]

Adorno's nostalgic lament for the condition of an earlier age refers to the lost language and lyricism of tonality, the loss operating on a personal level

---

[41]  Behler makes the case that the entire programme is subject to re-examination and reassessment in the wake of the horrors of National Socialism in the twentieth century.

[42]  I borrow the phrase from Spencer, 'Lateness and Modernity in Theodor Adorno', 229.

[43]  Theodor W. Adorno, *Beethoven. Philosophie der Musik: Fragmente und Texte*, ed. Rolf Tiedemann (Berlin: Suhrkamp Verlag, 2004); Adorno, *Beethoven: The Philosophy of Music*, trans. Edmund Jephcott (Cambridge: Polity Press, 1998).

[44]  See Gordon McMullan and Sam Smiles, 'Introduction: Late Style and Its Discontents' in *Late Style and Its Discontents*, ed. McMullan and Smiles, 1–12 (3).

[45]  Spencer, 'Lateness and Modernity in Theodor Adorno', 224.

[46]  Adorno's nostalgic view of Brahms as expressed in *Beethoven* resonates with earlier views of the composer by his contemporaries that recognize a sense of melancholy and nostalgia in his music. For a survey of such views, see Daniel Beller-McKenna, 'The Construction of Nostalgia in Brahms's Late Instrumental Music', in *Spätphase(n)? Johannes Brahms' Werke der 1880er und 1890er Jahren. Internationales musikwissenschaftliches Symposium, Meiningen 2008*, ed. Maren Goltz, Wolfgang Sandberger, and Christiane Wiesenfeldt (Munich: G. Henle Verlag, 2010), 256–67 (257–8).

in that this was a cherished element of Adorno's enchanted upbringing, and on a metaphorical level in that it engages with the aesthetic humanism that runs as a thread through the present book, with its archetypal journey from a paradise lost to one that is regained. The question of how this language has been lost invites an exploration of Brahms's use of tonality in these works, an analysis which opens onto a discussion of aesthetic failure. In Chapter 5, then, hermeneutic analysis and formal analysis join hands once more as a number of the pieces Adorno refers to as 'returning to the land of childhood' are explored in relation to both Adorno's and Hepokoski's respective understandings of the aesthetics of failure. These include the Sonata for Violin and Piano in G Major, Op. 78, the Sonata for Violin and Piano in A Major, Op. 100, and the Piano Trio in C Minor, Op. 101. Viewed in relation to the theory of formal functions, each of these three pieces defies its generic and tonal expectations. The poetics of loss is inscribed into the very fabric of the works not only in the intricate relationships Brahms builds between his Lieder and his instrumental music (Opp. 78 and 100) but also through the manner in which he manipulates formal functions, and vexes generic expectations for how these pieces unfold.

Although the metaphor that governs Adorno's view of Brahms – one that stems from their shared intellectual heritage – resonates on manifold levels with the poetic aspects of Brahms's music, Adorno himself seems to have been unaware of or unwilling to articulate such resonance. For instance, he does not pursue the question of whether Brahms's singular approach to traditional musical form and his capacity to delay, if not to eschew, tonal resolution registers the antagonistic nature of bourgeois society in the late nineteenth century. Whereas he acknowledges the sense of loss in Brahms's music, he is unwilling to dignify its failure in the way that he does with the music of Mahler, for instance. This is perhaps because, despite admiring Brahms's 'splendid resignation', Adorno was less emphatic in his embrace of what he perceived to be the composer's sense of reconciliation. Whatever the reason, this in no way diminishes Adorno's powerful metaphor of Brahms's music returning to the land of childhood which speaks to the aesthetic sensibility common to Brahms's Elegies, to which we have access only if we understand the intricate relationship between Brahms's music, German Idealism, and the notion of *Bildung*.

This book is both interpretive and documentary in its approach, embracing a hermeneutic method and a historicist method, neither of which is mutually exclusive. The hermeneutic method allows me to plumb the great interpretive depths of this repertoire, engaging with Brahms's powerful learnedness, and questioning the degree to which his music courts the cultivation and learning of the listener in terms of the composer's musical, literary, philosophical, and artistic models. The historicist method traces Brahms's indebtedness to an array of composers, literary and philosophical thinkers, and artists. It employs music analysis as a way to explore his engagement with musical forms and with broader hermeneutic contexts. The study embraces music's formalist nature, but it does not accept formalism's hermetic claims as understood by the anti-formalist New Musicology.[47] While I am faithful to the conviction that music is culturally embedded, rather than an object that is remote from its cultural context, I am also faithful to the conviction that it discloses cultural and social aspects of the world through its own forms. For, although literature, poetry, and art are intricately interwoven in the rich hermeneutic tapestry of this music, ultimately, as Brahms confessed to Clara Schumann in 1868, 'it is through my music that I speak' ('in meinen Tönen spreche ich').[48]

---

[47] For an overview of how the New Musicology relates to Brahms studies, see my Introduction to *Rethinking Hanslick: Music, Formalism, and Expression*, ed. Nicole Grimes, Siobhán Donovan, and Wolfgang Marx (Rochester, NY: University of Rochester Press, 2013), 4–5.

[48] Johannes Brahms to Clara Schumann, 5 September 1868, in Clara Schumann and Johannes Brahms, *Briefe aus den Jahren 1853–1896*, I, 595; this translation in *Johannes Brahms: Life and Letters*, selected and annotated by Styra Avins, trans. Josef Eisinger and Styra Avins (Oxford: Oxford University Press, 1997), 366.

# 1 | Brahms's Ascending Circle: Hölderlin and *Schicksalslied*

More you also desired, but every one of us | Love draws earthward, and grief bends you with still greater power; | Yet our arc not for nothing | Brings us back to our starting place.[1]

– Friedrich Hölderlin

Now it seems to me you return cultivated and ripe back to your youth, and will unite the fruit with the blossom. This second youth is the youth of the gods, and immortal, like them.[2]

– Johann Christoph Friedrich von Schiller

Brahms's *Schicksalslied*, Op. 54, a setting of the poem 'Hyperions Schicksalslied' from Hölderlin's *Hyperion*, is one of a number of distinctly elegiac works by Brahms. Although many of his instrumental compositions fit into this broad category, *Schicksalslied*, along with *Nänie*, Op. 82, and *Gesang der Parzen*, Op. 89, can be distinguished from the larger group on account of the nature of their poetic texts. All three compositions are concerned with the legends of classical antiquity as mediated through the turn-of-the-century New Humanism of Goethe, Schiller, and their contemporaries. Furthermore, when viewed as a group, these works speak to the poetics of loss in German culture that runs from before these Hellenic humanists up to figures such as Martin Heidegger and Theodor Adorno.[3]

Brahms's interest in the renaissance of Greco-Roman civilization was not merely a passing intellectual phase. His love for and deep appreciation of the literature of Greek antiquity is evidenced not only by the well-

---

[1] 'Größeres wolltest auch Du, aber die Liefe zwingt | All' uns nieder, das Leid beuget gewaltiger, | Und es kehrt umsonst nicht | Unser Bogen, woher er kommt.' Friedrich Hölderlin, 'Lebenslauf', as translated in Friedrich Hölderlin, *Selected Poems and Fragments*, trans. Michael Hamburger, ed. Jeremy Adler (London: Penguin, 1998), 59–60.

[2] 'Jetzt däucht mir kehren Sie, ausgebildet und reif, zu Ihrer Jugend zurück, und werden dir Frucht mit der Blüthe verbinden. Diese zweite Jugend ist die Jugend der Götter und unsterblich wie diese.' Letter from Schiller to Goethe, 17 January 1797. This translation is taken from *Correspondence between Schiller and Goethe from 1794 to 1805*, trans. George H. Calvert (New York, NY and London: Wiley and Putnam, 1845), I, 220–1.

[3] A very useful, and recent, source dealing with this aspect of German culture is found in Mary Cosgrove and Anna Richards, eds, *Sadness and Melancholy in German-Language Literature and Culture. Edinburgh German Yearbook* (Rochester, NY: Camden House, 2011).

worn copies of the writings of Sophocles, Aeschylus, and Homer in his library,[4] but also by the fact that his friend, the philologist Gustav Wendt, dedicated his 1884 translation of Sophocles to Brahms.[5] The idea of looking back to antiquity that these Hellenic humanists advocated resonates with Brahms's own focus on musical styles of the past as representative of a lost golden age.[6] As is the case with many of Brahms's compositions, however, the form of nostalgia found in these poetic texts also looks toward the future.

Brahms's library testifies to the depth of his involvement with the writings of Hellenic humanism.[7] He shared his profound interest in Schiller and Goethe with those in his circle of cultivated and learned friends in Vienna. His continued interest in the writings of Hölderlin was, however, somewhat more unusual. This Swabian poet, born in Lauffen am Neckar, near Stuttgart, in 1770, was little understood or appreciated in the nineteenth century. Although he was catapulted to fame in the early years of his adult life, in the second half of the nineteenth century he was largely viewed with scholarly scepticism because of the madness that isolated him from society for the last forty years of his life, until his death in 1843.[8] As a result his work was almost entirely forgotten, and his translations of the texts of classical antiquity were regarded as the fruits of madness, until the pioneering efforts of early twentieth-century editors.[9] Brahms is perhaps the only nineteenth-century

[4]  In addition to the 1884 Wendt edition of Sophocles listed in n. 5, Brahms also owned Friedrich Wilhelm Georg Stäger, *Sophokles. Tragödien* in the original and translated by Stäger, 2 vols (Halle: Verlag von Richard Mühlman, 1841) and a number of titles by Aeschylus and Homer. See Kurt Hofmann, *Die Bibliothek von Johannes Brahms* (Hamburg: Wagner, 1974).

[5]  Sophokles, *Tragödien*, trans. Gustav Wendt, 2 vols (Stuttgart: Verlag der J. G. Cotta'schen Buchhandlung, 1884).

[6]  For a discussion of the relationship between Brahms's compositional output and early music, see, for instance, Elaine Kelly, 'An Unexpected Champion of François Couperin: Johannes Brahms and the "Pièces de clavecin"', *Music and Letters* 85/4 (2004): 576–601; Elaine Kelly, 'Evolution versus Authenticity: Johannes Brahms, Robert Franz, and Continuo Practice in the Late-Nineteenth Century', *19th-Century Music* 30/2 (2006): 182–204; William Horne, 'Brahms's Düsseldorf Suite Study and His Intermezzo, Op. 116 No. 2', *Musical Quarterly* 73/2 (1989): 249–83; William Horne, 'Through the Aperture: Brahms Gigues WoO4', *Musical Quarterly* 86/3 (2002): 530–81; and Virginia Hancock, *Brahms's Choral Compositions and His Library of Early Music* (Ann Arbor, MI: UMI Research Press, 1983).

[7]  Most of these books can now be found in the Brahms library at the archive of the Gesellschaft der Musikfreunde in Vienna. For a catalogue of Brahms's library, see Kurt Hofmann, *Die Bibliothek von Johannes Brahms*.

[8]  Michael Hamburger provides a compassionate account of what he refers to as Hölderlin's 'self-alienation' in the Preface to Friedrich Hölderlin, *Friedrich Hölderlin: Poems and Fragments*, 4th edn (London: Anvil Press Poetry, 2004), 14 in particular.

[9]  These include Berthold Litzmann (1896), Wilhelm Böhm (1905), Norbert von Hellingrath (1913–23), and Franz Zimmermann (1914–26). It was in Böhm's edition that many of Hölderlin's theoretical essays and fragments became available for the first time. On the reception

composer to have set Hölderlin, a poet who seems instead to have captured the imagination of many twentieth-century composers and thinkers.[10]

Brahms's interest in Hölderlin predates the composition of *Schicksalslied*. We find Hölderlin in the pages of the notebooks that Brahms compiled in his youth to record quotations he especially liked.[11] Annotations to his 1846 edition of Hölderlin's *Sämmtliche Werke*, and the eventual setting of 'Hyperions Schicksalslied', bear witness to his continued preoccupation with this poet. Although there are no markings on the pages of *Hyperion*, the *Thalia* fragment, or the poem 'Hyperions Schicksalslied' itself, we can learn much from Brahms's annotations to Hölderlin's other poems in this volume.[12] Singled out for attention are 'Die Nacht' (extracted from 'Bread and Wine' in Brahms's 1846 edition), 'Die Heimath' ('Home'), and 'Lebenslauf' ('The Course of Life'), all of which are concerned with the human condition, and more specifically with the dichotomy between nature and civilization, with the cycle of benevolence and loss portrayed through the antithesis between the human and the divine, and with humankind's ultimate destiny.[13]

The nature and extent of Brahms's preoccupation with fate-related texts is immediately evident in Figure 1.1, where his underlining of certain words and, at some points, even particular letters (presumably with an eye to prosody) in Hölderlin's poem 'An die Parzen' ('To the Fates') suggests that he considered setting this to music.[14]

---

history of Hölderlin's writings, see Dieter Henrich, *The Course of Remembrance and Other Essays on Hölderlin* (Stanford, CA: Stanford University Press, 1997), 2. See also Robert Savage, *Hölderlin After the Catastrophe: Heidegger–Adorno–Brecht* (London: Camden House, 2008).

[10] Laura Tunbridge reports that Schumann thought highly of Hölderlin's poetry and even to some extent identified with the poet on account of his psychological condition. He spoke of Hölderlin's mental illness 'with fear and awe'. Although Schumann's original title for *Gesänge der Frühe*, Op. 133 was *An Diotima*, he never set any of Hölderlin's poetry. See Laura Tunbridge, *Schumann's Late Style* (Cambridge: Cambridge University Press, 2007), 137–8.

[11] Brahms cites the last four lines of Hölderlin's 'Sokrates und Alcibiades'. See *The Brahms Notebooks: The Little Treasure Chest of the Young Kreisler*, ed. Carl Krebs, trans. Agnes Eisenberger, annotated by Siegmund Levarie (New York, NY: Pendragon, 2003), 204–5.

[12] Friedrich Hölderlin, *Sämmtliche Werke*, ed. Christoph Theodor Schwab, 2 vols (Stuttgart & Tübingen: J. G. Cotta'scher Verlag, 1846).

[13] Brahms includes references in the poetry of the first volume at the poems 'Die Heimath' and 'Lebenslauf' to a discussion of these poems in the second volume, in a section called 'Hölderlin's Leben' (presumably written by the editor, Christian Theodor Schwab), 265–333 (298).

[14] This translation is taken from Hölderlin, *Friedrich Hölderlin: Poems and Fragments*, trans. Hamburger, 71. I have not underlined Brahms's annotations seen here in the original in the translation as they seem often to relate to matters of alliteration in the German.

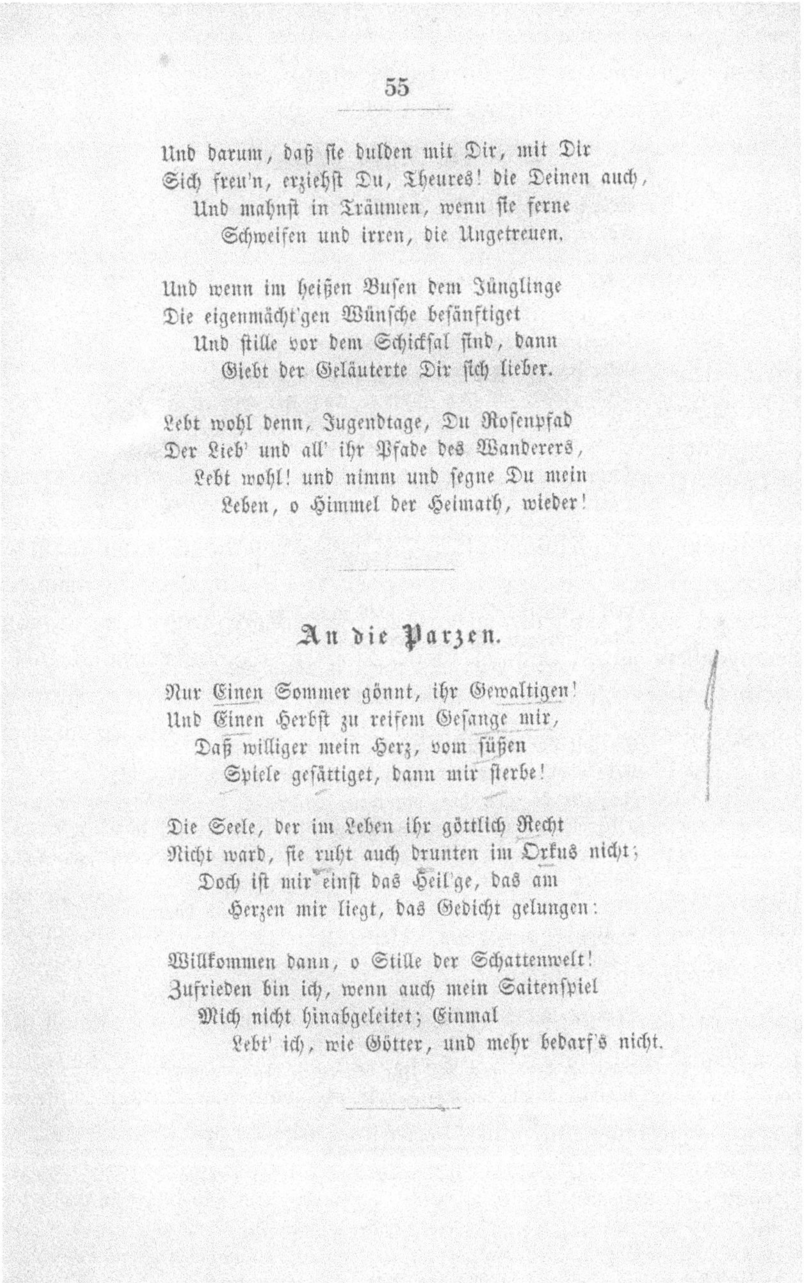

55

Und darum, daß sie dulden mit Dir, mit Dir
Sich freu'n, erziehst Du, Theures! die Deinen auch,
   Und mahnst in Träumen, wenn sie ferne
      Schweifen und irren, die Ungetreuen,

Und wenn im heißen Busen dem Jünglinge
Die eigenmächt'gen Wünsche besänftiget
   Und stille vor dem Schicksal sind, dann
      Giebt der Geläuterte Dir sich lieber.

Lebt wohl denn, Jugendtage, Du Rosenpfad
Der Lieb' und all' ihr Pfade des Wanderers,
   Lebt wohl! und nimm und segne Du mein
      Leben, o Himmel der Heimath, wieder!

### An die Parzen.

Nur Einen Sommer gönnt, ihr Gewaltigen!
Und Einen Herbst zu reifem Gesange mir,
   Daß williger mein Herz, vom süßen
      Spiele gesättiget, dann mir sterbe!

Die Seele, der im Leben ihr göttlich Recht
Nicht ward, sie ruht auch drunten im Orkus nicht;
   Doch ist mir einst das Heil'ge, das am
      Herzen mir liegt, das Gedicht gelungen:

Willkommen dann, o Stille der Schattenwelt!
Zufrieden bin ich, wenn auch mein Saitenspiel
   Mich nicht hinabgeleitet; Einmal
      Lebt' ich, wie Götter, und mehr bedarf's nicht.

**Figure 1.1** A copy of Brahms's annotations to Hölderlin's poem 'An die Parzen' as found in his copy of Friedrich Hölderlin, *Sämmtliche Werke*, ed. Christoph Theodor Schwab (Stuttgart & Tübingen: J. G. Cotta'scher Verlag, 1846), I, 55. This book is housed in the Archive of the Gesellschaft der Musikfreunde in Vienna

**To the Fates**

One summer only grant me, you powerful Fates,
And one more autumn only for mellow song,
    So that more willingly, replete with
        Music's late sweetness, my heart may die then.

The soul in life denied its god-given right
Down there in Orcus also will find no peace;
    But when what's holy, dear to me, the
        Poem's accomplished, my art perfected,

Then welcome, silence, welcome cold world of shades!
I'll be content, though here I must leave my lyre
    And songless travel down; for *once* I
        Lived like the gods, and no more is needed.

This resonates with his ongoing quest throughout the 1870s and 1880s to find suitable texts that deal with the poetics of loss in a secular manner, evidenced most explicitly in his correspondence with Elisabet von Herzogenberg. On a number of occasions in the years around 1880, Brahms expressed his dissatisfaction with his lot as a composer of spiritual music, and explicitly stated his wish to find 'heathen' texts for musical setting. On 14 July 1880, he wrote to Elisabet von Herzogenberg:

I am quite willing to write motets, or anything for chorus (I am heartily sick of everything else!); but won't you try and find me some words? One can't have them made to order unless one begins before good reading has spoilt one. They are not heathen enough for me in the Bible. I have bought the Koran but can find nothing there either.[15]

In August 1882 Brahms asked Herzogenberg, 'shall I never shake off the theologian?' Most likely referring to *Gesang der Parzen*, Op. 89, he wrote that 'I have just finished one which is actually heathenish enough to please me and to have made my music better than usual I hope'.[16]

---

[15] 'Motetten oder überhaupt Chormusik schreibe ich ganz gern (sonst schon überhaupt gar nichts mehr), aber versuchen Sie, ob Sie mir Texte schaffen können. Sie sich fabrizieren lassen, daran muß man sich in jungen Jahren gewöhnen, später ist man durch gute Lektüre zu sehr verwöhnt. In der Bibel ist es mir nicht heidnisch genug, jetzt habe ich mir den Koran gekauft, finde aber auch nichts.' Johannes Brahms to Elisabet von Herzogenberg, 14 July 1880, in Max Kalbeck, ed. *Johannes Brahms im Briefwechsel mit Heinrich und Elisabet von Herzogenberg,* I, 123. English translation in *Johannes Brahms: The Herzogenberg Correspondence,* ed. Max Kalbeck, *trans.* Hannah Byrant (London: Murray, 1909).

[16] Brahms to Elisabet von Herzogenberg, 8 August 1882, in *Johannes Brahms: The Herzogenberg Correspondence,* 174.

The Hölderlin poem that Brahms set – the artistic, structural, and formative heart of *Hyperion* – is written in three stanzas. The first directly addresses the gods, the 'blessed genii' who wander 'above in the light'; the second is a reflection on the condition of the gods, a consideration of the unattainable state of the naïve or the 'aorgic'; and the third is about 'suffering mortals' who – in contrast to the 'heavenly' ones – are 'hurled like water from ledge to ledge, downward for years to the vague abyss':[17]

| | |
|---|---|
| Ihr wandelt droben im Licht | You walk above in the light, |
| Auf weichem Boden, seelige | Weightless tread a soft floor, blessed |
|   Genien! |   genii! |
| Glänzende Götterlüfte | Radiant gods' mild breezes |
| Rühren euch leicht, | Gently play on you |
| Wie die Finger der Künstlerin | As the girl artist's fingers |
| Heilige Saiten | On holy strings. |
| Schicksaallos, wie der schlafende | Fateless the heavenly breathe |
| Säugling, athmen die | Like an unweaned infant |
|   Himmlischen; |   asleep; |
| | |
| Keusch bewahrt | Chastely preserved |
| In bescheidener Knospe, | In modest bud |
| Blühet ewig | For ever their minds |
| Ihnen der Geist, | Are in flower |
| Und die seeligen Augen | And their blissful eyes |
| Blicken in stiller | Eternally tranquil gaze, |
| Ewiger Klarheit. | Eternally clear. |
| | |
| | But we are fated |
| Doch uns ist gegeben | To find no foothold, no rest, |
| Auf keiner Stätte zu ruhn, | And suffering mortals |
| Es schwinden, es fallen | Dwindle and fall |
| Die leidenden Menschen | Headlong from one |
| Blindlings von einer | Hour to the next, |
| Stunde zur andern, | Hurled like water |
| Wie Wasser von Klippe | From ledge to ledge |
| Zu Klippe geworfen, | Downward for years to the vague |
| Jahr lang ins Ungewisse hinab. |   abyss. |

---

[17] The German and the English translation are taken from Michael Hamburger's edition *Friedrich Hölderlin: Poems and Fragments*, 121.

Hölderlin's potent *Götter/Menschen* antithesis is reflected in Brahms's setting, although with altered weight. The work is divided into two halves: the first is bound up with the gods, a setting of stanzas 1 and 2, and the second is concerned with the pitiful lot of humanity, a setting of

**Example 1.1**  Brahms, *Schicksalslied*, bars 94–103, showing the diminished triad at bars 102–3

Example 1.2a  Brahms, *Schicksalslied*, Introduction in E♭ major

**Example 1.2b** Brahms, *Schicksalslied*, Postlude in C major

J. B. 93

stanza 3, which is repeated in full. This cleft between the divine and the human, between youth and maturity, and nature and art, is delineated by the twice-repeated diminished triad at bars 102–3 (Example 1.1).

Brahms's setting is framed by an instrumental prelude and postlude. The former is twenty-eight bars long and tonicizes E♭ major. Its performance direction, 'Langsam und sehnsuchtsvoll' ('slow and full of longing'), is an unusual tempo designation for Brahms. The *Nachspiel* texturally elaborates the same thematic material, but now transposed down a minor third to C major. Moreover, in the postlude, following the articulation of the poem, the performance direction is 'Adagio' (Examples 1.2a and 1.2b). The text–music relationship outlined here has been one of the most contentious aspects of the work's reception.

## 1.1　Troubled Reception of *Schicksalslied*

As though cast in the shadow of its poet's maligned reputation, Brahms's *Schicksalslied* has had a troubled reception from the time of its premiere in Karlsruhe in 1871 to the present. The two principal reasons for this are precisely the points just raised, the first of which is the presence of the *Nachspiel* identified above. This is considered problematic, because Hölderlin's ostensibly despairing poem now ends with a section that is widely regarded as evoking comfort and reconciliation. Secondly, the instrumental postlude transposes the thematic material of the E♭ major introduction down a minor third to C major, thereby creating a progressive tonal scheme.

The largely positive responses to the work's early performances were mitigated by critics seeking to add another dimension to Hölderlin's poem, an imaginary continuation of its contents, in order to make sense of Brahms's setting. Hermann Kretzschmar, for instance, asserted that Brahms 'ethically wishes to imply an entire third part of the work', the interpretation of which required a hermeneutic leap on Kretzschmar's part beyond what is stated either in the poem or in Hölderlin's text. Voices would have been redundant in this *Nachspiel*, he argues, for they have already 'mourned, pleaded, and hoped. But the answer comes in other tones, it comes from above [. . .] The choir sang, "below it is dark", from above the comforting reminder urges perseverance, with the blessed promise: "Above is light."'[18]

Others understood the postlude as a supplement to Hölderlin's poetic message and interpreted the music as conquering or subjugating the words of the poem.[19] Eduard Hanslick pointed to such a discrepancy, interpreting Brahms's setting as conveying something that was beyond the expressive capacity of the poem:

In this hopelessness the poet finishes – but not so the composer. It is an extremely beautiful poetic turn, which reveals to us the whole transfiguring power of music. Brahms returns, after the final words sung by the choir, to the solemn, slow movement of the opening, and dissolves the confused hardship of human life in a long orchestral postlude, in blessed peace. In a touching and generally accessible way, Brahms conveys this train of thought via pure instrumental music, without the addition of a single word. The instrumental music here replenishes and complements the poem, and it articulates that which can no longer be expressed in words.[20]

Meanwhile in Leipzig, the anonymous critic of the *Allgemeine musikalische Zeitung* surmised that 'Such an ending [as Hölderlin's] could seem permissible to a musician. The poetic justice, however, demands resolution and reconciliation. And so enters a bright, comforting *Nachspiel* in C major, which takes the thoughts of the introduction and brings them to a satisfactory conclusion in a small orchestral section of really wonderful

---

[18] 'Was sollen die Menschen, die bis jetzt gesungen haben, hier noch weiter thun. Sie haben geklagt, gefragt und gehofft. Die Antwort aber kommt in anderen Tönen, kommt von oben, himmlische Mächte tragen ihnen im schönen Gesang (es ist der Einleitungssatz des Werkes; jetzt in C dur) das Bild, auf dem das Leben der Seligen geschrieben steht, entgegen. Der Chor sang: "unten ists dunkel", von oben mahnt es tröstend zum Ausharren, mit der seligen Verheissung: "Oben ist Licht"'. Hermann Kretzschmar, 'Neue Werke von J. Brahms', *Musikalisches Wochenblatt* 7 (1874): 95–7; 9 (1874): 107–11 (here at 110).

[19] Horstmann, *Untersuchungen zur Brahms-Rezeption der Jahre 1860–1880* (Berlin: Wagner, 1986), 197.

[20] 'In dieser Trostlosigkeit schließt der Dichter – nicht so der Componist. Es ist eine überaus schöne poetische Wendung, welche uns die ganze verklärende Macht der Tonkunst offenbart, daß Brahms nach den letzten Worten des Chors zu der feierlich langsamen Bewegung des Anfanges zurückkehrt und in einem längeren Orchesternachspiel das wirre Mühsal des Menschenlebens in seligen Frieden auflöst. In ergreifender, allen verständlicher Weise vollzieht Brahms diesen Gedankengang durch reine Instrumental-Musik, ohne Hinzufügung eines einzigen Wortes. Die Instrumental-Musik tritt also hier ergänzend und vollendend hinzu und spricht aus, was sich in Worte nicht mehr fassen läßt.' Eduard Hanslick, 'Brahms *Triumphlied* und *Schicksalslied*", in *Concerte, Componisten und Virtuosen der letzten fünfzehn Jahre, 1870–1885: Kritiken* (Berlin: Allgemeiner Verein für Deutsche Literatur, 1886), 51–4 (53).

harmonic and instrumental effect.'[21] None of these critics, however, countenanced the notion that Brahms's setting was faithful to the broader context of Hölderlin's novel in which this poem plays a central role, as we will see below.

Such divisive views persist in more recent commentary, which charge Brahms with either fundamentally misunderstanding or consciously contradicting Hölderlin's poetic message. Michael Musgrave argues that the text 'posed a problem for Brahms in ending in despair, with mankind plunged "headlong into the abyss", thus denying him the opportunity, always exploited in the texts of his own selection, for ending with consolation, with a hope of some kind'.[22] Malcolm MacDonald is convinced that Brahms has been faithful to the despondent nature of the ending of Hölderlin's poem. He finds 'the "hopeless longing" aroused in the postlude' to underscore 'the impassability of the divine/human cleft in Hölderlin's poem. Brahms's ultimate decision to close without recourse to words thus reinforces the conviction that verbal recall would create only a false sense of comfort.'[23]

Similarly, James Webster notes that 'despite Brahms's love for the poem', it lacked 'some hope of consolation', with the result that Brahms's setting 'violates no fewer than three fundamental aesthetic principles: fidelity to the sense of the text, tonal coherence, and the assurance of closure by the use of all performers at the end'.[24] Christopher Reynolds adds that whereas 'Brahms ultimately rejected the notion that the choir should repeat the earlier verses at the end', his 'qualms' did not prevent him 'from patching on a seemingly unmotivated reprise of the opening instrumental music, which even without words bewildered listeners struggling to understand what Brahms's conciliatory ending contributed to Hölderlin's despairing text'.[25] Peter Petersen puts it most forcefully by asserting that the postlude is 'a rare instance of a composer not merely placing an

---

[21] Anon., *Allgemeine musikalische Zeitung*, 46 (1871), 730. Hermann Levi suspected this anonymous critic to have been Frau Hofrath Henriette Feuerbach, the stepmother of Ludwig Feuerbach, to whom Brahms's *Nänie*, Op. 82, was dedicated. See the letter from Levi to Brahms, 30 November 1871, in *Johannes Brahms im Briefwechsel mit Hermann Levi, Friedrich Gernsheim, sowie den Familien Hecht und Fellinger* (Tutzing: Hans Schneider, 1974).

[22] See Michael Musgrave, *The Music of Brahms* (Oxford: Clarendon Press, 1985), 88.

[23] See Malcolm MacDonald, *Brahms* (New York, NY: Schirmer, 1990), 203.

[24] James Webster, 'The *Alto Rhapsody*: Psychology, Intertextuality, and Brahms's Artistic Development', in *Brahms Studies*, ed. David Brodbeck (Lincoln, NE: University of Nebraska Press, 2001), III, 19–46 (26).

[25] Christopher Reynolds, 'Brahms Rhapsodizing: The *Alto Rhapsody* and its Expressive Double', *Journal of Musicology* 29/2 (2012): 191–238 (223).

arbitrary interpretation on words but explicitly contradicting a poet's statement'.[26]

This fraught reception can be attributed to two related scholarly tendencies, the first to underestimate the sophistication of Brahms's appreciation of the poetic texts he set, the second for musical commentators to attempt to force Brahms's literary settings into an existing formal scheme.[27] For, unlike much of Brahms's instrumental output that evinces a closed form, this choral work is open-ended and does not meet such formal requirements. The resistance to viewing *Schicksalslied* in this manner is perhaps bound up with how scholars view the poem itself.

Commentators on *Schicksalslied* have regarded the interpolated poem that Brahms set as a self-contained entity, a fragment that is divorced from the broader context of Hölderlin's book. Yet 'Hyperions Schicksalslied', as we shall see, is the poetic nucleus of this epistolary novel. *Hyperion* belongs to the genre of the *Bildungsroman* – that is, the novel of formation. The poem that Brahms set, for reasons that will be elucidated below, is intricately bound up with the spiritual journey embarked upon in the book; the poem encapsulates the manifold contradictions and dissonances of the book and, in bringing these to their peak, clarifies the poetic, moral, and philosophical direction of the journey of hero and reader alike. Moreover, such a reading of this *Bildungsroman* might well have occurred to Brahms on account of his considerable knowledge of, and meaningful engagement with, the poetic and literary writings of Hölderlin and the Weimar Classicists.

This chapter, therefore, looks anew at Brahms's *Schicksalslied* and its ending in the full context of *Hyperion*, the literary and philosophical tradition to which it belonged, and Brahms's literary and intellectual preoccupations at the time of composition. Drawing on musical and

---

[26] 'In Brahms' Hölderlin-Vertonung begegnet uns der seltene Fall, daß ein Komponist einen vorgegebenen Text durch die Musik nicht nur eigenwillig interpretiert, sondern erklärtermaßen in Opposition zur Aussage des Dichters tritt.' Peter Petersen, 'Werke für Chor und Orchester', in *Johannes Brahms: Leben und Werke*, ed. Christiane Jacobsen (Wiesbaden, Breitkopf & Härtel, 1983). This translation by Mary Whittall in sleevenotes for Deutsche Grammophon, 'Johannes Brahms: Werke für Chor und Orchester', Cat. No. 449 651 2, 22–8 (25). Michael Steinberg's commentary on this work is one of few to avoid a reductive reading of the poem. See Steinberg, *Choral Masterworks: A Listener's Guide* (Oxford and New York, NY: Oxford University Press, 2005), 76–81.

[27] Margaret Notley considers similar difficulties with the reception of *Gesang der Parzen*, particularly issues that arise from underestimating the sophistication of Brahms's knowledge of poetic texts. See Notley, 'Ancient Tragedy and Anachronism: Form as Expression in Brahms's *Gesang der Parzen*', in *Expressive Intersections in Brahms: Essays in Analysis and Meaning*, ed. Heather Platt and Peter H. Smith (Bloomington, IN: Indiana University Press, 2012), 111–43.

hermeneutic analysis of *Schicksalslied*, on post-Kantian philosophy, on Brahms's annotations of pertinent books, and on literary theory, I dispute the notion that Brahms's setting is at odds with Hölderlin's poetic message. Rather, I make the case that precisely because of the tonal trajectory of its ending, amongst other features, we can meaningfully consider this work to assume the characteristically Romantic shape of the spiral. Consequently, Brahms's *Schicksalslied* can be understood as a musical manifestation of the notion of *Bildung* that prompts reflection and realization on the part of Brahms's listener akin to that of Hölderlin's reader. This proposed interpretation of *Schicksalslied* further prompts a reassessment of the extent to which Brahms's intellectual pursuits informed his compositional process.

## 1.2 Schiller, Goethe, and the Renaissance of Classical Antiquity

German Idealist aesthetics – especially in Schiller's formulation, which was to have such a profound impact on Hölderlin – was inspired by a perceived disjunction between imperfect reality and ideal. The imperfect reality refers to modern Germany, at the level of both the individual and society. It concerns the modern condition that has seen mankind as a unified whole fall into a state of fragmentation and opposition. This splintering of primordial unity was brought about with the mechanization of modern man, whereby the individual became increasingly highly developed in one faculty or function at the expense of the whole, at the cost of the *harmonisch gebildeter Mensch* (that is, a person who is well educated through culture). Schiller analyses the condition thus:

Enjoyment was divorced from labour, the means from the end, the effort from the reward. Everlastingly chained to a single little fragment of the Whole, man himself develops into nothing but a fragment; everlastingly in his ear the monotonous sound of the wheel that he turns, he never develops the harmony of his being, and instead of putting a stamp of humanity upon his own nature, he becomes nothing more than the imprint of his occupation or of his specialized knowledge.[28]

---

[28] Friedrich Schiller, *On the Aesthetic Education of Man: In a Series of Letters*, ed., trans., and with an introduction by Elizabeth M. Wilkinson and L. A. Willoughby (Oxford: Clarendon Press, 1967). The Sixth Letter discusses the fragmentation of unity, 31–43 (here at 35). M. H. Abrams discusses Schiller's 'diagnosis of the modern malaise'. See M. H. Abrams, *Natural Supernaturalism: Tradition and Revolution in Romantic Literature* (New York, NY and London: Norton, 1971), 198–217.

The ideal, on the other hand, refers to the perceived wholeness that existed prior to this destruction by modern civilization. It refers to a golden age of classical antiquity, when humans were creatures of instinct, unspoiled by reason.[29] A reimagination of the scriptural account of a paradise lost formed the basis for a secular philosophical humanism that would witness the recovery of the lost unity of the mind and spirit of humanity through the development of the intellect and culture. This conceptual design of the past, present, and future of human history was given powerful expression by Hellenic humanists for whom 'the right-angled Biblical pattern of Paradise–Fall–Redemption–Paradise Regained' was assimilated and reimagined in the post-Biblical circular pattern of 'Unity–Multiplicity–Unity Regained', that is, a 'Neoplatonic circular scheme of emanation and return'.[30]

Schiller provided a sophisticated theory of such unity in *On the Aesthetic Education of Man* and *On Naïve and Sentimental in Poetry*. In the latter, he makes a distinction between a naïve character – a childlike nature, a state of innocence, which is all but lost – and a sentimental character – a nature that seeks the naïve, and engages in a reflective, retrospective contemplation. Schiller clarifies that the naïve is unattainable for humanity: it requires a victory of art over nature, which entails both a heightened consciousness and an attempt to reflect on nature. The naïve, therefore, although it yearns for a state of innocence, is not comparable to innocence, because the naïve exists solely in one's awareness of it.

The dialectical thrust of Schiller's distinction is that 'neither the naïve nor the sentimental', taken alone, exhausts the 'ideal of beautiful humanity', which 'can only arise out of the intimate union of both'.[31] In order to heal the (self-)inflicted 'wound' – which has severed the 'inner union of human nature' – one must strive for wholeness.[32] This is to be found in Schiller's concept of the 'aesthetic', that is, a belief in education through art.[33]

---

[29] Friedrich Schiller, *On Naïve and Sentimental in Poetry*, trans. and with an introduction by H. B. Nisbet in *German Aesthetic and Literary Criticism: Winckelmann, Lessing, Hamann, Herder, Schiller, Goethe* (Cambridge: Cambridge University Press, 1985), 211.

[30] M. H. Abrams, 'Rationality and Imagination in Cultural History: A Reply to Wayne Booth', *Critical Inquiry* 2/3 (1976): 447–64 (453).

[31] Schiller, *On Naïve and Sentimental in Poetry*, 224.

[32] Schiller, *On the Aesthetic Education of Man*, trans. Wilkinson and Willoughby, 33.

[33] L. A. Willoughby, 'Schiller on Man's Education to Freedom through Knowledge', in Elizabeth M. Wilkinson and L. A. Willoughby, *Models of Wholeness: Some Attitudes to Language, Art and Life in the Age of Goethe*, ed. Jeremy Adler, Martin Swales, and Ann Weaver (Oxford and Bern, et al.: Peter Lang, 2002), 53–67 (61).

Here Schiller parted ways with the aesthetics of Kant. Although Schiller was indebted to Kant as a critic, both he and Goethe recognized a deficiency in the subjective basis of Kant's aesthetic system. Although convinced that pleasure in beauty must be disinterested, Schiller could not dissociate art from virtue. He and Goethe agreed that Kant's critical philosophy taught much about man but very little about art and beauty.[34] These Weimar Classicists aspired to a state of mind that would transform intellectual into moral virtue.

Thus, a moral imperative underpins the notion of *Bildung* that characterizes the work of these authors. Schiller and Goethe corresponded at length on this topic, which caught Brahms's attention – and captured his imagination – as he highlights and annotates many such passages in his copy of their correspondence. Of particular note is a letter from Schiller to Goethe of January 1797, which we might allow ourselves to imagine Brahms may have read as though it were addressed to him:

> I should wish particularly to know the chronology of your works. It would not surprise me, if, in the developments of your being, a certain necessary course in the nature of man were not traceable. You must have had a certain, not very short, epoch, which I might call your analytic period, wherein through division and separation you struggled toward wholeness; wherein your being was as if it were fallen out with itself and sought to reinstate itself again through Art and Science.
>
> Now it seems to me you return cultivated and ripe back to your youth, and will unite the fruit with the blossom. This second youth is the youth of the gods, and immortal, like them.[35]

The concept of *Bildung* encapsulated in this passage, and the literature it gave rise to, with its characteristic assimilation of philosophical thought, gripped the German artistic imagination throughout the nineteenth and twentieth centuries. At the heart of this philosophical and literary movement is what Constantin Behler terms 'nostalgic teleology' – that is, 'the classical German theory of modernity, in which typically an idealized image of ancient Greece anchors a critique of an alienated present that is to be dialectically overcome in a utopian third stage of

---

[34] Wilkinson and Willoughby, introduction to Schiller's *On the Aesthetic Education of Man*, xxvi.
[35] Letter No. 268 from Schiller to Goethe, 17 January 1797, in Brahms's copy of the *Briefwechsel zwischen Schiller und Goethe in den Jahren 1794 bis 1805*, (Stuttgart and Augsburg: J. G. Cotta'scher Verlag, 1856), I, 267, here translated by Calvert in *Correspondence between Schiller and Goethe*, I, 220–1. Brahms marked the second paragraph in this excerpt given as the second epigraph at the outset of this chapter.

history'.[36] Each of the texts Brahms chose for the works that espouse the poetics of loss engages in one way or another with this 'nostalgic teleology', confronting the dichotomy between the real and the ideal, between nature and a higher spiritual world. In this, he was following closely on Hölderlin's example.

## 1.3    The Caesura in Hölderlin's Theory of Tragedy

Hölderlin's *Hyperion or the Hermit in Greece* – as the full title reads – is written in the spirit of Sophoclean tragedy, a central tenet of which is an acceptance of circumstances endemic to the human condition over which mankind exerts no control. Hölderlin's translations of Sophocles, with which he was preoccupied for many years, profoundly influenced the writing of this novel and the theoretical writings on tragedy to which *Hyperion* is intimately connected.[37] A number of facets of this theory are crucial to understanding the structure and meaning of the novel.

First, central to the struggle of Greek tragedy, according to Hölderlin, are the conflicting drives of what he calls the 'aorgic' and the 'organic'.[38] The 'aorgic' is loosely comparable to Schiller's concept of the naïve. It is the 'condition of highest simplicity'[39] and represents nature prior to human intervention.[40] Also referred to as a 'Greek unicity', the aorgic is unattainable, because humanity's only access to it is through a conscious realization that it is lost.[41] The 'organic' (setting aside any connotations of organic

---

[36]  Constantin Behler, *Nostalgic Teleology: Friedrich Schiller and the Schemata of Aesthetic Humanism* (Bern and New York, NY: Peter Lang, 1995), 2.

[37]  Adler and Louth, introduction to Hölderlin, *Friedrich Hölderlin: Essays and Letters*, ed., trans., and with an introduction by Jeremy Adler and Charlie Louth (London: Penguin, 2009), xxxi.
      On Hölderlin's translations of Sophocles, and his theoretical writings on tragedy, see in particular the following essays in the Adler and Louth edition (page numbers for each of which are provided in parentheses): 'Being Judgement Possibility' (231–2), 'Hermocrates to Cephalus' (233), 'On Different Modes of Poetic Composition' (254–7), 'When the poet is once in command of the spirit . . .' (277–94), 'Notes on the *Oedipus* (317–24), and 'Notes on the *Antigone*' (325–32).

[38]  For a detailed discussion of the aorgic and the organic, see Hölderlin's essay 'Ground of the *Empedocles*', in *Friedrich Hölderlin: Essays and Letters*, 261–70, particularly 261–4. This is the only piece of Hölderlin's theoretical writings in the 1846 edition of the complete works that Brahms owned, where it is found on pages 253–62.

[39]  Elaine P. Miller, *The Vegetative Soul: From Philosophy of Nature to Subjectivity in the Feminine* (Albany, NY: State University of New York Press, 2002), 92.

[40]  'Aorgic' is probably a word of Hölderlin's own devising; see Adler and Louth, commentary on Hölderlin's essay 'Ground of the *Empedocles*' in *Friedrich Hölderlin: Essays and Letters*, 381, n. 46.

[41]  See David Farrell Krell, *The Tragic Absolute: German Idealism and the Languishing of God* (Bloomington, IN: Indiana University Press, 2005), 274–5, n. 16.

compounds or growth) is loosely comparable to Schiller's concept of the sentimental. It is the 'condition of highest development' that humans are capable of giving themselves.[42] It represents the peculiarly human activities of self-action, art, and reflection. Hölderlin considered what he refers to as the 'eccentric orbit of all human life' to run between the two poles of the aorgic and the organic.[43] The path of life for Hölderlin, therefore, entails contemplating the relation between reflection and being, between real and ideal, between art and nature.

In the published prologue to Book 1 of *Hyperion*, Hölderlin gave great emphasis to the notion of a 'resolution of dissonances in a particular character'.[44] Such dissonance, discernible on numerous levels in the novel, is most apparent in the struggles and hardships that face the protagonist (amongst them suffering and death), the antithesis between the divine and the human, and the tensions between past and present and youth and maturity, here played out in the contrast between modern society and the great heroic age of Greece.

Schiller's influence on the young Hölderlin was matched only by the latter's spiritual and intellectual exchange during the early 1790s with his friends and fellow students at the Tübingen seminary, Hegel and Schelling. Each not only identified with the spirit of the French Revolution but also shared a great deal of circumspection regarding Kant's critical philosophy.[45] The extent of their scholarly exchange and interaction was such that the exact authorship of their collaborative essay 'The Oldest Programme for a System of Idealism' remains unknown.[46]

In his own way, each of these men intuited and recorded a process 'from a world-embedded consciousness to a philosophically reflective one'.[47] This process, as Schelling explicates it, consists in the clarification 'of that which is utterly independent of our freedom, the presentation of an objective world which indeed restricts our freedom, through a process in which the self sees itself develop, through a necessary, but

---

[42] Miller, *The Vegetative Soul*, 92.     [43] Hölderlin, 'The Ground of *Empedocles*', 261–4.

[44] 'Die Auflösung der Dissonanzen in einem gewissen Karakter', in Friedrich Hölderlin, *Hyperion or The Hermit in Greece*, trans. Willard R. Trask (New York, NY: Frederick Ungar Publishing Co., 1965), 171.

[45] The spirit of the French Revolution was celebrated in the 'Liberty Tree' that the three planted in the market square in Tübingen on 14 July 1793.

[46] This essay is translated by Adler and Louth in *Friedrich Hölderlin: Essays and Letters*, 341–2.

[47] Michael Vater, introduction to Friedrich Wilhelm Joseph von Schelling, *System of Transcendental Idealism*, trans. Peter Heath with an introduction by Michael Vater (Charlottesville, VA: University Press of Virginia, 1978), xiv.

not consciously observed act of self-positing'.[48] The process to which Schelling refers would later acquire the name 'dialectic' and was to be taken up and perfected in Hegel's *Phenomenology of Spirit*.[49]

Hölderlin channelled the intellectual energy of this philosophical triumvirate into his poetry and literature. The result is the poet's singular thinking regarding beauty. His point of departure is that the great saying of Heraclitus 'εν διαφερον εαυτω (the one differentiated in itself) ... is the very being of Beauty, and before that was found there was no philosophy'.[50] For Hölderlin, beauty is manifest through unity-in-diversity and offers a resolution of difference in aesthetic experience. As the hero proclaims in the novel, 'Poetry [...] is the beginning and end of philosophical knowledge. Like Minerva from the head of Jupiter, philosophy springs from the poetry of an eternal, divine state of being. And so in philosophy, too, the irreconcilable finally converges again in the mysterious spring of poetry'.[51] Aspiring to the same concept of wholeness as Schiller – and anticipating Schopenhauer, Nietzsche, and Heidegger – Hölderlin believed in a dialectical scheme whereby 'division and difference', 'suffering and confusion', are the 'conditions of experiencing unity', and it is precisely in these conditions that 'unity or wholeness manifests itself'.[52]

It does so at the point at which the opposition between the aorgic and the organic reaches its highest peak. Hölderlin calls this the 'caesura', and in his notes on the tragedies of Sophocles he locates this watershed moment in the speeches of Tiresias.[53] He elaborates:

Hence the rhythmic succession of ideas wherein the *transport* manifests itself demands a counter-rhythmic interruption, a pure word, *that which in metrics is called a caesura*, in order to confront the speeding alternation of ideas at its climax, so that not the alternation of the idea, but the idea itself appears.[54]

---

[48] F. W. J. von Schelling, *Sämmtliche Werke*, ed. K. F. A. Schelling (Stuttgart and Augsburg: J. G. Cotta'scher Verlag, 1856–64), x, 97, here translated by Peter Heath in Michael Vater's introduction to Schelling, *System of Transcendental Idealism*, xiv.

[49] Following the halcyon days at the 'Stift' and the later fragmenting of their friendship, Schelling would contend that credit for the discovery of '*the* dialectic' is popularly misplaced. Vater, introduction to Schelling, *System of Transcendental Idealism*, xiii.

[50] Hölderlin, *Hyperion or the Hermit in Greece*, 93.

[51] Hölderlin, *Hyperion or the Hermit in Greece*, 93.

[52] Adler and Louth, introduction to *Friedrich Hölderlin: Essays and Letters*, xvii. For a detailed and considered study of the relationship between Hölderlin, Nietzsche, and Heidegger, see Babette Babich, *Words in Blood, Like Flowers: Philosophy and Poetry, Music and Eros, in Hölderlin, Nietzsche, and Heidegger* (Albany, NY: State University of New York, 2006).

[53] See Hölderlin, 'Notes on the *Oedipus*' and 'Notes on the *Antigone*', in Hölderlin, *Friedrich Hölderlin: Essays and Letters*, 317–32.

[54] Hölderlin, 'Notes on the *Oedipus*', in *Friedrich Hölderlin: Essays and Letters*, 318. The emphasis is in the original.

The caesura is comparable to a catastrophe in the literal sense: it entails a double-movement: the prefix 'kata' refers in Greek to a complete destruction or razing to the ground and the term 'strophe' means change, or an over-turning, thus opening onto a new beginning.[55] It does nothing to change the course of events. Rather, the moment of the caesura is a decidedly prophetic one. By crystalizing the moment of deepest tragedy and conflict, it is the catalyst for a fundamental change of perspective brought about by a piercing moral clarity, and thus marks the point at which humanity, through suffering, becomes wise. This crucial point of reversal or inversion speaks to the idea that 'a poem or a dramatic work turns on a moment of suspension or discontinuity'.[56] This literary device is a constant of Hölderlin's poetics.[57]

## 1.4   Fate and Tragedy in *Hyperion*

*Hyperion* comprises a series of letters written to the recipient Bellarmin, in which the hero records a spiritual journey of 'reflection and realization'. In what has become known as the *Thalia* fragment – published before the novel in 1794 in the journal *Thalia* and outlining the proposed trajectory for the complete work – Hölderlin charted the book as tracing the development of a character from a state of 'highest simplicity' (*höchste Einfalt*) brought about by the mere organization of nature, with no human intervention, to a state of 'highest formation' (*höchste Bildung*), through the organization that humans are capable of giving themselves.[58] The published book proceeds through three successive stages in each of which we become acquainted with one of the hero's three companions. By the end of the novel, Hyperion will have lost all three, and the reader will have shared in the numerous moments of fulfilment that end in his disillusionment or loss. Hyperion's relationships, therefore, involve a repetitive, increasingly intensified experience.

---

[55] On the concept of 'kata-strophé' in Greek theatre, see, for instance, Patrick Dove, *The Catastrophe of Modernity: Tragedy and the Nation in Latin American Literature* (Lewisburg, PA: Bucknell University Press, 2004), 32; and Carsten Meiner and Kristin Veel, eds, *The Cultural Life of Catastrophes and Crisis* (Berlin: de Gruyter, 2012).

[56] Charles Lewis, 'Hölderlin and the Möbius Strip: The One-Sided Surface and the "Wechsel der Töne"', *Oxford German Studies* 38/1 (2009): 45–60 (57).

[57] Adler and Louth, Introduction to *Friedrich Hölderlin: Essays and Letters*, xli.

[58] Hölderlin, 'Fragment von Hyperion' (*Thalia* Fragment), in Hölderlin, *Sämmtliche Werke*, ed. Friedrich Beißner (Stuttgart: Kohlhammer, 1943–85), iii (1957), 181. This fragment is not published in all recent editions of *Hyperion*. However, it is in the 1846 edition of Hölderlin's writings in the Brahms *Bibliothek*, which is undoubtedly the source that Brahms used.

There is, first, his revered mentor Adamas, who represents learning and awakens Hyperion's consciousness from a state of childlike innocence; second, his friend Alabanda, the guardian of his soul, who represents friendship, yet also conflict and dissonance; and third, his beloved Diotima, the ideal of beauty and perfection in the world. Diotima teaches Hyperion humility and shows him the path back to the natural beauty of the world and to the human realm, all of which she does through love.

Most eighteenth-century epistolary novels, from Rousseau's *La nouvelle Héloïse*, are characterized by subjective expression. In *Die Leiden des jungen Werther*, Goethe emphasized this subjectivism by including only letters by Werther himself and the voice of the editor. Hölderlin takes this one step further by making Hyperion his own editor.[59] We learn of this hero's tale through his first-person account to Bellarmin, in which he is both the subject and object of his own discourse in a way that Werther is not, because he always writes out of an immediate situation.[60] As Hyperion narrates his own life, the reader witnesses him coming to recognize patterns and discerning a coherence that was not at first evident to him at the time of his experience.[61] Consequently, the reader of *Hyperion* accompanies the character Hyperion on his spiritual journey and the artist Hölderlin–Hyperion on his artistic journey towards becoming a poet. The paths are fused, and the story of loss and disillusionment is 'recounted in a philosophically resigned but poetically transformative retrospect'.[62]

M. H. Abrams's explication of the Romantic notion of the ascending circle, or spiral, is apposite to the form of this book. *Hyperion* is written as a secular *Bildungsroman* in which the protagonist must earn his return to wholeness by striving incessantly along a circuitous path.[63] This model speaks to the spiral form that many Romantic figures considered to be the shape of all intellection, and in which they ordered their philosophies (for instance, Hegel's *Phenomenology of Spirit*), their histories (for instance, Carlyle's *Past and Present* and Karl Marx's writings on capitalism), and their poetry and fiction (for instance, Wordsworth's *The Prelude* and Goethe's *Wilhelm Meisters Lehrjahre*). Abrams provides a compelling and lucid account of how this Christian experience is intentionally

---

[59] Hölderlin's use of the first person, as Lawrence Ryan notes, represents a significant advance in the treatment of the subject in the novel from Goethe's epistolary novel *Die Leiden des jungen Werther*. See Ryan, 'Einleitung: von terra incognita im Reiche der Poësie', in *Hölderlins 'Hyperion': Exzentrische Bahn und Dichterberuf* (Stuttgart: Kohlhammer, 1965), 1–7(particularly 3–5).

[60] Michael Minden elaborates on this point in *The German Bildungsroman: Incest and Inheritance* (Cambridge: Cambridge University Press, 1997), 105.

[61] Minden, *The German Bildungsroman*, 117.    [62] Minden, *The German Bildungsroman*, 104.

[63] Abrams, *Natural Supernaturalism*, 185.

reconstituted into secular thinking in the works of Goethe, Schiller, Hegel, Hölderlin, Wordsworth, and T. S. Eliot, amongst others:

> The mind of man, whether generic or individual, is represented as disciplined by the suffering which it experiences as it develops through successive stages of division, conflict, and reconciliation, toward the culminating stage at which, all oppositions having been overcome, it will achieve a full and triumphant awareness of its identity, of the significance of its past, and of its accomplished destiny. The course of human life [. . .] is no longer a *Heilsgeschichte* [a story of salvation] but a *Bildungsgeschichte* [a story of cultural formation]; or more precisely, it is a *Heilsgeschichte* translated into the secular mode of a *Bildungsgeschichte*.[64]

The self-education of the mind is also a central trope of the Romantic philosophy of consciousness. The figure of the circuitous journey home-ward, as Abrams formulates it, is developed into a sustained vehicle for Hegel's *Phenomenology of Spirit* (1807), which recounts a spiritual journey from the 'moment' of departure of an alienated self until it finds itself 'at home within itself in its otherness'.[65] The ultimate goal of this spiritual journey is a recognition of the spirit's own identity.[66] This circuitous path is reimagined in *Hyperion*, which the author makes explicitly clear to the reader in the *Thalia* fragment of 1794:

> We all pass through an eccentric path, and there is no other way possible from childhood to consummation [*Vollendung*].
> The blessed unity, Being (in the only sense of that word) is lost to us, and we had to lose it if we were to gain it again by striving and struggle. We tear ourselves loose from the peaceful *en kai pan* of the world, in order to restore it through ourselves. We have fallen out with nature, and what was once one, as we can believe, is now in conflict with itself, and each side alternates between mastery and servitude . . . Hyperion too was divided between these two extremes.[67]

---

[64] Abrams, *Natural Supernaturalism*, 188.

[65] Hegel, *Phänomenologie des Geistes*, ed. Johannes Hoffmeister (Hamburg: Meiner Felix Verlag, 1987), 549, as translated and cited in Abrams, *Natural Supernaturalism*, 192.

[66] Abrams, *Natural Supernaturalism*, 230.

[67] Hölderlin, 'Vorrede' to the 'Vorletzte Fassung', *Sämmtliche Werke*, ed. Beißner, III, 236, translated and cited in Abrams, *Natural Supernaturalism*, 237. Terry Pinkard reports that Hölderlin entered the Greek phrase 'hen kai pan' (the 'one and all') in Hegel's yearbook in 1791 'to indicate their emerging view of a kind of synthesis of Kantianism, Spinozism, and an (idealized) Greek view of the world'. Terry Pinkard, 'Hegel: A Life', in *The Cambridge Companion to Hegel and Nineteenth-Century Philosophy*, ed. Frederick C. Beiser (Cambridge: Cambridge University Press, 2008), 15–51 (21–2). (The disparity in spelling lies in 'hen' being attributed to ancient Greek and 'en' being attributed to modern Greek.)

As we make our way through the novel, privy to the powerfully intimate nature of Hyperion's correspondence, we experience the increasing intensity of his joys and the depths of his grief. Because each stage in the development of the novel at once involves ongoing change and regression as well as growth and progression, *Hyperion* mediates upon identity, time, and memory.[68] This incorporates three temporalities: that of an earlier time to be recollected, the narrated present (the time at which the poet recalls the past – and the poem), and narrative time (when the poet formulates and tells of the multifaceted effect that such recollection has on him). In the course of composing this autobiographical narrative, as Abrams notes, 'Hyperion has recollected, faced up to, and to a degree comprehended his own past'.[69]

Hölderlin breaks the epistolary form only once in the book, to insert the interpolated song accompanied by a lute that Brahms would later set to music as *Schicksalslied*. This occurs in the fourth book at a juncture that marks the lowest ebb in Hyperion's fortunes. His hope in revolution has been dashed; due to his world-weariness, the elderly Alabanda has chosen to end his life by Romantic suicide; and Hyperion will soon learn of the death of his beloved Diotima. It is here that Hyperion recalls the song he had learnt from his revered teacher Adamas during an earlier, immature time and, in his time of loss, narrates it to Bellarmin. The recollection of the interpolated poem occurs in the letter that marks the chronological endpoint, but not the actual ending, of the novel. The poem itself is therefore supratemporal in its intersection of the three temporalities within the novel outlined above: an earlier time, the narrated present, and narrative time.

This poem, then, serves the crucial function of the caesura in Hölderlin's tragedy: it is the expression of catastrophe (*kata-strophé*), epitomizing that term's double meaning of both destruction and renewal. In experiencing the acute division and conflict between his self and his outer world, and suffering utter devastation and deprivation whilst at once feeling elation at his union with the universe, Hyperion reaches the furthest poles of his eccentric orbit. Lawrence Ryan points to the structural significance of the placement of the poem, observing that 'in the context of the novel, this song marks the very depth of suffering which soon turns into a new bliss (*Seligkeit*) [. . .] *Schicksalslied* is thus a turning point in the novel'.[70] From

---

[68] On this point, see Miller, *The Vegetative Soul*, 85.

[69] Abrams, *Natural Supernaturalism*, 243; see also Lawrence Ryan, *Hölderlins 'Hyperion'*, 223.

[70] Ryan, *Hölderlins 'Hyperion'*, 207–8. The translation is my own. Both this book and Lawrence Ryan, *Hölderlins Lehre vom Wechsel der Töne* (Stuttgart: Kohlhammer, 1960), are

here, Hyperion will turn back. Yet he does so self-consciously, aware that his suffering and anguish have afforded him a deeper insight into beauty and humanized nature.

The process of recollection, and the circularity that it entails, is crucial to understanding Hölderlin's novel and to our reading of Brahms's setting of its poetic nucleus, for the depth of despondency and dissonance that is articulated in this song is the agent of its own resolution. To put it more explicitly, the caesura of Hölderlin's *Hyperion* as articulated in this poem contains its own resolution, from which it cannot be separated.

Hölderlin's eccentric path (and perhaps also Brahms's) is both auto-biographical and vocational. The act of writing the novel is an intricate part of the autobiography, and the impulse to write the autobiography is integral to the vocation of the poet. Therefore, 'at the end of the novel Hyperion is beginning to be the poet Hölderlin himself now becomes'.[71] It is in this manner that *Hyperion* epitomizes 'the figure of autobiography redeemed by art'.[72] The passage with which Hölderlin has Hyperion introduce the poem is a testament to his redemption in that it bespeaks a level of maturity and wisdom that the younger Hyperion had not known:

I stayed by the shore and, wearied by the pains of parting, gazed silently at the sea, hour after hour. My spirit told over the sorrowful days of my slowly dying youth and waveringly, like the beautiful dove, flitted over the time to come. I wanted to strengthen myself, I took out my long-forgotten lute to sing a Song of Fate that once in happy, heedless youth I had repeated after my Adamas.[73]

Here Hölderlin inserts the poem. Significantly, the preposition with which the poem concludes – 'hinab' (downward) – 'signifies a direction, not an ending'.[74] This speaks to Hölderlin's understanding of a poem being as a metaphor. For Hölderlin, a poem literally 'carries' something 'across' into

    seminal texts and they continue to be at the forefront of scholarship on *Hyperion* and its relationship to Hölderlin's intellectual thinking.

[71] See both Abrams, *Natural Supernaturalism*, 243, and Minden, *The German Bildungsroman*, 118. John Daverio and Christopher Reynolds are amongst those who have read such biographical meanings into Brahms's *Schicksalslied*. See Daverio, 'The "Wechsel der Töne" in Brahms's *Schicksalslied*', *Journal of the American Musicological Society* 46/1 (1993): 84–113 (93); and Reynolds, 'Brahms Rhapsodizing', particularly 217–21.

[72] Minden, *The German Bildungsroman*, 118.

[73] Hölderlin, *Hyperion or The Hermit in Greece*, 153–4.

[74] As Walter Silz astutely notes in *Hölderlin's* Hyperion: *A Critical Reading* (Philadelphia, PA: University of Pennsylvania Press, 1969), 114.

sensible form.[75] In encapsulating and juxtaposing all of the extremes of this novel, 'Hyperions Schicksalslied' brings to bear the fact that Hölderlin's poetry integrates that which 'seems to lie outside it – the unpoetic – in order to be its "highest form"',[76] for, as he boldly expresses it in his famous 'Verfahrungsweise' essay ('When the Poet is at Once in Command of the Spirit . . .'), at 'this point the spirit is feelable in its infinity'.[77]

Following the poem, Hyperion continues to narrate his recollections to Bellarmin, paying particularly poignant attention to the letters in which Diotima reassured him that 'perfection' [*Vollendung*] is attainable in 'change' as well as in 'continuity'. The letter containing the poem (that is, the chronological endpoint of the novel) ends in a manner that speaks to a resolution of dissonance and an acceptance of suffering and conflict. The caesura results in the ensuing effusive paean to the naïve, which extols the rewards of sentimental reflection:

Ye airs that nourished me in tender childhood, and ye dark laurel woods and ye cliffs by the shore and ye majestic waters that taught my soul to surmise your greatness – and ah! ye monuments of sorrow, where my melancholy began, ye sacred walls with which the heroic cities girdle themselves, and ye ancient gates through which many a beautiful traveller passed, ye temple pillars and thou rubble of the gods! and thou, O Diotima! and ye valleys of my love, and ye brooks that once saw her blessed form, ye trees where she rejoiced, ye springtimes in which she lived, lovely with her flowers, depart not, depart not from me! yet if it must be, ye sweet memories! grow dim ye too and leave me, for man can change nothing and the light of life comes and departs as it will.[78]

The Sophoclean and the dialectical bent of the novel are given further powerful expression in Hyperion's exclamation to Bellarmin, that 'like nightingale voices in the dark, the world's song of life first sounds divinely for us in deep affliction'.[79]

---

[75] Adler and Louth, introduction to *Friedrich Hölderlin: Essays and Letters*, xxxvii. Ian Balfour draws attention to the use of this technique in Hölderlin's poem 'Wie wenn am Feiertage', wherein 'the poem insistently points to something beyond itself, yet it is in principle productive of whatever is beyond it, because it is itself the privileged site of mediation between the gods and the mortals'. Ian Balfour, *The Rhetoric of Romantic Poetry* (Stanford, CA: Stanford University Press, 2002), 180. On this topic, see also Alice A. Kuzniar, *Delayed Endings: Nonclosure in Novalis and Hölderlin* (Athens, GA: University of Georgia Press, 2008).

[76] Adler and Louth, 'Introduction', in *Friedrich Hölderlin: Essays and Letters*, xxxvii.

[77] Hölderlin, 'Über die Verfahrungsweise des poetischen Geistes', translated as 'When the poet is at once in command of the spirit . . .' by Adler and Louth in *Friedrich Hölderlin: Essays and Letters*, 277–94 (285).

[78] Hölderlin, *Hyperion or The Hermit in Greece*, 163.

[79] Hölderlin, *Hyperion or The Hermit in Greece*, 167

**Table 1.1** Summary of Jackson's formal outline of *Schicksalslied*

| Measure | 1–28 | 29–68 | 69–84 | 85–101 | 102–103 | 104–111 | 112–164 | 165–273 | 274–379 | 380–409 |
|---|---|---|---|---|---|---|---|---|---|---|
| Poem | | Stanza 1 | Stanza 2 | | | | Stanza 3 | | | |
| FF | | Exposition | | | | | | Development | Recap | |
| LSF | | First group/A | | B | | | Second group | | Second group | |
| Structural tonality | Eb | | | | Dim. triads | C minor | | | | C major |
| Passing tonality | | Eb → Bb (52) | → Bb | → Eb | | | C minor → G | C minor → V/c → | V/c → ped. on C | |

## 1.5   Form and Tonality in the *Song of Destiny*

Analytical discussion has tended to view *Schicksalslied* within the framework of sonata form. Timothy Jackson, for instance, considers this work to have a 'tragic reversed recapitulation' in which Brahms sacrifices the recapitulation of the first group (Table 1.1). This interpretation is based on formal features but avoids the hermeneutic elements of the piece, including the poetic text. It does not take into account the correspondence between the introduction and the coda that lie outside Jackson's sonata space, cyclic elements that are further bound up with the psychological journey of the piece and its attendant reflection and sense of contemplation. For Jackson, the circularity of this sonata space – which he sees as a metaphor 'for entrapment or flight without escape' – is attributable solely to the reversed sonata.[80] Nonetheless, this thematic material is never brought back in the tonic.

John Daverio analyses Brahms's *Song of Destiny* as a double-sonata form, whereby the first sonata form maps onto the first two verses of Hölderlin's poem, eschewing a development section, while the second sonata form, concerned with Hölderlin's depiction of the pitiful lot of mankind, ostensibly includes all of the formal functions of a sonata (Table 1.2). Daverio does not discuss the lack of a development section in what he deems to be the first of these conjoined sonata forms, nor does he address the lack of cadential structures demarcating the formal functions he outlines.[81] Regarding the text, he restricts his discussion of Brahms's setting to the poem as a self-contained entity divorced from the book. The hermeneutic gap that Daverio attempts to bridge, I propose, is not present if Brahms's composition is considered in relation to the entire novel.[82]

This is precisely because our understanding of the poem is integral to how we understand the piece. By limiting our field of vision to seeing the poem as a self-contained entity and interpreting the piece as a closed form, we severely limit the scope of our hermeneutic reading. This is borne out in

---

[80]  In their extensive study of sonata theory and sonata deformation, Hepokoski and Darcy reject the concept of the reversed recapitulation. If considered as part of the sonata paradigm, *Schicksalslied* is even more highly deformed than the model they reject, on account of the tonal anomalies and lack of resolution. See James Hepokoski and Warren Darcy, *Elements of Sonata Theory: Norms, Types, and Deformations in the Late-Eighteenth-Century Sonata* (Oxford and New York, NY: Oxford University Press, 2006), 383.

[81]  The first of Daverio's sonata forms fits into Hepokoski and Darcy's category of a Type 1 Sonata, that is, a sonata 'lacking a development, which is a "double-rotational" structure – an expositional rotation followed by a recapitulatory rotation'. Hepokoski and Darcy, *Elements of Sonata Theory*, 407.

[82]  Daverio refers to a 'gap that separates verbal utterance from musical elaboration'. See his 'The "Wechsel der Töne"', 91–2.

Daverio's hermeneutic interpretation. Although he goes so far as to acknowledge that the poem is a '*mise en abyme*, an encapsulated summation of the contraries informing the novel as a whole', he does not take the next step, which is to recognize that the purpose of the poem within the novel is to bring about a resolution of dissonance, although Hölderlin's theory of poetics is diagnostic, not prescriptive.[83] Daverio uses it in a prescriptive manner and restricts his discussion to a reading of the poem as a self-contained entity divorced from the book. Hence his conclusion: 'Only with the reflective orchestral *Nachspiel* do we come up against a problem, for here Brahms does overstep the structural bounds of his text. The music [...] modulates, so to speak, out of the fundamental tone of Hölderlin's text, closing as it does with suffering humanity's blind plunge into the abyss.'[84]

Attempts to make *Schicksalslied* fit the sonata mould (or even the double-sonata mould) are not only problematic, but also hinder hermeneutic analysis. An examination of Brahms's Op. 54 in relation to sonata theory shows the piece to be distant from this formal paradigm for two fundamental reasons. First, the dominant is never firmly established in the first half of the piece; second, the material heard on (as opposed to in) the dominant in the first half of the work is never later heard in the tonic. Thus Brahms's *Schicksalslied* does not establish the polarization or opposition that Charles Rosen sees as fundamental to the sonata-form paradigm.[85] Nor does it meet the 'obligation for tonal resolution' that James Hepokoski and Warren Darcy deem to be the defining feature of a sonata, displaying an absence of the mid-expositional closure ('medial caesura' or MC), the point of cadential punctuation that secures the secondary tonality (the 'essential expositional closure' or EEC), and the cadential structure that marks a return to the tonic (the 'essential structural closure' or ESC).[86]

If we think of *Schicksalslied* as a setting of the poetic nucleus of Hölderlin's novel as articulated in this poem, charges of the violation of aesthetic principles and of arbitrary interpretations that contradict the poet's statement no longer stand. A nuanced and sophisticated reading of Hölderlin's poem in its narrative context opens a window onto a more compelling reading of Brahms's composition, particularly given that Brahms was

[83]  Adler and Louth, 'Introduction' to *Friedrich Hölderlin: Essays and Letters*, xxx.
[84]  Daverio, 'The "Wechsel der Töne"', 96.
[85]  See Charles Rosen, *Sonata Forms* (New York, NY and London: Norton, 1988), ch. 8, 'Motif and Function'.
[86]  The terminology provided here in brackets is that of James Hepokoski and Warren Darcy, *Elements of Sonata Theory*, ch. 2. See also 243.

**Table 1.2** Summary of Daverio's formal outline of *Schicksalslied*

| Measure | 1–22 | 23–28 | 29–40 | 41–51 | 52–68 | 69–95 | 96–101 | 102–103 | 104–111 | 112–194 | 194–2–83 | 284–3–79 | 380–409 |
|---|---|---|---|---|---|---|---|---|---|---|---|---|---|
| Poem | | | Stanza 1 | | | Stanza 2 | | | Stanza 3 | | | | |
| Formal function | Intro | Frame | Sonata form I | | | | Frame | Axis | Sonata form II | | | | Coda |
| LSF | | | Expo/A | TR | B | Recap | | | | Expo | Dev | Recap | |
| Tonality | E♭ | | | | | B♭ → E♭ | | Dim. triads | C minor | | | | C major |

For all of the tables, the following abbreviations apply: FF = formal function; LSF = large-scale function; Expo = exposition; Dev = development; Recap = recapitulation; after William Caplin, I:PAC is a perfect authentic cadence in the tonic. Where cadences are indicated, they occur at the end of the given span of measures.

conversant with the spiritual journey of the *Bildungsroman* and was evidently quite taken with the philosophy of consciousness in its literary guise.[87]

By way of a new interpretation of this work, I propose that Brahms's *Schicksalslied* evinces a hybrid form singularly placed to accommodate its directional tonality: a large binary structure with an introduction-and-coda frame. Table 1.3 summarizes these findings. The introduction and the coda serve framing functions within Brahms's setting. As such, they are not designated with letters or numbers by which to denote their formal sections and subsections, because they stand outside the binary form, occupying what Hepokoski and Darcy refer to as 'parageneric space', that which lies outside of the generic form.[88]

At a cursory level, this binary form seems to provide a musical corollary of the potent *Götter/Menschen* antithesis of Hölderlin's novel. The A section can profitably be conceived of as a setting of the first and second verses of the poem. Brahms's A1 music has a close affinity to Hölderlin's concept of the aorgic – an unattainable state of innocence. Following the establishment of the tonic at bar 39, the optimistic mediant rise at bar 41 reflects Hölderlin's mention of the 'mild breezes' of the 'radiant gods' that 'gently play on you'. This is shortly followed by a further mediant rise to B♭ at bar 52. The dominant is never firmly established here, however (as is shown in the structural tonality, passing tonality, and cadential structure rows of Table 1.3). A return to the realm of the tonic is implied in the A2 material beginning at bar 69, which contemplates the heavenly life of the gods, before the B section addresses the human condition, the 'organic'. It is in this latter section, as we shall see below, that the music is at its most dissonant, perhaps expressive of all the division and conflict experienced in the eccentric orbit of human life. Encapsulating this binary opposition is the frame of the introduction and orchestral postlude, a framework that gives musical expression to the process of recollection fundamental to the genre of the *Bildungsroman*.

Although shifting tonality was nothing new by 1871, the tonal design of *Schicksalslied*, with its directional tonality, is highly innovative in Brahms's œuvre. A late nineteenth-century trajectory from E♭ major to

---

[87] Evidence for this is found not only in Brahms's sensitive musical setting of Hölderlin's *Hyperion* and his appropriation of Goethe's *Die Leiden des jungen Werther* (in the Piano Quartet No. 3 in C Minor, Op. 60), but also in many of the annotations he made to the Goethe–Schiller correspondence, as noted throughout this chapter.

[88] See James Hepokoski and Warren Darcy, *Elements of Sonata Theory*, ch. 13.

**Table 1.3** Formal outline of *Schicksalslied*

| Measure | 1–22 | 23–28 | 29–68 | 69–84 | 85–96 | 96–101 | 102–103 | 104–111 | 112–193 | 194–273 | 274–379 | 380–402 | 403–409 |
|---|---|---|---|---|---|---|---|---|---|---|---|---|---|
| Poem | | | Stanza 1 | Stanza 2 | | | | | Stanza 3 | | | | |
| Tempo | Langsam und sehnsuchtsvoll | | | | | | | Allegro | | | | Adagio | |
| Structural tonality | E♭ | | | | | | | C minor | | | | C major | |
| Passing tonality | | | | B♭ → E♭ | | | | C minor | → V/V/C minor | C minor → | V/C minor → | | |
| | | | | (V:IAC at 62) | | | | | | V/C minor → | Pedal on C | | |
| Form | Introduction (Cyclic form) | | Binary form | | | | | | | | | Coda (Cyclic form) | |
| | | | A | | | | | B | | | | | |
| | | | A1 | | A2 | | | B1 | | B2 | B1 | | |
| Cadential structure | ⇒ I:PAC | Post-cadential | ⇒ I:PAC | | ⇒ I:PAC | Post-cadential | | | | | | ⇒ I:PAC | Post-cadential |

After Williams Caplin, I:PAC indicates a perfect authentic cadence in the tonic. All cadences occur at the end of the given span of bars.

C minor within this binary structure will elicit few remarks; it is the fact that Brahms framed this structure with the correspondence yet simultaneous alienation of the introduction and coda (by turns E♭ major and C major) that marks this work apart and vexes Heinrich Schenker's theory of monotonality.[89] For the implied symmetry of the thematic recollection is not mirrored in the tonal plan. An exploration of the significance each of these tonalities held for Brahms will give a further dimension to this analysis.

I am inclined, with Michael C. Tusa, to dismiss scepticism at 'prior associations of key with character', instead thinking of such associations as 'part of the background of expectations, conventions, traditions, and individual works that informed the creation and reception of new works in the nineteenth century', even if only within the œuvre of a single composer.[90] The E♭ major in which *Schicksalslied* begins is a key Brahms had used on only three occasions in his compositional output before Op. 54. Each of these works is elegiac in nature. The Variations in E♭ on a Theme by Schumann (a theme that Schumann composed shortly before his suicide attempt in February 1854) end with a ceremonial funeral march;[91] the Trio for Piano, Violin and Horn, Op. 40 has as its second movement an elegy on the death of Brahms's mother in the tonic minor, whilst the whole work was written in her memory;[92] and the

---

[89] A possible model for the tonal trajectory of Brahms's *Schicksalslied* is Schumann's *Requiem für Mignon*, Op. 98b. For a cogent exploration of the unique tonal design of Schumann's *Requiem*, see Julian Horton, 'Schumann's *Requiem für Mignon* and the Concept of Music as Literature', in *Goethe: Musical Poet, Musical Catalyst*, ed. Lorraine Byrne (Dublin: Carysfort Press, 2004), 242–71. Regarding the issue of directional tonality, see also Kevin Korsyn, 'Directional Tonality and Intertextuality: Brahms's Quintet Op. 88 and Chopin's Ballade Op. 38', in *The Second Practice of Nineteenth-Century Tonality*, ed. William Kindermann and Harald Krebs (Lincoln, NE and London: University of Nebraska Press, 1996), 45–86; and Harald Krebs, 'Alternatives to Monotonality in Early Nineteenth-Century Music', *Journal of Music Theory* 25/1 (1981): 1–16.

[90] Michael C. Tusa, ' Beethoven's "C-Minor Mood": Some Thoughts on the Structural Implications of Key Choice', in *Beethoven Forum II*, ed. Lewis Lockwood and James Webster (Lincoln, NE and London: University of Nebraska Press, 1993), 1–27.

[91] Schumann's original composition was first published in 1939 (with the theme having been brought out by Brahms in 1893 as the final entry in the Collected Edition of Schumann's works). Brahms's library, however, contained 'an old copy of Schumann's Piano Variations in E♭ Major, the famous "last work", on which the composer had been working shortly before his suicide attempt in February 1854'. See Karl Geiringer, *On Brahms and His Circle*, rev. and enlarged by George Bozarth (Sterling Heights, MI: Sterling Heights Press, 2006), 16.

[92] Kalbeck was the first to put forward this interpretation of Op. 40 as being associated with the death of Brahms's mother and as being associated with memories of the composer's youth. Peter Jost takes issue with Kalbeck's reading, which, Jost asserts, relies too heavily on biographical issues and not enough on musical analysis. See Peter Jost, 'Klang, Harmonik, und Form, in Brahms' Horntrio, Op. 40', in *Intentionaler Brahms-Kongress Gmunden 1997: Kongreßbericht*, ed. Ingrid Fuchs (Tutzing: Hans Schneider, 2001), 59–71.

fourth movement of *Ein deutsches Requiem*, Op. 45, 'Wie lieblich sind deine Wohnungen', shares the key of E♭ major. Although it was composed later than *Schicksalslied*, the Violin Sonata No. 1 in G Major, Op. 78, with its central Adagio in E♭ major, is also suggestive in this context. The closing theme from the opening Allegro reappears in the slow second movement, expressively transformed into a funeral march that Brahms explicitly associated with the death of Felix Schumann.[93] We can therefore designate E♭ major as a tonality to which Brahms repeatedly turned in works associated with loss and bereavement, with each of these works being decidedly wistful and melancholic in nature.[94]

These E♭ major pieces, moreover, tend to transition out of the realm of mourning. The *Requiem* provides a particularly interesting case as, before Brahms added the fifth movement, 'Ihr habt nun Traurigkeit', the tonal trajectory from the fourth movement to the next (now sixth), 'Denn wir haben hie keine bleibende Statt', would have corresponded to that of *Schicksalslied*.[95] The E♭ that celebrates the dwelling place of the gods would have given way to the tumultuous C minor that gives voice to the woes of humanity, ultimately ending with the triumph of victory over death in C major. In the Violin Sonata, the theme expressively transformed as the funeral march in the second movement reappears one last time in the G minor finale, a movement that ends in the major.[96] All four works inhabit the same emotional sphere that prompted Adolf Schubring rather candidly to describe Brahms's Schumann

---

[93] See Michael Struck, 'Revisionsbedürftig: Zur gedruckten Korrespondenz von Johannes Brahms und Clara Schumann: Auswirkungen irrtümlicher oder lückenhafter Überlieferung auf werkgenetische Bestimmungen (mit einem unausgewerteten Brahms-Brief zur Violinsonate Op. 78)', *Die Musikforschung* 41/3 (1988): 235–41, translated in part by Ben Kohn and George Bozarth in 'New Evidence of the Genesis of Brahms's G Major Violin Sonata, Op. 78', *American Brahms Society Newsletter* 9/1 (1991): 5–6. On the relationship between music and poetry in Brahms's Op. 78, see Dillon R. Parmer, 'Brahms: Song Quotation, and Secret Programs', *19th-Century Music* 19/2 (1995): 161–90. For a consideration of the intricate relationship between Schumann's late Violin Concerto in D Minor (1853), Brahms's Variations in E♭ on a Theme by Schumann, and Brahms's Op. 78, see David Brodbeck, 'Medium and Meaning: New Aspects of the Chamber Music', *The Cambridge Companion to Brahms*, ed. Michael Musgrave (Cambridge: Cambridge University Press, 1999), 98–132 (especially 117–18).

[94] Of course, there are various keys that are associated with bereavement and loss in Brahms's output. I do not suggest that E♭ major is the sole key associated with this realm. Rather, I am highlighting an aesthetic quality that these E♭ major works have in common.

[95] This aspect of Brahms's *Ein deutsches Requiem* is discussed in James Webster, 'The *Alto Rhapsody*', and Christopher Reynolds, 'Rhapsodizing Brahms', 96–7.

[96] For a more in-depth discussion of this theme and its various manifestations in Brahms's Op. 78, see Chapter 5.

Variations, Op. 23 in terms of a 'determined pulling oneself together, shared with outbreaks of quivering pain'.[97]

The two diminished triads heard in the winds and horns that directly precede Brahms's setting of Hölderlin's third verse (as already shown in Example 1.1), and delineate the cleft between the human and the divine could go either to E♭ major or C minor. Brahms's choice of the latter key for this turbulent setting of the third verse afforded him the opportunity to employ a long-range tonal trajectory from C minor to C major over the second half of the work. This progression is redolent of the characteristically expressive course from sorrow or struggle to comfort and reconciliation that was common currency in the nineteenth century. Nonetheless, from Haydn's time on, as James Webster argues, resolutions into C major constituted the most important class of this topos, for this progression 'retained a special character, especially in conjunction with notions of the sublime and of transcendence'.[98] Webster categorizes the most meaningful C minor to major progressions since Haydn that must have been highly significant to Brahms including, but not limited to, Haydn's 'Chaos' from *The Creation*, Beethoven's Fifth Symphony, the finale of Schubert's String Quintet, and Act I of Wagner's *Tristan und Isolde*.[99] In Brahms's own output, we find this progression not only in *Schicksalslied*, but also in the *Alto Rhapsody*, the Symphony No. 1, and the sixth movement of *Ein deutsches Requiem*.

Brahms's extraordinary and intricately linked choices of form and tonality – from the elegiac E♭ major, via the turbulent C minor, to the transcendent C major – resonate closely with three characteristics that are central to Hölderlin's *Hyperion*, each of which has far-reaching implications for this musical setting: first, the three temporalities within the poem explored above, which can be further understood in terms of 'torrential time' (*reißende Zeit*, a term Hölderlin associated with revolutionary turmoil[100]) and a 'time of maturity' (*reifenden Zeit*);[101] second, the

---

[97] Adolf Schubring, 'Die Schumann'sche Schule: Schumann und Brahms: Brahms's vierhändige Variationen', *Allgemeine musikalische Zeitung* 3 (1868): 41–2, 49–51.

[98] Webster, 'The *Alto Rhapsody*', 23.

[99] The use of this C minor to C major topic in Brahms has been explored in great detail by James Webster and Peter Smith, amongst others. Webster traces its influence, particularly to Act I of *Tristan and Isolde*, which also has a psychological progression from C minor to C major. See James Webster, 'The *Alto Rhapsody*', 19–46. See also Peter H. Smith, *Expressive Forms in Brahms's Instrumental Music: Structure and Meaning in His Werther Quartet* (Bloomington, IN: Indiana University Press, 2005). Later instances of this same tonal trajectory include the Piano Trio in C Minor, Op. 101 and the Lied 'Auf dem Kirchhofe', Op. 105 No. 4.

[100] Robert Savage, *Hölderlin After the Catastrophe: Heidegger–Adorno–Brecht* (London: Camden House, 2008), 14.

[101] Ryan, *Holderlins Lehre vom Wechsel der Töne*, 22.

'resolution of dissonance' within the novel; and, third, the manner in which the articulation of this dissonance – the caesura or rupture – is the agent of its own resolution. These formal features of Hölderlin's poetry resonate in the details of Brahms's musical setting.

## 1.6   The Caesura in *Schicksalslied* and Brahms's Ascending Circle

With deep artistic affinity to Hölderlin's poetry, and in keeping with the rebirth of a new identity at the end of a secular *Bildungsroman*, Brahms's circle is incomplete. The beginning of *Schicksalslied*, as Christopher Reynolds astutely notes, 'sounds like a culmination, like a well-prepared conclusion',[102] whereas, because the final measures do not employ all of the instrumental and vocal forces heard up to this point, the ending evades a full sense of closure. This is entirely appropriate for a composition written in the spirit of the *Bildungsroman* whose journey is circuitous by necessity. As Hegel explains, 'It is a circle that returns into itself, that presupposes its beginning, and reaches its beginning only in its end'.[103]

The work opens with an arrestingly beautiful melody on muted violins supported harmonically by strings and winds, with pulsating timpani ostinato on the tonic. Brahms gives new meaning to this music upon its return in the coda with the use of a number of subtly sensitive alterations. When the opening melody reappears (as shown in Examples 1.2a and 1.2b), the restless timpani ostinato has ceased. The composer intended the erstwhile violin melody, now heard on the flute, to be played upon its return with 'passion and beauty', its ethereal tones transcending the 'large section of violins'.[104] The strings, now *dolce*, play an undulating arpeggio figure, serving to enhance the 'Er-Innerung'[105] of this ending, that is, the manner in which it remembers, internalizes, and reparticipates in its evolving consciousness.

---

[102]   Reynolds, 'Rhapsodizing Brahms', 222.

[103]   Hegel, *Phenomenology of Spirit*, as cited in Abrams, *Natural Supernaturalism*, 235.

[104]   Brahms to Karl Reinthaler, 24 October 1871, in *Johannes Brahms im Briefwechsel mit Karl Reinthaler, Max Bruch, Hermann Deiters, Friedr. Heimsoth, Karl Reinecke, Ernst Rudorff, Bernhard und Luise Scholz*, ed. Wilhelm Altmann (Berlin: Deutsche Brahms-Gesellschaft, 1907, repr. Tutzing: Hans Schneider, 1974), 42.

[105]   Hegel hyphenates the first occurrence of this word in the *Phenomenology of Spirit* in order to draw attention to its double-meaning of 'remembering' and 'internalizing', as noted by Abrams in *Natural Supernaturalism*, 235.

The Allegro C minor section that lies between this E♭ major opening and its ethereal C major return has a furious energy not found elsewhere in the piece. This is brought about by a number of factors. As Jackson observes, Brahms does not, in fact, establish the tonic of C minor, but rather suggests it by prolonging its dominant.[106] The unfulfilled nature of the music is intensified by the relentless quaver motion in the strings, reminiscent of the sixth movement of the *German Requiem*, combined with the oppressive four-part choir singing here for the first time in strict unison. All this characterizes the music that flanks the B2 section (that is, the music from bars 104–78 and 274–332, as outlined in Table 1.3). What lies between is music with developmental tendencies: it is at once the most harmonically free within the piece, and yet it is also tonally directed, as it establishes the unique tonal trajectory of the ending.

The overlapping circular figures in the strings from bar 179 announce the dominant of the dominant whilst at once providing respite from the frenzied pace. The fugal rendition of the first two lines of verse three has an eddying motion redolent of the transformation and regression as well as growth and progression that characterize Hölderlin's novel (bars 194–251). The swirling arpeggios that ushered in the secondary dominant now introduce the dominant of the ultimate tonic. The relentless quaver motion and the unison voices of the choir return as the suffering mortals fall headlong into the abyss. The texture is saturated with diminished seventh chords, which are at their most pronounced on the word 'blindlings' (headlong or blindly) before the hemiolas that evoke the symbolism of water thrown from ledge to ledge culminating in the terrifying *fortissimo* 'jahrlang' (for years) of bars 314–16. This takes place over a sustained pedal on C, posed as the dominant of F. Its energy spent, and the dynamic reduced from the *fortissimo* outbursts to a sustained *piano*, the music hovers here for no fewer than fifty-four bars (bars 326–79). Contemplating the vague abyss, and conscious of the division and conflict between the self and the outside world, the dissonance of Brahms's setting is now at its most acute.

Rather than continuing in the tonal direction adumbrated thus far, however, the music turns back, opening onto a new beginning. This is the definitive moment of the caesura in Brahms's composition, the 'pure word', as Hölderlin would have it. It marks the very moment when the

---

[106] Timothy Jackson, 'The Tragic Reversed Recapitulation in the German Classical Tradition', *Journal of Music Theory* 40/1 (1996): 61–111 (78).

subject has been objectified and now recognizes itself. As Hegel formulates it:

On the one hand . . . [consciousness] alienates itself and in this alienation sets itself off as object . . . On the other hand there is in this very process the other moment in which [self-consciousness] has equally transcended this alienation and objectification and taken it back into itself, and so is at home with itself in its otherness as such – This is the movement of consciousness.[107]

Brahms was certainly conversant with the Romantic plot archetype that underpins the philosophy of consciousness, for he highlights a lengthy passage in the Schiller–Goethe correspondence in which Schiller, taking issue with Schelling's *System of Transcendental Idealism*, addresses precisely the dichotomies central to Hölderlin's *Hyperion* between the conscious and the unconscious, between what Hölderlin would later term the aorgic and the organic, the two extremes of the 'eccentric orbit of all human life':

I fear, however, that these Gentlemen of Idealism [such as Schelling is] pay too little attention to experience in their ideas, and in experience the poet also begins with the Unconscious. Indeed, he may consider himself lucky if, in the completed work he only comes so far through the clearest Consciousness of his operations as to once again find the first, obscure total-idea of his work unweakened.[108]

The return to the thematic material of the introduction in this altered manner, I propose, transfers the poetic idea to the object of music, thereby giving musical form to the movement of consciousness, so that the listener can now experience the orchestral postlude from a different and much enhanced perspective. When considered in this way, this moment plays out just as Foucault characterizes it in his discussion of Hölderlin's *Hyperion*, as 'the improbable unity of two beings as closely aligned as a figure and its reflection in a mirror'.[109] In listening to (and experiencing) the postlude to

---

[107] Hegel, *Phenomenology of Spirit*, cited in Abrams, *Natural Supernaturalism*, 197.

[108] 'Ich fürchte aber daß diese Herren Idealisten ihrer Ideen wegen allzuwenig Notiz von der Erfahrung nehmen, und in der Erfahrung fängt auch der Dichter nur mit dem Bewußtlosen an, ja er hat sich glücklich zu schätzen, wenn er durch das klarste Bewußtsein seiner Operationen nur so weit kommt, um die erste dunkle Totalidee seines Werks in der vollendeten Arbeit ungeschwächt wieder zu finden'. Letter No. 809 from Schiller to Goethe, 27 March 1801, on 338–40 of Brahms's copy. This translation is my own.

[109] Michel Foucault, 'The Father's "No"', in *Language, Counter-Memory, Practice: Selected Essays and Interviews*, ed. and with an introduction by Donald F. Bouchard, trans. Donald F. Bouchard and Sherry Simon (Ithaca, NY: Cornell University Press, 1977), 68–86 (79).

*Schicksalslied* thus, we 'arrive where we started | And know the place for the first time'.[110]

Taken together, the unique tonal trajectory of this work, the refined alterations in orchestration and expression, and the consummate treatment of form, invite the listener to experience the musical material of the introduction anew, and with heightened awareness. This ending, therefore, calls to mind a moulding of musical material into the characteristically Romantic shape of an ascending circle or spiral. Brahms's musically 'eccentric path', like Hölderlin's, leads us away from the original unity in order to restore it, in a heightened manner, through ourselves. This postlude prompts reflection and realization on the part of Brahms's listener akin to that of Hölderlin's reader.

## 1.7   Epilogue: Brahms and the Literature of Humanity

The composer's well-known indecision throughout 1871 regarding this ending to *Schicksalslied* has undoubtedly vexed the question as to the work's hermeneutic meaning. He addressed this subject in a number of letters to his friend Karl Reinthaler that year, in the elusive manner that characterizes his enigmatic correspondence. Writing in October, he confesses that where his setting of Hyperion's song is concerned, 'I certainly say something that the poet does not say and, to be sure, it would be better if what's missing were in fact his main concern'.[111]

Commentators have taken this as an indication that Brahms granted himself poetic licence to 'overstep the structural bounds of [Hölderlin's] text'.[112] His comment can be interpreted differently, however, in light of our recognition of the structural significance of the caesura in Hölderlin's writings. Ian Balfour clarifies that at this pivotal juncture in much of Hölderlin's output 'the one truth ... must not be written or spoken, only "circumscribed", literally written around'.[113] Might Brahms, therefore, have been paying tribute to this very quality in Hölderlin's writings, that which Carola Nielinger-Vakil eloquently terms the poet's characteristic 'art

---

[110]  The reference is to T. S. Eliot, 'Little Gidding', from *Four Quartets*.

[111]  'Ich sage ja eben etwas, was der Dichter nicht sagt, und freilich wäre es besser, wenn ihm das Fehlende die Hauptsache gewesen wäre.' Johannes Brahms to Karl Reinthaler, 24 October 1871, in *Johannes Brahms im Briefwechsel mit Karl Reinthaler*, 42. This translation slightly amended from Michael Steinberg, *Choral Masterworks*, 80.

[112]  I borrow the phrase from Daverio, 'The "Wechsel der Töne"', 96.

[113]  Balfour, *The Rhetoric of Romantic Prophecy*, 242.

of leaving things unsaid'.[114] In that case, we might more usefully interpret his comment as 'I certainly say something that the poet does not *explicitly* say and, to be sure, it would be better if what's missing were in fact his main concern'.

Furthermore, throughout Brahms's deliberations, there is no evidence to suggest the slightest uncertainty regarding either the tonal trajectory or the formal structure of the ending of this work. He initially composed a coda that included the choir singing excerpts from the first two lines of the poem, 'Ihr wandelt droben im Licht | auf weichem Boden', in homophonic chords from what would have been bars 390–5, and a polyphonic interweaving of voices on the words 'selige Genien' from bars 402–6. It was this ending that Brahms shared with Hermann Levi in May 1871, and of which Levi copied a piano reduction, which is reproduced in Figure 1.2 and transcribed as Example 1.3. The composer subsequently thought better of including these words, and wondered if the solution might not be to let the choir instead hum 'ah' in the specified bars. Max Kalbeck reports that following his discussion with Levi, Brahms took a pencil and scratched the choir out of the postlude altogether.[115]

The question of the extent of Levi's influence on the final composition has never been fully addressed. A newly discovered letter from the conductor to Brahms, which is found on the reverse of Levi's piano reduction in Figure 1.2, currently housed at the Brahms-Institut in Lübeck, seems to indicate that Levi's input concerned only matters of instrumentation and choral and orchestral balance (Figure 1.3). The fact that Brahms had on an earlier occasion paid attention to 'some of the remarks that [he] mumbled shyly at the piano', Levi writes, had given him the courage to offer some further suggestions. Here the conductor proposes, for instance, adjustments to the balance of timpani and bass in the opening, and a reconsideration of a flute entry that he deems to look better on paper than it sounds in practice (at bars 56–7). Nowhere, however, does he make any suggestions regarding matters of large-scale form or tonality. Nor does he give any indication that such matters had arisen in earlier conversations.[116] Evidence seems to suggest,

---

[114] Carola Nielinger-Vakil, 'Quiet Revolutions: Hölderlin Fragments by Luigi Nono and Wolfgang Rihm', *Music and Letters* 81/2 (2000): 245–74 (247).

[115] Max Kalbeck, *Johannes Brahms* (Berlin: Deutsche Brahms-Gesellschaft, 1909), ii, 365.

[116] In the published correspondence of 1871, only two letters mention *Schicksalslied* prior to its premier on 18 October. In the first, without a specific date in September 1871, Brahms writes, 'should Simrock need the orchestral parts (for *Schicksalslied*) I have referred him to you'.

Example 1.3 Hermann Levi's transcription of Brahms's proposed ending for *Schicksalslied* in May 1871 in piano reduction. Transcribed from the original held at the Brahms-Institut in Lübeck. This would have followed on from bar 380

therefore, that Levi's influence was limited to helping Brahms reach his decision regarding the absence of the choir in the postlude. Indeed, both the *Stichvorlage* in Levi's hand and the autograph score of the

In the second letter of 27 September 1871, Brahms refers to Levi's 'puzzling correspondence' ('räthselhafte Zuschrift'). There is no way to ascertain whether Brahms was referring to this newly discovered letter.

**Example 1.3** (cont.)

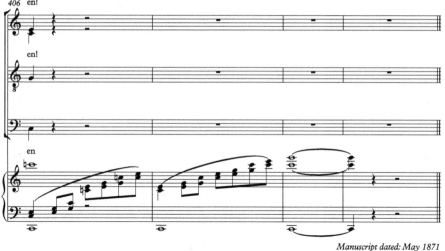

*Manuscript dated: May 1871*

composition, now housed at the Library of Congress, confirm that matters of form and tonality were finalized by May 1871.[117]

In Christmas of that same year, Brahms's yuletide greeting to Reinthaler picked up on their earlier exchange when the composer quipped that 'Hyperions Schicksalslied' is 'not the kind of poem to which one can tack

---

[117] The autograph score of *Schicksalslied* housed at the Library of Congress, Washington, DC, has the shelf mark Music 1178, item 4.

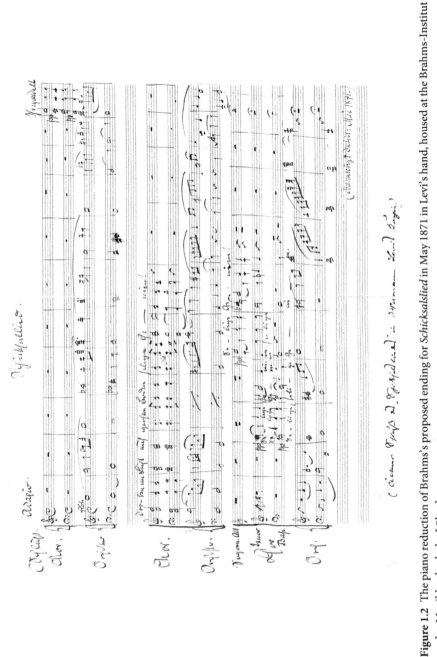

**Figure 1.2** The piano reduction of Brahms's proposed ending for *Schicksalslied* in May 1871 in Levi's hand, housed at the Brahms-Institut an der Musikhochschule, Lübeck

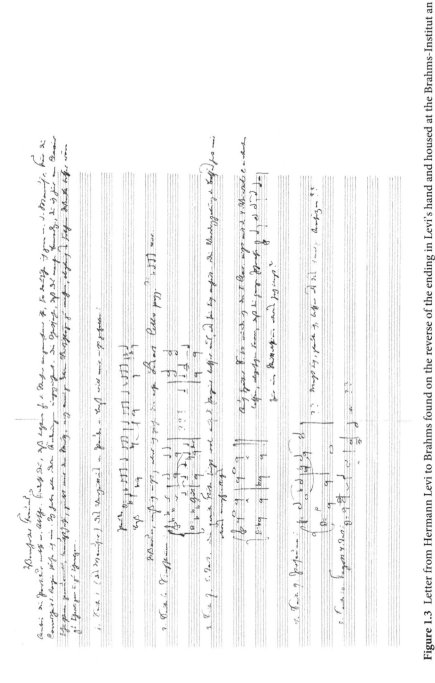

**Figure 1.3** Letter from Hermann Levi to Brahms found on the reverse of the ending in Levi's hand and housed at the Brahms-Institut an der Musikhochschule, Lübeck

**Figure 1.3** (cont.)

something on'.[118] I venture that this statement indicates Brahms's full appreciation of the completeness (or perfection – *Vollendung*) of Hölderlin's poem. By Christmas 1871, Brahms was happy to allow his wordless and tonally anomalous ending stand on its own merit as a representation of a heightened consciousness, for the ontological implications of his ascending circle were at that point entirely clear to him. We can profitably think of his last utterance to Reinthaler regarding the inappropriateness of words in his *Nachspiel* in the same spirit as the maxim with which Heidegger would later preface his commentaries on Hölderlin: 'for the sake of what has been composed, commentary on the poem must strive to make itself superfluous'.[119]

I bring together here the artistic voices of Brahms and Heidegger not by way of happenstance, but to highlight the poetic vision with which Brahms chose, interpreted, and set Hölderlin's poetry. It took literary critics more than a century to discover the structure of *Hyperion*, 'since it is folded into the thematic and philosophical texture of the book'.[120] Yet in his setting, Brahms intuited its complex poetic and philosophical meaning with an artistic sensitivity to Hölderlin that was not to be equalled until the late twentieth century. In the intervening years, the poet's reputation suffered as a consequence of what Robert Savage refers to as his 'state of spiritual benightedness'.[121] Following his rehabilitation in the early twentieth century, the misappropriation of his poetry by the National Socialists saw a renewed crisis in Hölderlin's reputation.[122] Both Heidegger and Adorno were key figures in the postwar re-evaluation of this poet.[123] Their writings, in turn, were instrumental in attracting numerous composers to the works of Hölderlin in the late twentieth century including Hanns Eisler, Heinz

---

[118] Johannes Brahms to Karl Reinthaler, 25 December 1871, in *Johannes Brahms im Briefwechsel mit Karl Reinthaler*, 44.

[119] Martin Heidegger, *Erläuterungen zu Hölderlin's Dichtung* (Frankfurt am Main: V. Klostermann, 1951), 7ff, quoted in Theodor W. Adorno, 'Parataxis: On Hölderlin's Late Poetry', in *Notes to Literature*, ed. Rolf Tiedemann, trans. Shierry Weber Nicholsen, (New York, NY: Columbia University Press, 1992), ii, 109–49 (114).

[120] Minden, *The German Bildungsroman*, 119. Lawrence Ryan is largely considered to have been the first critic to unlock Hölderlin's *Hyperion* in his 1965 text on that work. See Ryan, *Hölderlins 'Hyperion'*.

[121] Robert Savage, *Hölderlin After the Catastrophe*, 6.

[122] On this subject, see Savage, *Hölderlin After the Catastrophe*. On Heidegger's reception of Hölderlin, see in particular ch. 1, 'Conversation: Heidegger, Das abendländische Gespräch'.

[123] Particularly influential in this regard was Theodor Adorno's essay 'Parataxis: Zur späten Lyriks Hölderlins', *Neue Rundschau* lxxv (1964), included in Adorno's *Noten zur Literatur* (Frankfurt am Main: Suhrkamp, 1974), ii, 447–91 and translated in *Notes to Literature*, 109–49.

Holliger, Luigi Nono, Wolfgang Rihm, György Ligeti, Hans Werner Henze, and Benjamin Britten.[124]

What these late twentieth-century composers were undoubtedly drawn to in Hölderlin, as was the case with Brahms in the late 1860s, was 'the literature of humanity'. This entails 'a belief in the possibility and significance of formation, "Bildung", which applies equally to the individual human life and to the individual work of art'.[125] By intricately interweaving compositional process in *Schicksalslied* with intellectual tradition and philosophical thought, Brahms bestowed upon posterity a musical manifestation of *Bildung* in the form of a quintessentially Brahmsian fabric.

---

[124] I refer to Hanns Eisler, *Ernste Gesänge* (1962), Heinz Holliger, *Scarandelli-Zyklus* (1978–91), Wolfgang Rihm, *Hölderlin-Fragmente* (1977), Luigi Nono, *Fragmente-Stille, an Diotima* (1979–80), György Ligeti, *Hölderlin Phantasien* (1982), and Hans Werner Henze, Seventh Symphony (1983–4).

[125] Minden, *The German Bildungsroman*, 125.

## 2 | The Ennoblement of Mourning: *Nänie* and the Death of Beauty

> All peoples with a history have a paradise, a state of innocence, a Golden
> Age; yes, each individual has his paradise, his Golden Age that he recalls
> with more or less ecstasy depending on whether he has a more or less
> poetic nature.[1]
>
> – Friedrich Schiller

> Here then was nostalgia, not as a longing for conditions of a primitive
> origin but rather for the simple order of the world of art, for the realm of
> beauty and poetry.[2]
>
> – Helmut Schneider

Following *Schicksalslied* of 1872, Brahms waited nine years before he
returned to composing elegiac choral works with *Nänie*, Op. 82 of 1881.
The death of the artist Anselm Feuerbach (1829–1880) on 4 January 1880
provided the ostensible reason for Brahms's choice to set the last of
Schiller's elegies written in 1800, the poem 'Auch das Schöne muß
sterben'.[3] The poem is based on Book 24 of Homer's *Odyssey*, from
where Schiller took the image of the gods and goddesses who weep for
seventeen days following the death of Achilles.[4] In Brahms's copy of *The*

---

[1] Friedrich Schiller, *Sämmtliche Werke*, 5 vols, ed. Gerhard Fricke and Herbert G. Göpfert, 7th edn
(Darmstadt: Wissenschaftliche Buchgesellschaft, 1984), here translated in David Pugh, *Dialectic
of Love: Platonism in Schiller's Aesthetics* (Montreal & Kingston: McGill-Queen's University
Press, 1996), 401.

[2] 'Hier also gab es Nostalgie, aber nicht als die Sehnsucht nacht primitive Ursprungsverhältnissen,
sondern nach der einfachen Ordnung der Welt der Kunst, nach dem Reich der Schönheit und
der Dichtung.' Helmut Schneider, ed., *Deutsche Idyllentheorien im 18. Jahrhundert* (Tübingen:
Narr, 1988), 21. This translation is taken from Pugh, *Dialectic of Love: Platonism in Schiller's
Aesthetics* (Montreal & Kingston, McGill-Queen's University Press, 1996), 400.

[3] On Feuerbach's death, see Max Kalbeck, *Johannes Brahms* (Berlin: Deutsche Brahms-
Gesellschaft, 1909), III, 290; John A. James, 'Johannes Brahms's *Nänie*, Op. 82: A Study in
Context and Content', DMA Dissertation, Eastman School of Music (2001), 24.

[4] We know from a letter that Schiller wrote to Körner that he had been immersed in Homer's
*Odyssey*, in the translation by Johann Heinrich Voß (1781). See letter from Schiller to Körner, 20
August 1788, as mentioned in Wilkinson and Willoughby's notes in Friedrich Schiller, *On the
Aesthetic Education of Man: In a Series of Letters*, ed., trans., and with an introduction by
Elizabeth M. Wilkinson and L. A. Willoughby (Oxford: Clarendon Press, 1967), 294 (in
reference to letter XXVII). Many scholars consider Book 24 of *The Odyssey* to be a later addition

*Odyssey*, he highlighted three lines that fall within this song (lines 47–9), precisely the passage that sees Thetis, the mother of Achilles, rising from the sea in grief:

Hearing the news, your mother, Thetis, rose from the sea,
  immortal sea-nymphs in her wake, and a strange unearthly cry
  came throbbing over the ocean.[5]

This one-movement work for choir and orchestra exemplifies German Idealism in the musical realm.

Idealism is a synonym for 'idealist aesthetics', an aesthetic norm based on the belief that the purpose of art (poetry, writing, literature, music) is to edify, uplift, and ennoble, to point the way to the ideal.[6] The literary scholar Toril Moi understands it to be 'a historically and culturally significant intersection of philosophy and literature'[7] that emerged from German Idealist philosophy at the end of the eighteenth century in the idealist aesthetics of figures such as Kant, Hölderlin, Schiller, Novalis, Schlegel, and Hegel. The seemingly noble aspirations of German Idealism might strike us today as being quaint and naïve, if not hopelessly utopian. They are related to the Platonic idea that the *beautiful*, the *true*, and the *good* are one. This sentiment is given voice in Schiller's poem 'Die Künstler', which reads: 'But through the morning gate of Beauty | Did you enter the realm of Truth'.[8] Unlike the Platonic idea, however, aesthetic idealism extols artistic beauty as the most important of this triad of virtues. The widespread disenchantment in the wake of the French Revolution gave rise to much of the poetic output written in a German Idealist vein at the turn of the nineteenth century. It

---

  to the poem. See Bernard Knox, 'Introduction' to Homer, *The Odyssey*, trans. Robert Fagles, introduction and notes by Bernard Knox (London: Penguin, 1997), 9. On this point, see also Joachim Wohlleben, 'Ein Gedicht, ein Satz, ein Gedanke – Schiller's "Nänie"', in Klaus Deterding, ed., *Wahrnehmungen in Poetischen All. Festschrift für Alfred Behrmann* (Heidelberg: Winter, 1993), 54–72 (59).

[5] 'Auch die Mutter entstieg mit den heiligen Nympfen dem Meere, | Als sie die Botschaft vernahm; von lautwehklagenden Stimmen | Hallte die Flut: und Entzetzen ergriff das Heer der Achaier.' Homer, *Homers Odysee*, trans. Johann Heinrich Voß. Reprint of the first edition from 1781 with an introduction by Michael Bernays (Stuttgart: J. G. Cotta'schen Buchhandlung, 1881), 433–4.

[6] See Toril Moi, 'Idealism', in *The Oxford Handbook of Philosophy and Literature*, ed. Richard Eldridge (Oxford: Oxford University Press, 2009), 271–97.

[7] Moi, 'Idealism', 272.

[8] Schiller, 'Die Künstler'; this translation taken from Constantin Floros, Constantin Floros, *Johannes Brahms, 'Free but Alone': A Life for a Poetic Music*, trans. Ernest Bernhardt-Kabisch (Frankfurt am Main: Peter Lang, 2010), 168.

'offered the world an ecstatic, revolutionary vision of art as the embodiment of human freedom'.[9]

Moi provides a reminder of 'how strong [idealism's] hold on nineteenth-century writers, artists, critics, and audiences was'.[10] It exerted a powerful influence on the German artistic imagination during the period between the demise of Romanticism and the rise of modernism. We may attribute the death of idealism to its failure to deal with the modern world, particularly during the period 1870–1914. Nonetheless, pervasive and ever-changing, the concept of Idealism continued to operate during this time, assuming a somewhat altered identity at the end of the nineteenth century to that which emerged in the wake of the French Revolution. This change of identity goes hand in hand with the changing role of music as it relates to romanticism, which Carl Dahlhaus outlines as follows:

Early nineteenth-century music could be said to be romantic in an age of romanticism, which produced romantic poetry and painting and even romantic physics and chemistry, whereas neo-romanticism of the later part of the century was romantic in an unromantic age, dominated by positivism and realism. Music, *the* romantic art, had become 'untimely' in general terms, though by no means unimportant; on the contrary, its very dissociation from the prevailing spirit of the age enabled it to fulfil a spiritual, cultural, and ideological function of a magnitude which can hardly be exaggerated: it stood for an alternative world.[11]

The positivism and realism of the later part of the century is the result of industrialization and political disillusionment following the failure of the 1848 revolutions and the horrors of the Franco-Prussian war and the Paris Commune (1870–1). At this juncture, idealism yielded to the nostalgia that characterizes much of Brahms's late output. In the late nineteenth-century, 'disenchantment' is used synonymously with 'pessimism', and is associated with the pessimistic philosophy of Schopenhauer. For the sake of clarity, I will refer to these two temporalities of the aesthetic concept as 'idealism' in the early part of the century and 'new idealism' in the second half of the century, the latter being characterized by a further intensification of nostalgia.

*Nänie* is one of Brahms's most pronounced contributions to the tradition of thought in which Schiller features prominently. It is a paean to art that not only ruminates on time and the nature of musical memory but can also be understood as a musical manifestation of the Schillerian 'idyll'. An idyll, by

---

[9] Toril Moi, 'Idealism', 272.    [10] *Ibid.* 271.

[11] Carl Dahlhaus, *Between Romanticism and Modernism: Four Studies in the Music of the Later Nineteenth Century*, trans. Mary Whittall and Arnold Whittall (Berkeley, CA and London: University of California Press, 1980), 5.

definition, is an attempt to recover a pastoral mode. It conjures up a pastoral conception of a former state of innocence. A Schillerian idyll, as we will see in greater detail in Section 2.3, is a poetic genre in which the real and the ideal are united. Here again the two temporalities of idealism and new idealism are relevant to when Brahms composed this elegiac work towards the end of the nineteenth century. For Brahms, therefore, a 'late idyll' relates to the melancholy of century's end. It conjures up a much more recent image of the 'nature' of the pastoral element that Brahms has lost.

Erhard Bahr discusses the manner in which Schiller established 'a fixed point in history for the death of Beauty' in 'Auch das Schöne muß sterben'. He explains that 'even in classical Greece individual representatives of Beauty had to die, but due to the presence of the Greek gods and goddesses poetry was able to keep it alive in songs'.[12] Constantin Floros puts the matter clearly when he states that 'classical antiquity was to [Schiller] the lost "beautiful world", in which culture was harmoniously at one with nature'.[13] Schiller's poem 'Die Götter Griechenlands' ('The Gods of Greece', 1888) laments the vanishing beauty of Greek mythology in the Christian age.[14] Schiller perceived classical Greece with its living mythology as an enchanted world. 'For the modern period', however, as Bahr further contends, Schiller was one of the first to acknowledge what Max Horkheimer and Theodor W. Adorno would later in 1944 refer to as the 'disenchantment of the world' in *Dialectic of Enlightenment* (to which we will return in Chapter 5).[15]

That Brahms associated his composition *Nänie* with idealist sentiments is indicated in particular by the last verse of his setting, which ends with an homage to art whose role, as Peter Petersen suggests, is 'not only to console the bereaved but also to ensure life beyond death'.[16] There is also a trace of

---

[12] Ehrhard Bahr, 'Death and Mourning in Friedrich Schiller's Aesthetics: The Viability of Art in the Modern Age', in *A View in the Rear Mirror: Romantic Aesthetics, Culture, and Science Seen from Today: Festschrift for Frederick Burwick on the Occasion of His Seventieth Birthday*, ed. Walter Pape (Trier: Wissenschaftlicher Verlag, 2006), 107–20 (115).

[13] Floros, *Johannes Brahms, 'Free but Alone'*, 167.

[14] The issue of the death of beauty in the art of classical antiquity in the Christian age is raised again by Nietzsche in *The Antichrist*, as we will see in Chapter 4, in a passage that would capture Brahms's attention.

[15] Bahr, 'Death and Mourning in Friedrich Schiller's Aesthetics', 115. See also Max Horkheimer and Theodor W. Adorno, *Dialektik der Aufklärung: Philosophische Fragmente* (Frankfurt am Main: Fischer-Taschenbuch-Verlag, 1944), or Horkheimer and Adorno, *Dialectic of Enlightenment: Philosophical Fragment*, trans. Edmund Jephcott (Stanford, CA: Stanford University Press, 2002).

[16] Peter Petersen, 'Works for Chorus and Orchestra', Liner Notes for *Johannes Brahms, Werke für Chor und Orchester*, Deutsche Grammophon 449 651–2, 22–8 (27).

Idealist thinking in a comment he made to Julius Allgeyer on 10 May 1895 following the death of Henriette Feuerbach, to whom this piece is dedicated, that 'time alleviates, death transfigures'.[17]

In the opening line of Schiller's poem 'Auch das Schöne muß sterben', he opposes beauty and death in immediate and close proximity, thereby elevating death and the beautiful to the status of the ideal, 'one in the past as a lost ideal, the other in the future to be sought after'.[18] The trajectory to expression of mourning – and therefore immortality – unfolds through the course of the poem. Gerhard Kaiser's formulation enhances our understanding of this trajectory:

> The dead Achilles in 'Nänie' is the glorified son, and only in the lament of death is he glorified. The beauty of Achilles, Adonis, and Euridice as survivors is nothing more than a premonition of early death which lies over their forms. It is only the brilliant Achilles of the *Iliad* who appears intended for early death.[19]

Brahms's *Nänie* is concerned with three intellectual figures, all of whom were preoccupied with German Idealism as it relates to their respective art forms: for Schiller, the literary; for Feuerbach, the visual; and for Brahms, the musical. Whereas each art form is mutually independent, their shared Idealist aesthetic of the ennoblement of mourning allows Brahms to seamlessly interweave all three in his richly textured composition.

In this chapter, I consider Brahms's setting of this poem in relation to Schiller's aesthetic theory of mourning, whilst also exploring Schiller's poem in relation to matters of form in Brahms's setting. I situate *Nänie* in relation to the Schillerian idyll, thereby opening up new perspectives on the intertextual nature of this composition and its frame of allusive reference. These allusions are bound up with particular moments in time. The literary allusions go beyond Schiller and, through his poem, extend to Homer, just as Brahms's musical allusions go beyond self-allusion and extend to Beethoven. The visual realm is elegantly depicted in Schiller's descriptions of the figures of classical antiquity, an aspect of this poem that is every bit as vivid as Feuerbach's depictions of classical antiquity in his paintings.

The nucleus of German Idealism and its two temporalities is further underpinned by the crucial connection that exists between a group of

---

[17] 'Die Zeit lindert, der Tod verklärt.' Letter from Brahms to Allgeyer, 10 May 1895, in Alfred Orel, *Johannes Brahms und Julius Allgeyer: Ein Künstlerfreundschaft in Briefen* (Tutzing: Hans Schneider, 1964), 126.

[18] Gerhard Kaiser, *Vergötterung und Tod: Die thematische Einheit von Schillers Werk* (Stuttgart: J. B. Metzlersche Verlagsbuchhandlung, 1967), 34.

[19] Kaiser, *Vergötterung und Tod*, 34–5.

artists known as the *Deutsch-Römer* (German Romans, of whom Feuerbach was a key member) operating at the end of the nineteenth century, and their preoccupation with the new humanism of Schiller, Goethe, and Hölderlin. A consideration of this connection will deepen our understanding of the artistic affinity that exists between Brahms and Feuerbach. The focus on Feuerbach, furthermore, allows us to explore the vital role that visual art played in Brahms's intellectual world as he composed his elegiac choral works in the 1870s and 1880s, the impact of which is particularly pronounced in *Nänie* and *Gesang der Parzen*, as we shall see in Chapter 3. Although the visual, the literary, and the musical are intricately interwoven in Brahms's composition, I will consider each one in turn before considering how Brahms's *Nänie* brings all three together in what I argue, with recourse to the theories of Reinhold Brinkmann, is a musical manifestation of a Schillerian idyll.

## THE VISUAL

### 2.1   Feuerbach, Brahms, and the Realm of Classical Antiquity

During the years 1864–75, Brahms spent his summers in Baden (now Baden-Baden) along the northwestern border of the Black Forest. It was here in 1865 that he made the acquaintance of the artist Anselm Feuerbach. Kalbeck asserts that it was during this time that 'ancient art gained its special importance' for Brahms, which is evident in the nature of his elegies:

It is not only the compositions which are already rooted in antiquity by their texts that testify to this – such as *Schicksalslied*, *Nänie*, and *Gesang der Parzen* – but rather almost all of Brahms's late masterpieces which, in the sculpture of their compact form, the precision and simplicity of their urgent expression, the measured beauty of their deeply passionate movement, and in the characteristic individualization of their typical ideas, turn from the temporal to the eternal.[20]

---

[20] 'In der durch Feuerbachs Gegenwart befruchteten Lichtentaler Periode gewann die antike Kunst ihre besondere Bedeutung für unseren Tondichter, und übte sie auch mehr einen ergänzenden als grundlegenden Einfluß auf ihn aus, so war dieser doch durchaus kein vorübergehender, sondern wurde auf den italienischen Reisen des Meisters immer wieder aufgefrischt und befestigt. Dafür zeugen nicht allein die schon durch ihre Texte in antiken Anschauungen wurzelnden Kompositionen, wie "Schicksalslied", "Nänie" und "Parzengesang", sondern fast alle späteren Brahmsschen Meisterwerke, die in der Plastik ihrer gedrungenen Form, in der Genauigkeit und Einfachheit ihres zwingenden Ausdrucks, in der gemessenen Schönheit ihrer tief leidenschaftlichen Bewegung und endlich in der charakteristischen Individualisierung ihrer typischen Ideen sich vom Zeitlichen ab und dem Ewigen zuwenden.' Kalbeck, *Brahms*, ii, 2, 306–7.

In his description of *Nänie*, Kalbeck explores the nature of the relationship between artist and composer, and the degree to which this is based on their attitudes toward form:

The masculine fury of death, filled with the ancient spirit in the major key, is a great artistic achievement, which, without antiquarian velleities, by virtue of its idiosyncratic expression alone, brings us back to the time and place that Goethe/ Feuerbach's Iphigenia sought with her soul. It is Greek music, not from the Romanized period of the soft 'Graeculi', but from the classical age of Pericles.[21]

Feuerbach was an idealist-humanist who was raised in an atmosphere saturated with the high-minded ideals of humanistic philosophy. He was tutored in Latin and Italian, read the *Iliad* and the *Odyssey*, and was familiar with texts such as Goethe's *Iphigenia in Tauris* and Grillparzer's *Medea*. His family moved in cultured circles: he was the son of Josef Anselm Feuerbach, Professor of Classics and Ancient Studies at Freiburg University (whom the poet Georg Friedrich Daumer referred to as his 'dearest and most true friend'[22]); the grandson of the historian of law and criminal law Johann Paul Anselm Feuerbach; and the nephew of the philosopher Ludwig Feuerbach.

Being almost exact contemporaries, a number of uncanny similarities emerge in the biographies of Feuerbach and Brahms that illuminate the friendship that existed between these two people. At the outset of their professional lives, they each had an intellectual benefactor who would exert a great influence on the path of their careers. Historical consciousness is a defining feature of the nineteenth century, and in each case, this benefactor would play a pivotal role in the historicization of their artistic output. In Brahms's case, Robert Schumann penned the laudatory essay 'Neue Bahnen' in 1853, in which he introduced the young Messiah of music to the world.[23] Having spent much time in the Schumann household from

---

[21] 'Eine hohe Errungenschaft der Tonkunst verdient die männliche, von antikem Geiste erfüllte Totenklage in Dur genannt zu werden, welche ohne antiquarische Velleitäten, kraft ihres eigentümlichen Ausdrucks allein, uns in die Zeit und jenes Land zurückversetzt, das Goethe-Feuerbachs Iphigenie mit der Seele sucht. Es ist griechische Musik, und zwar nicht aus der romanisierten Periode der verweichlichen "Graeculi", sondern uns dem klassischen Zeitalter des Perikles.' Kalbeck, *Brahms*, III, 1, 291.

[22] Jürgen Ecker, *Anselm Feuerbach: Entwicklung und Interpretation seiner Gemälde, Ölskizzen und Ölstudien im Spiegel eines kritischen Werkkatalogs* (Munich, 1991), here cited in Natasha Loges, 'Exoticism, Artifice and the Supernatural in the Brahmsian Lied', *Nineteenth-Century Music Review* 3/2 (2006): 137–68 (138). Feuerbach's father was the author of the archaeological-aesthetic script *Der vatikanische Apoll*. See Christoph Heilmann, ed., *'In uns selbst liegt Italien': Die Kunst der Deutsch-Römer* (Munich: Hirmer Verlag, 1987), 383–93 (385).

[23] Robert Schumann, 'Neue Bahnen', *Neue Zeitschrift für Musik*, 28 October 1853, 185–6.

1853 to early 1854, Brahms was heavily influenced by Clara and Robert's attitudes to the music of the past, and Robert's espousal of the notion that the study of the work of past masters was not to 'muster erudite astonishment at every minute detail', but 'to trace the expanded artistic means of today back to their sources, and to discover how they can be intelligently employed'.[24] Following Schumann's suicide attempt and hospitalization at Endenich in February 1854, Brahms spent much time in the Schumann home as a deputy head of the household. Clara Schumann played a pivotal role in Brahms's intellectual development at this time, adding 'richly to Brahms's library during the 1850s'.[25] Amongst the volumes that she gave him as gifts were the tragedies of Sophocles and Aeschylus, Shakespeare, *The Dramatic Works*, Dante's *Divine Comedy*, the poems of Ossian, Plutarch's *Lebensbeschreibungen*, the complete works of Jean Paul and Schiller, and *The Thousand and One Nights*.[26] Brahms also used this time to embark upon a study of counterpoint, immersing himself in the resources of the Schumanns' library, and devoting himself to the study of the Renaissance and Baroque music he found there. Albert Dietrich refers to the years 1854–60 as 'Brahms's years of withdrawal', for it was during this time that he composed nothing and turned his attention instead to studying the works of composers including Durante, Lotti, Corsi, Palestrina, Byrd, Schütz, and J. S. Bach.[27]

Feuerbach underwent a comparable period of serious study to that of Brahms at the outset of his career. From 1844 he studied with the former Nazarene Wilhelm von Schadow at the Düsseldorf Academy, moving in 1848 to Munich, where he copied the old Masters at the Pinakothek, and from there to Paris where he worked under Thomas Couture from 1852 to

---

[24] Schumann, translated and quoted in Leon Plantinga, *Schumann as Critic* (New Haven, CT: Yale University Press, 1967), 85.

[25] Johannes Brahms, *Johannes Brahms: A Life in Letters*, ed. Styra Avins, trans. Josef Eisinger (Oxford: Oxford University Press, 2001), 68.

[26] George Bozarth, 'Brahms's Lieder-Inventory of 1859–60 and Other Documents of His Life and Work', *Fontes Artis Musicae* (1983): 98–117.

[27] On Brahms's study of early music, see Virginia Hancock, 'The Growth of Brahms's Interest in Early Choral Music, and its Effect on His Own Choral Compositions', in *Brahms: Biographical, Documentary and Analytical Studies*, ed. Robert Pascall (Cambridge: Cambridge University Press, 1983); Hancock, *Brahms's Choral Compositions and His Library of Early Music* (Ann Arbor, MI: UMI Research Press, 1983), 27–40; and David Brodbeck, 'The Brahms–Joachim Counterpoint Exchange: or, Robert, Clara, and "the Best Harmony between Jos. And Joh."', in *Brahms Studies*, ed. David Brodbeck (Lincoln, NE: University of Nebraska Press, 1994), I, 30–80. See also Albert Dietrich, *Erinnerungen an Johannes Brahms in Briefen besonders aus seiner Jugendzeit* (Leipzig: O. Wigand, 1898), 27–8. On Brahms's historical consciousness, see Mark Burford, '"The Real Idealism of History": Historical Consciousness, Commemoration, and Brahms's "Years of Study"', unpublished PhD dissertation, Columbia University (2005).

1854.[28] Similar to Schumann's very public introduction of Brahms to the musical world in 1853, the recommendation of the painter Johann Schirmer (1807–1863) led to Feuerbach being awarded a prestigious travel stipend from the prince regent of Baden in 1854 to go to Venice the following year for the purpose of copying Titian's *Assumption of the Virgin* (1516–18).[29] Feuerbach frequently created landscapes, but his principal interest was in the idealist depiction of predominantly classical scenes in a style that was reminiscent of the artists of the Italian Renaissance, such as Titian, Michelangelo, Rafael, Domenichino, Guido Reni, Correggio, Tintoretto, and Paul Veronese.[30] His visualizations of the great figures of antiquity and the Renaissance have an outward form of measured calmness that perfectly serves the ideal of harmonious balance and a return to timeless beauty espoused by the art historian Johann Joachim Winckelmann (1717–1768).[31]

In his seminal text *Thoughts on the Imitation of the Painting and Sculpture of the Greeks*, published in 1755, Winckelmann considered classical art to possess 'a noble simplicity and tranquil grandeur, both in posture and expression',[32] words that Feuerbach used to describe his own work.[33] He proposed the idea that the only way for artists to become great 'was by imitating the ancients'.[34] Feuerbach was no mere imitator of classical antiquity, however, and he too 'strove to achieve "soul" and "poesy"' in his paintings.[35] Much of the reverence for past masters amongst German artists of the late eighteenth and early nineteenth century can be traced back to Winckelmann. His historicist writings awakened consider-

---

[28] Peter Selz, *German Expressionist Painting* (Berkeley, CA and London: University of California Press, 1957), 23.

[29] Annegret Hobert and Margarete Benz-Zauner, 'Biographien', in Heilmann, ed., *'In uns selbst liegt Italien': Die Kunst der Deutsch-Römer*, 385.

[30] Julius Allgeyer, *Anselm Feuerbach: Sein Leben und Kunst, mit Selbstbildnis des Künstlers* (Bamberg: Buchner, 1894; rev. edn Berlin and Stuttgart: Neumann, 1904), 362. See also Peter Clive, *Brahms and His World: A Biographical Dictionary* (New York, NY: Scarecrow Press, 2006), 141.

[31] Heilmann, 'Einleitende Anmerkungen zur Kunst der Deutsch-Römer', in Heilmann, ed., *'In uns selbst liegt Italien'*, 16.

[32] Leon Botstein, 'Brahms and Nineteenth-Century Painting', *19th-Century Music* 14/2 (1990): 154–68 (159).

[33] Floros, *Johannes Brahms, 'Free But Alone'*, 173.

[34] Johann Joseph Winckelmann, *Thoughts on the Imitation of the Painting and Sculpture of the Greeks*, trans. H. B. Nisbet, in *German Aesthetic and Literary Criticism: Winckelmann, Lessing, Hamann, Herder, Schiller, Goethe*, ed. H. B. Nisbet (Cambridge: Cambridge University Press, 1985), 29–54 (33).

[35] Allgeyer, *Anselm Feuerbach: Sein Leben und seine Kunst*, I: 102.

**Figure 2.1**  Anselm Feuerbach, *Iphigenie* (1862), Hessisches Landesmuseum, Darmstadt

able enthusiasm in the art of classical antiquity, paving the way for the Hellenic ideal in art and literature at the turn of the nineteenth century that would later characterize the artworks of Feuerbach. The latter's painting *Iphigenie* (Figure 2.1) exemplifies Winckelmann's longing for ancient Greece and his notion of beauty and grace, as depicted by Iphigenia staring out at the Black Sea in longing and 'searching for the land of the Greeks with her soul'.[36]

Brahms and Feuerbach had in common a propensity toward the great, the exalted, and the ideal in classical figures. Both prized the importance of form, rigour of thought, dominance of the line, and sculpted design.[37] Writing in 1937, Walter Niemann refers to Feuerbach as the 'greatest of German neo-classic painters', considering his paintings to be 'pure music in their tranquil stateliness', their 'rugged beauty', and 'the poetic magic of their atmosphere'.[38] In a similar vein, he considered the compositions of Brahms ('the greatest German neo-classic in music') to demonstrate, 'by their choice of words and their titles – *Schicksalslied, Nänie, Gesang der Parzen, Rinaldo* – how peculiarly at home and at ease the composer felt in the world of antique or Italian beauty, which was that of the painter of "Iphigenie" or "Plato's Symposium"'.[39]

Niemann perceptively identified both Brahms and Feuerbach as having 'transfigured, revived, and renewed the antique spirit in poetic fashion and with modern sentiment'.[40] During Brahms's lifetime, the Viennese music critic Eduard Hanslick had also outlined 'the similarity in the *Kunstanschauung* that connected Feuerbach and Brahms', as 'their same imperturbable direction toward the great, the exalted and the ideal that often led to sharp severity and seclusion'.[41] Hanslick considered the words that Feuerbach used to describe his own painting 'Poetry' to apply equally well to the uncompromising artistic integrity of Brahms:

It is no picture dictated by fashion; it is severe and unadorned. I expect no understanding of it, but I can do nothing else. And he who takes the trouble to consider it for a long time becomes somewhat overcome, as though the picture is not a picture of our time.[42]

Brahms's enthusiasm for Feuerbach's paintings was often prompted or refreshed by the intervention of Julius Allgeyer, a copper engraver, photographer, and author of art-historical writings. In his *atélier* in Karlsruhe,

---

[36] Feuerbach cited in James J. Sheehan, *Museums in the German Art World: From the End of the Old Regime to the Rise of Modernism* (Oxford: Oxford University Press, 2000), 193.

[37] Ekkehard Mai, 'Im Widerspruch zur Zeit oder von der Tragik der Ideale. Feuerbachs Kunstwürfe', in Heilmann, ed., *'In uns selbst liegt Italien'*, 80.

[38] Walter Niemann, *Brahms*, trans. Catherine Alison Phillips (New York, NY: Tudor Publishing Company, 1937), 140.

[39] Niemann, *Brahms*, trans. Phillips, 140.     [40] Niemann, *Brahms*, trans. Phillips, 140.

[41] Eduard Hanslick, 'Brahms: "Nänie"', in *Concerte, Componisten und Virtuosen der letzten fünfzehn Jahre, 1870–1885: Kritiken* (Berlin: Allgemeiner Verein für Deutsche Literatur, 1886), 345–7.

[42] Feuerbach, as cited in Hanslick, 'Brahms: "Nänie"', 345–7.

Allgeyer dealt in photographic reproductions of Feuerbach's works. Brahms not only bought copies of these but also championed the artist to his intellectual circle. Shortly after the death of his mother, Christiane Johanna Brahms, in 1865, he wrote to Hermann Levi requesting that he tell 'Allgeyer that he has given me the greatest joy with the Feuerbachs; I would almost say that I have a need for them, because I don't feel like playing [the music of] dead musicians all the time'.[43] That same month, he asked Allgeyer to send copies of these reproductions through the music publisher Gotthart to a selection of 'other people'.[44]

Brahms's list of paintings tells us much about what he valued in Feuerbach's output, for he was repeatedly drawn to those paintings that connect the artworks of the Italian Renaissance with the German continuation of Greek humanity. Along with one copy of Allgeyer's complete catalogue of Feuerbach's work, the recipients of Brahms's gifts were each to be sent two copies of '*Hafis, Arentino, Dante,* Christus im Grab, das Liebespaar, das Gastmahl des *Plato, Medea, Iphigenie,* dem Kleinen an der Küste'.[45] So impressed was Brahms with Allgeyer's scholarship on Feuerbach that he was instrumental in arranging for the publication of his first article, 'Anselm Feuerbach', in the *Österreichische Wochenschrift für Wissenschaft und Kunst* in 1872.[46] Here Allgeyer writes in a Schillerian manner of the 'real and ideal moments' in Feuerbach's

[43] 'Sage z.B. Allgeyer, daß er mir die größte Freude gemacht hat mit den Feuerbachs; ich habe sie geradezu nötig, den alleweil tote Musiker spielen mag ich nicht.' Brahms to Hermann Levi, February 1865, in Kalbeck, *Johannes Brahms,* ii, 1: 173.

[44] A letter from Brahms to Allgeyer, January 1872, in Orel, *Johannes Brahms und Julius Allgeyer,* 73.

[45] 'Sei doch so gut mir für einige dieser "andre Leute" durch die Musik-Handlung Gotthart folgendes zukommen zu lassen. Einmal sämmtliche Blätter und zweimal: *Hafis, Arentino, Dante,* Christus im Grab, das Liebespaar, das Gastmahl des *Plato, Medea, Iphigenie,* und das Mädchen mit dem Kleinen an der Küste. Letzgenannte 9 Blätter also im Ganzen 3 mal, die übrigen 1 mal.' Brahms to Feuerbach, January 1872, in Orel, *Johannes Brahms und Julius Allgeyer,* 73 (italics in the original.) Constantin Floros provides a helpful clarification of what these paintings actually are: '"Hafis" refers either to "Hafis outside the Tavern" of 1852 or to "Hafis at the Well" of 1866. "Arentino" is short for the painting "The Death of Aerntino" (1854), a work known to exist in two versions. "Dante" indicates the picture "Dante and the Noble Woman of Ravenna" of 1857/58. "Christ ennobled" must mean the "Pietà" of 1863. The phrase "The Lovers" refers either to "Paolo and Francesca" or to "Romeo and Juliet", both of 1864. The title of the work depicting the "girl with the little one at the seacoast" is "Children at the Beach" of 1867. "Plato's Symposium", "Medea" and "Iphigenia", finally, are three of Feuerbach's most famous paintings, all existing in different executions'. Floros, *Johannes Brahms, 'Free but Alone',* 171.

[46] Julius Allgeyer, 'Anselm Feuerbach', *Österreichische Wochenschrift für Wissenschaft und Kunst* (1872): 641–52. Much later, Brahms also acquired a copy of Allgeyer, *Anselm Feuerbach: Sein Leben und seine Kunst,* now housed at the Brahms *Bibliothek* at the archive of the *Gesellschaft der Musikfreunde.*

output.[47] Much later, when Allgeyer published his monograph on Feuerbach in 1894, Brahms would write to Allgeyer to say that he simply 'could not thank [him] enough for the very rare and exalted artistic profit *your Feuerbach* means to me'.[48] In keeping with numerous other commentators during Feuerbach's lifetime, Allgeyer also identified the integrity in Feuerbach's art. This comment on the artist is also equally applicable to Brahms: 'It is difficult to convince and conquer the Germans by grace and charm. Hopefully pathos and passion, combined with beauty and grace, will do that.'[49]

## 2.2   The *Deutsch-Römer* and the Revival of the Classical Spirit in Germany

Despite the focus on Greece amongst the New Humanists, the historian Damian Valdez notes that none of the German Philhellenes of Schiller's generation actually visited Ottoman-ruled Greece, but instead, 'the German experience of Greece in the late eighteenth century was ultimately mediated by Italy'.[50] The artistic means by which the Germans gained access to this portal may have changed over time. As Valdez notes, 'the most salient Italian portal to the Greek world for Winckelmann remained sculpture', whereas 'for Goethe, that portal, at least until his second visit to Rome, was landscape'.[51] Regardless of the form in which it presented itself, however, Italy and, more specifically, the art of the Italian Renaissance, remained the tangible point of contact between the ancient Hellenic and the modern German worlds for Germany's Philhellenes, both at the end of the eighteenth and at the end of the nineteenth centuries.

Having lived in Rome for seventeen years from 1856 to 1873, Feuerbach had much time to nurture his reverence for the Italian Renaissance. He, along with Arnold Böcklin (1827–1901), Hans von Marées (1837–1887),

---

[47] Allgeyer, 'Anselm Feuerbach', 642.

[48] 'Ich aber kann Dir nicht herzlich genug danken für den überaus seltenen, hohen künstlerischen Gewinn, den mir *dein Feuerbach* bedeutet.' Letter from Brahms to Allgeyer, November 1894, in Orel, *Johannes Brahms und Julius Allgeyer*, 124. Emphasis in the original. On Brahms's estimation of this book, see also Richard Heuberger, *Erinnerungen an Johannes Brahms: Tagebuchnotizen aus den Jahren 1875 bis 1897* (Tutzing: Hans Schneider, 1971), 74.

[49] 'Es ist schwer die Deutschen durch Grazie und Anmuth zu überzeugen und zu besiegen, hoffentlich tut's das Pathos und die Leidenschaft, vereint mit Schönheit und Grazie.' Julius Allgeyer, on Feuerbach's fate, as cited in Orel, *Johannes Brahms und Julius Allgeyer*, 70.

[50] Damian Valdez, *German Philhellenism: The Pathos of the Historical Imagination from Winckelmann to Goethe* (New York, NY: Palgrave Macmillan, 2014), 162.

[51] Valdez, *German Philhellenism*, 163.

and the sculptor Adolf von Hildebrand (1847–1921), were part of a group known as the *Deutsch-Römer*, mostly German artistic personalities who lived in Rome and Florence in the second half of the nineteenth century and whose work was shaped by their time in Italy and by their impressions of that country's art and landscape. The *Deutsch-Römer* sought their roots in the art of the Italian masters in an effort to bring about an intellectual revival in painting.

The phenomenon of the *Deutsch-Römer* goes beyond a reverence for Italy and its artworks, however. In a seminal text called *'In uns selbst liegt Italien': Die Kunst der Deutsch-Römer ('Italy Lies in Our Selves': The Art of the German Romans)*, Christoph Heilmann asserts that this artistic movement owes a great deal to the time of the new humanism of Goethe, Hölderlin, Schiller, and German Romanticism and the idealism that was born with the Enlightenment. The *Deutsch-Römer* were also referred to as the 'New Idealists' in the 1890s by art historians such as Richard Muther and Cornelius Gurlitt.[52] The term explicitly linked these artists to Schiller and the German Idealist tradition, although it assumes a lateness that comes with the end of the nineteenth century and its political disillusionment and sense of disenchantment. It refers to artists who grounded their work in the study of nature but who were nonetheless 'painters of thought (*Gedenkenmaler*) "because the German is by birth a man of ideas"'.[53] These commentators adopted Schiller's language to describe the artistic output of this group in general and of Feuerbach in particular: 'The austerity of the antique spirit [. . .] is tempered by the melancholy of the modern intellect'. Olympus is filled 'with the light, the mist, the colour and the melancholy of a later and more neurotic age, the modes of which are more rich in *nuances* – an age which is sadder and more disturbed by human problems than was ancient Greece'.[54]

Heilmann probes the nature of this fascination with Italy, providing further context for the network of historical and intellectual connections between the new humanism and the reverence for Italian Renaissance

[52] See Cornelius Gurlitt, 'Adolf Hildebrand', *Die Kunst unserer Zeit: Eine Chronik des modernen Kunstleben* (Munich: Franz Hanfstaengel Kunstverlag, 1893), II, 76, as cited in Mitchell B. Frank, 'Painterly Thought: Max Liebermann and the Idea of Art', *Racar* 37/2 (2012): 47–59 (47).

[53] Karl Scheffler, *Deutsche Maler und Zeichner im Neunzehnten Jahrhundert* (Leipzig: Insel-Verlag, 1911), 3, here translated in Frank, 'Painterly Thought: Max Liebermann and the Idea of Art', 47.

[54] Richard Muther, *The History of Modern Painting* (London: Henry & Co., 1896) III, 558 and 472, cited in Frank, 'Painterly Thought: Max Liebermann and the Idea of Art', 49 (emphasis in the original).

art.[55] Venice and Rome meant far more than just biographical stages in the lives of these artists. These cities provided a living experience of the condition to which they aspired in their art. As Ekkehard Mai suggests, these cities were synonymous with a state of existence between longing and fulfilment; they gave the artist's life a calming certainty between inspiration and contentment.[56]

Botstein has persuasively argued that the passion for art and painting during the late nineteenth century in Vienna nearly rivalled that for music among the educated middle classes. Brahms shared with many of his immediate milieu an 'interest in collecting, visiting museums, and travelling to see art'.[57] This passion gave rise to his many trips to Italy between 1878 and 1893. It was at an auspicious time in the composer's life when he made the first of these eight trips together with his long-time friend Theodor Billroth, who had an exhaustive knowledge of the fine arts. In advance of these trips, Brahms travelled vicariously through Adolf Friedrich von Schack's (1815–1894) evocative descriptions of his travels in Italy, which he recommended to Billroth.[58]

Feuerbach is intimately connected with Brahms's love of art, and particularly with his love of Italian Renaissance art and classical antiquity. 'With him', as Max Kalbeck notes, 'we see Brahms entering into a similar artistic relationship with Greek and Roman antiquity as Feuerbach in his antiquating creations. These are not imitations of classical models, for which the musician is lacking any reliable tradition, but the revival of the classical spirit.'[59] Brahms's friend, the philologist Josef Viktor Widmann, provides evidence of the lasting association in Brahms's mind between Feuerbach and the art of Renaissance Italy in his recollection of one of the Italian journeys that he shared with Brahms in 1888. Widmann reports that in honour of Feuerbach's memory Brahms visited 'the former *Café* of the German artists, the "Genio" near the Fontana Trevi', and he initiated an

---

[55] Heilmann, 'Einleitende Anmerkungen zur Kunst der Deutsch-Römer', in Heilmann, ed., *'In uns selbst liegt Italien'*, 12.

[56] Ekkehard Mai, 'Im Widerspruch zur Zeit oder von der Tragik der Ideale. Feuerbachs Kunstwürfe', in Heilmann, ed., *'In uns selbst liegt Italien'*, 80–110 (80).

[57] Botstein, 'Brahms and Nineteenth-Century Painting', 156.

[58] See Natasha Loges, *Brahms and His Poets* (Rochester, NY: Boydell and Brewer, 2017), 355.

[59] 'Mit ihm sehen wir Brahms in ein ähnliches künstlerisches Verhältnis zum griechischen und römischen Altertum eintreten, wie Feuerbach in seinen antikisierenden Schöpfungen. Es handelt sich dabei nicht um Nachahmungen klassischer Vorbilder, für welche dem Musiker ohnehin jede zuverlässige Tradition fehlt, sondern um die Wiederbelebung klassischen Geistes.' Kalbeck, *Brahms* ii, 2: 305.

**Figure 2.2** Anselm Feuerbach, *Medea* (1870), Peter Horree/Alamy Stock Photo

excursion to Nettuno and Porto d'Anzio, where Feuerbach had made studies for his *Medea* (Figure 2.2).[60]

Although the two friends had been estranged since 1876, Feuerbach's death in 1880 came as a blow to Brahms, and it took him some time to process the loss.[61] In what has been perceived to be a breach of social etiquette, Brahms failed to send a note of condolence to Feuerbach's stepmother, Henriette Feuerbach, following the artist's death.[62] It was over a year and a half later, on completion of the composition of *Nänie* in August 1881, when Brahms wrote to Frau Feuerbach to ask if he might dedicate the piece to her. He confessed his desire 'to dedicate my music to [the artist's] memory' and his wish to see 'the name of your son joined to mine'.[63]

In setting Schiller's elegiac poem to music, Brahms created a lasting relationship between composer, artist, and poet,[64] all of whom, to varying degrees, may be understood as heirs to Winckelmann's neoclassicism in

---

[60] Josef Viktor Widmann, *Recollections of Johannes Brahms*, trans. Dora E. Hecht (London: Seeley & Co. Limited, 1899), 169.

[61] On the estrangement of Brahms and Feuerbach, see, for instance, Brahms's letter to Julius Allgeyer, 18 March 1876 in Orel, *Johannes Brahms und Julius Allgeyer*, 109. See also Floros, *Johannes Brahms, 'Free but Alone'*, 170–2.

[62] Kalbeck is most forgiving of Brahms's behaviour in this instance, asserting that the relationship between Brahms and Feuerbach (and, by extension, Brahms and Feuerbach's stepmother) was 'too high for an ordinary letter of condolence'. Kalbeck, *Brahms*, III, 1: 293. Siegfried Kross considers it to have been 'inexcusable' for Brahms to have ignored his friend's death, particularly in the context of the social formalities of the time. Kross attributes this behavior to Brahms's need 'to gain temporal distance from the shock of immediate experience'. See Siegfried Kross, *Die Chorwerke von Johannes Brahms* (Berlin: Max Hesses Verlag, 1963), 378.

[63] Brahms to Henriette Feuerbach, August 1881. The translated excerpts are from Avins, *Johannes Brahms: A Life in Letters*, 582–3.

[64] It is significant that Brahms heard Hermann Goetz's (1840–1876) setting a month after Feuerbach's death when it was performed in Vienna on 14 February 1880. Brahms had earlier, in 1875, been drawn to Schiller's poem 'Nänie', when he encountered Goetz's composition – also called 'Nänie' – but deferred setting it at that time out of respect for his younger colleague. Goetz died tragically and prematurely the following December. I am not concerned here with a comparative analysis of these two compositions. Numerous other scholars have embarked on this project, their studies indicating a strong likeness between the two. See, for instance, Hinrichsen, '"Auch das Schöne muß sterben" oder Die Vermittlung von biographischer und ästhetischer Subjektivität im Musikalisch-Schönen. Brahms, Hanslick und Schillers *Nänie*', in *Johannes Brahms oder die Relativierung der 'absoluten' Musik*, ed. Hanns-Werner Heister (Hamburg: Von Bockel Verlag, 1997), 121–54; James A. John, 'Johannes Brahms's *Nänie*'; Michael Musgrave, *The Music of Johannes Brahms* (Oxford: Clarendon, 1985), 168; and Floros, *Johannes Brahms, 'Free but Alone'*, 174–5. Brahms was certainly moved by the untimely death of his young friend and wrote a heartfelt note of condolence to Laura Goetz, the composer's widow. See Marek Bobéth, *Herman Goetz: Leben und Werk* (Winterthur: Amadeus Verlag, 1995), 507. See also Eduard Kreuzhage, *Hermann Goetz: Sein Leben und seine Werke* (Leipzig: Breitkopf & Härtel, 1916).

the visual, literary, and musical realms. These three figures are further united around their varying relationships to German Idealism, with their focus predominantly fixed on the reflective conception of ideas (*Begriffe*) rather than perception (*Anschauung*).[65] The preoccupation with form that they shared is readily discernible in their respective outputs and is particularly notable in Schiller's 'Auch das Schöne muß sterben', Feuerbach's *Iphigenie*, and Brahms's *Nänie*, all three of which exhibit an outward calm redolent of Winckelmann's writings.

## THE LITERARY

### 2.3 Idyll and Elegy in Schiller's Aesthetic Paradigm

Schiller's late elegy 'Auch das Schöne muß sterben' is concerned with the notion that through lamentation, art becomes immortal. This aesthetic ideal, which is also espoused in his theoretical writings, is bound up with the battle between reason and sensuality, and the effort to unite those two facets of the human mind. It is central to Schiller's series of letters in *On the Aesthetic Education of Mankind* (1794/5). Giving voice to the perennial concern of a lost paradise and the neo-Platonic dialectic of fall and return to which M. H. Abrams gives powerful expression, in the Eighth Letter Schiller suggests that art and culture have destroyed the totality in our nature. This position is related to the circuitous journey homeward, explored in Chapter 1, that describes humanity's alienation from nature and the attempt to return to nature:

Reason has purged herself of both the illusions of the senses and the delusions of sophistry, and philosophy itself, which first seduced us from our allegiance to nature, is now in loud and urgent tones calling us back to her bosom.[66]

The notion of unity is central to Schiller's conception of nature and humanity. Within his dialectical formulation, the wholeness to be found in nature can only be reconstituted by a higher art. In the Sixth Letter he asserts that 'if the cultivation of individual powers involves the sacrifice of wholeness', then 'it must be open to us to restore by means of a higher Art

---

[65] This distinction was made by Karl Scheffler in the context of defining the difference between French Naturalism, characterized by perception (*Anschauung*), and German art criticism, which is bound up with concept (*Begriff*). See Frank, 'Painterly Thought: Max Liebermann and the Idea in Art', 47.

[66] Schiller, *On the Aesthetic Education of Man: In a Series of Letters*, 49–51.

the totality of our nature which the arts themselves have destroyed'.[67] In Schiller's *Aesthetic Education*, we witness a dialectical turn from considering art to be the cause of lost wholeness to espousing it as a means through which this fragmented wholeness may once again be united and restored at a higher level: 'There must, therefore, since the cause does not lie in things themselves, be something of the disposition of men which stands in the way of the acceptance of truth, however brightly it may shine, and of the adoption of truth, however forcibly it may convince'. Echoing Kant's 1784 essay, 'Answer to the Question "What is Enlightenment"', Schiller continues:

**A sage of old felt what it was, and it lies concealed in that pregnant utterance:** *sapere aude*! Dare to be wise! It is energy and courage that are required to combat the obstacles which both indolence of nature and cowardice of heart put in the way of our true enlightenment.

Schiller lamented that his advice on aesthetic education went unheeded so that, rather than people looking inward for spiritual reflection, they relied 'on the state and on priests for their instruction'.[68] Brahms highlighted this passage in his copy of Schiller's complete works.[69] In the Ninth letter in the *Aesthetic Education*, Schiller encouraged writers to take inspiration from antiquity, indicating the degree to which this continues to be a living art form that endures in the manner of artistic responses to it. As David Pugh observes, 'modern art, if it is to be progressive in Schiller's sense, must paradoxically orient itself in some way on ancient Greek art'.[70] Consistent with the dialectical nature of Schiller's historical system, modern art 'must

---

[67]  Schiller, Sixth Letter; this translation by Wilkinson and Willoughby in Schiller, *On the Aesthetic Education of Man: In a Series of Letters*, 43.

[68]  Valdez, *German Philhellenism*, 194.

[69]  At this passage in Brahms's copy of Schiller's complete writings, there is a double line along the left outer margin of the Eighth Letter of *The Aesthetic Education of Mankind* that aligns most closely with the text given here in bold: 'Es muß also, weil es nicht in den Dingen liegt, in den Gemüthern der Menschen etwas vorhanden seyn, das der Aufnahme der Wahrheit, auch wenn sie noch so hell leuchtete, und der Annahme derselben, auch wenn sie noch so lebendig überzeugte, im Wege steht. **Ein alter Weiser hat es empfunden, und es liegt in dem vielbedeutenden Ausdruck versteckt:** *sapere aude.* Erkühne dich, weise zu seyn. Energie des Muths gehört dazu, die Hindernisse zu bekämpfen, welche sowohl die Trägheit der Natur als die Feigheit des Herzens der Velehrung entgegen setzten'. Friedrich Schiller, *Sämmtliche Werke*. Zwölf Bänden in sechs (Stuttgart und Tübingen: J. G. Cotta'scher Verlag, 1847), XII, 28. The translation is by Wilkinson and Willoughby in Schiller, *On the Aesthetic Education of Man: In a Series of Letters*, 51. See also Immanuel Kant, 'Answer to the Question "What is Enlightenment"', in Kant, *Political Writings*, ed. H. S. Reiss (Cambridge: Cambridge University Press, 1991), 54–60.

[70]  David Pugh, 'Schiller and Classical Antiquity', in *A Companion to the Works of Friedrich Schiller*, ed. Steven D. Martinson (Rochester, NY: Camden House, 2005), 57.

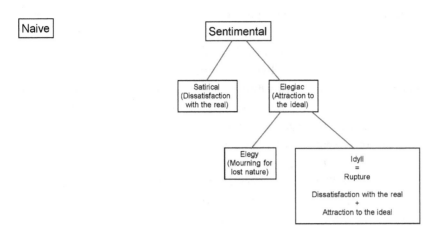

**Figure 2.3** Schiller's categorization of poetic genres

be both similar to and different from Greek art'.[71] Pugh explains the paradoxical role of the Greeks in Schiller's thought:

On the one hand, they represent a paradigm of unity and harmony to an age that has lost these qualities, and hence they are an object of aspiration and longing. On the other hand, and thanks to the intellectual and moral advances achieved in the modern age, any reconstituted unity and harmony must inevitably surpass all former achievements.[72]

In the *Aesthetic Education*, Schiller grappled with the fundamental question of 'how can we reasonably expect [art and aesthetic culture] to affect anything so great as the education of humanity'.[73] A year later, in his seminal treatise on modern literature, *On Naïve and Sentimental Poetry* (1795/6), he outlined two main categories of poetry that are of pivotal importance in his aesthetic of mourning and that serve well to illustrate this paradox: that is, the naïve, which is bound up with an imitation of nature, and the sentimental, which is bound up with the effort to regain a lost relationship to nature, a lost ideal. We encountered these categories in Chapter 1 and explored the degree to which they exerted an influence on Hölderlin's philosophical thought. It is worth probing them further here to gain a deeper understanding of Schiller's aesthetic of mourning.

For Schiller, the very capacity to seek the ideal (whether one looks to a recovery of the past or to attainment in the future) is precisely what

---

[71] Pugh, 'Schiller and Classical Antiquity', 57.
[72] Pugh, 'Schiller and Classical Antiquity', 55–6.
[73] This translation by Wilkinson and Willoughby in Schiller, *On the Aesthetic Education of Man: In a Series of Letters*, 63.

designates an individual as a poet, for art is opposed to nature (actuality). Schiller's theory illuminates Brahms's composition *Nänie*, which, I will argue, is informed by Schiller's categorization of poetic genres through the 'modes of perception'.[74] 'Every sentimental poet', Schiller writes, 'will adhere to one of these two modes of perception: the "satirical" and the "elegiac"' (Figure 2.3).[75] As was the case with the naïve and the sentimental, these subcategories are governed by perceptions of the real and the ideal. If the mode of perception is dissatisfaction with the real, then poetry takes the form of satire, that is, literature that criticizes corrupt or sophisticated ways of life. Satirical literature sees actuality (or the real) as an object of antipathy. Satire describes a world in which the ideal is absent.[76] If the mode of perception is attraction to the ideal, however, then poetry takes the form of the elegiac – that which takes pleasure in the representation of the ideal as predominating over actuality.

Moving down one further level in Schiller's system, the elegiac in a broad sense can also take one of two forms: the 'elegy' (in a narrow sense) and the 'idyll'. The elegy is defined as literature that looks back nostalgically to a simpler past that has now vanished. Its defining characteristic is mourning and, more specifically, mourning for lost nature. The elegy in this narrow sense considers the ideal to be an object of sympathy. Schiller's second subcategory, the idyll, is the site where the real and the ideal come together. The mode of perception in the idyll is simultaneously dissatisfaction with the real and an attraction to the ideal.

The idyll, therefore, is a synthesizing concept in which the representation of the ideal predominates over actuality (the real). It expresses what Paul Alpers refers to as a 'dissatisfaction with modern society and the individual's desire for harmony within himself and with his environment'.[77] From a formal point of view, the defining feature of the idyll is a contradiction, or a rupture, which has great significance for Brahms's setting, as we will see in Section 2.4. This contradiction, Schiller explains, comes about because the idyll will 'implement an ideal, and yet retain the narrower indigent pastoral world'.[78] Schiller provides further clarification on the idyll in a lengthy footnote:

---

[74] Schiller, *On Naive and Sentimental Poetry*, note K, 292–3.   [75] *Ibid.* 196.

[76] Moi, 'Idealism', 280.

[77] Paul Alpers, 'Schiller's Naïve and Sentimental Poetry and the Modern Idea of Pastoral', in *Cabinet of the Muses: Essays on Classical and Comparative Literature in Honour of Thomas G. Rosenmeyer*, ed. Mark Griffith and Donald J. Mastronarde (Atlanta, GA: Scholars Press, 1990), 319–31 (323).

[78] Schiller, *On Naive and Sentimental Poetry* in H. B. Nisbet, *German Aesthetic and Literary Criticism: Winckelmann, Lessing, Hamann, Herder, Schiller, Goethe* (Cambridge: Cambridge University Press, 1985), 213.

That I account the idyll as an elegiac category does seem to require justification. It should be recalled, though, that here I speak only of that kind of idyll that is a species of sentimental poetry, to the essence of which belongs the notion that nature is *opposed* to art, and the ideal to actuality. Even if this is not rendered explicit by the artist and he offers to our view a pure and spontaneous portrait of unspoiled nature or of the ideal fulfilled, yet that opposition is still within his heart and will betray itself in every stroke of the brush, even against his will.[79]

The idyll highlights the tension that exists between the real and the ideal, and between nature and art more strongly than any of Schiller's poetic categories. Whereas these oppositions are presented as simple binaries, their role in Schiller's dialectic reveals a more complex relationship. Nature represents a lost paradise, yet it is also an ideal to be attained in the future. Art is the cause of this lost paradise, yet it is only through art that we will see the recovery of nature. Constantin Behler evocatively refers to the simultaneously retrospective and teleological nature of Schiller's concept as 'nostalgic teleology', a schemata in which we find 'a recovery and reconstitution of "nature" by means of art'.[80] Schiller's aesthetic programme, as we witnessed Behler argue in Chapter 1, is built around 'the three-stage figure of origin and return; nature versus culture; the whole and its parts; the interior versus the exterior'.[81] A key passage in Schiller's writings summarizes and brings together the 'triadic history of genres' as they figure within this aesthetic programme:

Either nature and the ideal are an object of sadness if the first [nature] is treated as lost and the second [the ideal] as unattained. Or both are an object of joy represented as actual [the real]. The first yields the elegy in the narrower sense, and the second the idyll in the broader sense.[82]

Turning his focus more explicitly to Schiller's theory of mourning, Ehrhard Bahr notes that death and destruction 'function as essential elements of Schiller's aesthetics'. Grief about the destruction of Beauty constitutes Schiller's theory of mourning.[83] This aesthetic theory is explicated in his elegiac poetry, including the poem that Brahms set, 'Auch das Schöne muß sterben'.

---

[79] Schiller, *On Naïve and Sentimental Poetry*, 200, here at note K, 292–3. All of Schiller's examples are male. None are female and, as numerous authors have noted, Schiller offers a sexist and regressive view of women, one of the 'inner and ultimately destructive faultlines' of his aesthetic writings, as Moi asserts. On Schiller's treatment of sexuality in general and women in particular, see Moi, 'Idealism', 276–7. See also Constantin Behler, *Nostalgic Teleology: Friedrich Schiller and the Schemata of Aesthetic Humanism* (Bern and New York, NY: Peter Lang, 1995), ch. 2, 'The Hidden Violence of Bildung'.

[80] Behler, *Nostalgic Teleology*, 4.     [81] *Ibid.*, 4.

[82] Schiller, *On Naïve and Sentimental Poetry*, 200.

[83] Bahr, 'Death and Mourning in Friedrich Schiller's Aesthetics', 109.

## 2.4    From the Naïve to the Sentimental: Schiller's Theory of Mourning

Schiller's reception of Homer in his poetic and theoretical writings can be understood as part of a movement that witnessed renewed attention on the Homeric epics, prompted partly by Johann Heinrich Voß's hexameter translation of the *Iliad* and the *Odyssey* into German in 1781.[84] Schiller and Goethe both owned copies of this translation, the same edition that Brahms later owned.[85] For them, as Valdez observes, 'the ethical import of Greek tragedy and epic hinted at a pure humanity', one 'whose insights had to be distilled by a modern poet'.[86] Within this configuration, Homer serves as the naïve source for Schiller's sentimental reflection. Yet, as we have seen, Schiller's conception is dialectical. Nature, as Pugh explains, is not only 'the first but also the third term in humanity's dialectical progress'. Within Schiller's poetic production, Pugh considers this dialectical formula 'to be best borne out by his series of exceptional poems in the elegiac meter', which is exemplified by 'Auch das Schöne muß sterben'.[87]

The poem is in the form of the classical elegy with seven 'elegiac distiches', that is, pairs of lines that alternate between hexameter and pentameter (Table 2.1). Kevin F. Hilliard interprets a reflexive and self-reflexive structure in this poem.[88] Distich 1 is a reflection of the lament of the gods that concludes in distich 6, a feature of the form that has strong implications for Brahms's setting.

Schiller repeatedly conceives of Homer as a naïve poet, not a sentimental one, and praises him in *On Naïve and Sentimental Poetry* for his 'unadorned narrative style'.[89] As Schiller sees it, a naïve poet 'moves us by nature, by sensuous truth, by living presence', whereas a sentimental poet moves us 'by ideas'.[90] In other words, as Bahr remarks, 'poets of classical Greece were naïve because they simply imitated nature, while the modern poets were sentimental because they sought to regain a relationship to

---

[84] Brahms's library contains the following: Homer, *Odyee*, trans. Johann Heinrich Voß (Reutlingen: Im Comptoir der deutschen Classiker, 1819); Homer, *Homers Werke*, trans. Johann Heinrich Voß, 1 (Stuttgart & Tübingen: J. G. Cotta'scher Verlag, 1839); and Homer, *Homers Odyee*, trans. Johann Heinrich Voß. Reprint of the first edition from 1781 with an introduction by Michael Bernays (Stuttgart: J. G. Cotta'schen Buchhandlung, 1881).

[85] Valdez, *German Philhellenism*, 201–2.    [86] Valdez, *German Philhellenism*, 203.

[87] Pugh, 'Schiller and Classical Antiquity', 58. (Pugh lists poems such as 'Die Singer der Vorwelt', and 'Das Ideal und das Leben'.)

[88] K. F. Hilliard, '"Nänie": Critical Reflections on the Sentimental in Poetry', *Publications of the English Goethe Society* L75/1 (2006): 3–13.

[89] Pugh, 'Schiller and Classical Antiquity', 57.

[90] Schiller, *On Naive and Sentimental Poetry*, 194.

**Table 2.1** Formal outline of Schiller, 'Nänie'

| Distich | Line | Poem | Time signature | Tonality |
|---|---|---|---|---|
| 1 | 1 | Auch das Schöne muß sterben, das Menschen und Götter bezwinget! | 6/4 | D |
| | | Even beauty has to die; what overcomes men and gods | | |
| | 2 | Nicht die eherne Brust rührt es des stygischen Zeus. | | |
| | | Does not move the iron breast of the Zeus of Styx. | | |
| 2 | 3 | Einmal nur erweichte die Liebe den Schattenbeherrscher, | | |
| | | Only once did love soften the ruler of the shades, | | |
| | 4 | Und an der Schwelle noch, streng, rief er zurück sein Geschenk. | | |
| | | And even then he sternly called back his gift at the very threshold. | | |
| 3 | 5 | Nicht stillt Aphrodite dem schönen Knaben die Wunde, | | |
| | | Aphrodite cannot cure the lovely boy of the wound | | |
| | 6 | Die in den zierlichen Leib grausam der Eber geritzt. | | |
| | | The boar savagely ripped in his delicate flesh. | | |
| 4 | 7 | Nicht errettet den göttlichen Held die unsterbliche Mutter, | | |
| | | When the god-like hero falls at the Scaean gate and | | |
| | 8 | Wenn er, am skäischen Tor fallend, sein Schicksal erfüllt. | | |
| | | Falling fulfills his destiny, his immortal mother cannot save him. | | |
| 5 | 9 | Aber sie steigt aus dem Meer mit allen Töchtern des Nereus, | C | F♯ |
| | | But she rises from the sea with all the daughters of Nereus | | |
| | 10 | Und die Klage hebt an um den verherrlichten Sohn. | | |
| | | And laments her glorified son. | | |
| 6 | 11 | Siehe, da weinen die Götter, es weinen die Göttinnen alle, | | |
| | | Look, the gods are weeping, and all the goddesses too, | | |
| | 12 | Daß das Schöne vergeht, daß das Vollkommene stirbt. | | |
| | | Weeping that beauty must pass, that perfection must die. | | |
| 7 | 13 | Auch ein Klaglied zu sein im Mund der Geliebten ist herrlich, | 6/4 | D |
| | | There is splendor even in this – to be a lament in the mouth of those we loved, | | |
| | 14 | Denn das Gemeine geht klanglos zum Orkus hinab. | | |
| | | For what is common goes down to Orcus unsung. | | |

The English translation of the poem in this table is taken from Leonard Forster, ed., *Penguin Book of German Verse*, reprinted and with revisions (Harmondsworth: Penguin Books, 1959). I have slightly amended the translation.

nature that they had lost and were not able to recover'.[91] Ancient poets were 'characterized by an innocence of heart that entirely escapes their modern colleagues'.[92] By invoking Homer within his own poem, therefore, Schiller positions himself as the modern sentimental poet in relation to the ancient poet Homer.

Aspects of the form of Schiller's poem are reflected in the form of Brahms's setting. Germanists from the mid-nineteenth century to the present have argued that the anaphoric entry at line 13, distich 7 represents a revocation of the opening of the poem.[93] 'Auch ein Klaglied zu sein' is not only reminiscent of 'Auch das Schöne muß sterben' in its linguistic gesture; it heightens and conditions the sense of loss to which Schiller gave voice at the outset of the poem by reimagining this loss in relation to the power of art. In Schiller's formulation, 'Beauty has to cease to exist. Otherwise it would not be Beauty'.[94]

The dialectical process entailed in the death of beauty sees that which was a lament (*Klage*) undergo a crucial transformation to become a song of lament (*Klaglied*). In other words, the lament becomes the subject of the song: it is objectified and memorialized. As Hilliard explains, 'the positive [that is, beauty] cannot do without an explicit reference to its negative foil [that is, death]'.[95] As the third term in Schiller's dialectical process, we witness this negative foil validate, legitimize, and celebrate its own positive imprint. Bahr further explains that 'there will always be moments in history when Beauty will have to die, but these moments validate the mission of art'.[96]

That which is beautiful becomes truly immortal by virtue of being memorialized eternally in Schiller's poetry. Within its reflexive frame, the poem makes reference, whilst discreetly refraining from naming them, to three mythological characters who are not only beautiful, but

---

[91]  Bahr, 'Death and Mourning in Friedrich Schiller's Aesthetics', 116.

[92]  Toril Moi, 'Idealism', 277.

[93]  See, for instance, Wohlleben, 'Ein Gedicht, ein Satz, ein Gedanke – Schiller's "Nänie"'; Heinrich Düntzer, *Schiller's Lyrische Gedichte* (1856), cited in Wohlleben, 'Ein Gedicht, ein Satz, ein Gedanke – Schiller's "Nänie"', 61; and Kaiser, *Vergötterung und Tod*, 34.

[94]  Bahr, 'Death and Mourning in the Aesthetics of Schiller's Classicism', 177.

[95]  Hilliard, '"Nänie": Critical Reflections on the Sentimental in Poetry', 9.

[96]  Ehrhard Bahr, '*Wallensteins Tod* as a "Play of Mourning": Death and Mourning in the Aesthetics of Schiller's Classicism', *Goethe Yearbook* xv, ed. Simon Richter and Daniel Purdy (Rochester, NY: Boydell and Brewer, 2008), 171–86 (177).

are also young, and for each of whom a premonition of early death is provided. Distich 2 refers to the beautiful Eurydice, whose immortality is revoked by Hades because of her husband Orpheus's premature gaze; distich 3 refers to the death of Adonis, the son of Aphrodite, who is gored by a wounded boar; and distich 4 refers to Achilles, the godly hero and grandson of Zeus killed by Paris at the gates of Troy, despite the attempt by his mother, Thetis, the goddess of the sea, to make him invulnerable. In Schiller's poem all three of the verses that outline the destruction of beauty are introduced with the word 'nicht' ('not'), the negative declaration serving to heighten the sense of the loss of Beauty. When faced with the armoured heart of Zeus of Styx, Aphrodite cannot heal the wounds of the beautiful youth, nor can the deathless mother Thetis rescue her son: 'Nicht die eherne Brust rührt es des stygischen Zeus' (distich 1, line 2); 'Nicht stillt Aphrodite dem schönen Knaben die Wunde' (distich 3, line 5); and 'Nicht errettet den göttlichen Held die unsterbliche Mutter' (distich 4, line 7). Schiller elevates death and the beautiful to the status of the ideal, 'one in the past as a lost ideal, the other in the future to be sought after'.[97] By opposing beauty and death in this immediate and close proximity, Schiller composes the rupture that characterizes the idyll.

Schiller's definition of Beauty, moreover, does not refer to physical beauty but rather refers to 'the aura of beauty during a particular period of history' that was both remarkable and worthy of imitation. Beauty for Schiller, as Bahr formulates it, is 'a reference to the classical period of Greece as a model for modern art and literature, but at the same time a declaration of its historicity'. By establishing a fixed point in history for the death of Beauty, Schiller suggests that 'the Greek gods and all the Beauty they represented had become part of history that could not be recovered'.[98]

For a composer who was as preoccupied with matters of form as Brahms, Schiller's 'Auch das Schöne muß sterben' must have held great appeal, not

---

[97] Gerhard Kaiser, *Vergötterung und Tod*, 34.

[98] Bahr, '*Wallensteins Tod* as a "Play of Mourning"', 178. Bahr clarifies that the importance for Schiller is the loss of Greek Beauty, rather than the role of Christianity in the modern world. Nonetheless, where the latter in concerned and certainly in Schiller's earlier 1793 version of 'Das Götter Griechenlands', there is a continuity to be found here and in the passages of Nietzsche, *The Antichrist* that Brahms marked up in his copy of that book, as explored in Chapter 4.

only for its mastery of form but also for its capacity to articulate multiple degrees of loss at different moments in time. The lost Beauty to which 'Auch das Schöne muß sterben' refers finds concrete expression in Schiller's allusion to Homer. Schiller provides a sentimental reflection on Homer's naïve outpourings and in so doing memorializes lost beauty. Schiller's poetry, in turn, provides an allegory through which Brahms also addresses multiple levels of loss. In the first instance, Brahms memorializes the loss of literary beauty through Schiller's poetry and secondarily through classical antiquity as represented by Homer. Through the dedication of the piece to the artist's stepmother, Henriette Feuerbach, Brahms memorializes not only Feuerbach but also the loss of visual beauty in the form of classical antiquity and its surrogate, the art of the Italian Renaissance, which is celebrated in the paintings of Feuerbach and the *Deutsch-Römer*. Brahms's decision to include remarks in the programme note for the premiere of the piece for which he himself conducted the Zurich Tonhalle Orchestra on 6 December 1881 was highly uncharacteristic and therefore very telling.[99] It was clearly important to him that his audience understood the significance of Zeus, Eurydice, Adonis, Achilles, and Orcus, so that the listener could be afforded a deeper understanding of Schiller's poetic source.[100] His overt references to Homer, therefore, reinforced these classical associations and drew together the three strands of the visual, the literary, and the musical.

Notwithstanding the rich network of allusions to literature and the association with the world of art, the principal sense of loss that pervades this composition is the loss of musical beauty. By incorporating allusions not only to his own output but also to the music of Beethoven and

---

[99] The programme for this concert included Brahms, *Academic Festival* Overture, Op. 80, the Piano Concerto No. 2, Op. 83 (which Brahms himself played from the manuscript), the world premiere of *Nänie*, Op. 82, and the Second Symphony, Op. 73. I have been unable to locate a copy of the original programme.

[100] For a copy of Brahms's remarks in the programme note, see *Alte Brahms-Gesamtausgabe*, edited by the Gesellschaft der Musikfreunde in Vienna, xix (reprint of the Leipzig edition from 1927–8: Wiesbaden, 1965), as mentioned in Constantin Floros, '"Auch das Schöne muß sterben": Brahms's *Nänie*, Op. 82', in *Schiller und die Musik*, ed. Helen Geyer, Wolfgang Osthoff, and Astrid Stäber (Vienna: Böhlau, 2007), 395–407 (396). These annotations are included with the poem in most recent editions of Brahms's *Schicksalslied*. See, for instance, Brahms, *Alto Rhapsody, Song of Destiny, Nänie, and Song of the Fates in Full Score* (New York, NY: Dover, 2011), 63.

Schumann, Brahms evokes a sense of longing for the musical beauty of an earlier time and betrays a sense of dislocation with and alienation from his own age. *Nänie*, as we will see, occupies an important position as the last of Brahms's Elegies to celebrate tonality and the legacy of tonal music. In order to understand how, we will draw on the methodology of Reinhold Brinkmann and his probing exploration of the nature of melancholy in relation to Brahms's music.

## THE MUSICAL

### 2.5 An Aesthetic Rupture I: Framing Musical Beauty in Relation to Art

Reinhold Brinkmann's designation of Brahms as a 'late idyll' in *Late Idyll: The Second Symphony of Johannes Brahms* draws heavily on Schiller's theory of mourning, in particular the section concerning 'Sentimental Poets' in *On Naïve and Sentimental Poetry*.[101] 'For Brahms's symphonic idyll', he writes, 'is not – to adopt Schiller's terms – "naïve" but "sentimental"'. We recall that a poet 'either *is* Nature, or else he will *seek* her. The former is a naïve, the latter a sentimental poet.'[102] Nature, as we have now come to understand it, is a force that resists civilization, a force that is anti-historical.

Brinkmann's definition of idyll has much in common with Schiller's, but his category of 'late' conjures up a much more recent image of the 'nature' that Brahms has lost. Brahms's late style may be attributed to the composer's music-historic lateness within the nineteenth century, his lateness with regard to the age of tonality, his position at the end of the Austro-German symphonic tradition, and his place in a modern, historically self-conscious age, excluded from the innocence of an earlier one.[103] Schiller's category of sentimental is directly relevant to Brahms on the basis of cultural factors

---

[101] Reinhold Brinkmann, *Late Idyll: The Second Symphony of Johannes Brahms* (Cambridge, MA: Harvard University Press, 1997).

[102] *Ibid.*, 200.

[103] As well as Brinkmann, *Late Idyll*, see also Margaret Notley, *Lateness and Brahms: Music and Culture in the Twilight of Viennese Liberalism* (Oxford: Oxford University Press, 2007).

such as the increased scepticism and disillusionment that followed the failed revolutions in 1848 in Europe, and the industrialization and increased secularization that increased as the century progressed.

In his focused study on cultural melancholy, Brinkmann applies Schiller's late eighteenth-century philosophical thought to a late nineteenth-century context. It is precisely on account of the loss of naivety that Brinkmann considers Brahms to be a melancholic composer.[104] Following Schiller, he relates the idyll to an attempt to recover a pastoral mode, an Arcadian state of former innocence, for which he cites Brahms's increasing propensity from the 1870s onward to spend time away from the metropolis of Vienna in idyllic country retreats such as Baden-Baden or Pressbaum, where Brahms completed the composition of *Nänie*. Considering Brahms from Brinkmann's post-Schillerian perspective allows us to position him in relation to a series of modernist composers in *fin-de-siècle* Vienna who similarly sought refuge from the modern, industrial world in idyllic country retreats, such as Mahler, Bruckner, and Webern.[105] The sense of melancholy that we discern in the output of these composers is closely related to Svetlana Boym's concept of nostalgia, which, she cogently argues, is 'not anti-modern'. What appears to be 'a longing for a place' is actually 'a yearning for a different time'. Yet this is 'not always retrospective; it can be prospective as well'.[106] Attributing to it overtones of Horkheimer and Adorno's 'disenchantment of the world', Boym asserts:

Modern nostalgia is the mourning for the impossibility of mythical return, for the loss of an 'enchanted world' with clear borders and values. It could be a secular expression of a spiritual longing, a nostalgia for an absolute, for a home that is both physical and spiritual, for the edenic unity of time and space before entry into history.[107]

Boym's observation on 'modern nostalgia' illuminates Brinkmann's exploration of melancholy and the 'late idyll', which we can understand in relation to the disenchantment of the late nineteenth century. Brahms's very lateness is indicative of the broken idyll that he inhabits along with a number of his contemporaries. These include the novelist and poet Theodor Fontane

---

[104] For Brinkmann's discussion of Brahms's melancholy, see *Late Idyll*, 125–44.

[105] See Thomas Peattie, *Gustav Mahler's Symphonic Landscapes* (Cambridge: Cambridge University Press, 2015); Julian Horton, 'Brahms, Bruckner and the Concept of Thematic Process', in *Irish Musical Analysis* (Dublin: Four Courts Press, 2014), 78–105; Julian Johnson, *Webern and the Transformation of Nature* (Cambridge: Cambridge University Press, 1999).

[106] Boym, *The Future of Nostalgia*, 8.      [107] Boym, *The Future of Nostalgia*, 12.

(1818–1898) and the artist Adolph Menzel (1815–1905). These 'three fellow artists of the same generation', Brinkmann avers, 'found that at the close of the nineteenth century – an epoch they regarded as a late period – basic preconditions of their understanding of life and their art were being called into question'.[108]

In keeping with the central tenet of Schiller's definition of the idyll as entailing a contradiction or rupture, Brinkmann makes the case that relevant works of art by all three figures manifest their lateness in 'darkenings', 'interruptions', and 'structural breaks' of one kind or another.[109] Such fissures would seem to fit well in works that correspond to Schiller's category of idyll, works that 'implement an ideal, and yet retain the narrower indigent pastoral world'.[110]

Brinkmann's evocative description of a number of Menzel's paintings serves to elucidate these structural breaks. Consider his account of Menzel's *Berlin-Potsdamer Eisenbahn* of 1847, in which he observes:

The diagonal bisecting of the picture by the railroad reflects the historical conflict between nature and the industrial world in two ways: critically, as an element in the destruction of an archaic landscape (virgin land, primitive arboreal growth) and ancient life-styles (farmstead, sandy lane), but also enthusiastically, in the dynamic progress stirringly evoked by the advancing steam locomotive.[111]

A temporal element is at play here. As Brinkmann puts it, 'the silhouette of metropolitan Potsdam provides the historical dimension, constituting the background from which the "interruption" emanates, both ideologically and formally'.[112]

Equally evocative of 'the idyll', yet much more relevant to our exploration of Brahms's *Nänie*, as we will see, is Menzel's 1845 painting *Das Balkonzimmer* ('The Room with a Balcony', shown in Figure 2.4), which contains both a 'perfect idyll' and an 'underlying disturbance'.[113] The idyll is seen in the tall mirror in the wooden frame that reflects a perfectly composed domestic setting – perhaps a scene that the mirror had witnessed at an earlier time. Within this frame, we see the fine striped fabric of the sofa, and a smaller picture in the gold frame. Widening our focus, the disturbance of this harmonious world is found in the fragmentary composure of the painting as a whole, with the sunlight that streams through the double door opening onto a room that is somewhat impoverished in its furnishings by comparison with the scene in the mirror. Here we see a half-

---

[108] Brinkmann, *Late Idyll*, 10.    [109] *Ibid.*
[110] Schiller, *On Naïve and Sentimental Poetry*, 213.    [111] Brinkmann, *Late Idyll*, 9.
[112] *Ibid.*, 9.    [113] *Ibid.*, 4–6.

**Figure 2.4** Adolph Menzel, *Das Balkonzimmer* (1845), ART Collection/Alamy Stock Photo

painted wall, only a rough outline of the sofa, and the absence of the framed picture, made all the more conspicuous by the shadow left in its place. In Brinkmann's interpretation of this less opulent scene, the painting serves to question the idyll reflected in the mirror.

Menzel's *Das Balkonzimmer* expresses the contradiction or the rupture that defines Schiller's category of the idyll where the real and the ideal come together (Figure 2.3). Menzel depicts a dissatisfaction with modern society, giving expression to the individual's desire for harmony within herself and her environment. There is also a temporal dimension at play in this composition, an awareness that that which is reflected – a former state – cannot be recaptured in the present time of the painting. This realization heightens the sense of loss and the yearning for its recovery.

In connecting Brahms to Schiller's theoretical writings, Brinkmann taps into the historical and cultural aspects of Brahms's reception of Schiller that are often overlooked in studies on Brahms's texted music, which tend instead to focus on the poetry alone.[114] Just as his critique of Fontane and Menzel is concerned with their paintings, his exploration of 'late idyll' in Brahms is concerned with the music wherein he identifies 'darkenings' and 'brokenness', particularly in relation to the Second Symphony (which we will explore in a different context in Chapter 3). Drawing the musical and philosophical strands of the Schillerian idyll together, Brinkmann proposes that 'etched on the Brahmsian idyll, with its reflective intensity, is the consciousness of a late period which is excluded from the pure representation of an Arcadian state, and which realizes this consciousness in its art'.[115] In other words, not only is Brahms's music nostalgic, but, like Menzel's *Das Balkonzimmer*, it is music that is aware of its own nostalgia and seeks to recover a lost ideal. In keeping with Schiller's notion of 'nostalgic teleology',[116] the composer who emerges from Brinkmann's *Late Idyll* looks backward to a lost ideal, whilst his music simultaneously looks forward to the modernism of the twentieth century. Let us now turn to Brahms's *Nänie* in order to explore how this is the case.

## 2.6   An Aesthetic Rupture II: Framing Beauty in Brahms's *Nänie*

Brahms's *Nänie* begins with a bold and obvious allusion to Beethoven that is strongly characterized by pastoral topics, underlining the self-conscious nature of the nostalgia in this work, and explicitly marking out one of the moments at which Beauty must die. The plaintive oboe melody at the outset gives voice to a well-known allusion to the opening motto of Beethoven's Piano Sonata No. 26 in E♭ Major, Op. 81a, the 'Lebewohl'. Beethoven's distinctive motif, 'reminiscent of the vanishing sounds of a

---

[114] Although Brahms studies have not pursued the relationship between his music and Schiller's theoretical writings, studies on Schubert provide a methodology for such investigations. See, for instance, Su Yin Mak, 'Schubert as Schiller's Sentimental Poet', *Eighteenth-Century Music* 4/2 (2007): 251–63.

[115] Brinkmann, *Late Idyll*, 200.     [116] Behler, *Nostalgic Teleology*.

**Example 2.1a** Beethoven, Piano Sonata No. 26 in E♭ Major, Op. 81a, 'Lebewohl', bars 1–16

posthorn', the historically distant instrument that signalled nostalgia to a Romantic sensibility, comprises a falling $\hat{3}$– $\hat{2}$– $\hat{1}$ in the upper voice.[117]

As Charles Rosen reminds us, 'horn calls are symbols of memory – or, more exactly, of distance, absence and regret'.[118] The corresponding I-V-I motion in the bass that we typically find in the horn call would have sounded forth a perfect authentic cadence, fulfilling the move toward the tonic that

[117] Maynard Solomon, 'The Violin Sonata in G major, Op. 96: Pastoral, Rhetoric, Structure', in *The Beethoven Violin Sonatas: History, Criticism, Performance*, ed. Lewis Lockwood and Mark Kroll (Urbana and Chicago, IL: University of Illinois Press, 2004), 110–28 (117).

[118] Charles Rosen, *The Romantic Generation* (Cambridge, MA: Harvard University Press, 1995), 117.

**Example 2.1b** Beethoven, 'Lebewohl' Sonata, outline of the cadential structures, bars 1–16

**Example 2.1c** Reduction of Brahms, *Nänie*, bars 1–2

horn fifths typically promise. Beethoven, however, underpins the falling 'Lebewohl' motto with a deceptive I-V-vi cadence. The slow introduction to the first movement of this sonata travels from the submediant in bar 2 to a more remote flat submediant in bar 8, before coming to rest in bar 16 on the subdominant, from where it initiates the main Allegro section (Example 2.1a).

Further to the horn call's association with memory to which Rosen draws our attention, there is a decidedly intimate nature to this particular horn call. The word 'Lebewohl', as Beethoven conceived it when he inscribed it above the opening motto in his score, has a deeply intimate quality, more evocative of 'German *Innigkeit*' in 1809 than 'French pomposity', as Stephen Rumph notes.[119] Beethoven was at pains to emphasize this sense of intimacy to his publishers Breitkopf & Härtel, whom he upbraided for having employed the wrong translation:

---

[119] Stephen Rumph, *Beethoven after Napoleon: Political Romanticism in the Late Works* (Berkeley, Los Angeles, CA and London: University of California Press, 2004), 101.

I have just received the 'Lebewohl' and so forth. I see that after all you have published other French c[opies] with a French title. Why, pray? For 'Lebewohl' means something quite different from 'Les adieux'. The first is said in a warm-hearted manner to one person, the other to a whole assembly, to entire towns.[120]

Despite the 'Lebewohl' reference being clearly identifiable at the outset of *Nänie*, Brahms alters the harmonic motion of Beethoven's initial gesture in his D major context. The falling $\hat{3}- \hat{2}- \hat{1}$ remains, but the tail end of the deceptive cadence here becomes I-V-iv$^{6-3}$. Brahms's brief 'Lebewohl' gesture establishes the tonic and retains the contour of the outer lines of Beethoven's motto, whilst short-circuiting the harmonic trajectory of Beethoven's sixteen-bar introduction, allowing the deceptive cadence to arrive immediately at the subdominant (Examples 2.1b and 2.1c).

This telescoping of the harmonic trajectory of Beethoven's introduction within the intimate confines of Brahms's 'Lebewohl' gesture provides an early indication of the important role that the subdominant region plays in *Nänie*, the full significance of which is realized only with the plagal cadence that ends the piece.[121] Plagal harmony, as Margaret Notley asserts, 'can suggest qualities or states not easily conveyed in tonal music through harmonic means: otherworldliness, distance, timelessness, possibly even alienation'.[122] The move at the outset toward the subdominant region (an area that typically prepares resolution), rather than the tension-building dominant, puts one in mind of the outward form of measured calmness extolled in Winckelmann's writings and exemplified in many of Feuerbach's paintings, to recall the visual realm explored above. The deep sensuality of Brahms's pastoral melody in the oboe also finds a kinship with the sensuous nature of Feuerbach's paintings, particularly *Medea* (1862) and *Iphigenia* (1871), both of which feature Anna Risi (known as Nanna) as their model.

If the instrumental sonority of the posthorn was obscured in Beethoven's pianistic configuration, its pastoral colour is restored in Brahms's opening gesture scored for horns (which sound out the 'horn fifths'), along with flute, oboe, clarinets, and strings. Employing this orchestration for Beethoven's 'Lebewohl' motto re-inscribes nature and history in the falling horn call and the corresponding rising figure in the

---

[120] Letter from Beethoven to Breitkopf & Härtel, 23 September 1810 (Briefwechsel, No. 468), as cited in Lewis Lockwood, *Beethoven: The Music and the Life* (New York, NY: Norton, 2003), 302.

[121] In bar 177, as Hinrichsen suggests, Brahms takes up once more the 'Lebewohl' gesture that was left hanging in bar 2. See Hinrichsen, '"Auch das Schöne muß sterben"'.

[122] See Margaret Notley, 'Plagal Harmony as Other: Asymmetrical Dualism and Instrumental Music by Brahms', *Journal of Musicology* 22/1 (2005): 90–130 (95).

clarinets, whilst at the same time augmenting Beethoven's 2/4 rhythm to accommodate an expressive 6/4 time signature.

The formal structure of Brahms's *Nänie* lends itself to multiple interpretations (Table 2.2). It has widely been interpreted as a ternary form, a reading that is supported by changes in thematic material, key signature, time signature, and Brahms's performance directions for each of three sections: Andante, Più sostenuto, and Tempo primo. And yet we might also understand the treatment of formal functions to be entirely at odds with such a ternary structure, eliciting instead a large-scale binary (much like *Schicksalslied*), framed on either side by an introduction and a coda. Fundamental to the coherence of this binary framework is the large-scale plagal cadence that bookends the entire piece.

The Andante is governed by the 'Lebewohl' material (Example 2.2). The fugal subject that ushers in the four-part chorus to the words 'Auch das Schöne muß sterben' arises out of the opening 'Lebewohl' motto with which we have been preoccupied. The melody heard at bar 25 in the soprano and bar 33 in the tenor mirrors the D–A–B motif in the cellos and basses of bar 1 that underpins the falling $\hat{3}-\hat{2}-\hat{1}$ of the 'Lebewohl' gesture (Example 2.1c). Likewise, the fugal answer is drawn from the same material at the fifth, heard previously in bar 9 of the orchestral introduction and now reconfigured as part of the four-part fugal entry heard in bar 29 in the altos and bar 33 in the tenor and bass.

Brahms offers a countermelody from the upbeat to bar 42, as the choir, largely *a capella*, sings of that which 'overcomes men and gods' ('Das Menschen und Götter bezwinget'). This melody returns at bar 59, here pushing toward F major at bar 65 as Schiller's poem outlines the destruction of beauty in distich 3 with its repeated emphasis on the word 'nicht'. The subsequent move to F♯ minor at bar 75 is significant. It retrospectively suggests a tonicization of F♯ within a $\hat{7}-\hat{1}$ motion that extends from bar 65 to the C♯:PAC at bar 85. This anticipates the long tonicization of D major's third in the Più sostenuto which, in turn, will have implications for the plagal harmony that plays a crucial role at the beginning and end of *Nänie*.

The Più sostenuto section at bar 85 sets distiches 5 and 6 of Schiller's 'Nänie', the part of the poem that is concerned with the divine mother Thetis and the death of her mortal son Achilles. With the word 'Aber' ('but') at distich 5 (line 9), the structure and tone of Schiller's poem pivots from lamentation to triumph as Thetis rises from the sea in mourning at the death of her son: 'Aber sie steigt aus dem Meer mit allen Töchtern des Nereus'. At this central point, Brahms alters the time signature from a lilting 6/4 to a more heroic and

**Table 2.2** Formal analysis of Brahms's *Nänie*, Op. 82

| Bar | 1–25.1 | 25–41 | 42–46 | 47–59.1 | 59–64 | 65–70 | 71–74 | 74–78 | 78– | 85–89 | 90–95 | 96–106 | 107–18 | 119–23 | 124–41.1 | 141 | 149–57 | 158–62 | 162–76 |
|---|---|---|---|---|---|---|---|---|---|---|---|---|---|---|---|---|---|---|---|
| Tempo | Andante | | | | | | | | | Più sostenuto | | | | | | Tempo primo | | | |
| Meter | 6/4 | | | | | | | | | C | | | | | | 6/4 | | | |
| Ostensible tonality | D major | | | | | | | | | F♯ major (C♯ allusion) A tonicization of D major's third | | | | | | D major | | | |
| Thematic form | A | | | | | | | | | B | | | | | | A | | | |
| LSF | Intro | A | | | | | | | | B | | | | | | | | | Coda |
| Allusion | | | Beethoven, 'Lebewohl' motto | | | | | | | (1) Brahms, fifth movement of *Ein deutsches Requiem* (2) Beethoven, *An die ferne Geliebte*, 'Nimm sie hin denn, diese Lieder' | | | | | | Beethoven, 'Lebewohl' motto | | | |
| Distich | | 1 | | 2 | | 3 | | 4 | | 5 | | 6 | | | | 7 | | | |
| Line | | 1 | 2 | 3 | 4 | 5 | 6 | 7 | 8 | 9 | 10 | 11 | 12 | 11 | 12 | 13 | 13 | 14 | 13 |
| Cadence | I:PAC | | | | | | | | C♯:PAC at 85 | | | | | | F♯:IAC at 129 | | I:IAC | | I:PAC at 162 & 175 / Plagal at 179 |

After William Caplin, IAC denotes an imperfect authentic cadence; and PAC denotes a perfect authentic cadence. The Roman numerals that prefix these acronyms here and throughout this analytical passage indicate the relationship of the cadence to the tonic, D major. See William Caplin, *Classical Form: A Theory of Formal Functions for the Instrumental Music of Haydn, Mozart, and Beethoven* (Oxford: Oxford University Press, 2000).

**Example 2.2** Outline of 'Lebewohl' entries in the Andante, *Nänie*

military common time, as all four voices join in rousing homophony. He also removes the hemiolas and syncopation that have characterized the preceding passage, making the rhythm more tautly sprung and four-square. Further, he changes the key signature to F♯ major, a large-scale tonicization of D major's mediant, although we never satisfactorily cadence in that key. Instead, we are poised to look longingly at F♯ from an extended prolongation of the dominant C♯ beginning with the V:PAC at bar 85 that inaugurates the Più sostenuto. In this B section, Brahms employs a series of allusions both to his own music and to that of Beethoven and Schumann. His treatment of musical allusions is analogous to Schiller's treatment of literary allusions in the poem, and it is redolent of Feuerbach's references to classical antiquity in his artistic output, all of which speaks to a potent sense of memory and nostalgia.

Benedict Taylor gives detailed consideration to the question of 'how memory works' in music and explores its possible interpretations and permutations. Musical memory, he asserts, requires both 'a human listener (the subject)' and 'music heard at some earlier point in time (the object)'.[123] Taylor invokes Aristotle's adage that 'memory relates to what is past', before dividing musical memory into two broad categories. The first is simple memory, when the subject hears or recalls music (the object) that they have heard before. The second, more complex and sophisticated category is the music itself remembering its own earlier themes. From there, he moves on to outline the different types of memory in music, composing a taxonomy that is of particular significance to Brahms's *Nänie*, because each kind of quotation or allusion to past music that Taylor enumerates may be found in Brahms's *Nänie*. The earlier historical style is found in Brahms's employment of pastoral musical topics, most explicitly in the horn calls that characterize the 'Lebewohl' motif; the specific earlier compositions conjured up by Brahms include Beethoven's 'Lebewohl' Sonata and, as we will see presently, Beethoven's song cycle *An die ferne Geliebte*; Brahms's *Ein deutsches Requiem* satisfies the category of the earlier works by the composer himself. Finally, with regard to the composition's own musical past, Brahms brings us back to the materials heard at the outset of the piece in an altered manner at the composition's end. This web of allusion, furthermore, has semantic associations and a verbal web of memory, bound up with Schiller and Homer, that provide further dimensions for its hermeneutic context.

### 2.6.1 Brahms's Self-Allusion to *Ein deutsches Requiem*

Along with Brahms's allusions to Beethoven's *An die ferne Geliebte*, which we will explore in the next section, there is a significant amount of self-allusion in the central B section of *Nänie*. The music that witnesses Thetis rise from the sea, as John A. James astutely observes, is saturated with motifs from the fifth movement of *Ein deutsches Requiem*, at the words 'Ich will euch trösten' ('Thee will I comfort').[124] The fifth movement of the *Requiem*, a passage from Isaiah woven around texts from John and Ecclesiastes, offers the line 'Ihr habt nun Traurigkeit' ('You now have sorrow'). This was added following the death of Brahms's mother in 1865, allowing the *Requiem* to expand from six to seven movements. Between the opening movement of the *Requiem* and the fifth movement in which the soprano solo sings, the baritone soloist of the third movement begins with a meditation in D minor on the transience of all human life

---

[123] Benedict Taylor, *The Melody of Time: Music and Temporality in the Romantic Era* (Oxford: Oxford University Press, 2015), 131ff.

[124] Translations of the text of *Ein deutsches Requiem* are from Michael Musgrave, *Brahms: A German Requiem* (Cambridge: Cambridge University Press, 1996), 16.

**Example 2.3a** Brahms, *Ein deutsches Requiem*, V, opening melody

**Example 2.3b** Brahms, *Ein deutsches Requiem*, V, bars 62–4

Example 2.3c  Brahms, *Nänie*, bass voice at bars 87–90

before briefly taking up the question of comfort in his last utterance, 'nun, Herr, wie soll ich mich trösten?' ('Now, Lord, how shall I find comfort?') This baritone outpouring expresses doubt and anxiety. It is only with the soprano solo in the fifth movement that the promise of comfort is delivered. The soprano begins by singing 'Ihr habt nun Traurigkeit' ('ye now have sorrow') but transitions to singing 'Ich will euch trösten, wie einen seine Mutter tröstet' ('Thee will I comfort as one whom a mother comforts'). From here until the end of the work, comfort, *Trost*, is the central theme of *Ein deutsches Requiem*.[125]

The opening melody of this fifth movement (Example 2.3a) is taken up at bar 62 by the solo soprano, who intones the words 'ich will euch wieder sehen' ('I will see you again') in the same register, doubled by the first violins. Against this, the tenor voice in the choir, doubled by the horn, augments the rhythm of this melody, to sing the words 'ich will euch trösten' in quaver motion (Example 2.3b).

This rhythmically augmented melody comprises just one strand in the rich tapestry of Brahms's self-allusion in *Nänie*. At bar 87 of the latter, as early as the first phrase of the allusion-soaked Più sostenuto, the bass invokes the words 'mit allen Töchtern des Nereus' ('with all the daughters of Nereus') from distich 5 to the rhythmically augmented melody taken from the tenor voice of *Ein deutsches Requiem* (Example 2.3c).

### 2.6.2  Brahms's Beethoven Allusions

At the same time as Brahms infuses *Nänie* with reminiscences from the *Requiem*, he engages in further allusion, once again invoking Beethoven, but this time appealing to the intimate lyricism of the Romantic Lied. In bars 93–5, the melody to which the soprano sings 'um den verherrlichten

---

[125] Brahms began work on the *Requiem* most likely in response to the death of his mentor and dear friend Schumann in 1854 with whom it is likely that the funeral march in the second movement is associated. Most of the work on this composition, however, dates from 1865–66, following the death of Brahms's mother on 31 January 1865. Throughout the course of its composition, a mother image assumed ever greater significance, particularly with the addition of the fifth movement in 1868, following the premiere of the work at Bremen on 10 April 1868. For further details, see Beller-McKenna, *Brahms and the German Spirit* (Cambridge MA: Harvard University Press, 2004), ch. 3, 65ff.

**Example 2.4a** Beethoven, 'Nimm sie hin denn, diese Lieder', *An die ferne Geliebte*, Op. 98, bars 1–10

Sohn' ('for her glorified son') conjures up the motto of 'Nimm sie hin denn, diese Lieder' ('Take them then, these songs'), the final song of *An die ferne Geliebte*, Op. 98, the song cycle Beethoven wrote in the last decade of his life. This motto is bracketed in Example 2.4a as it appears in both the piano and voice parts of the opening strophe of Beethoven's song cycle.[126] The end of Brahms's allusion at bar 95, which retains Beethoven's melodic contour but alters the rhythm (Example 2.4b), sounds forth an authentic cadence in C♯ major, the dominant of the ostensible F♯ major tonic for this central B section. By invoking *An die ferne Geliebte*, Brahms also conjures up Schumann's celebrated allusion to the final song of Beethoven's cycle in the first movement of the *Fantasie*, Op. 17. The allusion to Beethoven's *An die ferne Geliebte* may also be connected to Schumann through a route other than the *Fantasie*, for 'Nimm sie hin denn, diese Lieder' provides what Brinkmann refers to as 'the lyrical nerve centre' of the finale of Schumann's Second Symphony, an 'intimate, biographically transmitted Beethoven quotation' that Brahms was undoubtedly aware of.[127]

---

[126] I note that both the Beethoven compositions that Brahms alludes to within his transfigured lament, that is, Beethoven's 'Lebewohl' sonata and *An die ferne Geliebte*, are each in the key of E♭ major, a tonality that is bound up with issues of loss and bereavement for Brahms, as we saw in Chapter 1.

[127] See Brinkmann, *Late Idyll*, 43. On the relationship between Beethoven's *An die ferne Geliebte* and Schumann's *Fantasie*, see Nicholas Marston, *Schumann: Fantasie, Op. 17* (Cambridge: Cambridge University Press, 1992).

**Example 2.4b** Brahms, *Nänie*, bars 85–95, choral parts only

Through his use of musical allusions, Brahms gives voice to the disenchantment of the modern world within a musical sphere. The nature of the musical allusion in Op. 82 goes beyond motivic allusion, allowing the three strands of the visual, the literary, and the musical to come together. The structure of Beethoven's cycle elicits a strong parallel with Brahms's *Nänie* whilst also resonating with the spirit of Schiller's poem. Both *An die ferne Geliebte* and *Nänie* look to a lost ideal in the past by way of attaining a future ideal. Both, therefore, may be understood in relation to the paradigm of nostalgic teleology, the Schillerian schema that traces a journey from naïve recollection to sentimental reflection. The self-reflexivity of Beethoven's cycle, which returns to the first song in the last, has a kinship with the self-reflexive nature of Schiller's poem 'Auch das Schöne muß sterben', particularly with its anaphoric entry at line 13, a trajectory that is also reflected in Brahms's setting of 'Auch das Schöne muß sterben'. The poetry of Alois

Isidor Jeitteles (1794–1858) that Beethoven set in *An die ferne Geliebte*, moreover, acquires a particular significance when considered in relation to Schiller's aesthetic project, the aim of which, as we have seen, is to address the question of how we can 'reasonably expect [art and aesthetic culture] to effect anything so great as the education of humanity',[128] and to restore the wholeness of nature 'by means of a higher Art'.[129]

The final song in Beethoven's song cycle, 'Nimm sie hin denn, diese Lieder', records a narrative of lost beauty and, more significantly, is concerned with the capacity to seek beauty, to 'attain what a loving heart has earned', not only through art but specifically through song. The text of this song, from which Brahms's allusion is drawn, reads as follows:

| | |
|---|---|
| Nimm sie hin denn, diese Lieder, | Take these songs now which I sang to you, my love, |
| Die ich dir, Geliebte, sang, | sing them over to yourself in the evening |
| Singe sie dann abends wieder | to the sweet sound of the lute! |
| Zu der Laute süßem Klang! | When the red glow of evening then passes |
| Wenn das Dämmrungsrot dann ziehet | to the still blue lake, |
| Nach dem stillen blauen See, | and the last ray flashes to its end |
| Und sein letzter Strahl verglühet | behind those mountain heights; |
| Hinter jener Bergeshöh'; | And [when] you sing what I sang, |
| Und du singst, was ich gesungen, | what issued from my over-flowing heart |
| Was mir aus der vollen Brust | without an artist's ostentation |
| Ohne Kunstgepräng' erklungen, | (I was conscious only of my longing): |
| Nur der Sehnsucht sich bewußt: | Then all that parted us |
| Dann vor diesen Liedern weichet, | is surmounted by these songs, |
| Was geschieden uns so weit, | and a loving heart attains |
| Und ein liebend Herz erreichet, | that which a loving heart has |
| Was ein liebend Herz geweiht! | hallowed.[130] |

---

128  Schiller, Tenth Letter, this translation by Wilkinson and Willoughby in Schiller, *On the Aesthetic Education of Man: In a Series of Letters*, 63.

129  Schiller, Sixth Letter, this translation by Wilkinson and Willoughby in Schiller, *On the Aesthetic Education of Man: In a Series of Letters*, 43.

130  This translation is slightly amended from *The Penguin Book of Lieder*, 25–8. The amendments are taken from Nicholas Marston, 'Voicing Beethoven's Distant Beloved', in *Beethoven and His World*, ed. Scott Burnham and Michael Steinberg (Princeton, NJ: Princeton University Press, 2000), 124–47 (127).

**Example 2.5** Beethoven, 'Nimm Sie hin denn, diese Lieder', *An die ferne Geliebte*,
bars 38–41

The subject of Beethoven's songs is the distant beloved as identified in
the title of the song cycle. In this last song, the poet implores his beloved to
sing the songs that he has sung, so as to lessen the distance between them.
Beethoven's cycle espouses a circular key scheme (E♭, G, A♭, A♭, C, and E♭).
Further cyclical elements are found when the last verse of the final song,
'Nimm sie hin denn, diese Lieder', recalls both the music and text of the
final verse of the first song, 'Auf dem Hügel sitz ich, spähend'.

What happens between the penultimate and the final verses of 'Nimm
sie hin denn, diese Lieder' (bars 38–41) encapsulates the circular form of
the entire cycle and is at once redolent of the dialectical journey of
Schiller's aesthetic paradigm, here played out in a three-stage process.
First, the forlorn lover claims that their songs are 'without an artist's
ostentation' ('Ohne Kunstgepräng' erlkungen'), their natural simplicity
finding a kinship with nature as opposed to art. In the second stage, the
singer reflects on their situation – 'I was conscious only of my longing'
('Nur der Sehnsucht sich bewußt') – before the piano interlude between
the third and fourth verses quotes the opening material of the final verse
of the first song. This quotation reveals the irony of the protagonist's
claim to natural simplicity in stage one, that is, the claim that the songs are
'without an artist's ostentation', whilst underlining the deeply considered
artistry of this song cycle (Example 2.5). As Nicholas Marston argues, *An
die ferne Geliebte* at once evinces a cyclical key scheme, enhances its
overall coherence by means of linking transitions between songs, and
endorses its artistic invention through a rich network of self-allusion.[131]

---

[131] In this discussion, I draw on Marston, 'Voicing Beethoven's Distant Beloved'. Marston further
notes that Beethoven first planned to set the last song to the same music as 'Auf dem Hügel sitz
ich, spähend', citing Beethoven's 'Scheide' sketchbook and Gustav Nottebohm's investigation
of the sketches. See Gustav Nottebohm, *Zweite Beethoveniana. Nachgelassene Aufsätze*, ed.
Eusebius Mandyczewski (Leipzig: 1887). For a detailed study of the motivic links and instances

The third stage of this dialectic comes as the fourth verse of 'Nimm sie hin denn, diese Lieder' carries on in its uninhibited *Volkstümlich* manner, once again quoting the opening material of this song from which Brahms would later draw his allusion.

The final verse of the first song in Beethoven's cycle, 'Auf dem Hügel sitz ich, spähend' ('I sit on the hill, gazing') runs thus:

| | |
|---|---|
| Denn vor Liebesklang entweichet | For sounds of love can put to flight |
| Jeder Raum und jede Zeit, | all space and all time; |
| Und ein liebend Herz erreichet, | And a loving heart attains |
| Was ein liebend Herz geweiht! | that which a loving heart has consecrated.[132] |

This song marks both the beginning of *An die ferne Geliebte* and the endpoint of Beethoven's cycle when it returns in an altered manner in the last song.

Numerous scholars have argued that Beethoven's nostalgia points simultaneously toward the past and the future. Joseph Kerman suggests that in Beethoven's cycle we 'regard space-distance as a metaphor, gradually clarified by the poet, for time-distance', for this final verse of the first poem begins by 'bringing together space and time',[133] just as it brings together nature and art. Nicholas Marston writes of the 'essential pastness' of Beethoven's cycle, but he too clarifies that 'the real temporal dimension of these poems [. . .] lies not in the past but in the future', one that wills the former happiness of the lovers to be attained again.[134] Charles Rosen acclaims Beethoven as 'the first composer to represent the complex process of memory – not merely the sense of loss and regret that accompanies visions of the past, but the physical experience of calling up the past within the present'.[135] Taylor goes a step further, suggesting that in Beethoven's *Liederkreis*, 'the effect is not just of passive memory but a linking of past and present; the memory of the past grows out of the present and indeed becomes part of the present, the two converging into a new variant which

---

of self-allusion within this cycle, see Christopher Reynolds, 'The Representational Impulse in Late Beethoven, I, *An die ferne Geliebte*', *Acta Musicologica* 60 (1988): 43–61.

[132] This translation is slightly amended from S. S. Prawer, ed. and trans., *The Penguin Book of Lieder* (London: Penguin, 1977), 25–8.

[133] Joseph Kerman, 'An die ferne Geliebte', *Beethoven Studies*, ed. Alan Tyson (New York, NY: Norton, 1973), I, 123–57 (129).

[134] Marston, 'Voicing Beethoven's Distant Beloved', 126.

[135] Charles Rosen, *The Romantic Generation*, 166.

combines memory and actuality into one'.[136] Taylor clarifies that within the Romantic conception of cyclicism, 'a return to something past may yet be part of an onward, teleological trajectory', a journey that 'introduces a new conception of time and narrative process'.[137]

The manner in which time and memory are treated in Beethoven's *An die ferne Geliebte* has a significant bearing on Brahms's allusions to past material in the memory-laden B section of *Nänie*, not least of which is an allusion to this very song cycle. This, in turn, as we shall see, informs our interpretation of *Nänie* as giving musical voice to a Schillerian idyll.

Returning to the formal structure of *Nänie*, if we conceive of Brahms's composition as being in ternary form, as suggested by the tempo designations, time signatures, and key signatures summarized in Table 2.2, then the Tempo primo constitutes nothing more than a simple return to the A section of the Andante. Yet the treatment of formal functions and musical texture frustrates this reading, suggesting instead that the B section has an onward, teleological trajectory that reaches beyond the end of the Più sostenuto section that ends at bar 141.

In distich 6 of Schiller's poem, as Hilliard argues, 'sorrow finds a voice',[138] as the gods and goddesses are united, along with Thetis, in mourning at the transience of beauty and the death of perfection. Brahms accorded great significance to distich 6 of Schiller's poem, as indicated by his choice to repeat these pivotal lines that witness the common grief of the gods and humanity: 'Siehe, da weinen die Götter, es weinen die Göttinnen alle, | daß das Schöne vergeht, daß das Vollkommene stirbt' ('Look, the gods are weeping, and all the goddesses too | weeping that beauty must pass, that perfection must die'). The repeat of this poetic distich is not accompanied by a repeat of the music to which it was first set in bars 97–117, however. Rather, the transcendent music that saw Thetis rise from the sea in her lament in distich 5 (bars 85–96, Example 2.3b) is reconfigured in the setting of distich 6 to express this shared sense of grief.

Noticeable by its absence in this repeat is the allusion to *Ein deutsches Requiem*. Thetis does not feature in distich 6 of Schiller's poem, and the bass line in the chorus is altered at bar 119 so that it no longer sounds out the allusion to the maternal fifth movement of *Ein deutsches Requiem*. Situated within this repeated material once again, however, is the allusion to *An die ferne Geliebte* in bars 127–9. The polyphonic outpouring by the

---

[136] Benedict Taylor, *Mendelssohn, Time and Memory: The Romantic Conception of Cyclic Form* (Cambridge: Cambridge University Press, 2011), 39–40.

[137] *Ibid.*, 40.     [138] Hilliard, '"Nänie": Critical Reflections on the Sentimental in Poetry', 5.

**Example 2.6** Brahms, *Nänie*, bars 137–42: a distorted echo of the Beethoven 'Lebewohl' motto (137–41) elides with the Brahmsian 'Lebewohl' motto (141–2)

choir singing 'daß das vollkommene stirbt' ('that perfection dies') is set to the melody with which Beethoven intones the words 'Nimm Sie hin denn, diese Lieder' ('Take them, then, these songs'), here sounding out once again the song the poet implored his lover to sing to lessen the time between them.

At bar 141 we once again hear the 'Lebewohl' gesture, now for the second time, coinciding with the Tempo primo direction. Those who hear this piece as being in ternary form consider this formal demarcation to signal a return to the A section.[139] The absence of a firm cadential structure, however, means that the return to the tonic is merely rhetorical. Rather than modulating back to the Andante with a strong perfect authentic cadence in the tonic, Brahms instead allows the tonic D major to simply reassert itself through a weakly articulated interrupted cadence in the apparent F♯ major which elides with the new D major phrase (Example 2.6). Here, the outer voices of the choir approach the tonic chord by stepwise motion from measure 139, although at the level of the phrase there is still an F♯–C♯–D/I-V-VI motion in the bass. Above this, the soprano intones the distinctive falling $\hat{3}$– $\hat{2}$– $\hat{1}$ 'Lebewohl' gesture.

Rather than pointing toward the subdominant region characteristic of Brahms's idiosyncratic '*Nänie* cadence', it moves toward the global tonic D major, here spelled as the submediant region of F♯. There is a beautifully poetic turn in that, as the choir alone laments the death of perfection, the words 'vollkommene stirbt' ('that perfection dies') witness a distorted echo of the Beethoven 'Lebewohl' progression give way to the Brahmsian 'Lebewohl' progression.

In this analytical reading, the B section extends not from measures 85 to 141, as a ternary reading would have it, but instead it extends from measures 85 to 162, ending with the cadence that punctuates the onset of the coda. The reflection of A within Brahms's B section can be understood as the aesthetic rupture that characterizes the Schillerian idyll. The re-emergence of D major as the tonic, devoid of the cadential structures required for a return to the formal function A, conjures up the memory of that which was heard earlier, that which is past, without allowing us to actually return to that material. The Tempo primo, therefore, is the site of an allusion to the opening, an allusion that is self-consciously framed within the B section. This manipulation of form in Brahms's composition is redolent of Menzel's painting, where the mirrored image in the wooden frame reflects an earlier, pastoral setting, a scene that the mirror had witnessed at an earlier time. Brahms's (self-)allusion framed within the B section, I propose, provides an instance

[139] See, for instance, Peter Petersen, 'Werke für Chor und Orchester', in *Johannes Brahms: Leben und Werke*, ed. Christiane Jacobsen (Wiesbaden, Breitkopf & Härtel, 1983); and James, 'Johannes Brahms's *Nänie*, Op. 82: A Study in Context and Content'.

of Taylor's category of 'music (as subject, having somehow attributed agency) remembering its own earlier themes (as object of its memory)'.[140]

As we hear the plaintive, pastoral oboe melody once again in a D major context, set to the familiar lilting 6/4 time and unfolding with the characteristic deceptive cadence that evokes Beethoven's intimately personal 'Lebewohl', we become conscious of a sense of loss, a sense of time, and a sense of memory. This temporal context is significant: we recall, with Bahr, that 'there will always be moments in history when beauty will have to die'.[141] As it moves from Beethoven to Brahms, the 'Lebewohl' motto that underpins *Nänie* accrues further meaning. In Brahms's composition, this nostalgic horn call conjures up a state of existence between longing and fulfilment. The recollection of earlier material in an altered manner, framed within the B section, presents us simultaneously with elements of the past and the present, or, one might suggest, with elements of the real and the ideal, the naïve and the sentimental. The one reflects on the other in this aesthetic rupture.

Brahms's setting of Schiller's anaphoric entry, 'Auch ein Klaglied zu sein', at bar 149 is derived from the D–A–B 'Lebewohl' motto that underpins the melodic and harmonic shape of the opening of *Nänie*. Upon its return, the music that sounds this anaphoric choral entry eschews the fugal treatment of the opening, however, and is instead characterized by a less strict contrapuntal interweaving of the three remaining voices from bar 153 onward. The low strings that were heard at the first entry of the chorus at bar 25 are absent at bar 149, where the four-part chorus now joins the ethereal upper register of the winds.

The cadential confirmation of the tonic that we expected to hear at bar 141 arrives belatedly on the downbeat of bar 162 as we reach the end of Brahms's setting of Schiller's poem, that is, the end of the large-scale B section (Table 2.2). From a tonal and formal point of view, then, everything that follows this perfect authentic cadence is post-cadential. The coda in bars 162–81 serves as the corresponding framing function to the introduction in bars 1–25. The long-overdue cadence in the tonic at bar 162—the first tonic confirmation since the end of the introduction—elides with the end of Brahms's anomalous repeat of the penultimate line of Schiller's poem, 'Auch ein Klaglied zu sein im Mund der Geliebten ist herrlich'. It is precisely this part of Brahms's *Nänie* that has proven most controversial in

---

[140] Taylor, *The Melody of Time*, 132. Walter Frisch also attributes agency to the music itself, in his thoughtful reading of memory in Schubert across a multi-movement work. See Walter Frisch, '"You Must Remember This": Memory and Structure in Schubert's String Quartet in G Major, D. 887', *Musical Quarterly* 84/4 (Winter 2000): 582–603.

[141] Bahr, '*Wallensteins Tod* as a "Play of Mourning"', 177.

the critical reception for not allowing the piece to draw to a close on the note of despondency with which Schiller's poem ends, but rather returning to the penultimate line of the poem.[142]

The distinction between the realm of lament (*Klage*) and the realm of elegy (*Klaglied*) that underpins the structure and meaning of Schiller's 'Nänie' plays a further role in Brahms's setting. In line 14, the choir alone warns that 'that which is common goes down to Orcus unsung', implicit in which is a warning that the worst fate would be to disappear *klanglos* to Orcus. Further reflecting the dialectical nature of the enterprise, 'the creation of the poem's own beauty', as Hilliard argues, 'depends on an elision of what is not beautiful' with 'what is "gemein" [common] in its source'.[143] The two lines of poetry in distich 7 are therefore interdependent: 'Auch ein Klaglied zu sein im Mund der Geliebten ist herrlich, | denn das Gemeine geht klanglos zum Orkus hinab'. Together these lines give voice to Schiller's conception of aesthetic humanity which, as Kaiser argues, bears the reflection of a freedom and joy that are only possible in light of death.[144]

A final consideration in our hermeneutic exploration of *Nänie* is the plagal harmony with which it began. The third and final iteration of the 'Lebewohl' gesture at bar 176 occurs within the post-cadential framing function. The full significance of Brahms's treatment of the 'Lebewohl' gesture throughout *Nänie* emerges only in relation to the larger formal process at play in this composition. It is only in retrospect that we recognize what Hans-Joachim Hinrichsen refers to as the 'reminiscent echo of a finite break-through [to be] the goal of the composition'.[145] We recall that in altering Beethoven's 'Lebewohl' motto in bars 1–2 of *Nänie*, Brahms short-circuited Beethoven's harmonic motion, telescoping the harmonic sequence of V-vi to V-bvi to V-IV$^{6-3}$ of bars 1–16 of Beethoven's slow introduction (Example 2.1b) to the distinctive '*Nänie* cadence' I-V-IV$^{6-3}$ that leads directly to the subdominant region. This idiosyncratic cadence is heard twice in *Nänie*, at bars 1–2 and at 141–2, marking both the opening of the piece and the reflection of this opening, which is heard as if within its own frame within the extended B section.

This farewell gesture is taken up one last time in the coda. It seems that the third and final 'Lebewohl' cadence sounded out at bar 176 is directed

[142] See, for instance, Eduard Hanslick, 'Brahms: "Nänie"', in *Concerte, Componisten und Virtuosen*, 345–7.
[143] Hilliard, '"Nänie": Critical Reflections on the Sentimental in Poetry', 9.
[144] Kaiser, *Vergötterung und Tod*, 34.
[145] Hinrichsen, '"Auch das Schöne muß sterben"', 151–2.

Example 2.7 Brahms, *Nänie*, bars 1–2 and 176–81

Example 2.7 (cont.)

not to the subdominant region, as the other two were, but instead to the tonic. Brahms, it would appear, is finally being faithful to the horn fifths that have called out for tonic resolution since the start of the piece. Yet the tonic at bar 177 is undermined by the C♮s that infiltrated the harmony in the preceding bar. Avoiding the pitch C♯ that is integral to the major dominant A major and which was the basis of the B-section prolongation, and instead veering toward the subdominant G major region, the final 'Lebewohl' gesture that Brahms offers culminates not with chord I but instead with chord $I^7$. This perpetuates the subdominant and leads to the plagal cadence from bars 178–9 that ends the piece, once again taking up and drawing to a close the plagal harmony with which *Nänie* began (Example 2.7). Above this plagal texture, the last echo of the 'Lebewohl' motto, now heard in the flutes, falls through the thin ether of the last page of Brahms's score, before the choir intones the word 'herrlich' ('glorious') one last time.

The last melodic note heard in the wind instruments that have signalled the pastoral mode throughout this composition is F♯ (bar 179). This recalls an important key area in both the middle of the A section (bar 65) and the entire B section. F♯, the upper-pitch of the 'Lebewohl' third, is also the leading note of the subdominant chord, which makes it perhaps a gently ambivalent note on which to end, given the stress, right up to this final page of Brahms's score, on the subdominant. Just four bars earlier, this F♯ had served as the leading note of G, and it continues to play a role in the final plagal cadence. We might suggest that Brahms retains something of Schiller's note of despondency, albeit one that hovers over an essentially more positive ending.

Hinrichsen gives elegant expression to the significance of Brahms's plagal ending:

If one considers Brahms's *Nänie* in the context of the relationship of factors external as well as internal to the work, then it turns out to a certain extent to be an expression of 'Innerlichkeit' supported by form (*formgeschützter Innerlichkeit*), to put a spin on Thomas Mann's famous formulation about the late nineteenth century. Schiller's epochal farewell gesture from the end of the Weimar period of art is radically privatized by Brahms for a personal lament of mourning. This privatization is signalled specifically in the first two bars of the composition but also it is a priori aesthetically objectified through its quoted position in a traditional reference, and in the further course of the composition it is less transcended than 'sublated' in Hegel's tripartite sense of the word.[146]

---

[146] 'Betrachtet man die Brahmssche *Nänie* in ihren werkinternen wie-externen Beziehungen und Zusammenhängen, dann erweist sie sich gewissermaßen als Ausdruck formgeschütter

Brahms's personal lament of mourning is not only for Feuerbach. It also pays homage to the many moments in history when Beauty must die, that is, the visual, the literary, and the musical moments alluded to in this richly textured composition. The Schillerian idyll provides a fitting platform on which Brahms could explore the tension that exists between the real and the ideal, between nature and art, and between the past, the present, and the future. On the one hand, Brahms's sense of intimacy in this choral work is very different to that of Beethoven in the intimate genres of the Lied and the piano sonata. On the other hand, the formal process through which Brahms's references to the works of Beethoven (and Schumann) are moved from their position outside the work to the very interior of *Nänie* has much in common with both the 'Lebewohl' sonata and *An die ferne Geliebte*.[147]

Attitudes toward German Idealism, as we saw at the outset of this chapter, changed substantially throughout the nineteenth century. The power of its aesthetic force at the beginning of the century is matched only by the degree to which it then completely disappeared as an aesthetic category at century's end. After the horrors of the Franco-Prussian war and the Paris Commune (1870–1), idealism seemed to be an impossible utopian project that was entirely out of touch with political and social events as they unfolded in Europe. It is remarkable that, within the space of a year, in his elegiac choral output, Brahms could represent both the early and the late stages of this continuum of German Idealism. *Nänie* is a paean not only to the position of art in the triad of virtues with which Idealism is concerned – the good, the beautiful, and the true – but most especially, it is a paean to musical beauty. By the time Brahms turned to composing *Gesang der Parzen* in 1882, his position on musical beauty and his approach to tonality would have altered considerably.

There are many ways in which we might understand the change that Brahms's aesthetic and compositional process was about to undergo in his elegiac output. For instance, we might question whether the composer's

Innerlichkeit, um die berühmter Formel Thomas Manns über das späte 19. Jahrhunderts zu variieren. Schillers epochale Abschiedsgeste vom Ende der Weimarer Kunstperiode wird von Brahms radikal zur persönlichen Trauerklage privatisiert, diese Privatisierung ihrerseits wird in den ersten beiden Takten der Komposition eigens angezeigt wie aber auch durch ihre zitierende Einstellung in einen Traditionsbezug a priori ästhetisch objektiviert und im weiteren Verlauf der Komposition weniger transzendiert als vielmehr im dreifachen Hegelschen Wortsinne aufgehoben'. Hinrichsen, "'Auch das Schöne muß sterben'", 154.

[147] See, for instance, Carl Dahlhaus's discussion of Beethoven's 'Lebewohl', the Piano Sonata No. 26 in E♭ Major, Op. 81a in Dahlhaus, *Ludwig van Beethoven: Approaches to his Music*, trans. Mary Whittall (Oxford: Clarendon Press, 1991), 34–42.

realization of the increasing failure of idealism to deal with modern life and modern problems was a contributing factor in this change. We might also consider that he became increasingly aware of the very facets of his own late age: his music-historic lateness within the nineteenth century, his lateness with regard to the age of tonality, his position at the end of the Austro-German symphonic tradition, and his place in a modern, histori-cally self-conscious age, excluded from the innocence of an earlier age. That which he—self-consciously—conjured up through allusive reference within the poetic realm of *Nänie* provided a momentary reprieve from the unstoppable march of time. When he turned to composing the *Gesang der Parzen* one year later, it would seem that Brahms was no longer seeking Schillerian harmony in an ever less harmonious world.

# 3 | A Disembodied Head for Mythic Justice: *Gesang der Parzen*

Do you believe, then, in no destiny? No power that rules over us and directs all for our ultimate advantage?[1]

– Johann Wolfgang van Goethe

[It conveys] something to do with human life and all its ambiguities and all its horrors and terrors and misery and at the same time there is something beautiful, and something also to do with the entry of the spiritual into the human situation and the closeness of the gods.[2]

– Iris Murdoch

Shortly after the composition of *Nänie* in 1881, Brahms once again turned his attention to confronting the ancient Greek opposition between the human and the divine. On this occasion, he returned to the dramatic output of Goethe, this time settling upon an independent and self-standing poem from the play *Iphigenie auf Tauris*: the bleak and desolate 'Song of the Fates', *Gesang der Parzen*. As was the case with *Schicksalslied* and would also come about in the *Vier ernste Gesänge*, the perceived sense of consolation found at the end of Brahms's *Gesang der Parzen* is largely considered to be at odds with the unremitting hopelessness of this poem. In this, the darkest of Brahms's Elegies, scholars have been confounded in their efforts to understand its hermeneutic meaning: whereas there is little consensus on the form of the piece, issues regarding its tonality, in particular the deployment of the major mode at the most acutely desolate point in the poem, has perplexed scholars. The lack of congruity between the poetic text and Brahms's setting remains something of an unanswered question.

---

[1] 'So glauben Sie kein Schicksal? keine Macht, die über uns waltet und alles zu unsern Besten lenkt?' This passage is highlighted in Brahms's copy of Goethe, *Wilhelm Meisters Lehrjahre*, housed at the Brahms library at the archive of the Gesellschaft der Musikfreunde, Vienna. Here translated by Thomas Carlyle in Goethe, *Wilhelm Meister's Apprenticeship and Travels* (Boston, MA: Ticknor and Fields, 1865), 61.

[2] Iris Murdoch talks with Eric Robson, *Revelations*, Border Television for Channel 4, broadcast, 22 September 1984. Quoted in Cheryl K. Bove, *Understanding Iris Murdoch* (Columbia, SC: University of South Carolina Press, 1993), 77.

This chapter attempts to answer that question. I argue that the key to understanding this complex composition lies in exploring its rich intertextuality. Whereas Goethe's play provided an important vehicle for delivering a beautifully poetic rendering of the tale of the fall of Tantalus, the play itself outside of this poem was of no interest to the composer. Rather, Brahms's intertextuality reaches back to numerous versions of this myth in classical mythology, reaching from Homer, Aeschylus, and Sophocles to Ovid.

A fundamental constituent of Goethe's 'restless maritime drama', as Edith Hall evocatively describes it, is the 'imagining of journeys, past and future',[3] the most remote of which is the tale of Tantalus found in the 'Song of the Fates'. The mythical figure Tantalus was an intimate friend of the gods and a frequent guest at their golden table. He is better known for the punishments that were meted out to him than for the transgressions that aroused the divine anger. These transgressions, the myth has it, may include abusing divine favour by revealing to mortals secrets he had learnt in heaven, offending the gods by killing his son Pelops and feeding him to them by way of testing their powers of observation, and stealing nectar and ambrosia from the gods to give to humans. Whatever the transgression(s), the punishment for Tantalus involved being banished to the Underworld. There, according to Homer, he was immersed in water and situated beneath hanging fruits. The water would recede when he tried to drink it, and the wind would waft away the fruits when he attempted to eat them. The curse placed on Tantalus as he was cast down to the Underworld would reign for generations. This is the most remote of the 'imagining of journeys' to which Edith Hall refers, precisely because the transgressions of Tantalus in Greek mythology are analogous to the concept of original sin in the Christian realm. Both provoke eternal punishment, both give rise to the dividing wall between heaven and hell, and both are bound up with the question of divine justice.

This mythical tale of transgression and eternal punishment was frequently associated in Brahms's correspondence with passages from the Old Testament book of *Job*. This juxtaposition of Biblical and mythical tales finds a further intertextual resonance with certain artworks of the Italian Renaissance, with which Brahms was particularly preoccupied at the time he was writing *Gesang der Parzen*.

---

[3] Edith Hall, *Adventures with Iphigenia in Tauris: A Cultural History of Euripides' Black Sea Tragedy* (Oxford: Oxford University Press, 2013), 51.

Our intertextual exploration will begin, therefore, with a historical and literary contextualization of Goethe's 'Song of the Fates'. From there, we broaden our inquiry to consider Goethe's Italian journey, on which he came upon the Head of Juno Ludovisi, which has critical importance for Brahms's understanding of Goethe's poem as a disembodied head – an independent poem that can be extracted from the play and that recounts the tale of the fall of Tantalus. I make the case that Brahms inscribes the myth of the fall of Tantalus across the surface and depth of his own *Parzenlied*, such that composer and listener alike are tantalized by it. That which seems to be within our grasp, from the tonality of the piece to its perceived sense of consolation, is never actually within our reach. To begin to discover how this is the case, we start our exploration with a crucial distinction between the concepts of fate and destiny in Brahms's elegiac choral works.

## 3.1   Distinguishing Between Destiny and the Fates

In Chapter 1, I made the case that in order to fully understand the hermeneutic context of Brahms's *Schicksalslied* we must look beyond the interpolated poem that he set in order to consider the wider implications of Hölderlin's *Hyperion* from which this poem is extracted. Doing so allows us to conceive of this piece within the poetic framework of an ascending circle: the fact that *Schicksalslied* ends in a key other than that in which it began is bound up with the spiritual journey of the protagonist in this novel and, as such, finds a poetic resonance with the Romantic philosophy of consciousness, which is central to the philosophy of Hegel and the poetry of Hölderlin, to cite just two examples. In short, in our reading of *Schicksalslied*, I make the case for a widening of the lens from Hölderlin's interpolated poem to the broader confines of his novel.

I argue for the reverse procedure in our reading of *Gesang der Parzen*, a setting of the 'Song of the Fates' that Iphigenia sings in Act ɪᴠ, Scene 5 of Goethe's play *Iphigenie auf Tauris*. To the extent that this song gives voice to the protagonist's attempt to come to terms with the conflicting demands of heavenly decree and worldly practicality, it has much in common with the poem 'Schicksalslied' that occupies a pivotal position in Hölderlin's novel. In their concentrated expression of deepest despair, they each address what Nietzsche refers to in *The Birth of Tragedy* as 'the very first philosophical problem', that is, 'a painful and irresolvable contradiction between man and god'.[4] Each poem expresses the protagonist's utter hope-lessness, and each ends on an air of unremitting bleakness. Both poems are bound up with memory and recall seminal events that took place earlier in the protagonist's tale. In the case of 'Schicksalslied', the poem was recited to Hyperion in his youth by his mentor Alabanda. In *Iphigenie auf Tauris*, the protagonist recalls the 'Song of the Fates' being sung to herself and her siblings in childhood by their nurse.

The similarities end there, however. Numerous factors clearly differenti-ate the aesthetic character of these two poems, not least of which is the nature of their respective endings. Hölderlin's 'Schicksalslied', as we recall, ends with a question mark. The preposition with which the poem con-cludes – 'hinab' ('downward') – 'signifies a direction, not an ending',[5] which has significant implications for the role the poem plays in Hölderlin's novel and Brahms's composition. Goethe's 'Song of the Fates', on the other hand, has a closed ending, for the narrator of the poem's sixth stanza – the unnamed exile (*der Verbannte*) who was hurled from the table of the gods – merely bows his head in acceptance of the ongoing mythic justice recorded in the poem.

The differences in the aesthetic trajectory of the two poems can be further illuminated with reference to their titles. 'Schicksalslied' may be freely translated as 'Song of Destiny'. This title, together with the poem's open-endedness, offers a sense of promise; 'Gesang der Parzen', on the other hand, explicitly conjures up death in the title in referring to the 'Fates' (the Moira in Greek mythology, the Parcae in Roman mythology, 'the uncompromising minions of death'[6]), that is, the three female personifica-tions of fate who, in turn, spun the thread of life from a distaff (the Weaver), measured the thread of life (the Apportioner), and cut the thread of life and chose the manner of a person's death (the Inflexible One). More recent manifestations of the 'Fates' are found in Shakespeare's three witches in *Macbeth* and Wagner's Norns in *Der Ring des Nibelungen*. Where *Schicksalslied* as a title seems to imply an aspect of personal choice and is bound up with a process of *Bildung* or cultivation of the individual whereby the protagonist has a hand to play in their own destiny, *Gesang der*

---

[4] Friedrich Nietzsche, *The Birth of Tragedy* and *The Case of Wagner*, trans. Walter Kaufmann (New York, NY: Vintage, 1967), 70–1, here cited in Kevin C. Karnes, *A Kingdom Not of This World: Wagner, the Arts, and Utopian Visions in Fin-de-Siècle Vienna* (Oxford: Oxford University Press, 2013), 57.

[5] Walter Silz, *Hölderlin's* Hyperion: *A Critical Reading* (Philadelphia, PA: University of Pennsylvania Press, 1969), 114. See Chapter 1 for a full discussion of Brahms's *Schicksalslied*.

[6] Damien Valdez, *German Philhellenism: The Pathos of the Historical Imagination from Winckelmann to Goethe* (New York, NY: Palgrave Macmillan, 2014), 173.

*Parzen* as a title introduces the notion of predestination, removing any question of self-determination and replacing it with an imperative for acceptance, eliciting a sense of resignation to that which cannot be altered and to questions that cannot be answered.

The passage that Brahms set opens with the lines 'In fear of the Gods shall ye dwell, sons of men', as the gods hold dominion over humanity in their eternal hands. Goethe warns humanity that, despite being exalted by the gods, they live in constant peril of being plunged, abused and shamed, into the nocturnal depths. In fact, the higher one is exalted, the further one may fall. There is little indication of a proportionate relationship between transgression and punishment in this poem, for the gods are indiscriminate in terms of who suffers and why, particularly as the curse descends from one generation to the next. While humanity remains bound in darkness in the hope of justice being served, the gods turn their blessed eyes away from an entire, once beloved race of people. Tantalus, plunged in the depths of Tartarus, hears this song, thinks of his descendants, and shakes his guilty head.

The recitation of the 'Song of the Fates' in the course of Goethe's play is followed by an air of redemption that is not indicated in the poem itself, nor does it find a parallel in Brahms's setting.

| | |
|---|---|
| Es fürchte die Götter | Beware of the gods in |
| Das Menschengeschlecht! | Their friendship with us! |
| Sie halten die Herrschaft | The power they hold is |
| In ewigen Händen, | Eternally theirs. |
| Und können sie brauchen | They are able to use it |
| Wie's ihnen gefällt. | According to whim. |
| | |
| Der fürchte sie doppelt, | For those they exalt |
| Den je sie erheben! | The danger is doubled. |
| Auf Klippen und Wolken | At tables of gold the |
| Sind Stühle bereitet | Chairs are arranged in |
| Um goldene Tische. | The clouds as on cliff edge. |
| | |
| Erhebet ein Zwist sich: | Should quarrels arise, |
| So stürzen die Gäste | The guests are abused and |
| Geschmäht und geschändet | Disgraced. When they fall to |
| In nächtliche Tiefen, | The depths of the darkest |
| Und harren vergebens, | Abyss they then languish; |
| Im Finstern gebunden, | They wait there in vain for |
| Gerechten Gerichtes. | Their cause to be heard. |

| | |
|---|---|
| Sie aber, sie bleiben | The gods keep on feasting, |
| In ewigen Festen | Eternal, secure at |
| An goldenen Tischen. | Their tables of gold. |
| Sie schreiten vom Berge | They live their exalted |
| Zu Bergen hinüber: | Lives on the peaks, |
| Aus Schlünden der Tiefe | And out of the chasms, |
| Dampft ihnen der Athem | Arising as steam, |
| Erstickter Titanen, | The breath of the Titans, |
| Gleich Opfergerüchen, | And choked cries as of victims, |
| Ein leichtes Gewölke. | Ascend to their ears. |
| | |
| Es wenden die Herrscher | The rulers avert then |
| Ihr segnendes Auge | Their gaze, with its blessing, |
| Von ganzen Geschlechtern, | From all of our line, |
| Und meiden, im Enkel | Refusing to see in |
| Die ehmals geliebten | The grandchildren's features |
| Still redenden Züge | The silent reminders |
| Des Ahnherrn zu sehn. | Of those they once loved. |
| | This song of the fates |
| So sangen die Parzen; | |
| Es horcht der Verbannte | Is heard by the exile |
| In nächtlichen Höhlen | Grown old in dark caverns. |
| Der Alte die Lieder, | He thinks of his line of |
| Denkt Kinder und Enkel | Descendants and sighs |
| Und schüttelt das Haupt. | With a shake of his head.[7] |

Throughout its performance and reception history, this poem has been repeatedly extracted from the context of the play for which it was composed. The literary historian Günther Müller argues that the *Parzenlied* forms an 'erratic boulder' in Goethe's play, protesting that it is not Iphigenia's song, but rather it is the 'Song of the Fates'. In a 2015 performance at London's Rose Playhouse theatre, the director omitted the 'Song of the Fates' entirely from the end of Act IV. Instead, a melodic fragment served as a leitmotif connecting two of the three occasions that the Germanist Erich Heller outlines as those when the 'reality of evil asserts itself poetically' in *Iphigenie auf Tauris*: first, the reference to the gruesome prehistory at the outset of the play; second, Iphigenia's brother Orestes's account of the murder of his mother

---

[7] This translation is from Dan Farrelly, *Under the Curse: Goethe's 'Iphigenie auf Tauris'* (Dublin: Carysfort Press, 2007).

Clytemnestra with the rage of madness that follows; and third – the subject of Brahms's setting – Iphigenia's attempt to come to terms with the demands of heavenly decree and worldly practicality.[8]

An example of removing the poem from the context of the play that is closer to Brahms's time involves a performance by the actress Charlotte Wolter, who became renowned for her début role as *Iphigenie* at Vienna's Burgtheater in 1862. Wolter was one of the great tragic actresses of the late nineteenth century, celebrated for her melodious and powerful voice. She achieved her most brilliant success in precisely the title role of Goethe's *Iphigenie*.[9] Ludwig Speidel, the theatre critic who covered the Burgtheater for the *Neue Freie Presse* for almost forty years, reports that the most notable and contentious aspect of her interpretation was that she stepped out of character to 'declaim the song with the force with which [. . .] the Fates may have sung it'.[10] Max Kalbeck provides a richly evocative account of Wolter's performance:

She stepped up to the altar in the middleground of the antiquated scene and, leaning against the marble, intoned the mighty words of the song with her deep, versatile and richly inflected voice (*modulationsfähigen Stimme*) to a house of breathless listeners, her body draped in stylishly flowing pleated garments, her head crowned as the personified idea of the deity enthroned, almost like a statue of Polyhymnia or Melpomene, and her recitation almost a song. The tragic chorus, banished from the modern stage, seemed to have returned and to have arisen again to new life in this one, who presided over her task with priestly

---

[8]  See Erich Heller, *The Disinherited Mind: Essays in Modern German Literature and Thought* (Harmondsworth: Penguin, 1961). The performance concerned is *Iphigenia in Tauris* by Johann Wolfgang von Goethe, trans. Roy Pascal, directed by Pamela Schermann, Rose Playhouse Theatre, London, 16 June–4 July 2015. The omission of the 'Song of the Fates' is not part of Pascal's translation but rather was the decision of the director.

[9]  Goethe's *Iphigenie auf Tauris* marked Charlotte Wolter's début at Vienna's Burgtheater in 1862. A quarter of a century later, it also marked the final performance staged at Vienna's old Burgtheater at Michaelerplatz in 1887, with Wolter again in the title role, before the theatre closed and reopened in a new and imposing building on Vienna's Ringstrasse. At her own request, Charlotte Wolter was buried in the costume she wore in the title role of *Iphigenie*. See W. E. Yates, *Theatre in Vienna: A Critical History, 1776–1995* (Cambridge: Cambridge University Press, 2005), 81, and Ludwig Speidel, *Schauspieler*, in *Ludwig Speidels Schriften* (Berlin: Meyer & Jessen, 1911), IV, 277.

[10]  Ludwig Speidel, *Kritishce Schriften*, ed. Julius Rütsch (Zurich: Artemis Verlag, 1963), 304, as cited in Margaret Notley, 'Ancient Tragedy and Anachronism: Form as Expression in Brahms's *Gesang der Parzen*', in *Expressive Intersections in Brahms: Essays in Analysis and Meaning*, ed. Heather Platt and Peter H. Smith (Bloomington, IN: Indiana University Press, 2012), 111–45, 138, n. 8. Speidel belonged to the numerous critical voices in Vienna at this time who were opposed to the cult of personality in the Burgtheater. Regarding Wolter's role as Iphigenia, he felt he had to emphasize that actors are only reproductive artists, not creative ones. See Yates, *Theatre in Vienna*, 81.

dignity and artistic grace. Without knowing it and wanting it, and simply by virtue of being inspired, the ingenious artist unlocked the myths of the deeper intention of the poet.[11]

In his study of the 'The Voice of Truth and Humanity' in Goethe's *Iphigenie*, Sigurd Burckhardt analyses the spheres of speech in the play. His findings help us to understand Wolter's performance as rendered by Kalbeck: 'Iphigenia sings when she is "possessed"', Burckhardt writes, 'not in the sense of being "deeply moved" (she is often so elsewhere) but in the literal sense: whenever she becomes the mouthpiece from above or below'.[12] Kalbeck's report of her unknowingly 'being inspired' seems to indicate such a possession of her character by the Fates. It was this performance, Kalbeck argues, that inspired Brahms's setting of the poem.[13]

Brahms made the case that his *Parzenlied* (as he called *Gesang der Parzen*) was not *Iphigenie*.[14] In correspondence regarding *Gesang der Parzen* with his close friend, the surgeon and gifted musical amateur Theodor Billroth, Brahms explained that he would prefer to conceal any association with Goethe's *Iphigenie* on the title page of his published score. Already in August 1882 he could anticipate the critic Speidel saying 'That isn't Goethe's *Iphigenie*'. 'And it's quite true', Brahms agreed, 'that *Parzenlied* is not *Iphigenie*'.[15] Goethe's play achieved great popularity in the late nineteenth century, to the extent that much of Brahms's audience would have already been familiar with it. Perhaps as a result of this familiarity, Brahms scholarship has been slow to take the composer at his word on this matter and has persisted in associating Brahms's composition with Goethe's modern drama (and, accordingly, with Euripides's play).[16] To understand Brahms's statement, we must begin to peel back the many layers of his rich intertextuality, for which reason we turn to the composition of the Second Symphony, some five years earlier than *Gesang der Parzen*.

---

[11] Max Kalbeck, *Johannes Brahms*, (Berlin: Deutsche Brahms-Gesellschaft, 1909), III, 355.

[12] Sigurd Burckhardt '"The Voice of Truth and of Humanity": Goethe's *Iphigenie*', in *The Drama of Language: Essays on Goethe and Kleist*, ed. Sigurd Burckhardt (Baltimore, MD and London: Johns Hopkins University Press, 1970), 33–56 (43).

[13] Kalbeck, *Johannes Brahms*, III, 355.

[14] Brahms to Theodor Billroth, 6 August 1882, in *Billroth und Brahms im Briefwechsel*, ed. Otto Gottlieb-Billroth (Berlin and Vienna: Urban & Schwarzenberg, 1935), 337.

[15] Brahms to Billroth, 6 August 1882, translated in *Brahms and Billroth: Letters from a Musical Friendship*, 123.

[16] See, for instance, Notley, 'Ancient Tragedy and Anachronism'.

## 3.2   A Genealogy of Dissonance

Styra Avins characterizes the years from 1877 onward in Brahms's life as those when the composer 'hit full stride'.[17] His income rose considerably after the publication of *Ein deutsches Requiem*, affording him a quality of life and a level of comfort he had not known until then. This brought with it financial independence, creative independence, and many opportunities to travel, which the composer capitalized upon to the great benefit of posterity. From this time onward, he regularly took the opportunity to escape Vienna for a more tranquil summer dwelling. His three summer trips to Pörtschach on the Wörthersee of 1877–9 inaugurated a period of great creativity beginning with the composition of the Second Symphony, of which Billroth would effuse, 'Why, it is all blue sky, babbling of streams, sunshine and cool green shade! By the Wörther See it must be so beautiful.'[18] The composition of the Second Symphony, as Reinhold Brinkmann observes, witnessed a significant shift for Brahms from 'the anxiety of influence', that characterizes the 'misreading' in the First Symphony – with, amongst other features, its thinly veiled allusion to Beethoven's Ninth in the finale – to Brahms's 'act of liberation' with the 'self-discovery in the Second'.[19]

Along with a rich harvest of instrumental works, the lakeside Austrian idyll also saw the birth of the first motet, 'Warum ist das Licht gegeben den Mühseligen', Op. 74/1, Brahms's longest *a capella* piece, which as we will see has a close relationship to the composition of *Gesang der Parzen*.[20] The first of Brahms's ten summers spent at Bad Ischl in 1880, another tranquil lakeside retreat, augmented this already rich output with the addition of the *Academic Festival Overture* and the *Tragic* Overture.[21]

It was at this auspicious time in Brahms's life that he made the first of nine trips to Italy in 1878.[22] Eftychia Papanikolaou notes that one of the main characteristics of German philhellenism was that it 'captured the

---

[17]   Styra Avins, *Johannes Brahms: A Life in Letters*, trans. Josef Eisinger (Oxford: Oxford University Press, 2001), 507.

[18]   Theodor Billroth to Brahms, 14 November 1877, translated in Reinhold Brinkmann, *Late Idyll: The Second Symphony of Johannes Brahms*, trans. Peter Palmer (Cambridge, MA: Harvard University Press, 1995), 13.

[19]   Brinkmann, *Late Idyll*, 141.

[20]   The instrumental works include the Ballades, Op. 75, the Capricci and Intermezzi, Op. 76, the Violin Concerto, Op. 77, the Two Rhapsodies, Op. 79, and the Sonata for Violin and Piano, Op. 78.

[21]   The summers of 1882, 1889, and 1896 were spent in the same house.

[22]   He and Billroth would again visit Italy in 1881, and Brahms and Widmann went together in 1880, 1890, and 1893. Brahms's last trip to Italy was in 1893.

Greek spirit indirectly through Rome'. This is evident, for instance, in the writings of Winckelmann, the German art historian and architect who pioneered the study of classical art. It is also reflected in the work of Jacob Burckhardt (1818–1897), the historian of art and culture who turned from 'romantic to classical art after making trips to Italy and becoming acquainted with Greco-Roman art'.[23] Papanikolaou cites the popularity of Burckhardt's *Die Kultur der Renaissance in Italien* as evidence of the extent to which Italy, for many 'romantic Grecophiles', had become 'the mirror through which nineteenth-century Germans – Brahms among them – perceived classical art and satisfied their lifelong passion for classical antiquity'.[24]

Brahms's Italian journeys informed his appreciation of the greatness of Greek art, whilst also playing a very important part in his friendships, particularly with Billroth and the writer and pastor Josef Viktor Widmann (1842–1911). Much of their correspondence during these years was bound up with either a sense of anticipation for or a wistful recollection of their trips to the land of ancient monuments and serene landscape. During his Italian journey, Brahms experienced the artworks he had read about and studied in numerous books, including Burckhardt's popular volume Wilhelm Lübke's *History of Architecture*,[25] Hermann Grimm's study of Michelangelo,[26] and the very fine poetry of his friend Paul Heyse, with whom Brahms shared a love of Italy, 'not just as a wellspring of Classical art', as Natasha Loges writes, 'but its landscape, language and people'.[27] Widmann would go on to publish numerous books on the fine art of Italy throughout the 1880s.[28] In his memoir of Brahms, he especially appreciated the composer's fine sensibility for Italian art, attributing his love for Italy to a spiritual kinship between Brahms's own artistic sensibility and the masters of the Italian Renaissance:

---

[23] Eftychia Papanikolaou, 'Brahms, Böcklin, and the *Gesang der Parzen*', *Music in Art: International Journal for Music Iconography* 30/1–2 (2005): 155–65 (155 and 158).

[24] Papanikolaou, 'Brahms, Böcklin, and the *Gesang der Parzen*', 158. Brahms owned a copy of Jacob Burckhardt, *Die Cultur der Renaissance in Italien: Ein Versuch*. Dritte Auflage besorgt von Ludwig Geiger (Leipzig: E. A. Seemann, 1877/78).

[25] Wilhelm Lübke, *Geschichte der Architektur von den ältesten Zeiten bis auf die Gegenwart*. Dritte stark vermehrte Auflage (Leipzig: E. A. Seemann, 1865).

[26] Hermann Grimm, *Leben Michelangelo's*. Zweiter Theil (Hannover: Carl Rümpler, 1863).

[27] Natasha Loges, *Brahms and His Poets* (Rochester, NY: Boydell and Brewer, 2017), 199.

[28] See, for instance, Josef Viktor Widmann, *Rector Muslins Italiänische Reise* (Zürich: Caesar Schmidt, 1881), and *Jenseits des Gotthard: Menschen, Städte und Landschaften in Ober- und Mittel-Italien* (Frauenfeld: J. Huber, 1888), in the first of which Brahms took a particularly keen interest.

Their buildings, their statues, their pictures were his delight and when one witnessed the absorbed devotion with which he contemplated their works, or heard him admire in the old masters a trait conspicuous in himself, their conscientious perfection of detail ... even where it could hardly be noticeable to the ordinary observer, one could not help instituting the comparison between himself and them.[29]

Brahms's good fortune from 1877 onward extended to the practical aspects of his working life, with an invitation from Hans von Bülow in July 1881 to use the Meiningen orchestra to rehearse new compositions without the pressure of performances.[30] This placed an immensely valuable resource in the composer's hands. Brahms's contentedness with his creative life was undoubtedly also related to some of his personal relationships having become especially rich and warm during this period. Brahms's correspondence shows a flourishing friendship with Billroth and Widmann, as well as with Elisabet and Heinrich von Herzogenberg, with whom Brahms resumed regular contact and correspondence from 1877;[31] also significant at this time was the composer's relationship with Emma Brandes Engelmann, a gifted pianist, and her husband, Theodor Engelmann, a professor of medicine; the philologist Gustav Wendt; and Bertha (née Porubsky) and Arthur Faber, the daughter and son-in-law of the pastor to the Protestant community in Vienna.

These years of personal and professional contentment, nonetheless, are the same years characterized by Brinkmann as Brahms's years of melancholy. In his powerfully perceptive study of the darkness that characterized the composer and his music at this time, Brinkmann (borrowing a phrase from Wolf Lepenies) evocatively describes Brahms as 'one of the nineteenth century's "great melancholic lone wolves"', the evidence for which he finds in the composer's 'creative doubts', 'an artistic self-questioning', and 'a skepticism about his own artistic existence'.[32] Such traits also leave a trace on the compositional output in the late 1870s and early 1880s, as we shall see, so that even in works such as the apparently cheerful Second

---

[29] Widmann, as cited in Florence May, *The Life of Johannes Brahms* (London: Arnold, 1905), ii, 229.

[30] See Avins, *Johannes Brahms: Life and Letters*, 580.

[31] A strain on this relationship from 1882 meant that Brahms and the Herzogenbergs would become increasingly estranged in the ensuing years. On Brahms's relationship to the Herzogenbergs, see Walter Frisch, 'Brahms and the Herzogenbergs', *American Brahms Society Newsletter* 4/1 (1986): 1–3. See also Paul Berry, *Brahms Amongst Friends: Listening, Performance, and the Rhetoric of Allusion* (Oxford: Oxford University Press, 2014), 109–13, and 149ff; and Antje Ruhbaum, *Elisabet von Herzogenberg. Salon–Mäzenatentum–Musikförderung* (Kenzingen: Centaurus, 2009).

[32] Brinkmann, *Late Idyll*, 134.

**Example 3.1** Brahms, Symphony No. 2 in D Major, Op. 73/I, bars 32–43

Symphony, Brahms kept his 'doubts alive about the friendliness of the world'.[33] Avins likewise attributes this dual aspect of the composer's demeanour to his 'understanding of the world', in which 'shadow is *never* far from light'.[34] In correspondence with Brahms in 1879, the

---

[33] Brinkmann, *Late Idyll*, 131.    [34] Styra Avins, *Brahms: A Life in Letters*, 552.

conductor and former Kapellmeister at Mannheim, Vincent Lachner, observed a decided darkness in the same symphony that Billroth had earlier celebrated for its sunny disposition.[35] Lachner took issue with the fact that Brahms interrupts the 'idyllically serene atmosphere with which the first movement begins' in order to sound forth the 'gloomy lugubrious tones of the trombones and tuba'.[36] Lachner was referring to the fleeting moment of darkness heard immediately before the statement of the second subject at bar 44 (Example 3.1).

This exchange of letters is by now well known to Brahms scholars, yet its content is worth revisiting for its direct relevance to the series of compositions Brahms wrote immediately after Symphony No. 2 which, taken together, trace a trajectory of melancholy that leads to *Gesang der Parzen*. Brahms's response to Lachner gives some indication of the dark shadow cast across these years and these works. In an unusually proprietorial tone, Brahms defended the first entrance of the trombones from bar 33 as 'mine', insisting that 'I can't get along without it', before offering uncharacteristically candid reasons for the disposition of this passage:

I would have to confess that I am, by the by, a severely melancholic person, that black wings are constantly flapping above us, and that in my output – possibly not entirely by chance – that symphony is followed by a little essay about the great 'Why'. If you do not know this (motet) I will send it to you. It casts the necessary shadow on the serene symphony and perhaps accounts for those timpani and trombones.[37]

If the 'black border' that Brahms claimed surrounded the Second Symphony permanently marked its joyous 'act of liberation',[38] then a darkness stemming from that time informed – if not engendered – a body of works reaching into the 1880s that share an aesthetic of despondency. These include the motet 'Warum ist das Licht gegeben den Mühseligen', a riddle canon of 1877–8 called 'Mir lächelt kein Frühling', and, ultimately, *Gesang der Parzen*. In these pieces, we discern a trajectory marked by an incremental sense of dissonance, both tonal and spiritual, and a lack of resolution, both harmonic and existential (Table 3.1).

Every piece in this select repertoire shares one or more of the following characteristics: a timbral darkness that exploits low voices and/or low

---

[35] Rinhold Brinkmann first published this letter in 1989 according to Michael Musgrave, Review of Reinhold Brinkmann, *Late Idyll: The Second Symphony of Johannes Brahms*, in *Music and Letters* 80/3 (August 1999): 465–9.

[36] This correspondence is translated in full in Brinkmann, *Late Idyll*, 126–9.

[37] Letter from Brahms to Lachner, August 1879, in Brinkmann, *Late Idyll*, 128.

[38] Brinkmann, *Late Idyll*, 141.

**Table 3.1** Trajectory of melancholy in Brahms's output from 1877 to the *Parzenlied*

| Work | Date | Text | Connection to 'Warum?' |
|------|------|------|------------------------|
| Symphony No. 2 | 1877 | None | Correspondence with Lachner |
| Motet, Op. 74/1, 'Warum?' | 1877–8 | Job 3:20–23 | Text is set |
| 'Mir lächelt kein Frühling' | 1877–81 | Brahms, after Goethe, 'Die erste Walpurgisnacht'[39] | Correspondence with Fritzsch |
| *Gesang der Parzen* | 1882 | Goethe, *Iphigenie auf Tauris*, Act IV, Scene 5 | Correspondence with Billroth |

instrumentation, with a particular emphasis on the trombone; a sense of historical reflection; an overt and self-conscious learnedness; and an increasingly acute lack of tonal resolution. Each of these pieces, further-more, is bound up with a sense of either mythic or Biblical justice, principally on account of Brahms's persistent association of each com-position with the leading text in the 'Warum?' motet, Job 3:20–23, which reads:

Warum ist das Licht gegeben dem Mühseligen, und das Leben betrübten Herzen? [Warum? Warum?] Die des Todes warten, und kommt nicht, und grüben ihn wohl aus dem Verborgenen? Die sich fast freuen und sind fröhlich, daß sie das Grab bekommen; [Warum? Warum?] und dem Manne, des Weg verborgen ist und Gott vor ihm denselben bedecket? [Warum? Warum?]

Why is light given to one in misery, and life to the bitter in heart, [Why? Why?] who long for death but it does not come, and dig for it more than for hidden treasures; who rejoice exceedingly and are glad when they find the grave? [Why? Why?] [And why is light given] to one who cannot see the way, whom God has fenced in? [Why? Why?][40]

Over a number of years, in Brahms's correspondence with a select few friends – the kind that Brinkmann refers to as the 'whole private game of disclosures and disguises' on account of its hidden allusions and secret meanings[41] – Brahms repeatedly called attention to the shared traits of these dissonant and desolate

---

[39] David Brodbeck convincingly makes the case that the text set in the canon 'Mir lächelt kein Frühling' is Brahms's own, written as a despondent response to Goethe's celebratory 'Die erste Walpurgisnacht'. See Brodbeck, 'On Some Enigmas Surrounding a Canon by Brahms', *Journal of Musicology* 20/1 (2003): 73–103.

[40] The opening of the text of 'Warum ist das Licht gegeben?' Op. 74/1, comprising the Book of Job 3:20–23. This translation is taken from Beller-McKenna, 'The Great *Warum?* Job, Christ, and Bach in a Brahms Motet', *19th-Century Music* 19/3 (Spring 1996): 231–51 (233).

[41] This phrase is borrowed from Brinkmann, *Late Idyll*, 133.

**Example 3.2**  Brahms, 'Warum ist das Licht gegeben den Mühseligen', Op. 74/1, bars 1–18

Job-related works, thereby drawing them together as a distinct collection of pieces. This collection exhibits a compositional and expressive trajectory that reaches a devastating point of culmination in *Gesang der Parzen* in the summer of 1882. A consideration of the treatment of dissonance in each of these works will clarify the course of this trajectory.

Although the Viennese public found the 'Warum' motet difficult to understand, Brahms ensured that those close to him were familiar with it. References to it dominate his correspondence throughout the second half of 1878 to an unusual degree. In early July, he warned Billroth that 'in these pages, you will perhaps not understand much because of the many different keys, but you can admire the beautiful text and respect the knowledge of the Bible'.[42] He was more direct regarding his compositional process in a letter to Hanslick in which he pointed to 'an

---

[42] Letter from Brahms to Billroth, July 1878, here translated by Hans Barkan, *Brahms and Billroth: Letters from a Musical Friendship* (New York, NY: Greenwood, 1977), 72.

**Example 3.2** (cont.)

open-ended sequence of imitative entries by descending fifths (D–A–E–B–F♯) [which reflects] the image of pointless striving that is implied by "the great Warum".[43] Daniel Beller-McKenna has observed that the implied leading note at the end of each fugal entry is only resolved onto the tonic of the ensuing voice and always at the wrong octave (Example 3.2).[44]

As though increasing the challenge for such a spiral of dissonance to resolve, soon afterward, and at the request of Elisabet von Herzogenberg, Brahms composed a riddle canon to a text of his own devising, as David

---

[43] Brodbeck, 'A Riddle Canon by Brahms', 92. These fifths always descend at the lower octave.

[44] Beller-McKenna, 'The Great *Warum?*', 244. The D♯ in the alto line in bar 9 resolves to the E in the tenor in bar 10; the A♯ in the tenor line in bar 13 resolves to the B♮ in bar 14; and the E♯ in the bass in bar 17 resolves to the F♯ in the soprano in bar 18.

Example 3.2 (cont.)

Brodbeck has convincingly argued, which amounts to a downhearted counterpart to Goethe's celebratory poem 'Die erste Walpurgisnacht', a pagan rite of spring. Brahms's poem reads, 'Mir lächelt kein Frühling | Mir strählt keine Sonne | Mir blüht keine Blumen | Für mich ist alles dahin' ('No spring smiles on me | No sun shines on me | No flower blooms for me | For me there is nothing left').[45] The unresolved canon was published anonymously in the *Musikalisches Wochenblatt* on 28 April 1881. Brahms's resolution to this canon, as Brodbeck indicates, is clearly related to the 'Warum?' motet. Not only do the two vocal works share a tempo designation of 'Langsam', and similar motivic contours (the motet begins $\hat{1}-\hat{3}-\hat{2}-\hat{6}-\hat{5}$ in D minor, whereas the canon begins $\hat{1}-\hat{3}-\hat{2}-\hat{1}-\hat{6}-\hat{5}$ in G minor), but both unfold 'a spiraling sequence of contrapuntal entries' in which the leading note plays a central role.[46] In the riddle canon, Brahms entirely vexes the potential for tonal resolution. Whereas in 'Warum?' the leading note that was seemingly left hanging at the end of each *dux* was in fact resolved with each succeeding imitative entry, in 'Mir lächelt kein Frühling', the leading note is repeatedly left unresolved. With each new entrance of the imitative voice, it is treated as the tonic of a new key, thus on each occasion $\hat{7}$ becomes $\hat{1}$, leading to an endless sequence of imitative entries descending in semitones (G–F♯–F–E–E♭–D) (Example 3.3).

When the editor of the *Musikalisches Wochenblatt* conveyed to Brahms a query from the reader who solved the anonymous riddle (the composer

[45] Brodbeck, 'A Riddle Canon by Brahms', 88. This translation is Brodbeck's.     [46] *Ibid.*, 92.

**Example 3.3** Brahms, 'Mir lächelt kein Frühling', WoO25, bars 1–22

Ferdinand Böhme) regarding the poetic text of the canon, Brahms again pointed to the connection with the 'Warum?' motet: 'Some day would you like to ask whether he knows the motets of mine that Simrock published? His mention of my canon text brought them to mind, and I would be pleased to send him those motets'.[47]

When, in July 1882, Brahms sent Billroth 'a little pencil sketch' of *Gesang der Parzen*, he advised his friend that 'it has a special relationship to you'.[48] In his lengthy response three days later, Billroth associated the piece with the Italian Renaissance, conceiving of its structure as 'three great medium-height arches, with two beautiful classical palaces such as one finds in

---

[47] Letter from Brahms to E. W. Fritzsch, *c.* 10 July 1881, here translated in Brodbeck, 'A Riddle Canon by Brahms', 89.

[48] Brahms to Billroth, 31 July 1882, here translated in *Brahms and Billroth: Letters from a Musical Friendship*, 120.

**Example 3.3** (cont.)

Veronese'. He further drew a connection between the 'harmonic sequences' that 'give the effect of a passionate desperation', and the 'abnormal hardnesses of the *Parzen*'.[49]

---

[49] Billroth to Brahms, 3 August 1882, here translated in *Brahms and Billroth: Letters from a Musical Friendship*, 121–2.

**Example 3.4** Brahms, *Gesang der Parzen*, Op. 89, bars 1–2 and 161–6

The following day, Brahms elaborated on this nexus of compositions once more with recourse to the 'Warum?' motet, as we might have come to expect: 'When you see it [the piano vocal score of *Gesang der Parzen*] once again and have yesterday's letter and the "Warum" in mind, you can no longer ask, like the prince in Shakespeare's tale, for enough sad music!'[50] He continued, 'Think over the first F♯ minor chord for a moment: how the modulation in the coda would be without effect, and would seem restless and artificial, if one had not heard this

---

**Example 3.4** (cont.)

same progression more often and more forcefully right at the beginning'.[51]

The significance of Brahms associating *Gesang der Parzen* with the pattern in the canonic motet would, at this stage, have been fully appreciated by Billroth. For he was by now aware of the open-ended sequence of imitative entries that reflect 'the image of pointless striving implied by "the great Warum"'.[52] In *Gesang der Parzen*, Brahms deploys a different harmonic pattern to achieve a similar expressive effect. The potency of the tonal instability heard as early as bar 2, where distant chords of D minor and F♯ minor are placed in jarring juxtaposition, determines the tonal plot for the entire piece, for it returns in an altered manner at the end (Example 3.4).

This tonal turbulence (which will be explored in greater detail in Section 3.5) gives rise to the large symmetrical design, the very facet that

---

[51] *Billroth und Brahms im Briefwechsel*, ed. Otto Gottlieb-Billroth (Berlin and Vienna: Urban & Schwarzenberg, 1935), 338–9. This translation is taken from Brodbeck, 'A Riddle Canon by Brahms', 89.

[52] Brodbeck, 'A Riddle Canon by Brahms', 92.

Brahms highlighted as governing the structure of *Gesang der Parzen*. Continuing the conversation with his friend, on 9 August 1882, lest his previous letters had not been sufficiently clear on the point, he once again associated the abrasive harmonic progression with the question of divine justice. Regarding Billroth's criticism of the 'passionate desperation' of these 'harmonic sequences',[53] Brahms advised, 'In the book of Job you will find that "Warum" – but no answer to it'.[54] Such a pronouncement on his own composition underlines the lack of resolution that characterizes every aspect of this most dissonant of Brahms's Elegies. His description of a formulation whereby a question is posed – in this instance, 'Warum?' – but never answered is entirely apposite to the unresolved nature of this richly intertextual composition. We will turn now to reconsider the poem that Brahms set, the 'Song of the Fates' from Act IV, Scene 5 of Goethe's play *Iphigenie auf Tauris*, in light of this trajectory of despondency and dissonance.

## 3.3   The Disembodied Head

Regarding Brahms's correspondence with Billroth, it is not merely a matter of taking the composer at his word that *Gesang der Parzen* is not *Iphigenie*, for we have compelling evidence to support this claim. In 1882, Brahms explicitly connected his composition to a particular statue that Goethe owned and which has a very specific meaning. He confessed to Billroth that 'I read the entire poem during my work and studied it as thoughtfully as Goethe in his day regarded his head of Juno'.[55] Although the 'Song of the Fates' forms an integral part of Goethe's play, it also lends itself readily – as we have seen – to being removed from that context. If we consider it as a self-standing poem, we begin to sense the appeal that Goethe's beautifully poetic rendering of this fable would have had for Brahms as a conduit for dealing with the irreconcilable gulf that exists between the gods and humanity. This association resonates on many levels, opening up important avenues of enquiry for our understanding of this complex piece. The first such avenue brings us to Italy at the time of Goethe's *Italian Journey* almost a century before Brahms's encounter with *Iphigenie*.

[53]  Billroth to Brahms, 3 August 1882, translated in *Brahms and Billroth: Letters from a Musical Friendship*, 122.

[54]  Brahms to Billroth, 9 August 1882, translated in Brodbeck, 'A Riddle Canon by Brahms', 89.

[55]  Letter from Brahms to Billroth, 6 August 1882, translated in *Brahms and Billroth: Letters from a Musical Friendship*, 123.

**Figure 3.1** The Junozimmer in Goethe's Town House in Weimar, LOOK Die Bildagentur der Fotografen GmbH/Alamy Stock Photo

During Goethe's sojourn in Italy from 1786 to 1788, he so admired a large sculpted head of the goddess Juno at the Villa Ludovisi that he had a copy made for his town house in Weimar (Figure 3.1). In his memoir of his *Italienische Reise*, amongst the myriad treasures of Greek and Roman antiquity and the masterpieces of the Italian Renaissance that he encountered, the poet prized this sculpture above all. Referring to it as his 'first Roman "sweetheart"', he enthused that 'No words can give the remotest inkling of it. It is like one of Homer's songs.'[56]

Schiller, convinced by Goethe's reverence for this colossal sculpture, was also undoubtedly influenced by Winckelmann, who believed that 'the Greeks expressed the innate harmony of their lives in the noble simplicity of their sculpture'.[57] In his 1755 essay 'Gedanken über die Nachahmung der griechischen Werke in Malerei und Bildhauerkunst' ('Thoughts on the imitation of the painting and sculpture of the Greeks'), Winckelmann

---

[56] 'Keine Worte geben eine Ahnung davon. Es ist wie ein Gesang Homers'. Goethe, *Italienische Reise*; JA xxvi.179 (6 January 1787).

[57] Elizabeth M. Wilkinson and Leonard Ashley Willoughby, 'Commentary' in Friedrich Schiller, *On the Aesthetic Education of Man in a Series of Letters*, trans. Wilkinson and Willoughby (Oxford: Oxford University Press, 1983), 254. On Winckelmann and sculpture see, for instance, 'Winckelmann: Thoughts on the Imitation of the Painting and Sculpture of the Greeks', in *German Aesthetic and Literary Criticism: Winckelmann, Lessing, Hamann, Herder, Schiller, Goethe*, ed. H.B. Nisbet (Cambridge: Cambridge University Press, 1985), 29–54.

proposed that 'the universal and predominant characteristic of the Greek masterpieces is a noble simplicity and tranquil grandeur, both in posture and expression'.[58] Even in such violent statues as those of the Laocoön group, Winckelmann found the embodiment of serenity and restraint. He exerted a strong influence on both Schiller's and Goethe's understanding of the Hellenic spirit,[59] for each of these humanist poets perceived the Greeks as an embodiment of wholeness. Applying Winckelmann's theory to the head of Juno, Schiller discerned in this statue the 'harmonious synthesis of spirit and matter', which he cast as the poetic counterpart to the fragmentation he deplored in the one-sided materialism of the moderns.[60] In Letter xv of the *On the Aesthetic Education of Mankind*, Schiller also acknowledged an irrational and pessimistic element contained in this ostensible serenity. By extolling the head of Juno as the epitome of ideal beauty, Schiller recognized its self-sufficiency and pointed to its capacity to contain an irrational nature within its outward impression of calmness:

> It is not Grace, nor is it yet Dignity, which speaks to us from the superb countenance of a Juno Ludovisi; it is neither the one nor the other because it is both at once. While the woman-god demands our veneration, the god-like woman kindles our love; but even as we abandon ourselves in ecstasy to her heavenly grace, her celestial self-sufficiency makes us recoil in terror. The whole figure reposes and dwells in itself, a creation completely self-contained, and, as if existing beyond space, neither yielding nor resisting; here is no force to contend with force, no frailty where temporality might break in. Irresistibly moved and drawn by those former qualities, kept at a distance by these latter, we find ourselves at one and the same time in a state of utter repose and supreme agitation, and there results that wondrous stirring of the heart for which mind has no concept nor speech any name.[61]

In this paean to the serene qualities of Greek sculpture, Schiller outlines a dialectic between the rational and the irrational that dwells beneath this apparently tranquil grandeur.

In positioning Goethe's 'Song of the Fates' in relation to the head of Juno, Brahms was making quite a statement about *Gesang der Parzen*. Like Goethe's statue, the poem lays a claim to independent interest outside of

---

[58] Winckelmann, 'Winckelmann: Thoughts on the Imitation of the Painting and Sculpture of the Greeks', in Nisbet, ed., *German Aesthetic and Literary Criticism*, 4.

[59] See, for instance, Goethe's essay 'Winckelmann', in Goethe, ed., *Winckelmann und sein Jahrhundert* (Tübingen: Cotta, 1905).

[60] Wilkinson and Willoughby, 'Commentary' in Schiller, *On the Aesthetic Education of Man*, 254. On Schiller and the fragmentation of modern society, see Chapter 1.

[61] Schiller, *On the Aesthetic Education of Man*, 109.

Goethe's play – 'a creation completely self-contained', as Schiller would have it. This representation of ideal beauty is characterized by both reason and instinct: an outward imprint of noble simplicity forms the outer façade within which resides the dissonance of a turbulent and deep sadness. By invoking the disembodied Juno in his declared intention to suppress any reference to *Iphigenie* on the title page of his score, Brahms enlisted both Schiller and Goethe in support of his aesthetic amputation.[62] To put it plainly, the head of Juno once belonged to a statue, just as the poem Brahms set once belonged to the larger body of Goethe's drama. The poem is worthy of aesthetic contemplation in and of itself, just as the colossal sculpture of Juno lays claim to interest and beauty independent of the mythology from which it originates. At the end of the first part of *Italian Journey*, Goethe acknowledged the independence of the statue as an object of aesthetic beauty when he considered three heads of Juno placed side by side for comparison and contemplation.[63]

Not only is this disembodied poem comparable to the sculpture of Juno as an object worthy of aesthetic contemplation; the composer seems to imply, at some level, that the 'Song of the Fates' is Juno. Brahms transfers the identity of the disembodied head onto the poem that is so readily extracted from the play, thereby inaugurating an afterlife for the 'Song of the Fates' that Goethe himself would not have anticipated. 'It did not occur to Goethe', Brahms continues in his letter to Billroth, 'that generations following his *Iphigenie* would honour Juno with the same respect that he honoured his head of the goddess!'[64] That disembodied head – then Goethe's, now Brahms's – would once again give voice to the dialectic of the rational and irrational that is concealed within its outward nobility. The sculpted head of Juno Ludovici would once again inspire grace and terror, repose and agitation.

The degree to which Brahms actually distanced the poem from Goethe's play is given potent symbolism in his Reclam edition of *Iphigenie auf Tauris*, housed at the Brahms-Institut in Lübeck, in which the pages where this text ought to appear have been torn out, most likely by the

---

[62] I borrow the term 'aesthetic amputation' from Mark Evan Bonds, who coined it to describe the deleted endings of Eduard Hanslick's *Vom Musikalisch-Schönen*. See Mark Evan Bonds, 'Aesthetic Amputations: Absolute Music and the Deleted Endings of Hanslick's *Vom Musikalisch-Schönen*', *19th-Century Music* 36/1 (2012): 3–23. The phrase is used here in an entirely different context.

[63] See Johann Wolfgang van Goethe, *Italian Journey [1786–1788]*, trans. W. H. Auden and Elizabeth Mayer (London: Penguin, 1962), ch. 7, 'Rome', letter of 21 February 1787.

[64] Letter from Brahms to Billroth, 6 August 1882, here translated in Barkan, *Brahms and Billroth*, 123.

composer himself. This is completely inconsistent with the treatment of the otherwise immaculate volumes in Brahms's library. Reflecting on the physical act of the composer tearing these pages from the book, and the imagined act of him carrying them around as he contemplated their setting, provides a powerful impression of Brahms as he embarked upon the process of composing this piece. This image will stay with us as we consider the nature of Brahms's symbolically disembodied head in greater detail.

## 3.4   Curating the Fall of Tantalus

Throughout the 1870s and 1880s, Brahms pursued an ongoing quest to find texts that deal with the poetics of loss in a secular manner. On a number of occasions in the years directly surrounding 1880, he expressed dissatisfaction with his lot as a composer of spiritual music, and explicitly stated his wish to find 'heathen' texts for musical setting. This is most pronounced in his correspondence with Elisabet von Herzogenberg, as for instance when he wrote on 14 July 1880 (as already seen in Chapter 1):

I am quite willing to write motets, or anything for chorus (I am heartily sick of everything else!); but won't you try and find me some words? [...] They are not heathen enough for me in the Bible. I have bought the Koran but can find nothing there either.[65]

Brahms's 1877 German translation of the Koran, housed at the Archive of the Gesellschaft der Musikfreunde, shows many of his characteristic markings, with the first twenty pages bearing his marginalia and markings, although these become increasingly less frequent as the chapters proceed.[66] Shortly after the beginning of Chapter 7 – the dividing wall between heaven and hell – the large sheets that were folded to produce Brahms's quarto edition remain uncut. In other words, these pages were never opened, and they remain unread. Chapter 7 of the Koran deals with the irreconcilable gulf between the divine and the human, precisely the issues with which Brahms was concerned in all of his elegiac choral works.

---

[65]  Johannes Brahms to Elisabet von Herzogenberg, 14 July 1880, in Max Kalbeck, ed. *Johannes Brahms im Briefwechsel mit Heinrich und Elisabet von Herzogenberg*, I, 123. English translation in *Johannes Brahms: The Herzogenberg Correspondence*, ed. Max Kalbeck, trans. Hannah Byrant (London: Murray, 1909).

[66]  *Der Koran. Aus dem Arabischen wortgetreu hin übersetzt und mit erläuternden Anmerkungen versehen von L. Allmann.* 7th edn (Bielefeld & Leipzig: Velhagen & Klasing, 1877).

The fact that the composer abandoned reading the Islamic text at this very point substantiates his claim to von Herzogenberg that in the Koran, as well as the Bible, his search for suitable texts with which to address this issue was vexed.

On 8 August 1882, Brahms again wrote to von Herzogenberg that 'I have just finished [a piece] which is actually heathenish enough to please me and to have made my music better than usual I hope'.[67] There is no reason to question Hanns Christian Stekel's deduction that Brahms was here referring to *Gesang der Parzen*.[68] The 'heathen' text that finally met his expressive requirements was, of course, the 'Song of the Fates' from Goethe's *Iphigenie auf Tauris.*

Act IV, Scene 5 of Goethe's drama comprises two parts. First, Iphigenie's soliloquy in the blank verse employed throughout the play sees her recall her hope, long since dimmed, that she would have any realistic prospect of leaving Tauris. She reflects on her 'solitude' and 'seclusion' and wonders whether the curse on the House of Atreus will 'reign for ever'. She had earlier hopes of 'wash[ing] from our house the evil stain of guilt'. The prospect of returning to Greece conjures up all of these memories and, with them, the ancient song that inaugurated the curse. Crucially, this is the song that 'the Parcae sang when Tantalus was hurled from the golden throne', she recalls, and that her nurse would sing to her in her youth.[69] The song, which speaks to the world of human attrition and destruction, forms the second part of Scene 5, and is the passage that Brahms set. Like the rest of the play, the poem is written in blank verse, although here Goethe changes the metre from iambic pentameter to dactylic dimeter, so arranged that each line begins with an anacrusis.[70]

Tantalus does not appear as a character in any surviving plays of classical antiquity, although his spectre looms large in many on account of the story of his eternal punishment. Amongst the three renderings of this legend that Brahms possessed in his library are Book XI (582–92) of Homer's *Odyssey* (of which Brahms owned three editions). This outlines Tantalus's alleged crimes and ensuing banishment from the golden table.[71] Brahms also

---

[67] Brahms to Elisabet von Herzogenberg, 8 August 1882, *Johannes Brahms: The Herzogenberg Correspondence*, 174.

[68] Hanns Christian Stekel, *Sehnsucht und Distanz: Theologische Aspekte in den wortgebundenen religiösen Kompositionen von Johannes Brahms* (Frankfurt am Main et al.: Peter Lang, 1997), 67.

[69] The quoted material in this paragraph is from Goethe, *Iphigenie in Tauris: A Drama in Verse*, trans. Roy Pascal (London: Angel Books, 2015), 87–8.

[70] Papanikolaou, 'Brahms, Böcklin, and the *Gesang der Parzen*', 161.

[71] Homer, *Odysee*, translated by Johann Heinrich Voß (Reutlingen: Im Comptoir der deutschen Classiker, 1819); Homer, *Homers Werke*, Von Joahann Heinrich Voß, I (Stuttgart & Tübingen:

owned Aeschylus's trilogy, *The Oresteia*, in which the curse on the House of Atreus forms the major plot line,[72] and Ovid's *Metamorphoses* (10.41–2), which tells that the punishment of the four great sinners (Tantalus, Sisyphus, Tityus, and Ixion) is stilled when Orpheus sings his lament for Eurydice.[73] Given that his friend Gustav Wendt dedicated his 1884 translation of Sophocles's *Tragedies* to Brahms, as we have seen, the composer might also have been aware that Sophocles had written a *Tantalus*, two fragments of which survive.

Tantalus is ever-present in Euripides's and Goethe's respective Tantalid tales, where he is woven into the narrative as the ancestor of Iphigenia. Goethe's play is a reworking of Euripides's drama. However, Brahms did not own (nor have we any evidence that he had read) either of Euripides's dramas *Iphigenia in Aulis* or *Iphigenia at Tauris*.[74] It is most likely, therefore, that upon reading the end of Act IV of Goethe's *Iphigenie auf Tauris*, the 'Song of the Fates' resonated with Brahms's prior knowledge of the fable as recounted in Homer, Aeschylus, Sophocles, and Ovid. It is in this context that we must understand Brahms's claim that *Gesang der Parzen* is not *Iphigenie*. Furthermore, it is for precisely this reason that I take issue with the legitimacy of the question of whether or not Brahms was faithful to Goethe's version (and secondarily to Euripides's version) of the Iphigenia legend, as posed by numerous scholars who have offered hermeneutic readings of this piece.

Margaret Notley, for instance, refers to the 'the tension between the two textual sources' (as though there were only two) and devotes much of her article on the *Parzenlied* to exploring the shape of tragedy in Euripides and Goethe's Tantalid tales. In what is otherwise a very perceptive analytical reading of the piece, however, Notley's endeavour to 'reimagin[e] the poem outside Goethe's play' is vexed, for she denies the independence of the 'Song of the Fates'. Notley argues that in 'going against the late eighteenth-century grain of Goethe's play',

---

J. G. Cotta'scher Verlag, 1839); and Homer, *Homers Odysee*, Von Joahann Heinrich Voß, Abdruck der ersten Ausgabe vom Jahre 1781 mit einer Einleitung von Michael Bernays (Stuttgart: J. G. Cotta'schen Buchhandlung, 1881).

[72] Aeschylos. Translated into the German by J. J. C. Donner, I (Stuttgart: Hoffmann'sche Verlags-Buchhandlung), 1854.

[73] Publius Ovid, *Verwandlungen nach Publius Ovidius Naso*. Von Johann Heinrich Voß (Reutlingen: Comptoir der deutschen Classiker, 1824).

[74] However, Brahms was familiar with Gluck's opera *Iphigenie in Aulis*, the libretto for which was based on Racine's *Iphigénie*, which in turn was based on the drama of Euripides. He transcribed a gavotte from the second act of Gluck's opera, which he dedicated to Clara Schumann. See Brahms, *Gavotte von Christ. W. Gluck*.

Brahms placed an 'anachronistic emphasis on human suffering and remorse'.[75]

Yet the evidence strongly suggests that Brahms was not at all concerned with the late eighteenth-century context of Goethe's play. Instead, he intentionally excised these lines for their poetic rendering of the tale of the fall of Tantalus. By recognizing the text that Brahms set to be this remote tale, we open up an entirely new way of looking at the *Parzenlied.* In this reading, we are no longer bound by the humanist ending of Goethe's play, nor is Brahms's focus on human suffering, remorse, or retribution anachronistic. In choosing this tale, Brahms found the perfect secular text to deal with the ethical and moral issues for which his search had been confounded in the Bible and the Koran. Brahms's persistent association of Juno's disembodied head with the great 'Warum?' takes on even further significance when considered in relation to Italian Renaissance art, with which he was deeply preoccupied at the time of writing *Gesang der Parzen.* Here we find an artistic analogy for the juxtaposition between the mythical and Christian realms that so powerfully informed the creation of Brahms's *Parzenlied.*

The Tantalus myth became well established in Italian Renaissance art, a particularly striking example being Titian's *Tantalus* (Figure 3.2), which forms part of Titian's cycle of the *Four Great Sinners* of antiquity, large-scale renderings of Tantalus, Sisyphus, Tityus, and Ixion, condemned to eternal torture in the depths of the Underworld in classical mythology for their transgressions against the divine order of the Olympian gods.

Titian's cycle (1549) was commissioned by Mary of Hungary to adorn the Great Hall of the Château of Binche in Flanders. 'Titian's paintings', we are told in a 1552 report by J. C. Calvete de Estrella, 'were hanging on the garden side of the hall, above the windows'. The report continues:

Opposite was a series of six tapestries with representations of six of the Deadly Sins, *Gluttony, Luxury, Anger, Envy, Avarice,* and *Sloth.* The seventh sin, *Pride* [...] appeared on the end wall above or near a daïs from where the emperor, queen and prince witnessed the spectacles. At the ends of the walls, and facing each other, were medallions of the Roman emperors Julius Caesar and Hadrian respectively, and above them, pictures of the *Contest of Apollo and Marsyas* and of *The Flaying of Marsyas* [Figure 3.3].[76]

---

[75] Notley, 'Ancient Tragedy and Anachronism', 117 and 113, respectively.

[76] J. C. Calvete de Estrella, *El felicíssimo viage del muy alto y muy poderoso Príncipe Don Phelippe, Hijo del Emperador Carlos Quinto* (Antwerp, 1552), here cited and translated in Thomas Puttfarken, *Titian and Tragic Painting: Aristotle's Poetics and the Rise of the Modern Artist* (New Haven, CT and London: Yale University Press, 2005), 80.

**Figure 3.2** Giulio Sanuto after Titian, *Tantalus* (*c.* 1565), Rijksmuseum Amsterdam

The four great sinners are the closest possible parallel in classical mythology to the Last Judgement and the eternal punishments of hell in the Christian realm. Titian's paintings were intended to be seen together at the Château of Binche in an arrangement where the brutal realism of eternal punishment in Tartarus was juxtaposed with the abiding horror of eternal punishment in hell.[77] This ensemble, P. P. Fehl asserts, was intended 'to awaken not compassion but awe. We are purged in the

---

[77] Puttfarken, *Titian and Tragic Painting*, 85.

**Figure 3.3** Titian, *The Flaying of Marsyas* (*c.* 1576), Lebrecht Music & Arts/Alamy Stock Photo

contemplation of this hell, from any sense of gloating or righteousness, whether in favour of this torture or of its condemnation.'[78]

More than three centuries later, another of the artists Brahms greatly admired, Max Klinger (1857–1920), would incorporate a comparable juxtaposition of a Biblical and a mythical fall from grace in his marble and bronze sculpture *Beethoven*, unveiled at the controversial Beethoven exhibition at the Vienna Secession in 1902 but on which he had been at work since 1886.[79] Kevin Karnes provides a rich exploration of the mythological

---

[78] P. P. Fehl, *Decorum and Wit: The Poetry of Venetian Painting: Essays in the History of the Classical Tradition* (Vienna: Irsa Verlag, 1992), 105–6.

[79] Alessandra Comini, *The Changing Image of Beethoven: A Study in Mythmaking* (Santa Fe, NM: Sunstone Press, 2008), 406–10.

and historical context of Klinger's *Beethoven*, observing that on alternate sides of Beethoven's throne he juxtaposed 'images of Adam and Eve, moments before the Biblical fall' with an image that Klinger described as *Tantalide*, 'a relief depicting the mythological figure of Tantalus, together with a female companion'. Karnes notes that Tantalus's companion was 'wholly Klinger's invention'. Apart from that, 'Klinger's rendering of Tantalus's tale follows closely that of Homer's *Odyssey*', as outlined earlier in this chapter.[80]

The visual emphasis of Titian and Klinger, over three centuries apart, and the aesthetic focus of these two curatorial projects is entirely different — with Mary of Hungary's Titian ensemble fixed on the juxtaposition between eternal punishment in hell and Tartarus, and Klinger's *Beethoven* capturing those moments immediately before the fall from grace and embodying 'perhaps *the* essential, artistic expression of *fin-de-siècle* utopian longing in the Austro-German artistic world'.[81] Nevertheless, they share with Brahms's *Gesang der Parzen* a very important perspective: all three are concerned with juxtaposing mythical and Biblical depictions of what Nietzsche terms 'the very first philosophical problem', that is, 'a painful and irresolvable contradiction between man and god'.[82]

This irremediable gulf between the ancient Greek opposition of the divine and the human lies behind each of Brahms's elegiac works with which this book is concerned. *Gesang der Parzen* provides the only example, however, where Brahms deliberately juxtaposed mythical and Biblical tales in the creation of the piece. The former constitutes the poetic source for the composition – the highly moralizing and self-professed 'heathen' text that Brahms mined from Goethe's *Iphigenie auf Tauris*. The latter constitutes the hermeneutic context that he created around *Gesang der Parzen* in what might well be described as a campaign that directed and controlled the reception of this work by persistently associating it with the great 'Warum?' of the book of Job. Stekel proposes that Brahms sought out the same difficult questions in his Biblical settings as he did in his secular choral and orchestral works in order to 'legitimize' them.[83] His choice of Biblical texts (whether direct, as for instance in *Ein deutsches Requiem* and the *Vier ernste Gesänge*, or indirect, as for instance in the implicit association of *Gesang der Parzen* with Job) speaks to Brahms's formidable theological knowledge. Yet we must also acknowledge a reciprocity to the

---

[80] Karnes, *A Kingdom Not of This World*, 57.     [81] *Ibid.*, 57.

[82] Friedrich Nietzsche, *The Birth of Tragedy and The Case of Wagner*, 70–1, here cited in Karnes, *A Kingdom Not of This World*, 57.

[83] Stekel, *Sehnsucht und Distanz*, 67.

relationship that Stekel outlines: if the Biblical settings legitimize the secular texts, the secular texts in turn give us a fresh perspective on these Biblical passages and remove them from the confines of religious dogma. Viewed in this wider context, Brahms's elegiac works form a fundamental part of the culture of philhellenism in the late nineteenth century. They comprise an integral part of an intellectual movement in the German-speaking lands at this time that viewed the Bible (and in Brahms's case, the Koran) and the tales of classical mythology as legitimate literary and philosophical sources to be drawn upon in a secular and humanist manner. The appeal of these Hellenic texts and their moralizing potential is addressed by Nietzsche in *The Birth of Tragedy*:

> It is as if the Olympian magic mountain had opened before us and revealed its roots to us. The Greek knew and felt the terror and horror of existence. That he might endure this terror at all, he had to interpose between himself and life the radiant dream-birth of the Olympians. That overwhelming dismay in the face of the titanic powers of nature, the Moira [or the Parcae] enthroned inexorably over all knowledge, the vulture of the great lover of mankind, Prometheus, the terrible fate of the wise Oedipus, the family curse of the Atridae which drove Orestes to matricide: in short, that entire philosophy of the sylvan god, with its mythical exemplars, which caused the downfall of the melancholy Etruscans – all this was again and again overcome by the Greeks with the aid of the Olympian.[84]

Where Brahms connects the myth of the fall of Tantalus to the suffering of Job, Nietzsche connects the Prometheus myth to the fall of Adam and Eve, considering the two to be 'related to each other like brother and sister'. As Karnes argues, 'clear parallels exist between the stories of Tantalus and Prometheus', for 'both were punished by a vengeful Zeus for attempting to bestow godly gifts on immortal men and women'.[85] Nietzsche elaborates on the compatibility between the Biblical and the mythical sources asserting that 'the best and highest possession mankind can acquire is obtained by sacrilege and must be paid for with consequences that involve the whole flood of sufferings and sorrows with which the offended divinities have to afflict the nobly aspiring race of men'.[86]

There is no evidence that Brahms had read Nietzsche by the time he completed his *Parzenlied* in 1882. It was 1887 when the philosopher sent him a signed copy of *On the Genealogy of Morals*, Brahms's copy of which is well used. The only other books by Nietzsche in Brahms's library are those published together in the 1895 collected writings, which would exert a great

---

[84] Friedrich Nietzsche, *Basic Writings of Nietzsche* (New York, NY: Random House, 2000), 42.
[85] Karnes, *A Kingdom Not of This World*, 57.    [86] Nietzsche, *Basic Writings of Nietzsche*, 71.

influence on the composition of the *Vier ernste Gesänge*, as we shall see in Chapter 4. Regardless of whether Brahms had read Nietzsche, the strategy employed in *The Birth of Tragedy*, whereby Nietzsche situates Greek and Biblical foundation myths next to one another, is of a piece with Brahms's curatorial enterprise in *Gesang der Parzen*, for these gestures form an integral part of a larger hermeneutic movement in the German-speaking lands of the late nineteenth century.

In drawing these strands together, there is much to be gained in our understanding of Brahms's *Parzenlied* in relation to the simultaneously secular and sacred curatorial projects explored above. Taken together, Mary of Hungary's allegorical programme of Titian's artworks in 1549, the complex of images incorporated in Klinger's *Beethoven* statue, and Nietzsche's juxtaposition of Greek and Biblical foundation myths present a concentrated study in adversity for those who have lost the majesty of their prior life and now know only misfortune and lost prosperity. All of these artistic projects focus on the irreconcilable conflict between suffering humanity at the mercy of forces beyond their control and the arbitrary power and caprice of the gods. In each case, the gods have nothing to offer those who seek justice. Art, on the other hand, does. Brahms's *Gesang der Parzen* does. And it does so with a compelling and remarkable resonance with Iris Murdoch's estimation of Titian with which we opened this chapter. Let us now return to the *Parzenlied* to find out how, like *The Flaying of Marsyas*, it conveys

something to do with human life and all its ambiguities and all its horrors and terrors and misery and at the same time there is something beautiful, and something also to do with the entry of the spiritual into the human situation and the closeness of the gods.[87]

## 3.5   *Gesang der Parzen*: 'Far Away from Tonality'

Due to their common source material in Goethe's *Iphigenie auf Tauris*, numerous commentators have understood the artist Anselm Feuerbach's paintings of *Iphigenia* to form an artistic analogy to Brahms's *Gesang der Parzen*.[88] A more suitable artistic analogy to the *Parzenlied* requires the

---

[87] Iris Murdoch in conversation with Eric Robson, as cited in fn. 2.

[88] The dissonance and despondency that characterize Op. 89 are difficult to perceive in these Feuerbach paintings. Instead, Feuerbach's *Iphigenia* settings, as we saw in Chapter 2, have an affinity with the ennoblement of mourning found in Brahms's *Nänie*.

depiction of a harsher landscape, however, one that conveys a sense of terror, dissonance and agitation apposite to Schiller's dialectical description of the head of Juno, such as that found in the artworks of the Italian Renaissance explored above. Mindful of Brahms's advice to Billroth that 'In the book of Job you will find that "Warum" – but no answer to it', I further suggest that the dissonance and lack of resolution that marks *Gesang der Parzen* resonates with the collective fates of Tantalus and Job, for the music in the *Parzenlied* cycles over and over and never finds a resting place.[89]

Regardless of which analytical technique we employ, or of how we conceive of this work harmonically, we – composer and listener alike – are vexed in our quest for resolution. We might go so far as to suggest that Brahms inscribes the myth of the fall of Tantalus onto the very fabric of this score, for the music steadfastly refuses to allow us to touch that which seems to be within our reach. This is the case across the work on numerous structural levels, and it is most evident in the treatment of tonality. (Throughout the analytical discussion that follows, refer to the tabular analysis found on Table 3.2.)

The ostensible tonality of *Gesang der Parzen*, D minor, is peculiarly absent in Brahms's composition. Upon hearing the Baroque-inflected opening material that Notley designates as the 'ritornello', which is characterized by dotted rhythms and an organ-like orchestral texture, the listener is immediately struck by an unconventional dominant emphasis on the downbeat, whilst the tonic is obstinately relegated to the anacrusis. Brahms's compositional choice here may be related to the dactylic dimeters of Goethe's poem whereby each line begins with an anacrusis: 'Es *fürch*-te die Götter | Das *Men*-schengeschlecht!' Yet the technique of reversing the conventional tonal functions of tonic and dominant takes on a greater large-scale significance. Throughout the piece, Brahms steadfastly evades cadential confirmation in D minor. The one structural tonic chord to occur at bar 31 is weakly articulated on account of $\hat{3}$ and $\hat{5}$ heard in the upper register in the winds, leading to a cadential structure that, following William Caplin, we can describe as i:IAC.[90] The cadence is heard half-way through the bar, rather

---

[89] Rosemarie P. Mauro, 'The *Gesang der Parzen* of Goethe and Brahms: A Study in Synthesis and Interpretation', unpublished MA thesis, University of Washington (1986), 33.

[90] After William Caplin, IAC denotes an imperfect authentic cadence; PAC denotes a perfect authentic cadence; and HC denotes a half cadence. The Roman numerals that prefix these acronyms in Table 3.2 and throughout this analytical passage indicate the relationship of the cadence to the tonic, D minor. See William Caplin, *Classical Form: A Theory of Formal Functions for the Instrumental Music of Haydn, Mozart, and Beethoven* (Oxford: Oxford University Press, 2000).

**Table 3.2** Formal outline of *Gesang der Parzen*, Op. 89

| Bars | 1–19 | 20–31 | 31–35 | 36–47 | 48–71 | 72–83 | 84–99 | 100–3 | 104–11 | 112–15 | 116–61 | 162–76 |
|---|---|---|---|---|---|---|---|---|---|---|---|---|
| Rotation | 1 | | 2 | | | | | | 3 | | | 4 |
| Stanza | | 1 | | 2 | 3 | 4 | | | 1 | | 5 | 6 |
| Topic | Ritornello | Processional (Refrain?) | Ritornello | | | | | Processional | | | A *capella* | Ritornell-o |
| Thematic material | A | B | A | B variant | | | A/B variant | B-based | B | | B-based | A |
| Cadences | | i:PAC (19–20) | i:IAC (31) | | iii:IAC (70) | III:IAC (72) | | | | Plagal (115) | I:PAC (160–1) | |
| Passing tonality | | | | → C maj | → C maj | F maj | F → C♯/D♭ → V/i | Standing V/i | Standing V/i | | | |
| Ostensible tonality | D minor | | | Other | | | | D minor | | | D major | D minor |

than on the first beat, as we come to the end of stanza 1, and it marks (and overlaps with) the onset of the second utterance of the ritornello. The persistent emphasis on the fifth scale degree in the bass, moreover, gives the effect of a large-scale prolongation of the dominant, not the tonic.

Whereas the mediant F (with mixed modality) seems like a conventional choice for the secondary tonal area, here the cadential confirmation is equally evasive. With the beginning of stanza 2 at bar 36, and its redoubled emphasis on the tyranny of the gods, the listener is brought to an 'other' as yet undefined tonal area, which seems to begin on the flat submediant, B♭. From bar 38, F major is prolonged (yet not cadentially secured), veering toward the secondary dominant (C) by way of a V:HC cadence at bar 47 in advance of stanza 3, which shifts the emphasis to a focus on suffering humanity. The restless nature of the music persists and this passage is heard, retrospectively, as a dominant preparation for the (again) weakly articulated cadence on the mediant minor (iii:IAC) at bar 51. This cadential pattern is repeated and extended at bar 69. If we consider the passage that sets the words 'gerechten Gerichtes' (which translates literally as 'a juster decree') with which stanza three ends to be a larger cadential progression – beginning with the C major chord on the upbeat to bar 69 and ending on the F major chord at the downbeat of bar 72 – then, despite the surge in dynamics from *pp* to *f*, here we have a weakly articulated cadence in the mediant minor (iii:IAC at bar 69), quickly followed by another in the mediant major (III:IAC at 72). Yet, Brahms makes the listener question whether there is a cadence at all, as the music is propelled forward into the following bars that prolong the dominant of F, C major.

Stanza 4 of Goethe's poem turns to the elysian world of the gods as they remain feasting at their golden tables. The music continues to inhabit the secondary tonality of F, but this is interrupted by a brief prolongation of C♯/D♭ major (the flat submediant of F♭), as the wide angular leaps in the strings and winds reflect the gods striding from one mountain top to the next. An apparent dominant preparation for a cadence in C♯ major ensues from bar 84, complete with a change of key signature. However, this is reconfigured by the interrupted cadence 'in' C♯ minor at bar 100, that is V of C♯ is interrupted by A, which is quickly revealed as the structural dominant chord of D at bar 100. This gesture seems to correct the errant path of the music, reinstating the key signature of the bleak key of D minor.

Here we encounter one of Brahms's most noteworthy pieces of text-setting in this composition. We return to the poetry of Goethe's first stanza complete with the processional music heard initially from bar 20, now also marked by the same destabilizing elements, that is, a lack of a structural tonic and the according prolongation of the dominant. Yet, on account of what directly precedes the abridged repeat of this first stanza, it is expressively transformed: the rousing, if not terrifying, ritornello heard at the outset of *Gesang der Parzen* contrasts greatly with the descending line that is faintly reminiscent of the ritornello but is nonetheless heard here with sparse orchestration and dynamics at bar 100ff. The effect is such that, despite similar vocal and orchestral forces in each iteration of the first stanza (TBB, alternating with SAA, *p* with timpani, bassoons, horns in D, cellos, and double basses at bar 20 altered only to have the voices sing *sotto voce* at bar 104), with its return at bar 104, this material undergoes a remarkable transformation from its harsh and ominous origin to a tone of wearied lament. Following what we may now hear as a faint retransition, the reiteration of stanza 1 is fleeting, never building to the majestic forte that brought back the ritornello at bar 31, but instead yielding, via a plagal cadence in D, to the fifth stanza with its evocation of the major modality (to which we will return below).

In the *Paths to the New Music*, Anton Webern called attention *Gesang der Parzen*, noting how its 'remarkable harmonies already take it far away from tonality'.[91] Mindful of J. P. E. Harper-Scott's definition of tonality, we can begin to understand why Webern might have conceived of the piece thus. In *The Quilting Points of Musical Modernism*, Harper-Scott maintains that:

> The central asseveration of tonality is that a musical configuration is either consonant or dissonant in one of an increasingly varied number of ways – but that ultimately the stable configuration, against which everything else will be judged more or less stable, is the consonant configuration.[92]

For this configuration to be 'tonal', it must have a diatonic relation at its heart: a V-i cadence that is either stated or implied. It is precisely this relation that Brahms undermines in *Gesang der Parzen*. At the opening of the work, we have an unambiguous V-i (bars 19–20). At the end, we also have the tonic (albeit without the third in the final sonority). However, with the exception of one weakly articulated i:IAC with double appoggiatura in bar 110, these two diatonic structures that bookend the piece are never connected by a crucial

---

[91] Anton Webern, *The Path to the New Music*, ed. Willi Reich, trans. Leo Black (Bryn Mawr, PA: Universal Edition, 1975), 46.

[92] J. P. E. Harper-Scott, *The Quilting Points of Musical Modernism: Revolution, Reaction, and William Walton* (Cambridge: Cambridge University Press, 2012), 172–3.

affirmatory gesture: the structural perfect cadence. In the *Parzenlied*, Brahms pays lip service to the rhetoric of tonality whilst at once undermining its very foundation. He does so, as we have seen, by inscribing the myth of the fall of Tantalus across the surface and the depth of every structural level of this desolate work. This makes the D minor at the end sound even more hollow than it would were it only the open fifths that made it so.

With the undermining of any satisfactory functions of tonality (by which I refer to cadential functions and tonal confirmation), musical topics play a crucial role in establishing the large-scale form of this piece.[93] Notley has given much attention to this aspect of Brahms's *Gesang der Parzen*, outlining a scheme of 'formal phases, formal functions, and topical allusions in Brahms's setting'.[94] I have incorporated her findings in the 'Topic' row of Table 3.2. Along with the historically conscious tone of the ritornello sections explored in relation to tonality above, Notley outlines a processional refrain that is more balanced in its phrase structure and more tonally stable than the ritornello. It is to this refrain that Brahms set the first stanza (associated with thematic material B in Table 3.2). These strongly contrasting but equally ceremonial themes contribute to what Notley perceives to be 'an aura of ancient theater'.[95] This archaic quality is further invoked in the dissonance and modal effects that contribute to the *Parzenlied*'s tonal instability.

A reiterative principle therefore takes hold in *Gesang der Parzen*, by which we might consider the work to evince a 'rotational form', that is, a series of rotations 'of a thematically composite, larger block' redolent of the approach to form that James Hepokoski applies to a number of Sibelius's symphonies.[96] 'Strictly considered', Hepokoski writes, 'a

---

[93] On the subject of topic theory in nineteenth-century repertoire, see Julian Horton, 'Listening to Topics in the Nineteenth Century', in *The Oxford Handbook of Topic Theory*, ed. Danuta Mirka (Oxford: Oxford University Press, 2014), 642–64; and Kofi Agawu, *Playing with Signs: A Semiotic Interpretation of Classical Music* (Princeton, NJ: Princeton University Press, 1991), ch. 2, 26–50.

[94] Notley, 'Ancient Tragedy and Anachronism', 119.     [95] *Ibid.*, 119.

[96] Numerous scholars have recognized the significance of the recurring themes in *Gesang der Parzen* and have cast the work in a variety of formal contexts, from rondo form (Malcolm MacDonald and Karl Geiringer) to a series of free variations (Christian Martin Schmidt and Janina Klassen). For these readings, see Malcolm MacDonald, *Brahms* (New York, NY: Schirmer, 1990), 289; Karl Geiringer, *Brahms: His Life and Work*, 3rd edn (New York, NY: Da Capo, 1981), 323; Christian Martin Schmidt, *Reclams Musikführer Johannes Brahms* (Stuttgart: Reclam, 1994), 211; and Janina Klassen, 'Parzengesang', in *Rezeption als Innovation: Untersuchungen zu einem Grundmodell der europäischen Kompositionsgeschichte – Festschrift*

rotational structure is more of a process than an architectural formula'. This involves 'a "referential statement" of contrasting ideas', such as 'a series of differentiated figures, motives, themes, and so on', which may either 'cadence or recycle back through a transition to a second broad rotation', with the 'second (and any subsequent) rotations normally rework[ing] all or most of the referential statement's material, which is now elastically treated'.[97] One of rotational theory's most useful character-istics, as Harper-Scott suggests, 'is its ability to bring almost instant clar-ification to complex structures, as a preliminary to hermeneutic inquiry'.[98]

Each of the rotations begins with the 'ritornello' topic. At the outset of each rotation, the music holds the promise of bringing us somewhere new, yet, each time, we are thrust back to the ritornello with which we began and its bleak D minor hue. Here again we think of the effect of the 'Warum?' motet and the 'Mir lächelt' canon never finding a resting place. If we consider all three works to share an aesthetic of despondency – as we are directed to do by the composer in his correspondence – we recognize an incremental intensification of the promise of that which cannot be deliv-ered, the presence of something that is just beyond our reach. Here, it is not only a case of the 'Why?' of the opening bars of the 'Warum' motet never being answered. In *Gesang der Parzen*, the 'answer' is repeatedly presented as a possibility, yet the composer consistently reneges on its delivery. This obtains right to the point of the final possible return of the ostensible tonic D minor in the fourth and last rotation.

Perhaps the most 'tantalizing' of all aspects of the *Parzenlied* is the setting of the fifth stanza. Here, Brahms's musical language has elicited most com-ment in relation to the incongruity between poetry and music. Brahms chose this peak of ruthlessness and mercilessness to introduce the parallel D major modality to the work for the first time, whilst also introducing a lilting triple time, evoking a tranquil hymn-like texture that brings a sense of serenity to the music not found elsewhere in this composition. The sense of consolation that is awakened with the introduction of the major mode at the fifth stanza is widely considered to be at odds with the unremitting bleakness of the

---

*für Friedhelm Krummacher zum 65. Geburtstag*, ed. Bernd Sponheuer, Siegfried Oechsle, Friedhelm Krummacher, Helmut Well (Kassel: Bärenreiter, 2001), 330.

[97] James Hepokoski, *Sibelius*, Symphony No. 5 (Cambridge: Cambridge University Press, 1993), 25. Hepokoski continues, 'Portions may be omitted, merely alluded to, compressed, or, contrarily, expanded or even "stopped" and reworked "developmentally". New material may also be added or generated. Each subsequent rotation may be heard as an intensified, meditative reflection on the material of the referential statement.'

[98] J. P. E. Harper-Scott, *Edward Elgar, Modernist* (Cambridge: Cambridge University Press, 2006), 67.

poem, which here makes it clear that the curse on Tantalus will last for generations. The jarring contrast between the cold severity of the poem at this point and the tender (yet devastating) beauty of Brahms's turn to the major is either deemed to be directly attributable to Goethe's humanism or else is attributed to some sort of a misreading of the poem. Walter Niemann, for instance, professed that 'with the gods, as with nature, there is *no* pity'. Brahms's soft and warm-hearted nature forced him to make what Niemann understands as an 'unintentional musical confession'.[99] Peter Petersen suggests that in this passage, Brahms betrays a 'lack of sympathy with the content of *Gesang der Parzen*'.[100]

Yet here too, the effect of the major modality is mitigated by the degree to which Brahms infuses 'the atmosphere with plagal harmonies' and places 'an expressive dissonance on every downbeat'.[101] Scott Burnham is the one commentator to have picked up on the bitter irony of this passage:

Is this *Seligkeit*? If so, it is *Seligkeit* in the contrary-to-fact subjunctive mood: were there to be *Seligkeit*, it would sound like this. Brahms's subdominant-drenched major mode is the sound of tenderness but this is now proffered for tenderness eternally withheld, in a kind of killing irony that goes beyond corrosive sarcasm to what Brahms himself called the 'utter misery of humanity'.[102]

Brahms's friend, the young lawyer Gustav Ophüls, asked him for his opinion on this passage. The composer's response gives no indication that by employing the major mode he attempted to ameliorate the psychological harshness of these poetic lines:

---

[99] 'Die niederdeutsche Bürgerlichkeit (im schönsten Sinne!) und Weichheit seiner angeblich so herben und harten, in Wirklichkeit tief gefühlsgesättigten, weichen und gemütvollen Natur zwingt ihn zu dem sicher ungewollten musikalischen Geständnis, daß er Universalität und wirkliche Größe nicht besitzt, daß er jene antike Ewigkeitsidee nur dadurch darstellen kann, daß er sie durch Mitleid mit den gestürzten Menschen ersetzen zu können glaubt, daß die unversöhnlichen Götter mit ihnen alle Zukunft bis in die entferntesten Enkel nicht haben. Die Größe zerrinnt in Gefühlssentimentalität – freilich in jene schwerblütige norddeutsche, die so edel und musikalisch Brahmsisch ist, wie nur irgend etwas'. Niemann, 'Brahms' *Gesang der Parzen* und Ophüls' Brahms-Erinnerungen', *Zeitschrift für Musik* 89/7 (1922): 156–60 (156–7).

[100] Peter Petersen, 'Werke für Chor und Orchester', 172. Translated by Mary Whittall in the Sleeve Notes for Deutsche Gramophon, 'Brahms Chörwerke mit Orchester', 449 651 2, 22–8 (27).

[101] Scott Burnham, 'Between Schicksalslied and Seligkeit: Morality as Music in Brahms', Keynote Lecture delivered at the Conference 'Brahms in the New Century', Graduate Centre, City University New York, 2012, 6. I am very grateful to the author for having shared an unpublished version of this paper with me.

[102] *Ibid.*, 6.

| | |
|---|---|
| Es wenden die Herrscher | From races ill-fated, |
| Ihr segnendes Auge | Their aspect joy-bringing, |
| Von ganzen Geschlechtern, | Oft turn the celestials, |
| Und meiden, im Enkel | And shun in the children |
| Die ehmals geliebten | To gaze on the features |
| Still redenden Züge | Once loved and still speaking |
| Des Ahnherrn zu sehn. | Of their mighty sire. |

Instead, at the end of his letter, once again engaging in 'the whole private game of disclosures and disguises',[103] Brahms points to a compelling precedent for his seemingly strange compositional choice:

I often hear people philosophizing about the fifth strophe of the *Parzenlied*. I think that, at the mere entry of the major key, the unsuspecting listener's heart must soften and his eyes become wet, only then does the whole misery of humanity take hold of him. At the end of Handel's *Saul* there is a whole Requiem with funeral march which, if memory serves, is in the major.[104]

Brahms was a great admirer of Handel, particularly of *Saul*, which he conducted in February 1873 during his first season as music director at the Gesellschaft der Musikfreunde. There are countless major-mode pieces marked by sorrow and poignancy that Brahms might have pointed toward here. One thinks immediately of the sense of irony deployed in numerous Schubert songs such as 'Die Post' or 'Die Nebensonne' from *Winterreise*.[105] Donald Francis Tovey's observation that 'Gluck's highest pathos is expressed in the major mode' is also relevant here.[106] Yet Brahms chose Handel's Dead March in C Major from *Saul*. The fact that Handel, as Peter Kivy observes, obviously made an effort to make this 'an unusual, if not strange, funeral march, which persistently calls attention to *itself*; to, in

---

[103] Brinkmann, *Late Idyll*, 133.

[104] Johannes Brahms as quoted in Gustav Ophüls, *Erinnerungen an Johannes Brahms* (Berlin: Verlag der Deutschen Brahms-Gesellschaft, 1921), 280. This translation is slightly amended from Papanikolaou, 'Brahms, Böcklin, and the *Gesang der Parzen*', 162. The last passage, not cited by Papanikolaou or in other recent Brahms scholarship, reads, 'Zum Schluß des "Saal" von Händel übrigens steht ein ganzes Requiem mit Trauermarsch, meines Erinnerns alles in Dur!' Kalbeck, *Johannes Brahms*, III, 360.

[105] Although she does not mention Brahms having envoked Handel's 'Dead March' in his letter to Ophüls, Notley offers bars 121–36 of the 'Forlane' of Ravel's *Tombeau de Couperin* as 'an example of the marked poignancy that the major mode can express in an overwhelmingly minor key piece'. Notley, 'Ancient Tragedy and Anachronism', 142, n. 48.

[106] Donald Francis Tovey, *Essays and Lectures on Music* (Oxford: Oxford University Press, 1949), 96–7.

other words, the musical medium'[107] was certainly not lost on Brahms. It was perhaps this very facet of his own composition that allowed him to propose to von Herzogenberg that in *Gesang der Parzen* his music was 'better than usual'.[108]

Brahms was abundantly aware, moreover, of the 'apparent mismatch' in this particular anthem, as Tim Carter puts it, 'between what a piece does and (anachronistic) modern expectations thereof, as with, for example, a "happy" – *recte* "grand" major key [. . .] rather than a "sad" minor one'.[109] What Brahms did not make explicitly clear to Ophüls was that, in playing with convention in the employment of the major mode at this most poignant juncture in Goethe's poem, he once again inscribed the myth of Tantalus. D major remains in sight but out of reach in the fifth stanza, just as D minor is beyond our grasp for the entire composition.[110]

When considered in this light, the perceived incongruity between Goethe's desolate poem and Brahms's achingly beautiful setting diminishes. The rich intertextuality of *Gesang der Parzen* demonstrates the composer's incisive perception of the manifold implications of Goethe's deeply poetic and quintessentially German rendering of this mythical tale of Tantalus. In this poem, Brahms found the perfect text with which to grapple with his own unanswered questions. Without shying away from the harshness and bleakness of Goethe's desolate lines and the depiction of human misery contained therein, he created a rich tapestry woven into which are the legends of classical antiquity, Biblical tales, and an artistic resonance with the Italian Renaissance. All of this, in Brahms's setting, is in dialogue with some of the most pressing philosophical and existential issues of the late nineteenth century. The fact that these questions remain unanswered in Brahms's work, and the fact that we, like Tantalus, cannot grasp that which seems to be within our reach, is a testament to the musical sensitivity of Brahms's *Parzenlied*.

---

[107] Peter Kivy, *Sounding Off: Eleven Essays in the Philosophy of Music* (Oxford: Oxford University Press, 2012), 156.

[108] Brahms to Elisabet von Herzogenberg, 8 August 1882, *Johannes Brahms: The Herzogenberg Correspondence*, 174.

[109] Tim Carter, 'The Search for Musical Meaning', in *The Cambridge History of Seventeenth-Century Music*, ed. Tim Carter and John Butt (Cambridge: Cambridge University Press, 2005), 158–96 (179).

[110] This is not least because of the persistent use of B♭s, which are 'borrowed' from the minor mode. On the subject of interchangeable major and minor modalities, J. P. E. Harper-Scott offers an interesting discussion of 'major-feel and minor-feel music' in relation to the music of Elgar. Harper-Scott, *Edward Elgar, Modernist*, 9, n. 16.

# 4 | The Last Great Cultural Harvest: Nietzsche and the *Vier ernste Gesänge*

Much like the endings to all three of Brahms's elegiac choral works explored in earlier chapters, *Schicksalslied*, *Nänie*, and *Gesang der Parzen* from the 1870s and 1880s, the song that ends Brahms's *Vier ernste Gesänge*, Op. 121 of 1896, has had a difficult reception, from the time of its initial publication to the present. This opus comprises four songs, each of which sets a passage from the Luther Bible. The first three set texts from the Old Testament, each addressing death and espousing varying shades of pessimism. Numbers 1 and 2 have frequently been associated with the philosophy of Schopenhauer, particularly 'On the Vanity and Suffering of Life', chapter 46 of *The World as Will and Representation*, which puts forward the view that death or non-existence is preferable to a desolate life.[1] The third and most famous song, 'O Tod, wie bitter bist du', traces a trajectory from fear of death for those who are young and healthy to considering death to be a welcome relief for the weary and suffering. The fourth and last song, a setting of the first letter of St Paul to the Corinthians, is a paean to love that is widely considered to be incongruous with the rest of the set. It is the only setting of a passage from the New Testament, and its rousing and uplifting countenance is at odds with the air of pessimism that pervades numbers one to three.

The fact that Brahms frequently described these songs as *Schnaderhüpfeln* (a Southern German term meaning harvesters' revels) has confounded efforts to solve what is by now a characteristically Brahmsian riddle.[2] At issue are a number of questions: first, why Brahms chose this last text; secondly, what its relationship is to the first three songs; and, thirdly, why he chose the bewildering term *Schnaderhüpfeln* to describe his self-styled *Serious Songs*.

---

[1] Arthur Schopenhauer, *World as Will and Representation*, trans. E. F. J. Payne, 2 vols (New York, NY: Dover, 1969).

[2] See, for instance, Wolfgang Sandberger, 'Spätwerk als selbstbezügliche teleologische Konstruktion: Die "Vier ernsten Gesänge" Op. 121', in *Spätphase(n)? Johannes Brahms' Werke der 1880er und 1890er Jahre*, ed. Maren Goltz, Wolfgang Sandberger, and Christiane Wiesenfeldt (Munich: Henle, 2010), 280–96.

A number of commentators have attempted to address the apparent discontinuity between the first three songs and the last. Malcolm Boyd's assertion that this fourth song 'really has no place in this cycle' seems to decline Brahms's invitation to grapple with the weight of the issues at hand.[3] Significantly more engaging is Daniel Beller-McKenna's proposal that the last song expresses Brahms's 'opposition to the pessimism of Schopenhauer', and his argument that the composer shaped his final published utterance into a coherent, if not masterful, work of art.[4] Yet, for each answer that Beller-McKenna provides, he opens a window onto further evidence of the complex nexus of ideas underpinning this composition, which in turn compounds the puzzle surrounding the genesis and meaning of this fourth song.

For instance, as we will see below, there is the notebook in which Brahms jotted down many of the Biblical texts he set over the course of his career, which provides direct evidence of the connection between Op. 121 and Brahms's ardent patriotism; there is the sketch of Op. 121 No. 4 found in the composer's apartment upon his death and now housed at the Archive of the Gesellschaft der Musikfreunde in Vienna. This sketch definitively shows that at the time of composition Brahms had in mind not only Biblical texts, but also German literature. The multiple texts in this sketch are related to Brahms's description of these songs as 'truly heathenish, but truly human'.[5] For he was not aiming to compose a set of Biblical songs, as Dvořák had done the previous year.[6] Brahms repeatedly referred to Op. 121 as 'godless' songs, a description that was not intended as mere provocation. The scholar who embarks upon a hermeneutic reading of the *Vier ernste Gesänge*, therefore, must attempt to answer what it is that unites these apparently disparate elements.

The answer, I propose, may well lie in the writings of Nietzsche and, more specifically, in his book *The Antichrist*, a copy of which Brahms obtained early in 1895. Brahms's confrontation with the candid and urgent

---

[3] Malcolm Boyd, 'Brahms and the *Four Serious Songs*', *Musical Times* 108/1493 (July 1967): 593–5 (595).

[4] Daniel Beller-McKenna, 'Brahms on Schopenhauer: The *Vier ernste Gesänge*, Op. 121 and Late Nineteenth-Century Pessimism', in *Brahms Studies*, ed. David Brodbeck (Lincoln, NE and London: University of Nebraska Press, 1994), I, 170–90.

[5] Richard Heuberger recalls the composer referring to the work as 'echt heidnisch, aber echt menschlich'. See Richard Heuberger, *Erinngerungen an Johannes Brahms*, ed. Kurt Hofmann (Tutzing: Hans Schneider, 1976), 105. The term 'heidnisch' should be understood here not in today's general vernacular sense of unenlightened or un-Christian, but instead in the literal sense meaning neither specifically Christian, Jewish, nor Muslim.

[6] Antonin Dvořák, *Ten Biblical Songs*, Op. 99 (1894).

nature of Nietzsche's pronouncements in this book is quite likely to have contributed to his final and most pronounced turn inward.

Brahms had much in common with Nietzsche's religious and philosophical outlook. As we shall see, the composer would have identified with Nietzsche's scepticism regarding the existence of God, and he would have shared his reverence for Greek classicism and the Bible, which both men approached with scholarly acumen and a critical bent. Despite such commonalities, however, in *The Antichrist* Brahms would have found much that challenged his own position on matters of faith and much thought-provoking material that prompted him to crystalize his thinking on these matters. Furthermore, Nietzsche's attack on Protestantism and, more importantly, on the cultural legacy of Lutheranism would have been an affront to Brahms. In this regard, Nietzsche's provocative little book flew in the face of this composer's unshakeable patriotism, his *Kulturprotestantismus* (cultural Protestantism), and his belief in the role of art in the German nation. When considered in this context, Brahms's late decision to set the first letter of St Paul to the Corinthians as the fourth of the *Serious Songs* obtains great significance. In relation to Nietzsche's *The Antichrist*, and in the context of the sketch for Op. 121, we may profitably conceive of this composition as Brahms's last great cultural harvest.

## 4.1   Brahms and Nietzsche in 1890s Vienna

In 1895, the latest instalment in Nietzsche's collected writings was published and made its way into Brahms's personal library. Included in this single book are *The Case of Wagner, Twilight of the Idols, Nietzsche contra Wagner, The Antichrist*, and a selection of poetry.[7] In a letter to Fritz Simrock of 6 February 1895, Brahms wondered whether the publisher still had a copy of Josef Viktor Widmann's review of Nietzsche's work.[8] His request came right at the time when the serious literary reception of Nietzsche's thinking was gaining strong currency in

---

[7]  Friedrich Nietzsche, *Der Fall Wagner. Götzen-Dämmerung. Nietzsche contra Wagner. Der Antichrist. Gedichte* (Leipzig: Druck und Verlag von C. G. Naumann, 1895). This is housed in the archive of the Gesellschaft der Musikfreunde in Vienna, shelf mark Brahms Bibliothek 10.237/131B. The whereabouts of this Nietzsche volume was first listed in Mark Peters, 'Introduction to, and Catalogue of Brahms's Library', unpublished Master's thesis, University of Pittsburgh (1999). I am grateful to David Brodbeck for drawing this thesis to my attention.

[8]  Brahms to Fritz Simrock, 6 February 1895 in *Johannes Brahms Briefe an P. J. Simrock und Fritz Simrock* (Tutzing: Hans Schneider, 1974), IV, 163.

Vienna in the 1890s.[9] Widmann, who introduced Brahms to Nietzsche's writings, had written three reviews of Nietzsche at this point, including 'Nietzsche's Dangerous Book' (1886), 'Nietzsche's Break with Wagner' (1888), and 'On Nietzsche's "Antichrist"' (1895).[10]

Nietzsche's enthusiasm for Brahms lasted roughly from 1874 to 1887, although in *Human, All Too Human* (1878) he criticizes recent music for becoming too intellectual, too 'modern', a censure possibly aimed at Brahms, whose First Symphony had received similar rebukes in the contemporary press.[11] In *The Case of Wagner* (1888), Nietzsche is just as hostile to Brahms as to Wagner, and it is here that he famously recognized a 'melancholy of impotence' in the music of Brahms.[12] Kalbeck presumed that Brahms was interested in the philosopher's famous and inflammatory remarks in *The Case of Wagner*.[13] Yet Brahms's annotations and marginalia indicate that he was drawn to another of the books Nietzsche wrote in 1888 (which was not published until 1895), the attack on Christianity and German culture with the provocative and somewhat ambiguous title *The Antichrist*.[14]

In the same month that Brahms requested Widmann's Nietzsche essay from Simrock, February 1895, he confided to Clara Schumann his wish to compose 'nothing more for the public, but only for himself'.[15] Following

---

[9] Carl Niekerk, *Reading Mahler: German Culture and Jewish Identity in Fin-de Siècle Vienna* (Rochester, NY: University of Rochester Press, 2010), 86. See also Steven Aschheim, *The Nietzsche Legacy in Germany, 1890–1990* (Berkeley, CA: University of California Press, 1994), 32–4.

[10] See Widmann, 'Nietzsches gefährliches Buch', *Der Bund* 256, 16 September 1886; 'Nietzsches Abfall von Wagner', *Der Bund* 321–2, 20–21 November 1888); and 'Über Nietzsches "Antichrist"', *Der Bund*, 11–12 January 1895. See also Widmann's book, *Jenseits von Gut und Böse* (Stuttgart, 1893). We do not know whether Simrock sent the review or whether Brahms kept it. It is not in his Nietzsche books in the Brahms *Bibliothek*.

[11] On this aspect of the reception of Brahms's First Symphony, see Walter Frisch, *German Modernism: Music and the Arts* (Berkeley and Los Angeles, CA: University of California Press, 2005), 20.

[12] Nietzsche, *The Case of Wagner*, in Walter Kaufmann, trans. and ed., *The Basic Writings of Nietzsche* (New York, NY: Random House, 2000), 643. (Kaufmann, for reasons he makes clear in this edition, translates 'Melancholie des Unvermögens' as 'melancholy of incapacity'. I have amended this translation.)

[13] Kalbeck's footnote to the letter containing Brahms's request to Simrock reads, 'Die über den "Fall Wagner" seinerzeit in Feuilleton des Berner "Bund" (20 u. 21 November 1888) veröffentlichte flammende Auseinandersetzung Widmanns mit Nietzsche'. Kalbeck in *Johannes Brahms Briefe an Fritz Simrock* (Tutzing: Hans Schneider, 1974), 163, n. 2. It appears Kalbeck was not aware that Brahms owned or had read a copy of this 1895 Nietzsche volume, as he never mentions it in his biography.

[14] The ambiguity arises from the fact that in German, *Der Antichrist* can mean either the 'Anti-Christ' or the 'Anti-Christian'. It is widely agreed that Nietzsche intended his title to mean both. There are no markings at all in Brahms's copy of *The Case of Wagner*.

[15] Max Kalbeck, 'Brahms's Four *Serious Songs*, Op. 121 (1914)', trans. William Miller in *Brahms and His World*, ed. Walter Frisch and Kevin C. Karnes (Princeton, NJ: Princeton University Press, 267–87 (268). See also Max Kalbeck, *Johannes Brahms*, IV, 391.

the composition of the *49 Deutsches Volkslieder*, for the first time in his adult life, Brahms wrote no music for a year.[16] On a number of occasions prior to this, he announced that he was retiring from composition, but never before had he either indicated or embarked upon such a retreat inward.

It was some years earlier that Brahms read *On the Genealogy of Morals*, which he had been sent in 1887 by Nietzsche himself.[17] Brahms's characteristic markings are found only in the third of the three essays, called 'What is the meaning of ascetic ideals?' Here, in a reversal of the familiar trope of reception throughout the nineteenth century, whereby Brahms was cast as a chaste composer – not least by Wagner – and Wagner was cast as a composer of sensual music, Nietzsche asks 'What is the meaning of ascetic ideals? – Or, to take an individual case that I have often been asked about: what does it mean, for example, when an artist like Richard Wagner pays homage to chastity in his old age? In a certain sense, to be sure, he had always done this: but only in the very end in an ascetic sense.'[18]

In this passage, which Brahms marked in his own copy of the book, Nietzsche was referring to what he perceived to be a shift in Wagner's thinking, from the former follower of Ludwig Feuerbach and advocate of sensuality to the preacher of Christian medieval piety, as evidenced not only in the opera *Parsifal*, but also in the prose writings that preceded it, including 'What is German?' (1878) and 'Religion and Art' (1880).[19] Nietzsche was further contributing to an ongoing late nineteenth-century discourse on art, religion, and nationalism. Wagner's 'Religion and Art', which sought to save religion, or to renew Christianity, was responding to Nietzsche's earlier writings and to a notable 1878 essay by Siegfried Lipiner, a founding member of the Pernerstorfer circle, called 'On the Elements of a

---

[16] Styra Avins, Johannes *Brahms: Life and Letters*, selected and annotated by Styra Avins, trans. Josef Eisinger and Styra Avins (Oxford: Oxford University Press, 1997), 723.

[17] For further background to the relationship between Brahms and Nietzsche that led up to the philosopher sending his book in 1887, see David Thatcher, 'Nietzsche and Brahms: A Forgotten Relationship', *Music and Letters* 54/3 (1973): 261–80.

[18] Friedrich Nietzsche, *The Basic Writings of Nietzsche*, trans. and ed. Walter Kaufmann, intro. Peter Gay (New York, NY: Modern Library, 2000), 534. On the fundamental struggle between notions of sensuality and purity in the reception of Brahms and Wagner, see Laurie McManus, 'The Rhetoric of Sexuality in the Age of Brahms and Wagner', unpublished PhD dissertation, University of North Carolina (2011).

[19] Richard Wagner, 'Was ist deutsch?' in *Sämtliche Schriften und Dichtungen* 10: 36–54; translated as 'What is German?' in *Richard Wagner's Prose Works* (London: Kegan Paul, 1895), IV, 149–69; and 'Religion und Kunst' in *Sämtliche Schriften und Dichtungen* X, 211–53, translated in *Richard Wagner's Prose Works*, VI, 211–52.

Renewal of Religious Ideas in the Present'.[20] Lipiner aimed to 'reinvigorate the present with a quasi-religious conception of reality: "to comprehend . . . the world as a work of art"'.[21]

We know from letters and the memoirs of his friends that, along with the famous surgeon Theodor Billroth and the poet Josef Viktor Widmann, Brahms was at the heart of a group of learned liberals who tried to reconcile the scientific materialism and positivism of the age in Vienna with an intelligent discourse on religion and matters of faith. Although there is no record of Brahms's circle having been in touch with the Pernerstorfer circle, each group was grappling with similar issues.[22] Brahms and Billroth had numerous conversations regarding the complex consequences for those who were raised Lutheran but, despite retaining its cultural trappings, had otherwise extricated themselves from this faith. Their conversations concerned the writings of figures such as Peter Rosegger and Ludwig Anzengruber whose work was concerned with finding what Widmann referred to as a 'godless' Christianity.

The consistent absence of dogmatic texts in Brahms's religious music is well documented, for example, *Ein deutsches Requiem* or the Motets, Op. 74.[23] In his secular settings of the legends of classical antiquity, as mediated through German Idealist poetry, Brahms consistently returned to the perceived gulf between divine and human. Here, as we saw in earlier chapters, he addresses issues of hope, fate, human suffering, and death, without relying on religious dogma or drawing on the notion of an afterlife.

---

[20] Siegfried Lipiner, 'On the Elements of a Renewal of Religious Ideas in the Present', trans. Stephen Hefling in *Mahler im Kontext: Contextualizing Mahler*, ed. Erich Wolfgang and Morten Solvik (Vienna: Böhlau, 2011), 91–114.

[21] Morten Solvik, 'The Literary and Philosophical Worlds of Gustav Mahler', in *The Cambridge Companion to Mahler*, ed. Jeremy Barham (Cambridge: *Cambridge University Press*, 2007), 21–34 (24).

[22] The Pernerstorfer Circle was a group of late nineteenth-century Viennese intellectuals who developed and espoused a collective outlook on matters of politics, religion, philosophy, poetry, music, and theatre. By the turn of the century, some of the most notable members included Mahler and Viktor Adler. See William J. McGrath, *Dionysian Art and Populist Politics in Austria* (New Haven, CT: Yale University Press, 1974).

[23] See, in particular, Jan Brachmann, *Kunst, Religion, Krise: Der Fall Brahms* (Kassel et al.: Bärenreiter, 2003); Brachmann, 'Stern, auf den ich schaue: Brahms' Arbeit mit der Bibel', in *Johannes Brahms*, Ein deutsches Requiem: *Ich will euch trösten: Symposium. Ausstellung. Katalog*, ed. Wolfgang Sandberger (Lübeck: Brahms Institut, 2012), 21–6; Daniel Beller-McKenna, *Brahms and the German Spirit* (Cambridge, MA: Harvard University Press, 2004); and Hanns Christian Stekel, *Sehnsucht und Distanz: Theologische Aspekte in den wortgebundenen religiösen Kompositionen von Johannes Brahms* (Frankfurt am Main, et al.: Peter Lang, 1997).

Brahms, therefore, would have understood, if not identified with, the distinction Nietzsche draws between the respective attitudes toward hope in the literature of Christianity and that of ancient Greece. He would likely have been intrigued by Nietzsche's denouncing of a worldview that is predicated on a future reward and his espousing instead of a return to a focus on this life. Indeed, he probably shared the philosopher's regret that the literature of Christianity had cast a shadow over the literature of Greek classicism, as indicated by a number of passages he marked in *On the Genealogy of Morals*, for instance:

Even in the midst of Graeco-Roman splendor, which was also a splendor of books, in the face of an ancient literary world that had not yet eroded and been ruined, at a time when one could still read some books for whose possessions one would nowadays exchange half of some national literatures, the simplicity and vanity of Christian agitators – they are called Church Fathers – had the temerity to declare 'we, too, have a classical literature, *we have no need of that of the Greeks*'; and saying this they pointed proudly to books of legends, letters of apostles, and apologetic tracts, rather as the English 'Salvation Army' today employs similar literature in its struggle against Shakespeare and other pagans.[24]

The prospect of reading Nietzsche's *The Antichrist* upon its publication eight years hence would surely have appealed to Brahms. Here was a fellow German who, like himself, was brought up in a traditional Lutheran family and whose faith had lapsed in adulthood. In reading this book, the ongoing conversation that Brahms had over many years with his cultivated friends on matters of religion and faith would continue, so to speak.

At the heart of Nietzsche's protest in *The Antichrist* is the conviction that Christianity as an organized religion not only was far removed from the principles and actions of the figure from whom it claimed its inspiration, but that it exploited the legacy of Jesus. Nietzsche asserted that the one true Christian, Jesus, died on the cross. He extolled the virtues of a life lived according to the legacy of Jesus. However, he regarded Christian religion to be of an entirely different order. The Apostle Paul, he charges, 'substituted faith in Christ for Christlike life', because he was incapable of living a genuinely Christian life.[25] Moreover, Nietzsche alleges that St Paul himself recognized this fact, and thus he interprets Pauline

---

[24] Nietzsche, *The Basic Writings of Nietzsche*, trans. Kaufmann, 579–80.
[25] Kaufmann's translation of *The Antichrist*, here cited in Kaufmann, *Nietzsche: Philosopher, Psychologist, Antichrist* (Princeton, NJ: Princeton University Press, 1974), 345.

Christianity to be merely an 'escape' and 'the perfect revenge' against true Christian law and those who were able to follow it.[26]

Nietzsche's protest, moreover, is not in the spirit of the German Reformation, for he also includes Luther's Protestantism in his indictment. His Lutheran upbringing would no doubt have taught him that although Luther extolled the virtues espoused by St Paul, he did not accept the second half of Paul's pronouncement, according to which the greatest virtue is love.[27] Luther insisted that 'although love ... is a beautiful ... virtue, faith is infinitely much greater and more sublime'.[28] Directing his ire at Luther's attribution of supreme importance to faith, Nietzsche deconstructs this Biblical passage – and everything he considers it to stand for – thereby bringing his critique of Christianity to a devastating culmination. He deems it to be 'a matter of absolute indifference' to Christians 'whether a thing be true, but a matter of the highest importance *to what extent* it is believed to be true'. To arrive at Christian belief, as he sees it, one must abandon reason and knowledge, for 'the road to truth becomes the *forbidden* road'.[29]

The question of truth further informs Nietzsche's analysis of the realms of happiness and hope in *The Antichrist* in a continuation of a theme addressed in *On the Genealogy of Morals*. Christian sufferers, Nietzsche observes, 'have to be sustained by a hope which cannot be refuted by any actuality – which is not *done away with* by any fulfilment: a hope in the Beyond'. Lamenting the irrational basis of such a position, Nietzsche rebuffs the very cornerstone of Christianity and the New Testament, declaring, 'So much for the three Christian virtues faith, hope, and love'. He deems it more appropriate to refer to these as 'the three Christian shrewdnesses'.[30]

Nothing so far departs radically from what Brahms would have already read in *On the Genealogy of Morals* eight years earlier. However, the extent and degree of the vociferous attack on the Reformation in *The Antichrist*

---

[26] Kaufmann, *Nietzsche: Philosopher, Psychologist, Antichrist*, 344.

[27] I Corinthians 13:13. In their translations of *The Antichrist*, Hollingdale and Kaufmann both adopt the traditional King James translation of the three Christian virtues as 'faith, hope, and charity'. I amend this throughout this chapter to 'faith, hope, and love', thereby reflecting the German 'Liebe' found in Luther, Nietzsche, and Brahms. No further amendments are made to the translation of *The Antichrist*.

[28] Kaufmann, *Nietzsche: Philosopher, Psychologist, Antichrist*, 348. I have amended the word 'charity' in Kaufmann's translation to 'love'.

[29] Nietzsche, *Twilight of the Idols and The Antichrist* trans. R. J. Hollingdale (London: Penguin, 1990), 145.

[30] Nietzsche, *Twilight of the Idols and The Antichrist*, 145.

had no precedent in Nietzsche's earlier writings. To Nietzsche's mind, the Renaissance provided an ideal opportunity for the revaluation, if not the abolition, of an exhausted Christianity. Yet the Germans wasted this opportunity, as he sees it. Instead of gratefully grasping the Renaissance and its attendant overcoming of Christianity, Nietzsche writes, '[Luther's] hatred grasped only how to nourish itself on this spectacle': the devastating consequence is that 'the German monk', as he pejoratively calls him, '*restored the Church*'.[31] In so doing, he 'robbed Europe of the last great cultural harvest'. The last passage that Brahms marked in his copy of the book – with a large exclamation mark – reads:

For almost a millennium they have twisted and tangled everything they have laid their hands on, they have on their conscience all the half-heartedness – three-eighths-heartedness! – from which Europe is sick – they also have on their conscience the uncleanest kind of Christianity there is, the most incurable kind, the kind hardest to refute, Protestantism . . . If we never get rid of Christianity, the *Germans* will be to blame.[32]

Although we might reasonably imagine Brahms to have been sympathetic to Nietzsche's diatribe against Christianity's childish faith and its lifelessness, this statement would have struck at the heart of Brahms's patriotic, cultural, and artistic identity.[33] The composer's German patriotism – as vividly represented, for instance, by the bronze relief of Bismarck that stood in his apartment at Karlsgasse, 4 in Vienna – never wavered throughout his life; he considered the Luther Bible to be the shining beacon of Lutheranism, and throughout his entire career he contributed in word and deed to the cultural Protestantism of German art.

Brahms read *The Antichrist* at a time when he was confronted with the death of many of his closest friends, when his own health was failing, and when his own musical fallowness was acting upon him. These factors, together with Nietzsche's calculated assault on Luther, seem to have prompted Brahms to return to a deep contemplation of the Luther Bible, which resulted in his last two works: the *Vier ernste Gesänge*, Op.

---

[31] Nietzsche, *Twilight of the Idols and The Antichrist*, 197.

[32] *Ibid.*, 198. Natasha Loges notes that Brahms marked a similar passage in Adolf Friedrich von Schack's art catalogue *Meine Gemäldesammlung* (1881) in which Schack complained that Germans were complete Philistines. See Natasha Loges, *Brahms and His Poets* (Rochester, NY: Boydell and Brewer, 2017), 346.

[33] The exclamation mark found here can be understood in the German tradition of providing an exclamation mark where we today usually use '[sic]' – that is, to flag and disclaim an obvious error in the text at hand.

121, which was published in his lifetime, and the Eleven Chorale Preludes, Op. 122, which he left to posterity and which were published posthumously. In order to fully appreciate how Brahms might have read and interpreted these pronouncements in *The Antichrist*, we now turn to an exploration of the composer's position on matters of faith and national identity.

## 4.2  A Question of Faith for Brahms and His Liberal Viennese Circle

We have no documentary evidence in the form of letters or memoirs that record Brahms's reaction to Nietzsche's *The Antichrist*. Most of the friends with whom he would have discussed such things had died in recent years. These included Elisabet von Herzogenberg, one of the few people with whom Brahms corresponded on the subject of Nietzsche and from whom he regularly sought advice on religious texts, and his close friend Theodor Billroth.[34] Josef Viktor Widmann, who had first introduced Brahms to Nietzsche's writings, was in ill health at this time, and so declined Brahms's invitation for another Italian journey in April 1895, during which the two might well have discussed Nietzsche's latest publication. Brahms would have had to make do, instead, with the review of *The Antichrist* that Widmann penned in January of that year.[35]

In the absence of documentary evidence, our interpretation of Brahms's setting of the first letter of St Paul to the Corinthians as it relates to Nietzsche's *The Antichrist* draws on the intellectual, cultural, religious, and biographical context in which Op. 121 was composed. This entails looking afresh at evidence concerning Brahms's views on organized religion, exploring how these views relate to his thoughts on the Bible, and inquiring anew into the nature of the relationship between religion and culture and, by extension, patriotism in Brahms's life, correspondence, and cultural milieu.

Pinning down Brahms's religious orientation is a difficult task, all the more so in the context of the culturally complex city of Vienna, to which he moved permanently in 1871.[36] Brahms was raised in a traditional Lutheran family in Hamburg and received an education that included lessons in

---

[34] The chronology of death is as follows: Elisabet von Herzogenberg (7 January 1892), Theodor Billroth (6 February 1894). The death of Hans von Bülow (12 February 1894) may also be pertinent.

[35] Widmann, 'Über Nietzsches "Antichrist"'.

[36] Beller-McKenna, *Brahms and the German Spirit*, 30.

Lutheran catechism and confirmation.[37] A fundamental change in religious outlook took place when the young composer left Hamburg in 1853, and came under the influence of Joseph Joachim and the Schumanns.[38] Robert Schumann's essay 'Neue Bahnen' and the death of its author fortified Brahms's interest in the Bible as a philosophical and cultural text that could be drawn upon for spiritual guidance.[39] Brahms's acquaintance with the artist Anselm Feuerbach and his burgeoning friendship with Billroth between 1865 and 1871 further influenced his thinking in this regard.[40]

The period during which Brahms lived in Vienna (intermittently from 1863 to 1871 and permanently from 1871 to 1897) witnessed the ascendancy of a new form of liberalism in that city. The most important opponents of the liberals in Vienna, as Jan Brachmann argues, were the political Catholics who became prominent through the priest and journalist Albert Wiesinger. The use of the adjective 'Christian' in his propaganda was intended to exclude liberals and Jews. At this time, therefore, the term 'Christian' did not merely reflect religious belief, but instead it was a campaign slogan that embraced anti-modernism, anti-intellectualism, and anti-Semitism.[41] Following the creation of the Dual Monarchy (Austria–Hungary) in 1867, the liberal Austrian Constitution went into effect in December 1867, granting a number of significant civic and social reforms. The liberals, as Jonathan Kwan notes, regarded religion as a personal concern with no place in state and legal matters.[42] The constitution included the guarantee of equal legal rights for all citizens, the curtailment of the power of the Catholic Church, the promotion of rationalism and science, and the primacy of German culture, the latter being celebrated further following Prussia's victory over France in 1871.[43] The

---

[37] *Ibid.*, 33.    [38] Stekel, *Sehnsucht und Distanz*, 25–40.

[39] Beller-McKenna, *Brahms and the German Spirit*, 34. See also Robert Schumann, 'Neue Bahnen', *Neue Zeitschrift für Musik*, 28 October 1853, 185–6.

[40] Stekel, *Sehnsucht und Distanz*, 41–6.

[41] Jan Brachmann, 'Brahms zwischen Religion und Kunst', in *Brahms Handbuch*, ed. Wolfgang Sandberger (Stuttgart: Metzler, 2009), 128–33 (129).

[42] Jonathan Kwan, *Liberalism and the Hamburg Monarchy, 1861–1895* (London: Palgrave Macmillan, 2013), 144.

[43] See Carl E. Schorske, *Fin-de-siècle Vienna: Politics and Culture* (New York, NY: Alfred Knopf, 1980), 5–10; for an in-depth study of the vicissitudes of liberalism and nationalism in Austria during this time, see Jonathan Kwan, *Liberalism and the Hamburg Monarchy, 1861–1895* (London: Palgrave Macmillan, 2013); Pieter Judson, *Exclusive Revolutionaries: Liberal Politics, Social Experience, and National Identity in the Austrian Empire, 1848–1914* (Ann Arbor, MI: University of Michigan Press, 1996), particularly chs. 5, 6, and 7. See also the introduction to William J. McGrath, *Dionysian Art and Populist Politics in Austria* (New Haven, CT and London: Yale University Press, 1974), particularly 7–13; and Margaret Notley, *Lateness and Brahms: Music and Culture in the Twilight of Viennese Liberalism* (Oxford: Oxford University Press, 2007), particularly 15–21 and 207–16.

law also recognized the autonomy of individual religions to administer their own internal affairs and – in a clause pointed at the hitherto privileged Catholic Church – stated that no citizen could be compelled to take part in a public religious function against their will.[44]

By 1872, the period of transition between absolute monarchy and modern democratic politics was well under way. Austria had been Catholic since the Counter-Reformation and had therefore been modernized through the Enlightenment, but not through religion, as was the case in northern Germany. The German inclination toward inward cultivation and *Bildung* was never as essential in Viennese culture as it had been in Germany. Brahms and his German circle, therefore, occupied something of an outsider position in Vienna in espousing this salient aspect of German Protestant and Romantic subjectivity.

What further set Vienna apart from the traditions of many German cities in the second half of the nineteenth century was the dominance of the natural sciences and medicine. Unlike the University of Berlin during the tenure of figures such as Humboldt, Hegel, and Ranke two generations earlier, after the reforms of 1848 the University of Vienna 'did not take shape as a modern university in the context of *Bildung*' but 'unambiguously in the context of the natural sciences and the ideological confidence of materialism'.[45]

This materialism and positivism that prevailed at the university informed the ongoing discourse on religion and matters of faith in Vienna at that time. Serious and critical exploration of this subject was part of the everyday conversation in modern Vienna. Engaging with the latest writings of religious criticism carried cultural cachet. It was in this spirit, for instance, that Brahms's friend Bertha Faber (née Porubsky), the lapsed Lutheran daughter of Vienna's pastor, Gustav Porubsky, gave the composer a volume of writings by David Friedrich Strauß, the German theologian famous for his book *Das Leben Jesu*, which portrayed the 'historical Jesus' and denied his divine nature.[46] Hanslick's like-minded espousal of 'the essence and foundation of religion' being 'only ethics' speaks to a shared mindset, which considered 'all faiths with the same moral principles [to be] of equal worth'.[47] Hanslick shared this outlook

---

[44] Judson, *Exclusive Revolutionaries*, 120–1. The legally recognized religions were Roman Catholicism, Calvinism, Judaism, Greek Orthodoxy, and Lutheranism.

[45] David S. Luft, *Eros and Inwardness in Vienna: Weininger, Musil, Doderer* (Chicago, IL: University of Chicago Press, 2003), 24.

[46] The volume Bertha Faber gave Brahms was David Friedrich Strauß, *Voltaire. Sechs Vorträge* (Leipzig: Hirzel, 1870), as documented in Brachmann, *Kunst, Religion, Krise*, 201.

[47] 'Wesen und Grundlage der Religion sei nur die Moral; bei gleichen moralischen Grundsätzen seien alle Bekentnisse gleichwertig. Die biblischen Geschichten lernten wir nur von ihrer

with his fellow liberal, Max Kalbeck, who, as Margaret Notley posits, 'prided himself on being a freethinker in religious matters'.[48]

Billroth's letters to Brahms regarding religion, moreover, go beyond the general statements of Hanslick and Kalbeck and probe what the implications are for persons like themselves who had been brought up as Lutherans but later lost their faith. As well as articulating why he no longer subscribes to a religious dogma, Billroth recognizes that the very act of extricating oneself from the faith in which one was raised brings with it a complex set of issues and consequences. Robert B. Pippin's formulation regarding Nietzsche's lost faith is equally applicable to Brahms and Billroth: 'It doesn't really matter if there had been a god or not; the psychological experience of secularization and disillusionment, the *experience of loss*, is certainly real enough and clearly characterizes a wide swath of modernist experience'.[49] The familiarity and ease with which Billroth addresses Brahms on these matters implies that these letters are only the written part of a larger, ongoing conversation between the two on this topic.

For instance, in June 1880 Billroth wrote to Brahms of his thoughts concerning his own funeral, as prompted by the objectionable oration of the clergyman at a Protestant funeral he attended. Referring to a similar conversation he had had with Brahms in the Café Bauer, Billroth states his preference to be carried out to the *Zentralfriedhof* (the Vienna Central Cemetery) in the Alserstadt in Vienna 'without a clerical escort and without a spiritual service'.[50] He insisted that he had 'nothing against religion, or confession, so long as it is alive in spirit only; but when it occurs in practice, I cannot help feeling an inner contradiction and deriving a trivial impression'.[51]

---

liebenswürdigen, gemütvollen und poetischen Seite kennen; die "Wunder" nur als Gleichnisse'. Hanslick, *Aus meinem Leben* (Berlin: Allgemeiner Verein für Deutsche Litteratur, 1894), I, 6–7. This translation is from Notley, *Lateness and Brahms*, 209. Also of interest here is Hanslick, 'Über Religionsverschiedenheit', *Beilage zum Morgenblätte der Wiener Zeitung*, 25 and 26 October 1848; reprinted in Hanslick, *Sämtliche Schriften: Historisch-kritische Ausgabe. Aufsätze und Rezensionen 1844–1848*, ed. Dietmar Strauß (Vienna: Böhlau, 1993), I, 189–201.

[48] Margaret Notley, 'Nineteenth-Century Chamber Music and the Cult of the Classical Adagio', *19th-Century Music* 23 (1999): 33–61 (36).

[49] Robert R. Pippin, 'Nietzsche and the Melancholy of Modernity', *Social Research* 66/2 (1999): 495–520 (504) (emphasis in the original).

[50] Billroth also made the not inconsiderable request of Brahms that the second movement of the Requiem might be arranged for wind instruments and male-voice choir for his funeral.

[51] Theodor Billroth to Johannes Brahms, 20 June 1880. *Billroth und Brahms in Briefwechsel: Mit Einleitung, Anmerkungen und 4 Bildtafeln* (Berlin: Urban & Schwarzenberg, 1935). The translation is my own.

The following year, in an exchange with their mutual friend Hanslick, Billroth expressed his conviction that God was a human construct, at once distancing himself from a belief in god(s) and religious dogma and embracing human spirituality:

Man has always created his gods or his god in his own image, and prays and sings to him – that is, properly speaking, to himself – in the artistic forms of the period. Since the so-called divine is always a mere abstraction or personification of one or several human attributes in the highest conceivable potency, it follows that human and divine, worldly and religious, cannot really be of differing natures. Man cannot, in fact, think anything supernatural, nor can he do anything unnatural, because he never can think or act without human attributes.[52]

Billroth was aware that this departure from the Lutheran faith came at a price. In January 1886, he continued to be concerned with the shared plight of like-minded lapsed, yet cultural, Lutherans, whose spiritual needs could not be adequately fulfilled by the positivism and materialism of the age. The religious denomination is not the defining feature, but rather the impact on one's life of the loss of faith. This fate would also apply to those, like Hanslick, for instance, who were raised as Roman Catholics. What Billroth was addressing here was the question of the limits of human knowledge in an age of reason and science, when figures such as Ludwig Feuerbach, Ludwig Büchner, David Friedrich Strauß, and Charles Darwin shaped intellectual thought. He wrote to Brahms to announce that he was sending him a copy of Peter Rosegger's 1883 book, *The God Seeker: A Tale of Old Styria*.[53] This book, which 'impressed [Billroth] enormously', portrays an ascetic Promethean hero who is excommunicated by the Church for murdering a tyrannical pastor, and seeks solitude in the mountains, eventually finding an altogether new religion for a 'godless' community there.[54] Billroth introduced the book thus:

The so-called materialists have the idea that sometime, instead of a religion, there will be something else more advanced and positive – or negative – of one kind or another. *The God Seeker* describes the rationalistic and nihilistic condition under which people suffer when torn out of the traditional religious atmosphere which has been a part of their land and their existence. I thought the writing excellent, and yet it seemed to me, as I think it does to the author himself, that there exists no clear

---

[52] Billroth to Hanslick, 21 February 1891, in Georg Fischer, ed., *Briefe von Theodor Billroth* (Hannover and Leipzig: Hahn, 1897), 501. As cited in Brachmann, *Kunst, Religion, Krise*, 258.

[53] Peter Rosegger, *Der Gottsucher* (Hamburg: Projekt Gutenberg, 2012).

[54] This description taken from James Billington, *The Icon and The Axe: An Interpretive History of Russian Culture* (London: Vintage, 1970), 763, fn. 51.

idea of the consequence of this social question. I, nevertheless, would compare the book to the best ones of Anzengruber. As far as I know people, they're always in a condition of infantilism and need fairy tales for their happiness.[55]

With the mention of Ludwig Anzengruber (1839–89), the Austrian playwright and novelist whose anti-clerical drama of 1870, *Der Pfarrer von Kirchfeld* (*The Pastor of Kirchfeld*), was a great success, Billroth continues his roll call of key Austrian figures who participated at that time in the ongoing and spirited debate in Vienna about the nature of atheism and the notion of creating 'a religion that does not believe in a god'.[56]

## 4.3   Brahms and Religion Beyond the Viennese Circle

Beyond Vienna, Brahms found another acquaintance – and soon to be close friend – in Widmann of Bern, with whom he could discuss the place of religion in society. He and the feuilleton editor of the Bernese newspaper *Der Bund* first met in 1874 at the home of the composer Hermann Goetz (1840–1876). The two had in common not only music, but also a love of literature, philology, and travel. From the outset, each recognized in the other a lively mind and spirit, and their friendship was characterized by candour and intellectual curiosity. Brahms had full access to his friend's impressive library, through which passed a constant stream of the latest publications waiting to be reviewed in *Der Bund*. The composer's satchel, filled with such volumes as he came to and from the Widmann home in Bern, would become a symbol of the highly cultured nature of their friendship.

The two spent a number of summers together between 1886 and 1888 at Thun overlooking the Bernese Alps. During the first of these summers, Brahms composed a wealth of chamber music, including the Cello Sonata No. 2 in F Major, Op. 99, the Violin Sonata No. 2 in A Major, Op. 100, and the Piano Trio No. 3 in C Minor, Op. 101. This same year, Widmann wrote

---

[55]  Billroth to Brahms, 13 January 1886. This translation from *Johannes Brahms and Theodor Billroth: Letters from a Musical Friendship*, trans and ed., Hans Barkan (Norman, OK: Oklahoma Press, 1957), 162–3.

[56]  Ludwig Anzengruber was an Austrian playwright and novelist highly acclaimed for his realistic portrayal of peasant life. The Brahms *Bibliothek* contains a copy of Ludwig Anzengruber, *Dorfgänge: Gesammelte Bauerngeschichten*, 2nd edn, ii, (Vienna: L. Rosner, 1880). It does not, however, contain a copy of Rosegger, *Der Gottsucher*. For a nuanced view of the similarities and differences in the outlook of Rosegger and Anzengruber on religious and spiritual matters, see *Peter Rosegger/Ludwig Anzengruber Briefwechsel: 1871–1889*, ed. Konstanze Fliedl and Karl Wagner (Vienna, Cologne et al.: Bölhau, 1995), in particular, the foreword.

his review of *Beyond Good and Evil* and, one year later, Nietzsche sent Brahms *On the Genealogy of Morals* and his choral composition *The Hymn to Life* through their mutual Bernese acquaintance. Brahms and Widmann's travels together also brought them on a number of trips to Italy in 1888, 1890, and 1893. All the greater pity, therefore, that Widmann was too ill to take Brahms up on the offer of a fourth Italian trip together in 1895, where the two might have discussed *The Antichrist* in person.

Parallels in their upbringing may have contributed to the affinity between Brahms and Widmann on spiritual and religious matters. Widmann, like Billroth, was also the son of a clergyman. He grew up with the liberal Protestant outlook of *Gefühlsreligiosität* inspired by Schleiermacher's 1799 address *On Religion: Speeches to its Cultured Despisers* and espoused the view that art and religion should be intimately connected.[57] Widmann's self-described undisturbed childhood in the spirit of Schleiermacher lasted only until his 'eyes were opened to the philosophical untenability of the dogmas of the church'.[58] Upon finishing his studies in Protestant theology at both Heidelberg and Jena, he came to the view that 'theology hides an empty reliquary'.[59] In autumn 1868, he retired as pastor and took up a post as the director of a school. In 1874, he also retired from this job, following complaints by parents regarding the atheist tone of the religious education he delivered. He joined the Swiss Theological Reform Movement, an organization concerned with the incompatibility between the traditional contents of faith, and modern experience and scientific knowledge.

It was on this very topic that Widmann had his first conversation with Brahms. When asked for his opinion, Brahms denounced the Swiss Reform Movement as 'a half-measure, unable to satisfy either religious yearnings on the one hand, or a philosophy striving for complete freedom on the other'.[60] Whether or not Widmann was influenced by Brahms's

---

[57] Friedrich Schleiermacher, *Über die Religion: Reden an die Gebildeten unter ihren Verächtern* (Berlin: Unger Verlag, 1799), translated as *On Religion: Speeches to its Cultured Despisers*, ed. Richard Crouter (Cambridge: Cambridge University Press, 1996).

[58] Max Widmann, 'Aus meiner theologischen Zeit: Lebenserinngerungen und kritische Betrachtungen von J. V. W.', *Der Bund* 319–21 (1891), in Max Widmann, *Josef Viktor Widmann. Ein Lebensbild. Zweite Lebenshälfte* (Leipzig: 1924), 349–68 (353), as cited in Brachmann, *Kunst, Religion, Krise*, 227. The discussion of Widmann contained in this section draws on Brachmann, 'Brahms und Josef Viktor Widmann', in *Kunst, Religion, Krise*, 226–41.

[59] Widmann, as cited in Brachmann, *Kunst, Religion, Krise*, 227.

[60] Josef Viktor Widmann, *Recollections of Johannes Brahms*, trans. Dora E. Hecht (London: Seeley & Co. Limited, 1899), 99. Jan Brachmann provides a detailed and engaging discussion of Widmann's changing relationship to his Protestant faith and his friendship with Brahms in *Kunst, Religion, Krise*, 226–41.

judgement, he shortly afterward broke with the Swiss Reform Movement, as he could no longer endorse its intellectual compromises. Although he and Brahms continued to correspond, they did not commit any of their conversations on religion to paper. Widmann's memoirs and his *Recollections of Johannes Brahms* give us some indication of the direction of his continuously developing views on religion. While this cannot be taken as being representative of Brahms's point of view, it is nonetheless instructive in terms of outlining the opinions of his close friends and the topics with which they were concerned.

As the years passed, Widmann's lack of belief in the deity came increasingly to the fore, and his journalism and polemical writings became ever more anti-clerical and anti-theological. His son, Max Widmann, recalls that his father came to doubt the existence of a personal god to whom one can turn in prayer as much as he doubted the divinity of Jesus, belief in miracles, or the resurrection of the dead. An attack on Christian dogma and ecclesiasticism occupied his life, in which he fought any religion that allegedly revealed the beyond, and he held the Judeo-Christian adoption of a noble nature created by God in disdain.[61]

Nonetheless, Widmann was acutely aware of the cultural and intellectual dimensions of religion. Moreover, his disillusionment with organized religion did not in any way alter or diminish his reverence for the Bible. Indeed, he considered 'Christian atheism' ['christlichen Atheismus'][62] to be entirely compatible with a reverence for the beauty of the Old and New Testaments. It was in an attempt to reconcile his non-belief with his longing for spiritual fulfilment that he turned to the philosophical writings of Nietzsche, penning a famous and largely positive review of *Beyond Good and Evil* in 1886.[63] Yet, as Nietzsche's attacks on Christianity became ever more pronounced and rancorous in his 1888 writings, Widmann began to turn his polemic against the philosopher.[64] Jan Brachmann characterizes Widmann at this point as launching 'a multi-front war: against piety, orthodoxy and reform theology in the evangelical camp, against the political organization of Catholicism, and against a modern philosophy, which – antidemocratic and elite – was engaged in

---

[61] Brachmann, *Kunst, Religion, Krise*, 230.

[62] Max Widmann, *Josef Viktor Widmann. Ein Lebensbild. Zweite Lebenshälfte* (Leipzig: Frauenfeld, 1924), 68.

[63] Widmann, 'Nietzsches gefährliches Buch'. Available in English translation as Widmann, 'Nietzsche's Dangerous Book', trans. Tim Hyde and Lysane Fauvel, *New Nietzsche Studies: The Journal of the Nietzsche Society* 4/1–2 (Summer/Fall 2000): 195–200.

[64] Although *The Antichrist* was written in 1888, it was not published until 1895 in the volume that Brahms owned. Widmann reviewed this book in January 1895.

a "reevaluation of all values"'. The balancing act that Widmann set himself in reconciling his beliefs with these developments in religious culture was based on a Christian atheism or, as Widmann himself called it, a 'god-free Christianity' ['gottfreies Christentum'].[65]

## 4.4  Brahms's Late Musings on the Nature of Immortality

The last two years of Brahms's life brought a candour regarding matters of belief not found in his letters and accounts of his life before he turned to composing the *Vier ernste Gesänge*. Richard Heuberger reports an intimate conversation in June 1895 in which Brahms reflected poignantly on all the members of his immediate family having died one after the other. Only his stepmother and her son from her first marriage were still alive. Heuberger quotes the composer: 'I often think to myself that I am almost to be envied because no one else, whom I love with all of my innermost heart, can die ... Apart from Frau Schumann, I am attached to nobody with all of my soul. We do not quite believe in the immortality beyond. The only true immortality lies in children.'[66]

Max Kalbeck reports Brahms's disclosure in 1896 that, already at the time of composing *Ein deutsches Requiem* in 1868, he no longer believed in the immortality of the soul.[67] At their meeting in March 1896, Brahms was taken aback at the unwavering and unquestioning nature of Dvořák's faith, which indeed must have seemed foreign to one who was accustomed to the intense and searching debates he and his circle had on the subject of religion. Brahms considered his Czech acquaintance to be a 'fanatical Catholic' and marvelled to Heuberger that 'such a hardworking person as Dvořák has no time to be bound up with doubt, but rather remains true throughout his life to what he was taught as a boy'.[68] Dvořák, for his part, found Brahms's position equally difficult to come to terms with, as witnessed by Josef Suk in a conversation between Brahms and Dvořák in Vienna in March 1896:

---

[65] Brachmann, *Kunst, Religion, Krise*, 230–1.

[66] 'Oft denke ich mir, daß ich fast zu beneiden bin, weil mir niemand mehr sterben kann, den ich so ganz von innersten Herzen heraus liebe ... Außer an Frau Schumann hänge ich an Niemanden mit ganzer Seele – Es ist doch eigentlich grauslich und man soll so was weder denken noch sagen. Ist das den ein Leben so allein! An die Unsterblichkeit jenseits glauben wir ja doch nicht recht. Die einzig wahre Unsterblichkeit liegt in den Kindern'. Brahms, as quoted in Richard Heuberger, *Erinnerungen an Johannes Brahms*, 82.

[67] Kalbeck, *Johannes Brahms*, iv, 445. For an interesting discussion of how Brahms chose the texts for the Requiem, see Jan Brachmann, 'Stern, auf den ich schaue: Brahms' Arbeit mit der Bibel', 21–6.

[68] Jan Brachmann *Kunst, Religion, Krise*, 214, Heuberger, *Erinnerungen an Johannes Brahms*, 95.

Then faith and religion were discussed. Dvořák, as everybody knows, was full of sincere, practically childlike faith, whereas Brahms's views were entirely the opposite. 'I have read too much Schopenhauer, and things appear much differently to me', he said ... Dvořák was very reserved on the way back to the hotel. Finally, after a very long time he said: 'Such a man, such a soul – and he believes in nothing, he believes in nothing!'[69]

Contrary to Beller-McKenna's characterization of this passage as 'Dvořák's overreaching assessment',[70] I suggest that it speaks to Brahms's scepticism regarding the existence of God and to the sharply anti-Catholic bias that Brahms shared with Kalbeck and others in his circle of German Protestant friends. This is most evident in his scorn for Bruckner, for instance, in a conversation that allegedly took place between Brahms and Heinrich Groeber in 1895: 'His piousness – that is his thing, and it does not affect me. But this *Meßvelleitäten* is disgusting and completely contrary to me.'[71] The word 'velleity' (used pejoratively in relation to late Wagner in Nietzsche, *On the Genealogy of Morals*[72]) can be understood as 'the fact or quality of merely willing, wishing, or desiring, without any action or advance toward action or realization'.[73] When Brahms combines this with the word '*Meß*' (holy mass) in *Meßvelleitäten*, he is making a pun, as Ronald Knox argues: 'The grotesque mismanagement of musical dimension (*Maß*) in Bruckner's music is a consequence of his *Pfaffen* piety'.[74] These tensions between Protestantism and Catholicism must be understood against the backdrop of the *Kulturkampf* in German-speaking central Europe in the late nineteenth century that witnessed the lasting anti-Catholic sentiment of Bismarck's empire and an anti-Protestant sentiment in Vienna, the latter often further associated with anti-liberalism and anti-Semitism.[75]

---

[69] Josef Suk, '*Aus meiner Jugend: Wiener-Brahms Erinnerungen von Josef Suk*', *Der Merker* 2/4 (1910): 149, as cited in Daniel Beller-McKenna, *Brahms and the German Spirit*, 31.

[70] Beller-McKenna, *Brahms and the German Spirit*, 31.

[71] 'Seine Frömmigkeit – das ist seine Sache, das geht mich nichts an. Aber diese Meßvelleitäten sind mir ekelhaft, ganz zuwider'. Brahms, as cited in Kalbeck, *Johannes Brahms*, III, 408–9. This entire passage is translated in Nicole Grimes and Dillon Parmer, '"Come Rise to Higher Spheres!" Tradition Transcended in Brahms Violin Sonata No. 1 in G Major, Op. 78', *Ad Parnassum: A Journal of Eighteenth- and Nineteenth-Century Instrumental Music* 6/11 (April 2009): 129–52, Appendix 4, 151–2. Brahms invented this word 'Velleität', a philosophical term referring to feeble, hesitant intentions.

[72] Nietzsche, *The Genealogy of Morals*, third essay, section 4.

[73] This definition is taken from the Oxford English Dictionary.

[74] Ronald Knox, 'Brahms as Wordsmith', in *Gli spazi della musica* 5/2 (2016): 17–27 (27). As Knox argues, Brahms's use of the word 'Pfaffen' expresses his 'sheer disdain' for Catholic clerics.

[75] Notley gives sustained consideration to these tensions in *Lateness and Brahms*, particularly in ch. 1, 'Brahms as Liberal: Bruckner as Other', 15–35.

## 4.5   Brahms's Godless *Schnaderhüpfeln* and the 'Last Great Cultural Harvest'

Throughout 1895 and 1896, Brahms frequently referred to the *Vier ernste Gesänge* as godless 'Schnaderhüpfeln'. Kalbeck, for instance, writes of Brahms's references to Op. 121 including the terms 'godless *Schnadahüpfeln*', the '*Schnadahüpferln* of May 7', or simply '*Schnadahüpferln*'.[76] On 21 July 1896, having earlier feared that Heinrich von Herzogenberg might disapprove of the godless nature of the songs, Brahms wrote to his friend upon hearing otherwise that he was 'extraordinarily happy' to hear that his *Schnaderhüpfeln* had met with his approval.[77] Three days later, in a typically self-deprecatory manner, he wrote to Julius Stockhausen of his 'somewhat sour *Schnaderhüpfeln*'.[78]

Scholars have never understood why such an obscure term – which denotes merry-making, and is usually associated with decidedly unserious yodelling in Bavaria – was chosen by Brahms to describe these most *Serious Songs*. The composer's fondness for riddles did not diminish as the years advanced. This characteristic trait of public versus private reception, whereby he revealed only a limited amount of information about a piece to a chosen few, is found, in an earlier instance, in his request to his publisher to add a picture of a man in a blue coat and yellow vest to the cover of the Piano Quartet in C Minor, Op. 60.[79] What is most poignant about Brahms's *Schnaderhüpfeln* reference is that those who were most likely to understand or decipher it had either died recently, or were in failing health. Indeed, in 1895, even Nietzsche himself, to whom I have no doubt the *Schnaderhüpfeln* reference was directed, lay between his two deaths, that of his mind in 1889 and that of his body in 1900. He was thus oblivious to Brahms's most substantive response to his writings.

---

[76] Kalbeck, 'Brahms's Four *Serious Songs*, Op. 121 (1914)', 268. See also Kalbeck, IV, 441. The spelling given by Kalbeck is phonetic, hence the discrepancy in spelling with the correct term '*Schnaderhüpfeln*'.

[77] Brahms to Heinrich von Herzogenberg, 21 July 1896, in *Johannes Brahms im Briefwechsel mit Heinrich und Elisabet von Herzogenberg*, ed. Max Kalbeck (Berlin: Deutschen Brahms-Gesellschaft, 1908), II, 275. This translation in Johannes Brahms, *The Herzogenberg Correspondence*, ed. Max Kalbeck, trans. Hannah Bryant (London: Murray, 1909), 418.

[78] Brahms to Julius Stockhausen, 24 July 1896, in Julia Stockhausen (ed.), *Julius Stockhausen: Der Singer des Deutschen Liedes* (Frankfurt am Main: Englert und Schlosser, 1927), 477.

[79] Dillon R. Parmer, 'Musical Meaning for the Few: Instances of Private Reception in the Music of Brahms', *Current Musicology* 83 (2007): 109–30. This Piano Quartet is frequently referred to as the 'Werther Quartet'. See, for instance, Peter H. Smith, *Expressive Forms in Brahms's Instrumental Music: Structure and Meaning in His Werther Quartet* (Bloomington, IN: Indiana University Press, 2005).

Max Kalbeck was the first to probe the godless nature of these so-called 'dance tunes', in the seminal essay on Brahms's Op. 121 in his biography of the composer.[80] In his analysis of the the *Vier ernste Gesänge*, which continues to be the most comprehensive piece of scholarship on that work, Kalbeck consulted the Bible, Brahms's pocket notebook of Biblical texts, and the texts the composer actually set in the published composition. Table 4.1 outlines all of these sources and clearly shows that not all of the texts in the notebook were included in the composition and that any reference to God, Christ, or Christian theology was systematically removed from those that were.

An important chronology that bridges the years 1888 and 1895 is fundamental to how these godless *Schnaderhüpfeln* can be understood as a cultural harvest. Apart from these years marking the respective dates of both the writing and subsequent publication of *The Antichrist*, they also give an indication of when Brahms entered the texts set in Op. 121 into his Biblical notebook (Table 4.1).[81] The general consensus is that Brahms entered the first four texts in 1888, the so-called *Dreikaiserjahr* of 1888 that saw the deaths of the German emperors Wilhelm I and Friedrich III and the accession of Wilhelm II.[82] These events had a profound impact on the composer, to such an extent that von Herzogenberg suggested in March 1888 that Brahms write an elegy for Wilhelm I.[83]

Immediately after Ecclesiastes 4:1–3, Brahms has written a reference to the *Wisdom of Solomon*, chapter 9 (Figure 4.1a). The heading above this chapter in Brahms's 1833 Bible reads 'Gebet zu Gott um Weisheit' ('prayer to God for wisdom'). Yet, in his Biblical notebook, Brahms has instead written 'Gebet eines Königs' ('Prayer of a King'). There is a blank leaf next to this and, over the page, there are further Biblical texts in different ink and handwriting, indicating that these were added at a later time (Figure 4.1b). I suggest that they were added in 1895, subsequent to Brahms having read *The Antichrist*. Whereas Brahms no doubt identified with many aspects of Nietzsche's critical stance on Christianity, the philosopher's assault on German culture also

---

[80] Kalbeck, 'Brahms's Four *Serious Songs*, Op. 121 (1914)'. I borrow the term 'dance tune', here at 268, from Kevin C. Karnes. See also Kalbeck, *Johannes Brahms*, IV, 441–60.

[81] Brahms's Biblical notebook is now housed at the Wienbibliothek im Rathaus, shelfmark HIN 55.733.

[82] Ryan Minor, *Choral Fantasies: Music, Festivities, and Nationhood in Nineteenth-Century Germany* (Cambridge and New York, NY: Cambridge University Press, 2012), 167 and Beller-McKenna, *Brahms and the German Spirit*, 137. The first four Biblical texts in Brahms's Biblical notebook are I Kings 6:11–14; Jesus Sirach (Ecclesiasticus) 41:1–4; Ecclesiastes 3:18–22; and Ecclesiastes 4:1–4.

[83] See Kalbeck, *Johannes Brahms*, IV, 188; Brahms to Elisabet von Herzogenberg on 3 March 1888 and her response on 28 March 1888 in *Johannes Brahms im Briefwechsel mit Heinrich und Elisabet von Herzogenberg*, II, 183 and 188.

**Table 4.1** Brahms's Bible Notebook and its relationship to the *Vier ernste Gesänge*, Op. 121 Texts are given in the order in which they appear in Brahms's notebook

| Biblical reference | Original in Brahms's 1833 Bible (orthography as in the original) | English translation, with text omitted by Brahms in the final composition crossed out | Location in Op. 121 |
|---|---|---|---|
| 1 Kings 6:11–14 | 11 Und es geschah des Herrn Wort zu Salomo, und sprach: <br> 12 Das sey das Haus, das du bauest. Wirst du in meinen Geboten wandeln, und auch nach meinen Rechten thun, und alle meine Gebote halten, darinnen zu wandeln, so will ich mein Wort mit dir bestätigen, wie ich deinem Vater David geredt habe. <br> 13 Und will wohnen unter den Kindern Israel, und will mein Volk Israel nicht verlassen. <br> 14 Also bauete Salomo das Haus, und vollendetes. | 11 Now the word of the Lord came to Solomon, <br> 12 'Concerning this house that you are building, if you will walk in my statutes and obey my rules and keep all my commandments and walk in them, then I will establish my word with you, which I spoke to David your father. <br> 13 And I will dwell among the children of Israel and will not forsake my people Israel'. <br> 14 So Solomon built the house and finished it.* | Not included |
| Jesus Sirach (Ecclesiasticus) 41:1–4 | 1 O tod, wie bitter bist du, wenn an dich gedenket ein Mensch, der gute Tage und genug hat, und ohne Sorge lebet; <br> 2 Und dem es wohl gehet in allen Dingen, und noch wohl essen mag! <br> 3 O Tod, wie wohl thust du dem Dürftigen, <br> 4 Der da schwach und alt ist, der in allen Sorgen steckt, und nichts Bessers zu hoffen, noch zu erwarten hat! | 1 O death, how bitter is the thought of you to the one at peace among possessions, who has nothing to worry about and is prosperous in everything, <br> 2 and still is vigorous enough to enjoy food! <br> 3 O death, how *sweet you are* to one who is *old* and failing in strength, worn down by age *and has nothing better to hope for or expect!* | Op. 121/3 |
| Ecclesiastes 3:18–22 | 18 Ich sprach in meinem Herzen von dem Wesen der Menschen, darinnen Gott anzeiget, und läßt es ansehen, als wären sie unter sich selbst wie das Vieh. | ~~18 I said in my heart with regard to the children of man that God is testing them that they may see that they themselves are but beasts.~~ | Op. 121/1 (Appears as Op. 121/2 in the autograph score) |

**Table 4.1** (*cont.*)

| Biblical reference | Original in Brahms's 1833 Bible (orthography as in the original) | English translation, with text omitted by Brahms in the final composition crossed out | Location in Op. 121 |
|---|---|---|---|
| | 19 Denn es gehet dem Menschen, wie dem Vieh; wie dieß stirbt, so stirbt er auch; und haben alle einerley Odem; und der Mensch hat nichts mehr, den das Vieh; den es ist alles eitel. | 19 For what happens to the children of man and what happens to the beasts is the same: as one dies, so dies the other. They all have the same breath, and man has no advantage over the beasts, for all is vanity. | |
| | 20 Es fährt alles in Einen Ort; es ist alles von Staub gemacht, und wird wieder zu Staub. | 20 All go to one place. All are from the dust, and to dust all return. | |
| | 21 Wer weiß, ob der Geist der Menschen aufwärts fahre, und der Odem des Veihes unterwärts unter die Erde fahre? | 21 Who knows whether the spirit of man goes upward and the spirit of the beast goes down into the earth? | |
| | 22 Darum sahe ich, daß nichts bessers ist, den daß ein Mensch fröhlich sey in seiner Arbeit: den das ist sein Theil. Denn wer will ihn dahin bringen, daß er sehe, was nach ihm geschehen wird? | 22 So I saw that there is nothing better than that a man should rejoice in his work, for that is his lot. Who can bring him to see what will be after him? | |
| Ecclesiastes 4:1–4 (4:1–4 are marked in the 1833 Bible, but only 4:1–3 are jotted down in the Bible notebook) | 1 Ich wandte mich, und sahe an alle, die Unrecht leiden unter der Sonne; und siehe, da waren Thränen derer, die Unrecht litten, und hatten keinen Tröster; und die ihnen Unrecht thäten, waren zu mächtig, daß sie keinen Tröster haben konnten. | 1 Again I saw all the oppressions that are done under the sun. And behold, the tears of the oppressed, and they had no one to comfort them! On the side of their oppressors there was power, and there was no one to comfort them. | Op. 121/2 (Appears as Op. 121/1 in the autograph score) |
| | 2 Da lobte ich den Todten, die schon gestorben waren, mehr, den die Lebendigen, die noch das Leben hatte; | 2 And I thought the dead who are already dead more fortunate than the living who are still alive. | |
| | 3 Und der noch nicht ist, ist besser, den alle beyde, und des Bösen nicht inne wird, | 3 But better than both is he who has not yet been and | |

**Table 4.1** (*cont.*)

| Biblical reference | Original in Brahms's 1833 Bible (orthography as in the original) | English translation, with text omitted by Brahms in the final composition crossed out | Location in Op. 121 |
|---|---|---|---|
| | das unter der Sonne geschiehet.<br>4 Ich sahe an Arbeit und Geschicklichkeit in allen Sachen, da neidet einer den andern. Das ist je auch eitel und Mühe. | has not seen the evil deeds that are done under the sun.<br>[4 ~~Then I saw that all toil and all skill in work come from a man's envy of his neighbor. This also is vanity and striving after wind.~~]* | |
| Reference to Song of Solomon 8, but no text provided | | | |
| 1 Corinthians 13:1–13 | 1 Wenn ich mit Menschen- und mit Engel-Zungen redete, und hätte der Liebe nicht; so, wäre ich ein tönend Erz oder eine klingende Schalle.<br>2 Und wenn ich weißagen könnte, und wüßte alle Geheimnisse, und alle Erkenntniß, und hätte der Liebe nicht, so wäre ich nichts.<br>3 Und wenn ich alle meine Habe den Armen gäbe, und ließe meinen Leib brennen; und hätte der Liebe nicht, so wäre mir nicht mütze.<br>4 Die Liebe ist langmüthig und freundlich, die Liebe eifert nicht, die Liebe treibet nicht Muthwillen, sie blähet sich nicht;<br>5 Sie stellet sich nicht ungeberdig, sie suchet nicht das Ihre, sie lässet sich nicht erbittern, sie trachtet nicht nach Schaden; | 1 If I speak in the tongues of men and of angels, but have not love, I am a noisy gong or a clanging cymbal.<br>2 And if I have prophetic powers, and understand all mysteries and all knowledge, and if I have faith, so as to remove mountains, but have not love, I am nothing.<br>3 If I give away all I have, and if I deliver up my body to be burned, but have not love, I gain nothing.<br>4 ~~Love is patient and kind; love does not envy or boast; it is not arrogant~~<br><br>5 ~~or rude. It does not insist on its own way; it is not irritable or resentful;~~ | Op. 121/4 |

**Table 4.1** (*cont.*)

| Biblical reference | Original in Brahms's 1833 Bible (orthography as in the original) | English translation, with text omitted by Brahms in the final composition crossed out | Location in Op. 121 |
|---|---|---|---|
| | 6 Sie freuet sich nicht der Ungerechtigkeit, sie freuet sich aber der Wahrheit. | 6 ~~it does not rejoice at wrongdoing, but rejoices with the truth.~~ | |
| | 7 Sie verträget alles, sie glaubet alles, sie hoffet alles, sie duldet alles. | 7 ~~Love bears all things, believes all things, hopes all things, endures all things.~~ | |
| | 8 Die Liebe höret nimmer auf, so doch die Weißagungen aufhören werden, und die Sprachen aufhören werden, und die Erkenntniß aufhören wird. | 8 ~~Love never ends. As for prophecies, they will pass away; as for tongues, they will cease; as for knowledge, it will pass away.~~ | |
| | 9 Denn unser Wissen ist Stückwerk, und unser Weißagen ist Stückwerk; | 9 ~~For we know in part and we prophesy in part,~~ | |
| | 10 Denn aber kommen wird das Vollkommene, so wird das Stückwerk aufhören. | 10 ~~But when the perfect comes, the partial will pass away.~~ | |
| | 11 Da ich ein Kind war, da redete ich wie ein Kind, und war klug wie ein Kind, und hatte kindische Anschläge; da ich aber ein Mann ward, that ich ab, was kindisch war. | 11 When I was a child, I spoke like a child, I reasoned like a child. When I became a man, I gave up childish ways. | |
| | 12 Wir sehen jetzt durch einen Spiegel in einem dunkeln Worte, dann aber von Angesicht zu Angesichte. Jetzt erkenne ichs Stückweise, dann aber werde ichs erkennen, gleichwie ich erkennet bin. | 12 For now we see in a mirror dimly, but then face to face. Now I know in part; then I shall know fully, even as I have been fully known. | |
| | 13 Nun aber bleibet Glaube, Hoffnung, Liebe, diese drey; aber die Liebe ist die größeste unter ihnen. | 13 So now faith, hope, and love abide, these three; but the greatest of these is love.[*] | |
| Wisdom of Solomon 9:1–12 | 1 O Gott meiner Vater, und Herr aller Güte! der du alle Dinge durch dein Wort gemacht, | 1 O God of my fathers, and Lord of mercy, who hast made all things with thy word, | Not included |

**Table 4.1** (*cont.*)

| Biblical reference | Original in Brahms's 1833 Bible (orthography as in the original) | English translation, with text omitted by Brahms in the final composition crossed out | Location in Op. 121 |
|---|---|---|---|
| | 2 Und den Menschen durch deine Weisheit bereitet hast, daß er herrschen sollte über die Kreatur, so von dir gemacht ist; | 2 And ordained man through thy wisdom, that he should have dominion over the creatures which thou hast made, | |
| | 3 Daß, er die Welt regieren sollte mit Heiligkeit und Gerechtigkeit, und mir rechtem Herzen richten: | 3 And order the world according to equity and righteousness, and execute judgement with an upright heart: | |
| | 4 Gib mir die Weisheit, die stets um deinen Thron ist, und verwirf mich nicht aus deinen Kindern. | 4 Give me wisdom, that sitteth by thy throne; and reject me not from among thy children: | |
| | 5 Denn ich bin dein Knecht, und deiner Magd Sohn; ein schwacher Mensch, und kurzes Lebens, und zu gering im Verstande des Rechtes und Gesetzes. | 5 For I thy servant and son of thine handmaid am a feeble person, and of a short time, and too young for the understanding of judgement and laws. | |
| | 6 Und wenn gleich einer unter den Menschenkindern vollkommen wäre, so gilt er doch nichts, wo er ohne die Weisheit ist, so von dir kommt. | 6 For though a man be never so perfect among the children of men, yet if thy wisdom be not with him, he shall be nothing regarded. | |
| | 7 Du hast mich erwählet zum Könige über dein Volk, und zum Richter über deine Söhne und Töchter; | 7 Thou hast chosen me to be a king of thy people, and a judge of thy sons and daughters: | |
| | 8 Und hießest mich ein Tempel banen auf deinem heiligen Berge, und einen Altar in der Stadt deiner Wohnung, der da gleich wäre der heiligen Hütte, welche du vor Zeiten bereiten ließest; | 8 Thou hast commanded me to build a temple upon thy holy mount, and an altar in the city wherein thou dwellest, a resemblance of the holy tabernacle, which thou hast prepared from the beginning. | |
| | 9 Und mit dir deine Weisheit, welche deine Werke weiß, und dabey war, da du die | | |

**Table 4.1** (*cont.*)

| Biblical reference | Original in Brahms's 1833 Bible (orthography as in the original) | English translation, with text omitted by Brahms in the final composition crossed out | Location in Op. 121 |
|---|---|---|---|
| | Welt machtest, und erkennt, was dir wohlgefällt, und was richtig ist in deinem Geboten. | 9 And wisdom was with thee: which knoweth thy works, and was present when thou madest the world, and knew what was acceptable in thy sight, and right in thy commandments. | |
| | 10 Sende sie herab von deinem heiligen Himmel, aus dem Thron deiner Herrlichkeit; sende sie, da sie bey mir sey und mit mir arbeite, daß ich erkenne, was dir wohlgefälle. | 10 O send her out of thy holy heavens, and from the throne of thy glory, that being present she may labour with me, that I may know what is pleasing unto thee. | |
| | 11 Denn sie weiß alles, und verstehet es. Und laß sie mich leiten in meinen Werken mäßiglich, und mich behüten durch ihre Herrlichkeit; | 11 For she knoweth and understandeth all things, and she shall lead me soberly in my doings, and preserve me in her power. | |
| | 12 So werden dir meine Werke angenehm seyn, und werde dein Volk recht richten, und würdig seyn des Throns meines Vaters. | 12 So shall my works be acceptable, and then shall I judge thy people righteously, and be worthy to sit in my father's seat. | |

\*   These translations taken from *Die Bibel/The Holy Bible, Übersetzung nach Martin Luther, Altes und Neues Testament/English Standard Version Containing the Old and New Testament* (Stuttgart: Deutsche Bibelgesellschaft and Wheaton, IL: Crossway, 2009), with the exception of Ecclesiasticus 41:1–4 and Wisdom of Solomon 9:1–12.

affected him to such an extent that he returned once more to the Biblical notebook, adding not only the *Wisdom of Solomon* text to which he alluded in the fateful year of 1888 but also the first letter of St Paul to the Corinthians.

Brahms's Biblical notebook includes the entire thirteenth chapter of 1 Corinthians. It is worth considering the significance of the verses Brahms left out of the song text, that is 1 Corinthians 13:4–11. Verses 4 to 10 describe

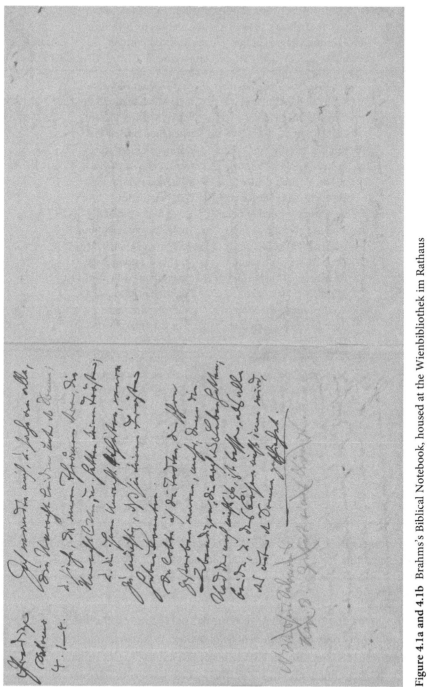

**Figure 4.1a and 4.1b** Brahms's Biblical Notebook, housed at the Wienbibliothek im Rathaus

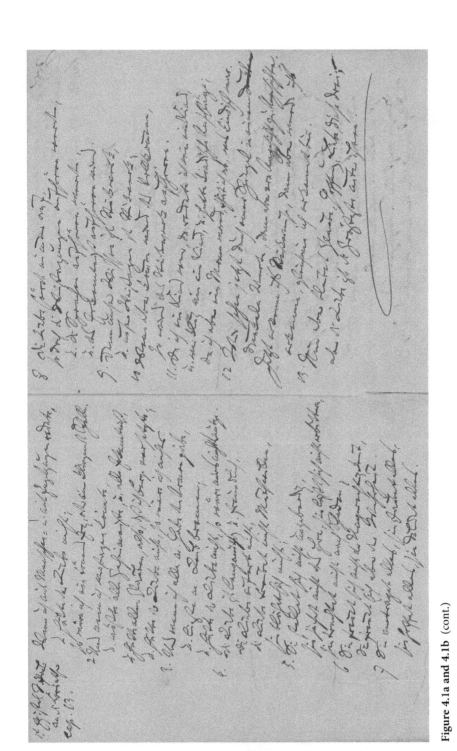

Figure 4.1a and 4.1b (cont.)

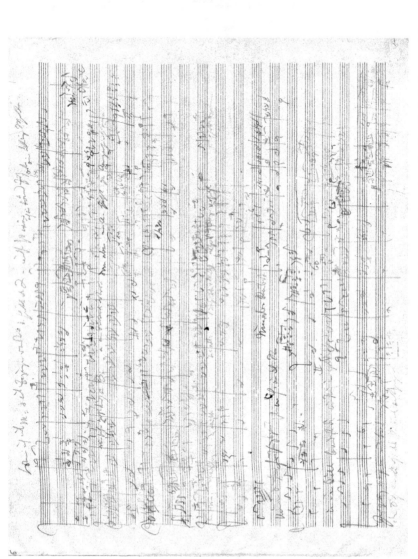

**Figure 4.2** Sketch of Brahms *Vier ernste Gesänge*, Op. 121, Autograph A122A at the Gesellschaft der Musikfreunde, Vienna

Example 4.1 Transcription of Autograph A122

**Example 4.1** (cont.)

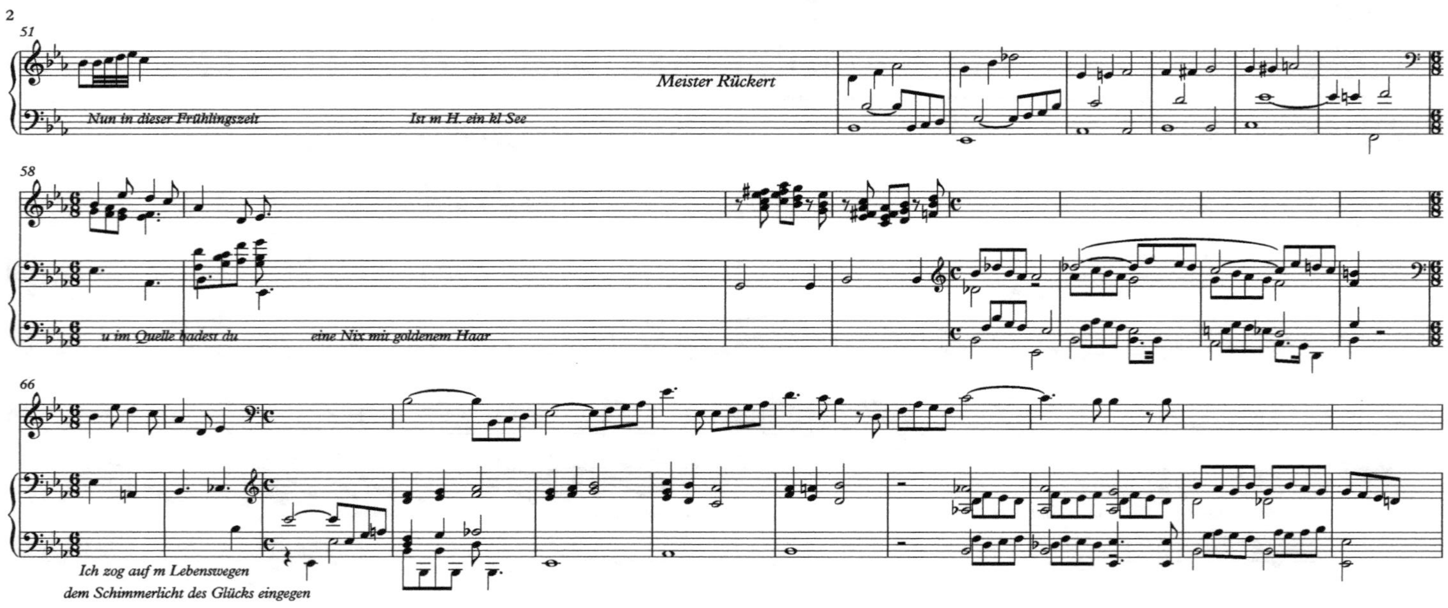

the qualities of love and, more specifically, the infallibility of Pauline, Christian love. Perhaps the omission of these lines amounts to a refusal on Brahms's part for his meditation on love to be circumscribed by St Paul's definition. Rather, as we will see, it is grounded in a celebration of German culture. Furthermore, despite Brahms's ongoing sense of nostalgia, as explored throughout this book, the lost golden age for which he yearned was not that of Christianity's childish faith. This might well explain his choice not to include the lines that speak of reasoning like a child and the 'childish ways' of verse 11.

The sketch of Op. 121/4 found in the composer's apartment upon his death, now catalogued as Autograph A122 in the Archive of the *Gesellschaft der Musikfreunde*, has gained some notoriety as Brahms's 'Janus-faced' sketch, owing to the fact that no one can say with certainty which side is the recto and which is the verso. Regardless of the order in which this sketch was composed, it reveals a great deal about the scale of conception of Brahms's *Vier ernste Gesänge*. Upon consulting this sketch, one first sees the page reproduced here as Figure 4.2 and transcribed as Example 4.1.[84] (This annotated transcription has key and time signatures not found in the original.) This sketch (hereafter referred to as A122/A) contains the main thematic ideas for both the E♭ major and B major sections of the fourth song, complete with excerpts from the Biblical text. In the bottom left corner of the page, Brahms also cites fragments from two German poems corresponding to this same musical material. 'Nixe im Grundquell', by Gottfried Keller, is followed by the first of Friedrich Rückert's *Trauerlieder*. In addition, in larger handwriting, Brahms has written 'Meister Rückert'.

Brahms and Keller struck up a friendship in 1866, the composer admiring the works of the Swiss writer and poet and holding his epistolary style in particularly high regard. He set three of Keller's poems to music, including the retrospective meditation 'Abendregen', Op. 70 No. 4, the anguished 'Salome', Op. 69 No. 8, and the poignant and nostalgic 'Therese', Op. 86 No. 1. Brahms's artistic response to the poetry of 'Meister Rückert' was more extensive than these Lieder in every respect, from genre, to the employment of instrumental and vocal forces, to the degree of intertextuality. In these Rückert settings he does not confine himself, as he did with Keller, to the Lied. Brahms's first Rückert setting is 'Fahrwohl', Op. 93a/4 (1883) for chorus of four mixed voices. In that same year, he reported to Kalbeck that his friend, the baritone Julius Stockhausen, was so overcome with emotion in rehearsing his profoundly moving setting of Rückert's

---

[84] In preparing the transcription in Example 4.1, I consulted Cornelia Preißinger's transcription and made a number of amendments. See Cornelia Preißinger, *Die vier ernsten Gesänge, Op. 121: Vokale und instrumentale Gestaltungsprinzipien im Werk von Johannes Brahms* (Frankfurt am Main et al.: Peter Lang, 1993), 231, 235.

'Mit vierzig Jahren', Op. 94/1, that 'he was unable to finish it'.[85] The year 1894 gave rise to the singular combination of alto, viola, and piano, in the *Zwei Gesänge*, Op. 91, the first of which sets Rückert's 'Gestillte Sehnsucht'.

In the fateful *Dreikaiserjahr* of 1888, which we recall lies on one side of the chronological bridge that extends to 1895, Brahms set two 'Nachtwache' texts by Rückert as the first two songs in his *Fünf Gesänge*, Op. 104. Whether or not by coincidence, these songs are respectively in the keys of B minor and E♭ major, global tonalities that would later hold great significance for the fourth of the *Serious Songs*. Indeed, there is great poetic resonance to the fact that the second of these two, as Walter Niemann reminds us, was sung at Brahms's own funeral. The composer's departure from this world, therefore, was shrouded in the key that is consistently associated with death and bereavement in his elegiac compositions.

The composer's final published setting of Rückert, before he inscribed the great German poet's name on his sketch of Op. 121/4, came in the final five of his thirteen canons for female voices, Op. 113 (although these canons originated at a much earlier date). All of the canons in this set deal in one way or another with the pain of love. The last canon is particularly interesting. Here, Brahms engages in an unusually forthright degree of intertextuality in setting Rückert's 1821 self-reflexive poem 'Einförmig ist der Liebe Gram' ('Humdrum are the woes of love'). Adding to the intensity of the lateness of Brahms's setting is the fact that the melody is not of his own devising but rather comes from the last song of one of Schubert's final, and most poignant, compositions: 'Der Leiermann' of *Winterreise*. Whereas Müller and Schubert's wanderer reaches the end of his internal monologue in this final poem, Rückert's narrator, in Brahms's most haunting setting, shares their pain amongst a chorus of women's voices. The cyclical structure of the canon encircles and encapsulates the perennial nature of the shared concerns of Müller, Schubert, Rückert, and Brahms, concerns that pervade the canon of great German literature and music.

It is against this rich backdrop that we must interpret Brahms's inscription of the poetry of Keller and Rückert, and the declaration 'Meister Rückert' in his sketch of the last of the *Vier ernste Gesänge*. Both of the poems cited in this sketch are bound up with reflection upon a life of striving, the elusive nature of love, and a conscious realization of the transience of beauty. Following the notation with poetic fragments, Brahms returns to the E♭ major material from the outset, thus precluding the possibility that the sections with the poetic texts might have been intended for another composition.

---

[85] Kalbeck, *Johannes Brahms*, I, 277.

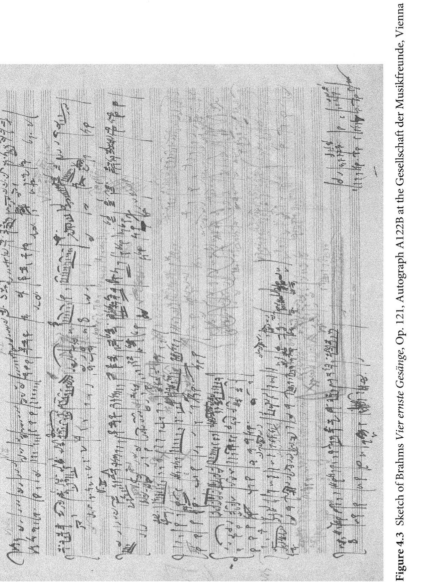

**Figure 4.3** Sketch of Brahms *Vier ernste Gesänge*, Op. 121, Autograph A122B at the Gesellschaft der Musikfreunde, Vienna

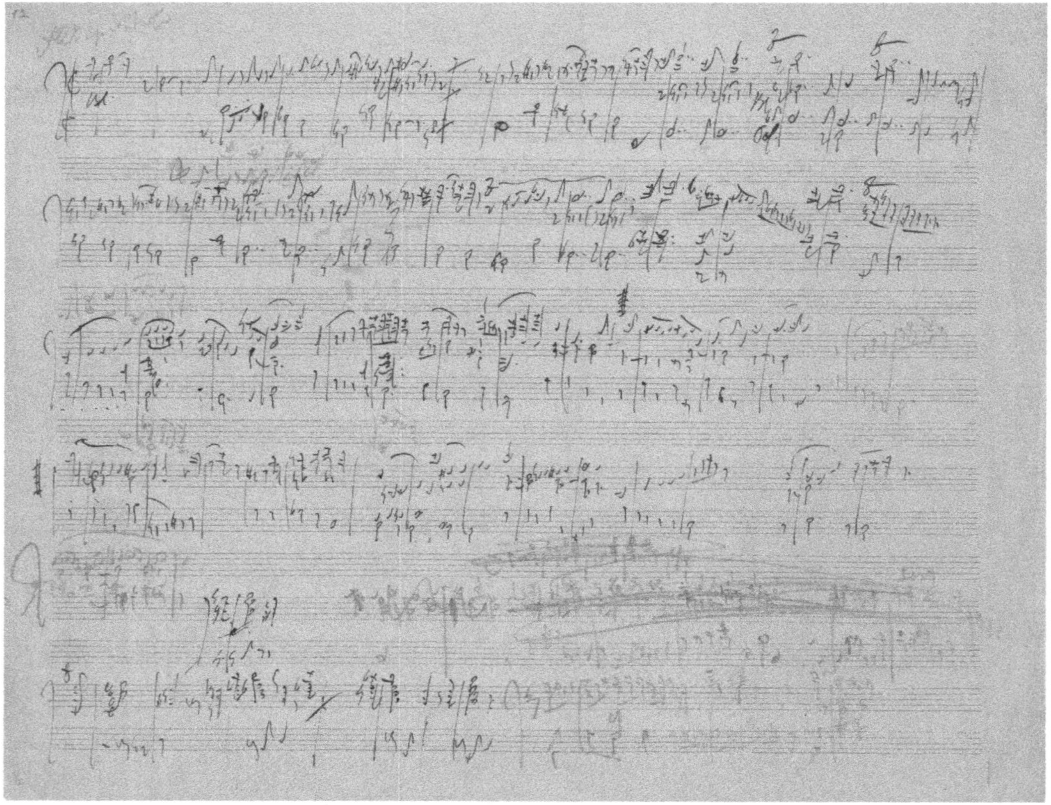

**Figure 4.4** Brahms orchestral sketch housed at the Archive of the Gesellschaft der Musikfreunde as part of A121

## Poems Referred to in Brahms's Sketch A122

**Gottfried Keller, *Nixe im Grundquell***

| | |
|---|---|
| Nun in dieser Frühlingszeit | In this springtime |
| Ist mein Herz ein klarer See, | My heart is a clear sea, |
| Drin versank das schwere Leid, | In it sank my heavy heart, |
| Draus verdampft das leichte Weh. | My pain vanishes coming out. |
| | |
| Spiegelnd mein Gemüthe ruht, | Mirrored, my soul rests |
| Von der Sonne überhaucht, | In the warm breath of the sun, |
| Und mit Lieb' umschließt die Fluth, | And the water lovingly embraces |
| Was sich in dieselbe taucht. | That which dives into it. |
| | |
| Aber aus dem Grunde sprüht | But from the seabed |
| Überdies ein Quell hervor, | bubbles a spring |
| Welcher heiß, lebendig glüht | glowing hot and sparkling |
| Durch die stille Bluth empor. | through the still water above. |
| | |
| Und im Quelle badest Du, | And in the spring, you bathe, |
| Eine Nix' mit goldnem Haar! | A mermaid with golden hair! |
| Oben deckt den Zauber zu | The water above deep and clear |
| Das Gewässer, glatt und klar. | Cloaks the magic below.[86] |

**Friedrich Rückert, *Trauerlieder* I**

| | |
|---|---|
| Ich zog auf meinen Lebenswegen | On my journey through life |
| Dem Schimmerlicht des Glücks eingegen | I encountered the shimmering light of happiness |
| Das mir nur vorwärts immer schien; | that always appeared to me to be ahead; |
| Und immer vorwärts mit Verlangen | and ever moving forth with desire |
| Kam ich dem Schimmer nachgegangen, | I came to pursue the shimmer, |
| Und sah ihn immer vorwerts fliehen. | and saw it flee ever onwards. |
| | |
| Auf einmal – wie ist mir geschehen? – | Suddenly – as has happened to me? – |
| Muß ich danach mich rückwerts drehen, | I must turn backwards, |
| Dort blinkt michs an wie Abendschein. | there, twinkling at me like the evening glow. |
| Wie bin ich denn vorbei gekommen? | |

---

[86] This translation in Max Kalbeck, 'Brahms's *Four Serious Songs*, Op. 121 (1914)', 275–6.

| | |
|---|---|
| Und hab' es noch nicht<br>    wahrgenommen?<br>Es muß im Traum gewesen seyn. | How have I come to pass it by?<br>And have I still not embraced it?<br>It must have been a dream.[87] |

Over the page in what is now the bound sketch is the outline of an orchestral work, complete with instrumental markings but no poetic or Biblical texts (hereafter A122/B) (Figure 4.3). Margit McCorkle, Max Kalbeck and, more recently, Cornelia Preißinger have all argued that A122/B contains fragments of motivic material from numbers 1, 2, and 3 of the *Serious Songs*.[88] The presence of material from the *Vier ernste Gesänge* in this sketch leads Kalbeck to two conclusions: first, that 'Brahms once intended to create an orchestral work in which motives from three of the four songs were present'[89] (in the manner of the violin sonatas Opp. 78 and 100 and the Piano Concerto No. 2 in B♭ Major, Op. 83); and, secondly, that the fourth 'uplifting resurrection song' – as he refers to it – was once intended to be part of a separate composition, a sketch for:

a symphonic cantata, different from Gustav Mahler's C Minor Symphony (which Koeßler showed [Brahms] in manuscript, at the request of the composer residing in Unterach, during one of his last Ischl summers), but illuminated and seized by a similar 'primal light' (*Urlicht*), which washed over him in 'eternal, divine life'.[90]

There is much dispute by scholars such as George Bozarth and Daniel Beller-McKenna regarding the veracity of Kalbeck's hermeneutic claims for Op. 121.[91] Both downplay the importance of the allusions to Op. 121 contained in A122/B, and thereby they dismiss Kalbeck's theory that Brahms may have had in mind either an orchestral work or symphonic cantata based on these songs. Drawing on Bozarth's evidence, Beller-McKenna argues instead that A122/B is more likely part of a larger orchestral work in E♭ major that Brahms never completed. Both scholars

---

[87] This translation is my own.

[88] Margit McCorkle, *Johannes Brahms: Thematisch-bibliographisches Werkverzeichnis*, ed. Margit McCorkle and Donald McCorkle (Munich: Henle, 1984); Kalbeck, *Johannes Brahms*, IV, 448–54; Preißinger, *Die vier ernsten Gesänge Op. 121*, 231.

[89] Kalbeck, 'Brahms's Four *Serious Songs*, Op. 121 (1914)', 274. See also Kalbeck, *Johannes Brahms*, IV, 448.

[90] Kalbeck, 'Brahms's Four *Serious Songs*, Op. 121 (1914)', 279. See also Kalbeck, *Johannes Brahms*, IV, 454. Hans Koeßler (1853–1926) was a German composer who worked predominantly in Budapest. In his recollections, Heuberger mentions Brahms, Mahler, and Koeßler socializing together in Ischl, where Brahms spent the summer of 1895. See Heuberger, *Erinnerungen an Johannes Brahms*, 84.

[91] See, for instance, George Bozarth, 'Paths Not Taken: The "Lost" Works of Johannes Brahms', *Music Review* 50 (1989), 185–205; and Daniel Beller-McKenna, 'Reconsidering the Identity of an Orchestral Sketch by Brahms', *Journal of Musicology* 13/4 (Autumn 1998) 508–37.

make a connection between the musical material on A122/B and that of the Brahms orchestral sketch now housed at the Archive of the Gesellschaft der Musikfreunde as part of A121 (Figure 4.4). Neither Bozarth nor Beller-McKenna, however, discusses the significance of the poetic texts alluded to in A122/A, nor do they scratch the surface of Kalbeck's enticing reference to Mahler.

We shall never be able to say with certainty which works Brahms's various sketches represent or to which compositions they might have given rise. What is certain is that Brahms's thoughts on Mahler's Second Symphony – as relayed by Kalbeck – are of great significance. For there are a number of interesting parallels between this symphony and the *Vier ernste Gesänge*. In composing these works, both Brahms and Mahler went back to German literary history. The Schopenhauerian stance of Brahms's first two songs in this set is somewhat akin to the Scherzo of Mahler's Second Symphony, of which the principal thematic material is derived from the *Wunderhorn* Lied 'Des Antonius von Padua Fischpredigt' ('St Anthony of Padua's Sermon to the Fishes') in which 'nature is chaotic and in movement and any attempt to read a moral message into it is futile'.[92] Such pessimism is followed in both works by a more uplifting utterance, which, in each case, alludes to a Nietzschean (and Aristotelian) transformation of tragedy into joy. Brahms's Op. 121, as Carl Niekerk observes of Mahler's Second, can be understood to 'question the possibility of a return to a naïve form of religious experience'.[93]

The very first known reference to *Schnaderhüpfeln* is found on a post-card from Brahms to Friedrich Hegar in September 1895, directly preceding that conductor's performance on 20 October of Beethoven's Ninth Symphony and Brahms's *Triumphlied*, Op. 55. Brahms confessed on that occasion that he was utterly preoccupied with Beethoven's symphony and his own *Schnaderhüpfeln*: 'I know only of the Ninth Symphony and my *Schnaderhüpfeln* – What else is new?'[94] Based on the date of this postcard, and the fact that the manuscript for Op. 121 had not yet been completed, Wolfgang Sandberger suggests that the term *Schnaderhüpfeln* here refers to the *Triumphlied*.[95] He questions whether Kalbeck and subsequent scholars

---

[92] Niekerk, *Reading Mahler*, 94.    [93] *Ibid.*, 96.

[94] 'Ich weiß immer nur von der 9t und meinem Schnaderhüpferl – Wie giebt's den sonst Gutes?' Postcard from Brahms to Friedrich Hegar, 22 September 1895, housed in the Zentralbibliothek Zurich, Musik- und Handschriftenabteilung, Signature AMG I 1106, as cited in Sandberger, 'Spätwerk als selbstbezügliche teleologische Konstruktion: Die "Vier ernsten Gesänge"', 280.

[95] Sandberger, 'Spätwerk als selbstbezügliche teleologische Konstruktion: Die "Vier ernsten Gesänge" Op. 121', 281–2.

are correct in associating such harvesters' revels with Op. 121 at all. Yet, given Brahms's consistent use of the term exclusively in relation to these songs, particularly the last of the four, it is more plausible that the composer was absorbed in the symphony that would appear on the October concert programme – Beethoven's Ninth – and the songs on which he was working at precisely that time.

Beethoven's Ninth Symphony, as with Mahler's Second, aspires to the same condition to which Mahler alluded in a letter of 1896 concerning his own Third Symphony: 'But now imagine such a *large* work that, in fact, mirrors the *entire world* – one is, so to speak, only an instrument upon which the universe plays'.[96] The fact that Brahms associated the *Vier ernste Gesänge* with both Beethoven's Symphony No. 9 and Mahler's Symphony No. 2 tells us nothing about the scale of the instrumental, vocal, or choral forces he intended to use. But, viewed together with the sketch A122/A (see Figure 4.2 and Example 4.1) and the poetic fragments contained therein, it reveals a great deal about the scale of conception he had in mind when composing this work, his artistic vision not unlike that of Mahler.

If, in fact, Brahms did intend this cycle to be his 'last great cultural harvest' – in response to Nietzsche's charge against Luther – this masterpiece of German art engages with the German musical canon, it sets texts from the German Luther Bible, it embraces German literary history, and it grapples with the German philosophical tradition from Schopenhauer to Nietzsche. It does all of this in the spirit of the German humanist writers to whom so much of Brahms's output is indebted. Furthermore, in keeping with the intensely private nature of Brahms's musings in the evening of his life, and with his wish to compose 'nothing more for the public, but only for himself',[97] he distilled the monumental scale of conception into that most intimate of forms, the Lied. Lest we forget the intense *Innigkeit* that gave rise to the creation of these songs, it took some persuasion on Kalbeck's part to convince the composer to send the set to his publisher. Brahms was particularly concerned that the fourth 'uplifting resurrection song' – to borrow Kalbeck's phrase – remain private.[98]

---

[96] Gustav Mahler to Anna von Mildenburg, 28 [?] June 1896, in Herta Blaukopf (ed), *Gustav Mahler Briefe*, 2nd edn (Vienna: Zsolnay, 1996), here trans. Solvik in 'The Literary and Philosophical Worlds of Gustav Mahler', 24.

[97] Kalbeck, 'Brahms's Four *Serious Songs*, Op. 121 (1914)', 268. See also Kalbeck, *Johannes Brahms*, iv, 391.

[98] Kalbeck, *Johannes Brahms*, iv, 441–2.

## 4.6   Epilogue

Having made the decision to offer the *Serious Songs* for publication, Brahms was genuinely concerned about how his 'truly heathenish, but truly human' work would be received.[99] In announcing these songs to Simrock on 8 May 1896, Brahms confessed that they were a birthday present he had given himself on 7 May and warned the publisher, 'they aren't exactly fun – on the contrary, they are damnedly serious and at the same time so impious that the police might prohibit them – if the words weren't all in the Bible!'[100] Writing to Max Klinger, to whom the songs were dedicated as an expression of gratitude for the *Brahmsphantasie*, Brahms confessed that 'while working on them I often thought of you, and of how deeply the momentous words, heavy with meaning, might affect you. Even if you are a reader of the Bible you may well be unprepared for them, and surely so with music.'[101] He feared the songs might cause Heinrich von Herzogenberg 'to attack my unchristian principles in your newspaper'.[102] The composer's reservations were not unfounded. At this time, the social and emotional structures of *Pietas Austriaca* – that is, the relationship of Catholic religious practices and symbols to the House of Habsburg – still had a strong intensity. Despite increased religious tolerance in liberal Vienna, there was a genuine cause for concern in performing such agnostic expressions in Austrian society.[103] These matters were certainly not to be taken lightly following the appointment of Karl Lueger as leader of the Austrian Christian Social Party and vice-mayor of Vienna in 1895.

Just a few weeks after he composed the *Vier ernste Gesänge*, the death of Clara Schumann dealt Brahms a blow from which he would not recover. He and a number of friends gathered both in mourning and in celebration of music following her funeral. It was here that he first played through the songs for a small, select audience. In his *Recollections of Johannes Brahms*, Gustav Ophüls, who was in attendance at that solemn celebration of Frau Schumann's life, again refers to Brahms's legal concerns in a deeply poignant account of this recital:

---

[99]  Heuberger, *Erinngerungen an Johannes Brahms*, 105.
[100]  Brahms to Fritz Simrock, 8 May 1896, in Avins, *Johannes Brahms: Life and Letters*, 733.
[101]  Brahms to Max Klinger, 28 June 1896, in *Ibid.*, 734.
[102]  Brahms, *The Herzogenberg Correspondence*, 415.
[103]  Avins, *Johannes Brahms: Life and Letters*, 733–4.

In the midst of a stimulating conversation, Brahms suddenly said: 'I have com-posed a few songs for my birthday, they are completely godless songs, but thank-fully the lyrics are in the Bible'. He spoke no more of it; and understandably we eagerly anticipated what type of songs these would be, whose essence Brahms so auspiciously announced and which he promised to show us that same day [...] Meanwhile Brahms took the manuscript out of his suitcase, pages in long land-scape format where, as I recall, early May 1896 was listed as the date of composi-tion. Then he began to play and also to sing the Lieder [...] It was more of a heightened declamation in tones of the words of the Bible that he gave forth from himself with his hoarse voice; and what we heard was anything but artsong. And yet no singer since then, not even Meschaert, can awaken in me the same powerful impression that the songs made on me in this improvised way by their creator. It was no different than if the prophet himself had spoken to us. Before the beginning of the first song, Brahms, who was clearly deeply stirred within himself and enraptured by the passionate splendor of the Biblical text, said 'do you see what powerful words these are: "For the fate of humans and the fate of animals is the same"!' Then in the fourth song – 'and if I give my body to be burned!' The third song – 'O death, how bitter thou are' gripped him so strongly while he was playing that in the poignant conclusion, 'O death how sweet you are', large tears rolled down his cheeks and he almost breathed these last words of the text into himself with tears in his voice. I will never forget the overwhelming impression of this song. It was characteristic of Brahms (who surrounded his soft heart with the armor of harshness, apparently to hide the inner emotion) that after the last note faded, he dealt me – sitting on his left – a blow on the leg and said: 'Young man, that is not yet for you, you must not think of such things!'[104]

Ophüls then accompanied the composer to his room to return the score, whereupon Brahms took the opportunity to ask his young friend, a lawyer by profession, 'whether the published version of the songs already printed by Simrock could be prohibited for religious reasons. What I replied I no longer remember exactly, but I do recall that I then gave my strong conviction that such a measure is not legally tenable and would be a shame and disgrace to art.'[105]

Brinkmann, in his incisive study regarding Brahms and melancholy, is amongst the few to acknowledge that Brahms was as much bound up with the cultural pessimism of the late nineteenth century as Schopenhauer and Nietzsche (and, indeed, Mahler) were.[106] What frustrated Brahms most in

---

[104] Gustav Ophüls, *Erinnerungen an Johannes Brahms: Ein Beitrag aus dem Kreis seiner rheinischen Freunde* (Munich: Langewiesche–Brandt, 1983), 19–20.

[105] *Ibid.*, 27–8.

[106] For a deeply insightful discussion of this aspect of Brahms's (compositional) persona, see the section called 'Melancholy' in Reinhold Brinkmann, *Late Idyll: The Second Symphony of*

the writings of these philosophers was not their diagnosis of such pessimism – with aspects of which he strongly identified. Rather, it was the fact that, having made such a diagnosis, they provided no mechanism with which humanity might come to terms with the harshness of reality.[107] This is precisely what Brahms offered in his final paean to love in the fourth and most uplifting of these *Serious Songs*.

Circumspection regarding Kalbeck's over-active hermeneutic imagination aside, the biographer elegantly encapsulates what Brahms was aiming to achieve in what we might profitably conceive of as his 'last great cultural harvest':

> The rigid, bleak, and merciless pessimism of the Old Testament encounters the New Testament's message of salvation, the gospel of all-believing, all-hoping, all-suffering love that teaches us unbounded, merciful, ideal optimism. The rational philosopher has bumped up against the limits of empirical science and human cognition, and now the mystic and the ecstatic, the artist and the poet, overcomes these things in a flight of fancy.[108]

What Brahms left to posterity in this collection of intensely intimate songs is a particularly German and characteristically Brahmsian testament to the strength of the human spirit.

*Johannes Brahms*, trans. Peter Palmer (Cambridge, MA: Harvard University Press, 1995), particularly pages 125–44.

[107] Another reading of this song is that it is a sarcastic response to the Catholicism that held an increasingly strong hold on Viennese cultural and political life following the election of Karl Lueger as Mayor of Vienna.

[108] Kalbeck, 'Brahms's Four *Serious Songs*, Op. 121 (1914)', 278.

# 5 | The Sense of an Ending: Music's Return to the Land of Childhood

Oh if I but knew the way, the sweet way back to the land of childhood![1]

– Klaus Groth

Artworks of the highest rank are distinguished from the others not through their success – for in what have they succeeded? – but through the manner of their failure.[2]

– Theodor W. Adorno

At its core, the present book is concerned with endings. The various compositions addressed in the preceding chapters share a crucial characteristic: they each have an apparently anomalous ending. Critics since Brahms's lifetime have had difficulty understanding why *Schicksalslied* ends in a key other than that in which it began – that is, the bright and buoyant C major that follows the E♭ major opening; the affirmative D major in which *Nänie* ends, with Brahms's return to the penultimate line of the poem, is thought of as a compositional miscalculation, for it seems to contradict Schiller's poetic message; the D major to which Brahms set the fifth stanza of *Gesang der Parzen* is thought to be incongruent with the unremitting bleakness of Goethe's poem; and the fourth song in the *Vier ernste Gesänge* is considered to be at odds with the first three, for it is the only one based on an uplifting passage from the New Testament and the only one in the collection to be set in a major key. In all four instances, as we have seen, hermeneutic readings tend to favour a trajectory from darkness into light, a trajectory that sees Brahms always taking the opportunity, in those pieces where he set texts of his own choosing, to end with consolation, reconciliation, or a hope of some kind.

I have sought to interrogate the complexity of these endings with a view to deepening our understanding of the expressive capacity of Brahms's

---

[1] Klaus Groth, 'O wüßt ich doch den Weg zurück', set by Brahms in *Neun Lieder und Gesänge*, Op. 63 No. 8.

[2] Theodor W. Adorno, *Beethoven. Philosophie der Musik: Fragmente und Texte*, ed. Rolf Tiedemann (Berlin: Suhrkamp Verlag, 2004), 99–100; translated in English as Adorno, *Beethoven: The Philosophy of Music*, trans. Edmund Jephcott (Cambridge: Polity Press, 1998). Hereafter Adorno, *Beethoven*.

music and demonstrating how the spiritual struggles that may be discerned in these works are intricately bound up with Brahms's treatment of form. All of the music with which we have been concerned up to this point sets literary texts – either poetic or Biblical. In this final chapter, I wish to turn to a series of instrumental pieces. These are not chosen at random. Rather, they are a series of Brahms pieces mentioned by Adorno in an important passage in his unfinished book on Beethoven written in 1934.[3] In this passage, Adorno is also concerned with endings, the question of whether those endings are failures or not, and, if they are, the question of whether the piece has earned its failure. Adorno, much like Samuel Beckett, came to believe that failure was an integral part of an artist's work. He developed this into a poetics of failure that is intricately linked to the poetics of loss with which we have been concerned throughout this book. The issues Adorno raises, as we shall see, resonate with the broader themes encountered in Brahms's Elegies: the notion of a disenchantment with the world, circular schemes of emanation and return, the notion of a paradise regained, or of a return to a metaphorical land of childhood.

Adorno wrote a second and more substantial piece in this same year called 'Brahms aktuell', his only piece of writing devoted exclusively to that composer. Viewing this together with the passage on Brahms in the Beethoven manuscript reveals the characteristically dialectical nature of Adorno's thought where Brahms is concerned. Margaret Notley makes an important distinction between logic and tone in Adorno's reception of Brahms.[4] Logic is concerned with compositional process, primarily thematic development, that which we may understand as the objective elements of music. Tone is concerned with the intellectual legacy of a work, its historical precedents, its influences and its expressive potential, that which we may understand as the subjective elements of music. 'Brahms aktuell' is predominantly concerned with the logic of Brahms's music, whereas the fragment from the Beethoven book takes up the question of its tone. Viewing both of Adorno's Brahms pieces of 1934 side by side, therefore, allows us to critique his philosophical evaluation of what he considered to be the truth or the untruth in Brahms's music in terms of the interaction of subjectivity and objectivity. Adorno's distinction between logic and tone, or objectivity and subjectivity, further maps onto the binary opposition between intellectualism and sensuality. This distinction will be important

---

[3] Adorno, *Beethoven*.

[4] Margaret Notley, *Lateness and Brahms: Music and Culture in the Twilight of Viennese Liberalism* (Oxford: Oxford University Press, 2007), 21ff.

as I widen the view, following Adorno's lead, to consider his writings on Brahms in relation to his writings on Mahler.

By considering Brahms's compositional output within the same framework as the music of Mahler or the writings of Nietzsche (as we also did in Chapter 4), we touch on a second broad theme of this book, which is the question of what Brahms's place is within the fabric of musical modernism. This is just as closely related to his technical innovation as it is concerned with broader cultural factors. Reinhold Brinkmann has shown how modernism, from the paintings of Adolph Menzel onward, is bound up with a world that was rapidly disappearing, a world that may never have existed at all. Brahms's music, much like that of Mahler, Schoenberg, Berg, Webern, Zemlinsky, and other composers of early twentieth-century Vienna, registers an uneasy relationship or an anxiety with the past. Much of this music is characterized by a longing to be reconnected with a past that is lost, one that is beyond the grasp of these composers, yet one for which they continue to yearn. One thinks, for instance, of the private inscriptions in the orchestral draft of Mahler, Symphony No. 9, 'O Jugendzeit! Entschwundene! O Liebe! Verwehte!' ('O Childhood! Vanished! Oh Love! Shattered!'),[5] or the last song in Schoenberg's 1912 composition *Pierrot Lunaire*, setting a translation of Albert Giraud as 'O alter Duft aus Märchenzeit' ('Oh ancient scent of fairytale times'), which, as Roger Marsh argues, 'yearns nostalgically for earlier times, and through which Schoenberg allows himself [. . .] a wistful nod in the direction of tonality'.[6] What Brahms has in common with these Viennese composers, therefore, is the capacity simultaneously to yearn for the past whilst reaching for the future, that notion which we have referred to throughout the book as nostalgic teleology. Before considering Brahms within this wider framework, we will first turn to Adorno's writings on Brahms, beginning with the essay 'Brahms aktuell'.

## 5.1   Adorno and Brahms

In his writings on music, Adorno was never primarily interested in Brahms. Unlike Beethoven and Mahler, on each of whom he developed

---

[5] Anthony Newcomb argues that this is not a lament for Mahler's own life but the lament for lost childhood that is an intrinsic part of *Bildung*. See Anthony Newcomb, 'Narrative Archetypes and Mahler's Ninth Symphony', in *Music and Text: Critical Inquiries*, ed. Peter Scher (Cambridge: Cambridge University Press, 1992), 118–36 (123–4).

[6] Roger Marsh, '"A Multicoloured Alphabet": Rediscovering Albert Giraud's *Pierrot Lunaire*', *Twentieth-Century Music* 4/1 (2007): 97–121 (98).

extensive theories, his writing on Brahms is confined to the three-page essay[7] and a few fragments scattered throughout his letters, books, and papers. Adorno wrote 'Brahms aktuell' one year after Schoenberg's now famous Brahms lecture was broadcast on Frankfurt Radio, the city where Adorno lived, although we have no way of knowing whether Adorno heard this broadcast.[8] The formalist bent of the essay has much in common with Schoenberg's view of Brahms, and it was written with the aim of creating a segue between Beethoven and twentieth-century music. Adorno wrote this essay not to promote Brahms, but for the sake of what he referred to as 'legitimate new music', which he considered to have been 'misconstrued and discredited' in recent music criticism.[9]

In 'Brahms aktuell', Adorno is concerned primarily with logic at the expense of tone. His '*historical* review' of 'the origin of the new music' provides a list of techniques that stem from Brahms's compositional process. These techniques resonate with Schoenberg's concept of developing variation.[10] They include 'the revision of absolute music in the context of the chamber music sonata, the self-contained [*in Griffen*] piano movement, [...] the technique of the thematic fragmentation of themes, its conversion through the pervasive principle of development, and above all the style of *harmonic* polyphony'.

Adorno's distinction between logic and tone in Brahms's music reveals the degree to which the Marxist critic's historical limitations are indebted to the nineteenth-century reception of Brahms, which was equally divided between those concerned with logic and those concerned with tone.[11] Schoenberg is a pivotal figure in this regard. There are clear continuities from nineteenth-century 'organic' thinking on music to Schoenberg's thinking on developing variation and, from there, to Adorno's writings on musical logic.

Schoenberg refers to the 'Brahmsian School' as those who employ the technique of 'connecting ideas through developing variation, thus showing

---

[7] Theodor W. Adorno, 'Brahms aktuell' appears in vol. XVIII of Theodor W. Adorno, *Gesammelte Schriften: Musikalische Schriften*, ed. Rolf Tiedemann and Klaus Schutz (Frankfurt am Main: Suhrkamp Verlag, 1984).

[8] For an annotated translation of Schoenberg's Brahms Lecture, see Thomas McGeary, 'Schoenberg's Brahms Lecture', *Journal of the Arnold Schoenberg Institute* 15/2 (November 1992): 5–99.

[9] All references to Adorno's 'Brahms aktuell' are from my own translation, as provided in the Appendix.

[10] Schoenberg's radio broadcast was later revised and published as 'Brahms the Progressive', in Arnold Schoenberg (ed. Leonard Stein), *Style and Idea* (London:8 Faber, 1975), 398–441.

[11] See Nicole Grimes, 'The Schoenberg/Brahms Critical Tradition Reconsidered', *Music Analysis* 31/2 (2012): 127–75.

consequences derived from the basic idea, and remaining within the boundaries of human thinking and its demands of logic'.[12] Central to the concept of developing variation is Schoenberg's assertion that 'in the succession of motive-forms produced through the variation of a basic motive, there is something which can be compared to development, to growth'.[13] Walter Frisch clarifies that 'Adorno's principal goal is to show how Schoenberg was the first twentieth-century composer to grasp and carry out the "historical tendencies" of Western art music. One of those tendencies is the continuous transformation or reshaping of musical material (an activity equated with "an autonomous aesthetic subjectivity" of a composer), which begins to dominate the external form (equated with objectivity).'[14] Adorno considers Brahms to be Beethoven's heir in the realm of continuous transformation. Prior to Beethoven, the thematic material was dictated by the overall form, whereas with Beethoven, the thematic material determines the overall form. Adorno considers Brahms to embody the next stage in this process, which is developing variation. 'Within the framework of tonality', Adorno writes, Brahms 'rejects the conventional formulae' and 'produces the unity of the work anew'. He is:

> simultaneously the advocate of a universally encompassing economy that quashes all contingent moments of music and still develops the greatest diversity – indeed, precisely this diversity – out of identically maintained materials. Nothing unthematic remains, nothing that is not understood as having derived from what is identical in however latent a fashion.[15]

Adorno's view of Brahms is coloured by the notion of lateness: lateness in Brahms's own works, Brahms's late position at the end of the period of tonal harmony, and Brahms's chronological positioning at the end of the nineteenth century, which has been widely perceived as a period inherently

---

[12] The theory of developing variation also appears in a number of his pedagogical writings, including *Fundamentals of Musical Composition* (London: Faber, 1970), and *Structural Functions of Harmony* (London: Faber, 1983, c. 1969). It is dealt with in a number of his essays, in particular his 1931 essay 'Linear Counterpoint', his 1946 essays 'Criteria for the Evaluation of Music' and 'Heart and Brain in Music', and, of particular interest to the present study, his 1947 essay 'Brahms the Progressive'. 'Brahms the Progressive', 'Linear Counterpoint', 'Criteria for the Evaluation of Music', and 'Heart and Brain in Music' are all reproduced in Schoenberg, *Style and Idea*, 398–441, 289–94, 124–36, and 53–75, respectively. Here at 130–1.

[13] Schoenberg, *Fundamentals of Musical Composition*, 8.

[14] Walter Frisch, *Brahms and the Principle of Developing Variation* (Berkeley and Los Angeles, CA: University of California Press, 1984), 19.

[15] Adorno, *Philosophy of New Music*, trans., ed., and with an introduction by Robert Hullet-Kentor (Minneapolis, MN: University of Minnesota Press, 2006), 47.

concerned with issues of sickness and decay.[16] Despite Brahms's formidable control of motivically driven form, in Adorno's Marxist reading, the
very culture of tonal music is stained by its own lateness. Because it lacks
the capacity to be separated from consciousness, it was deemed to have
come to a natural end. Consciousness, in turn, was considered to be bound
up with intentions, so that goal-directed, highly intentional tonal music
was considered by default to be utterly conventional. Adorno appropriates
the Marxist philosopher György Lukács's term 'second nature' in relation
to tonality. For Lukács in *The Theory of The Novel*, 'second nature' signifies
'the world of convention'.[17] For Adorno, as Andrew Bowie asserts, second
nature in music 'has its roots in first nature, via a supposed "natural"
connection' of the 'harmonic system to our responses'.[18]

The turn away from tonality was the most important development of
the Second Viennese School for Adorno, one which, to his mind, involves
moving away from that which 'through the generations has, as second
nature, instilled itself in people'. Post-tonal music, on the other hand,
'determines musical behavior largely independently of [its] consciousness
and [its] intention'.[19] Adorno draws a parallel, as Susan Gillespie observes,
between the tonal system and the traditional forms of Victorian poesy:

Both are based on accepted forms that have become second nature. They are
'merely' stylistic in their reliance on outward 'effects', rather than on the structural
whole, and they lull the reader or listener into a superficial, momentary appreciation that falls short of the Hegelian dictum Adorno placed at the beginning of the
*Philosophie der neuen Musik*: 'For in art we have to do not with some merely
pleasing or useful game, but . . . with an unfolding of the truth'.[20]

---

[16] On theories of degeneracy and decline as they relate to modernity and to Brahms, see Michael
von der Linn, 'Themes of Nostalgia and Critique in Weimar-Era Brahms Reception', *Brahms
Studies*, ed. David Brodbeck (Lincoln, NA: University of Nebraska Press, 2001), III, 231–48.

[17] Notley, *Lateness and Brahms*, 6, n. 7.

[18] Andrew Bowie, *Adorno and the Ends of Philosophy* (Cambridge: Polity Press, 2013), 86. Bowie
clarifies that the harmonic system is historically developed. In a 1956 essay Adorno clarifies why
he considers the tonal system – as part of second nature – to have become stagnant. See
Theodor W. Adorno and Susan Gillespie, 'Music, Language, and Composition', *Musical
Quarterly* 77/3 (Autumn, 1993): 401–14 (401–2). (This is a translation by Susan Gillespie of
Adorno's essay 'Musik, Sprache, und ihr Verhältnis im gegenwärtigen Komponieren',
*Gesammelte Schriften* (Frankfurt am Main: Suhrkamp, 1978), XVI, 649–64.)

[19] Adorno, *Gesammelte Schriften* (Frankfurt: Suhrkamp, 1997), XV, 193, cited and translated in
Bowie, *Adorno and the Ends of Philosophy*, 86.

[20] Susan Gillespie, 'Translating Adorno: Language, Music, and Performance', *Musical Quarterly*
79/1 (1995): 55–65 (57). See also Georg Wilhelm Friedrich Hegel, *Werke*, ed. Eva Moldenhauer
and Karl Markus Michel, III, *Phänomenologie des Geistes* (Frankfurt am Main: Suhrkamp,
1986), 38. The translation of the Hegel passage is also by Gillespie.

A consideration of Adorno's changing stance on Beethoven's output from the early works to the late ones forms a fundamental starting point for elucidating Adorno's position on Brahms. In the Beethoven manuscript, Adorno attempted to demonstrate that Beethoven represents the moment when music 'converges with philosophy', by invoking Hegel's definition of truth both for the content and the process of philosophy.[21] Truth can be understood to emerge from contradictions that apparently cannot be negated or resolved. As Daniel Chua notes, in remaining 'true to the thrust of Marxist theory', Adorno's 'historical narrative contextualizes Beethoven's music in a history that embraces both the political and intellectual upheavals of the early-nineteenth century'.[22] Adorno argues that in Beethoven's second period, his work 'attains an actual synthesis of subjectivity and objectivity'. Subotnik provides a number of reasons for this synthesis in her analysis of the manuscript:[23] first, the external reality was favourable to a dialectical synthesis between musical structure as a totality which could accommodate a concept (such as subject, individual, freedom) with its opposite (object, society, form) in a resolution which preserved the essence of each;[24] second, this music effected a momentary reconciliation not only between Beethoven and society, but also between the particular (individual man) and the abstract (social man, or man as a historical species); third, the persona within the music was accorded the status of a collective persona or 'universal subject' – the musical equivalent of a world-historical individual. This second period was therefore considered, as Subotnik formulates it, to be 'Utopian, ahead of its time, and more nearly whole than contemporaneous society'.[25]

In Beethoven's third period, however, 'the synthesis prefigured in the style of the second turned out to be impossible. His late style, according to Adorno, clearly acknowledges this reality and, for this reason, it is the most realistic of Beethoven's styles.'[26] Chua has likened Adorno's description of the 'expansion of time' that links these two opposing moments of historical compression for Adorno – from the synthesis of the second period to the fragmentation of the late style – to 'a Big Bang theory of music history':

Time, as it were, explodes under the pressure of the 'symphonic contraction' of Beethoven's heroic style, and the stuff of truth distends and disconnects until it falls

---

[21] Adorno, *Beethoven*, 29.

[22] Daniel Chua, 'Believing in Beethoven', *Music Analysis* 19/3 (October 2000): 409–21 (415).

[23] Rose Rosengard Subotnik, 'Adorno's Diagnosis of Beethoven's Late Style: Early Symptom of a Fatal Condition', *Journal of the American Musicological Society* 29/2 (1976): 242–75 (248–9).

[24] Subotnik, 'Adorno's Diagnosis of Beethoven's Late Style', 244.     [25] *Ibid.*, 250.

[26] *Ibid.*, 250.

apart under its own entropy to leave the debris of history as shrunken bits of truth strewn over inhuman landscape.[27]

As a poetic metaphor, this is an excellent way of describing Adorno's shattered historical conception, of articulating how the whole history of music from Beethoven's late period to Schoenberg exhibits what Subotnik calls 'a condition of "post-totality", an inability to recover this perceived [wholeness]'.[28] As Subotnik succinctly captures it, Adorno's post-Beethovenian history of music 'represents at once the winding down of human history and a prolegomenon to the music of a post-historical world, which since it continues to exist physically, Adorno considers to have entered into a meaningless, ahistorical stasis'.[29] In Adorno's view of music history, Beethoven is regarded at one end as a virtual year zero,[30] whilst at the other end Schoenberg's music heralds 'the end of dynamic human development'.[31] Beethoven occupied a privileged position in Adorno's historical scheme between the genius of Mozart and the expressive excesses of the Romantics, while Brahms occupied a position of privilege between the truth of Beethoven's early music and the end of human consciousness.

Adorno's 'Brahms aktuell' reflects this position. The developments in new music that Adorno has outlined would be 'unthinkable without Brahms', he asserts. 'The most radical' of Reger's achievements, which he defines as 'making prose by virtue of easing up on metre', is also considered to be inconceivable without Brahms. How much Schoenberg owes to Brahms was already evident in the early 'evolutionary period', he continues, whereas Hindemith's early compositions as far as Op. 10 'often grapple with Brahms'.[32] Framing his argument in decidedly Hegelian terms, Adorno recommends that consulting such music should 'suffice

[27]  Chua, 'Believing in Beethoven', *Music Analysis* 19/3 (October 2000): 409–21 (413).

[28]  Rose Rosengard Subotnik, 'The Historical Structure: Adorno's "French" Model for the Criticism of Nineteenth-Century Music', *19th-Century Music* 2/1 (July 1978): 36–60 (38).

[29]  Subotnik, 'Adorno's Diagnosis of Beethoven's Late Style', 245–6.

[30]  I acknowledge that from Adorno's perspective, the great achievement of human history took place in the bourgeois period which, as Subotnik notes, dates back approximately to Monteverdi. However, music history, to the extent that it really mattered for Adorno, extends back only as far as Beethoven. See Adorno, 'Bach Defended Against His Devotees', *Prisms*, trans. Samuel and Sherry Weber (London: 1967), 137; and Subotnik, 'Adorno's Diagnosis of Beethoven's Late Style', 243.

[31]  Subotnik, 'Adorno's Diagnosis of Beethoven's Late Style', 246.

[32]  These Hindemith works include chamber music (Andante and Scherzo for Clarinet, Horn and Piano, Op. 1, String Quartet No. 1, Op. 2, Piano Quintet, Op. 7), orchestral music (Merry Sinfonietta, Op. 4), concertos (Concerto for Violoncello Accompanied by Orchestra, Op. 3), piano music (Waltzes for Piano Four Hands, Op. 6), Lieder (Lieder in Aargau Dialect, Op. 5, 3 Songs for Soprano and Orchestra, Op. 9) and an unfinished opera (*The Cousin's Visit*, based on W. Busch).

historically' for any interested party to see that Brahms is not a 'superseded' composer.

Adorno considers the seriousness of the grand Beethovenian sonata construction of the second period to have been 'softened' by the 'melodious homophony' of the 'Schumannesque' for the sake of 'song and harmonic discovery'. This transformed the Beethovenian sonata construction into a 'lyrical *Liederspiel*'. As a result of Schumann's 'subjectivity and altered musical material', he considered an 'unmediated recourse to Beethoven', although desirable, to be no longer possible. Turning instead to the 'chromaticism of the New Germans and Chopin' – which at that point, he notes, had not yet found success in the theatre music of Wagner – in the area of 'sonata form' it offered only a 'mere increase of the Schumann situation'. It is therefore in the works of Brahms alone that he could discern the 'objective spirit of the sonata', to 'deliberate [...] upon itself'. 'Brahms's music', he extrapolates:

> examines its material – that of the high Romanticism of Schumann – profoundly in its self-motivation (*Selbstgegebenheit*) until it becomes objectified [...] What is achieved in Wagner through a dynamic tempest is achieved in Brahms through stubborn insistence. His results however have a more lasting quality [...] for the ensuing compositional practice.[33]

Brahms's major contribution, in Adorno's teleological scheme, is to have dissolved 'the harmonic discoveries' of Schumann 'from their expressive isolation' and to have determined 'harmonic structure anew' from these now cleansed harmonic discoveries. Adorno argues that Brahms 'further constructed and increased' Beethoven's 'specific developmental technique' and his 'art of variation'. The 'regeneration and reconstruction of the sonata' remain unresolved, in Adorno's opinion. Nonetheless, once again resorting to logic rather than tone, he takes consolation in the fact that Brahms's 'art of [the] economical fragmentation of themes into the smallest motives' reveals what he refers to as 'a magnificent, uncomfortable *Unnaïvetät* of composition [that Brahms commands] in today's heightened material consciousness'.[34]

In his last book, which was not completed at his death, *Aesthetic Theory*, Adorno uses the term 'Unnaïvetät' in several contexts. This has been variously translated as 'lost naïveté'[35] or 'absence of naïveté – a reflective

---

[33] See the Appendix.     [34] Adorno's emphasis. See the Appendix.

[35] 'Aber ihre Autonomie beginnt, ein Moment von Blindheit hervorzukehren. Es eignete der Kunst von je; im Zeitalter ihrer Emanzipation überschattet es jedes andere, trotz, wenn nicht wegen der Unnaïvetät, der sie schon nach Hegels Einsicht nicht mehr sich entziehen darf' is

posture'.[36] For Adorno, 'reflection means burdening artworks down with intentions'.[37] When he extols Brahms's 'magnificent *Unnaïvetät*', therefore, he celebrates the fact that, from a formal perspective and divorced from the perceived expressive excesses of Schumann and Bruckner, amongst others, Brahms's process of developing variation is entirely appropriate to an age that seeks to redress the balance between objectivity and subjectivity.

As a closing gambit, and by way of reorienting his readership to privilege the material elements in Brahms's music, he questions the legitimacy of 'influence' as a criterion for music history. This passage illuminates the issues that Adorno considered to govern the reception of Brahms's music in 1934:

Even if Brahms's tone is always without 'influence', what is this obvious influence in art? It has established *laws* whose obligatory exactitude competes with its waiting latency. The time will come when future Brahmsian performances that realize the laws (constructive principles), and not the academic heritage or the autumnal colours, will be uncovered, just as they have been so fruitful up to now.

If Adorno had heard Schoenberg's radio address on Brahms in 1933, he was selective in his borrowing, interested only in the fact that Schoenberg had 'anointed Brahms a "progressive" in the technical domain'.[38] He extols the merits of the technique identified by Schoenberg as developing variation and attempts to reenergize the reception of the composer's music by arguing that Brahms, as Max Paddison puts it, 'further stripped music of its "naivety" and increased its cognitive character (*Erkenntnischarakter*)'.[39] Yet, whilst he plays down the significance of the expressive and historical lineage of Brahms's works – the 'tone' associated with degenerate music in

---

translated as 'Indeed, art's autonomy shows signs of blindness. Blindness was ever an aspect of art; in the age of art's emancipation, however, this blindness has begun to predominate in spite of, if not because of, art's lost naïveté, which, as Hegel already perceived, art cannot undo.' Theodor W. Adorno, *Aesthetic Theory*, trans. Robert Hullot-Kentor (London: Continuum, 1997), 1.

[36] 'Unnaïvetät der Kunst gegenüber, als Reflexion, bedarf freilich der Naïvetät in anderem Betracht' is translated as 'absence of naiveté – a reflective posture toward art clearly also requires naiveté'. Adorno, *Aesthetic Theory*, 269.

[37] Adorno, *Aesthetic Theory*, 27.

[38] I borrow the phrase from James Webster, 'The *Alto Rhapsody*: Psychology, Intertextuality, and Brahms's Artistic Development', in *Brahms Studies*, ed. David Brodbeck (Lincoln, NE: University of Nebraska Press, 2001), III, 19–46 (34).

[39] Max Paddison, *Adorno's Aesthetics of Music* (Cambridge: Cambridge University Press, 1993), 256.

Weimar-era Germany – he takes no heed of the 'beauty', 'emotion', and 'expression' in which Schoenberg famously rejoiced in Brahms.[40]

Michael Spitzer's criticism of Adorno's music-historical limitations in the *Beethoven* book, particularly where eighteenth-century conventions are concerned, is fully applicable to 'Brahms aktuell'. Spitzer argues that 'Adorno's analytical tools are primitive and of their time, fixated on Schoenbergian thematic relationships at the expense of tonality'.[41] Despite the philosopher's awareness of the 'autumnal colours' and the 'academic heritage' of Brahms's music, he is reluctant to afford these qualities any historical significance.[42] As Notley summarizes the situation, despite extolling his treatment of thematic material, 'it appears that Adorno could not closely consider Brahms's style in all its complexity, much less the possibility of stylistic change, because the idea of music-historic lateness so strongly colored his perspective'.[43]

## 5.2    Music's Return to the Land of Childhood

Anything else Adorno wrote on Brahms after 1934 was of a fragmentary nature and tangential to substantial considerations of the music of other composers. Along with *Beethoven: The Philosophy of Music*, such passages are found in *Mahler: A Musical Physiognomy*,[44] and *The Philosophy of New Music*. One of the few instances in which Adorno discusses actual compositions by Brahms is in Fragment 185 of the incomplete book on Beethoven. In Fragment 183, he upbraids not only Schumann but also Schubert for 'the flagging of energy to be found' in their works, which 'is the price exacted for the attempted transcendence of form'. This symptom, found in Schubert in 'the unfinished works', and in Schumann in 'the mechanical element', is diagnosed as being 'the first manifestation of the decay of music as an objective language'. The result of such decay is that 'the language falls breathlessly behind the moment invoked, or is its empty shell'.[45]

---

[40] Schoenberg, 'Brahms the Progressive', 439.

[41] Michael Spitzer, 'Notes on Beethoven's Late Style', in *Late Style and Its Discontents: Essays in Art, Literature, and Music*, ed. Gordon McMullan and Sam Smiles (Oxford: Oxford University Press, 2016), 191–208 (204).

[42] Adorno, 'Brahms aktuell'. See the Appendix.    [43] Notley, *Lateness and Brahms*, 7.

[44] Theodor W. Adorno, *Mahler: A Musical Physiognomy*, trans. Edmund Jephcott (Chicago, IL and London: University of Chicago Press, 1992).

[45] Adorno, *Beethoven*, 73–4.

Adorno then reflects on Brahms's approach to form, making the particularly suggestive comment that with Brahms it is as if 'music were returning to the land of childhood'. Fragment 185 reads:

Brahms, with incomparable formal tact, faced the consequences of increasing subjectivity as it affected the large-scale form. The critical point in this regard is the finale. (N.B. It probably *always was*: the 'happy ending', the finale always gives an impression of embarrassment. Beethoven's great finale movements always have a paradoxical character – perhaps in the antagonistic world, music was *never* able to close, as has now become obvious. Compare the failure of the concluding movements of Mahler's Fifth and Seventh Symphonies.) Here, Brahms showed a splendid *resignation*: in principle, his best final movements go back to the *Lied*, as if music were returning to the land of childhood. For example, the Finale of the C minor Trio, above all the close in the major, like the last stanza of a *Lied*. Another example is the wholly lyrical Finale of the violin sonata in A major. The finale of the G major Sonata, on the 'Regenlied', acts like a key.[46]

Tonic harmony provides an obvious musical analogue for 'home' in the Romantic longing for childhood.[47] This relates to Novalis's aphorism that philosophy is really homesickness, 'the drive to be everywhere at home'.[48] Adorno's characterization of Brahms's music returning to the land of childhood taps into the deep vein of German modernist philosophy that runs as a thread throughout this book. A return to childhood is bound up with an attempt to recapture the enchantment of childhood in the aftermath of the modernist 'disenchantment of the world'. The conceptual paradigm of a return to childhood, a return 'home', is given powerful expression in Schiller's essay *On the Naïve and Sentimental in Literature*, as we have seen in earlier chapters. As Damian Valdez summarizes it, 'the naïve in poetry and in life was described by Schiller in terms of a proximity

---

[46] Adorno, *Beethoven*, 74 (emphasis in the original). Adorno would later use precisely this same imagery to admonish Stravinsky for 'extirpating memory' in *The Soldier's Tale*. He writes, 'The traces of this past, like the soldier's mother, are subject to a taboo. Brahms's way by which the subject returns "to the land of childhood" becomes the cardinal sin for an art that wants to reconstruct the presubjective aspect of childhood.' See Adorno, *Philosophy of New Music*, 192, n. 44.

[47] See Marjorie Hirsch, *Romantic Lieder and the Search for Lost Paradise* (Cambridge: Cambridge University Press, 2007), 162; Nicholas Marston, 'Schubert's Homecoming', *Journal of the Royal Musical Association* 125 (2000): 248–70; Charles Fisk, *Returning Cycles: Contexts for the Interpretation of Schubert's Impromptus and Last Sonatas* (Berkeley, CA: University of California Press, 2001); and the final chapter, called 'Coming Home' of Janet Schmalfeldt, *In the Process of Becoming: Analytical and Philosophical Perspectives on Form in Early Nineteenth-Century Music* (Oxford: Oxford University Press, 2011).

[48] Andrew Bowie, *Music, Philosophy and Modernity* (Cambridge: Cambridge University Press, 2007), 39.

to childhood and its spontaneous, harmonious, potentially all-embracing relationship with nature'.[49] In extending the metaphor to the twentieth century, Adorno indicates that the return to childhood is the quest of modern art more generally. This is in keeping with Lukács in *The Theory of the Novel* who finds 'transcendental homesickness' of the modern subject at the heart of modernity.[50]

The metaphor of a return to childhood also has a particular significance in relation to Adorno's biography, given that political events in the first half of the twentieth century left an indelible mark on his view of history and society. This informed his conception of music history wherein elements of social critique may be inscribed within musical processes. Adorno was acutely aware, as Richard Leppert points out, that he 'entered the world at a moment of enormous transformational change, too much of it dystopian, and especially, if hardly exclusively, for the country of his birth, whose once-liberal political traditions both defined and perpetuated cultural *Bildung*'.[51] Adorno's formative early experiences of playing four-handed piano duets with his mother and his aunt Agathe led him 'to connect the very principle of music to belonging – as it were, to *being home*'. Leppert asserts that 'music, both figuratively and literally defined the centre for Adorno of the utopian longing invoked in the conjunction of childhood and belonging that under ideal circumstances appends to "home"'.[52] Adorno's conception of Brahms's music returning to the land of childhood, therefore, registers both a personal and a musical loss, rendering Adorno – in the pivotal year of 1934, when he left his homeland for Oxford – both a literal exile and a figurative one. For the conception of a return to a naïve state of innocence, as we saw in Chapter 1, entails an acknowledgement that such a state of innocence does not exist except in one's yearning for it. We can understand Adorno's musical land of childhood – that is, the period of tonal harmony – in similar terms: this was his lost paradise to which, he was convinced, there was no return. Each of the Brahms pieces that he names in relation to this aesthetic paradigm registers a sense of loss in a distinctive way.

---

[49] Damian Valdez, *German Philhellenism: The Pathos of the Historical Imagination from Winckelmann to Goethe* (New York, NY: Palgrave Macmillan, 2014), 197.

[50] Georg Lukàcs, *The Theory of the Novel*, trans. Anna Bostock (London: Methuen Press, 1917), 93.

[51] Richard Leppert, 'The Cultural Dialectics of Chamber Music: Adorno and the Visual-Acoustic Imaginary of *Bildung*', in *Brahms in the Home and in the Concert Hall*, ed. Katy Hamilton and Natasha Loges (Cambridge: Cambridge University Press, 2014), 346–65 (346).

[52] *Ibid.*, 352.

An acknowledgement of the expressive tone in Brahms's music, which was so conspicuous by its absence in 'Brahms aktuell', pervades the passage in the Beethoven book, which is soaked with nostalgia and melancholy. These facets are perhaps nowhere more evident than in Brahms's Lieder, a genre that deals extensively with the Romantic nostalgia for childhood. With their sense of longing and their wish for a return to nature and naturalness, nineteenth-century Lieder, as Marjorie Hirsch argues, provide a 'lens of adult consciousness through which youth's domain comes into view'.[53] Brahms wrote numerous works that are explicitly engaged with themes of childhood, such as the *Volks-Kinderlieder* that he composed for the Schumann children in 1858, the famous 'Wiegenlied', Op. 49 No. 4, and the 'Geistliches Wiegenlied', Op. 91 No. 2. Hirsch explores how 'the path back to childhood winds its way through memory and imagination' in a select repertoire of Brahms's compositions, including the 'Heimweh' Lieder, Op. 63, Nos 7–9, settings of Klaus Groth's poems, one of which is cited at the outset of this chapter: 'O wüsst ich doch den Weg zurück' ('Oh, if only I knew the way back').[54] Groth suggested the title 'From the Paradise of Childhood' [*Aus der Kinderparadies*] for Brahms's collection.[55] Whilst these songs, as Hirsch avers, 'possess a childlike melodic charm', they 'are fundamentally about regret, loss, despair, isolation, confusion, and fading memories'.[56]

Having positioned Brahms's output in relation to the aesthetic paradigm of childhood, Adorno calls attention to three particular Brahms compositions in the *Beethoven* manuscript (Table 5.1). All three are chamber works, generically coded for intimacy and compositional experimentation. Two of the three works cited – the A Major Violin Sonata, Op. 100, and the Piano Trio No. 3 in C Minor, Op. 101 – were composed in what Notley refers to as 'Brahms's chamber-music summer of 1886', when, ensconced in the idyllic surroundings of Thun in the Bernese Oberland of Switzerland, he composed the Cello Sonata No. 2 in F Major, Op. 99, the Violin Sonata No. 2 in A Major, Op. 100, the Piano Trio in C Minor, Op. 101, and the Violin Sonata No. 3 in D Minor, Op.

---

[53] Hirsch, *Romantic Lieder and the Search for Lost Paradise*, 148.

[54] *Ibid.*, 148. It is worth noting that Adorno uses precisely this song as a means to admonish Stravinsky for rooting out and destroying memory in *The Soldier's Tale*. He writes: 'Stravinsky's infantilism knows the price to be paid. He scorns the sentimental illusion of "O wüsst ich doch den Weg zurück" and constructs the standpoint of the mentally ill in order to make the primitive contemporary world manifestIbid.' See Adorno, *The Philosophy of New Music*, 125–6.

[55] Hirsch, *Romantic Lieder and the Search for Lost Paradise*, 151.     [56] *Ibid.*, 149.

**Table 5.1** Adorno's Brahms finales

| Work | Movement 1 | Movement 2 | Movement 3 | Movement 4 |
|------|-----------|-----------|-----------|-----------|
| Brahms, Sonata for Violin and Piano in G Major, Op. 78 | *Vivace ma non troppo* G major | *Adagio–Piú andante–Adagio* E♭ major | *Allegro molto moderato* G minor (with coda in G major) | |
| | Sonata form | Ternary form | Rondo form | |
| Brahms, Sonata for Violin and Piano in A Major, Op. 100 | *Allegro amabile* A major Sonata form | *Andante tranquillo* F major Rondo form | *Allegretto grazioso* A major Rondo form | |
| Brahms, Piano Trio in C Minor, Op. 101 | *Allegro energico* C minor | *Presto non assai* C minor | *Andante grazioso* C major | *Allegro molto* C minor (→ C major) |
| | Sonata form | Ternary form | Ternary form | Sonata form |

108.[57] In a different permutation, two of the three works Adorno cites have well-documented relationships to Brahms's Lieder.[58] His settings of Groth's poems 'Regenlied' and 'Nachklang' from the *8 Lieder und Gesänge*, Op. 59, composed in 1873, pervade all three movements of the G Major Violin Sonata, Op. 78, composed five years later, and 'Regenlied' provides the main thematic material for the third movement. The A Major Violin Sonata, composed in Thun in 1886, is filled with allusions to three of the songs that Brahms wrote that same summer, 'Wie Melodien zieht es mir leise durch den Sinn' (first movement, second theme), the cradle song 'Immer leise wird mein Schlummer', and 'Auf dem Kirchhofe', all from the *5 Lieder*, Op. 105. Given the explicit mention of Lieder in Adorno's passage on Brahms's finales, this seems to be a likely key to understanding what brings all three works together.

---

[57]  Margaret Notley, 'Brahms's Chamber Music Summer of 1886: A Study of Opp. 99, 100, 101, and 108', unpublished PhD dissertation, Yale University (1992).

[58]  Both these song collections contain settings of Klaus Groth texts. On the friendship between Brahms and Groth, and with particular reference to their discussion of childhood in relation to these songs, see Hirsch, *Romantic Lieder and the Search for Lost Paradise*, 150–2. For a more comprehensive study of the relationship between Groth and Brahms, see Peter Russell, *Johannes Brahms and Klaus Groth: The Biography of a Friendship* (Aldershot: Ashgate, 2006). On the relationship between the songs and the instrumental works, see Dillon Parmer, 'Brahms, Song Quotation, and Secret Programs', *19th-Century Music* 19/2 (Summer 1995): 161–90, and Inge van Rij, *Brahms's Song Collections* (Cambridge: Cambridge University Press, 2006).

Yet there are no such allusions to song in the Piano Trio, Op. 101. The inclusion of two rondo finales with one finale in sonata form seems to disqualify large-scale form as the common denominator. Notwithstanding Adorno's disdain for the *per aspera ad astra* ending, explored in greater detail below, the fact that two of these works have a tonal trajectory from the minor to the major – either across the architecture of the whole work (Op. 101) or within the final movement alone (Op. 78) – also rules out tonal transcendence as our point of commonality. The question lingers: what prompted Adorno to extol Brahms's finales on the basis of these three works in the same breath that he derided two of Mahler's as a cause of embarrassment? A plausible answer, I propose, lies in their endings. Brahms's manipulative treatment of tonality and formal functions in these three finales continuously defers and destabilizes cadential structures, thereby frustrating their generic expectations.

Composers had played with and thwarted generic conventions throughout the period that Dahlhaus designates as the 'second age of the symphony'.[59] But there seems to be something more at play in these Brahms pieces, which may be attributed to the close relationship between two of them – the Sonatas for Violin and Piano – and Brahms's Lieder.

In a recent study, Steven Vande Moortele outlines two personas that emerge from Adorno's writings on music to whom he gives the titles 'musicology's Adorno' and 'music theory's Adorno'. The former, he argues, came of age along with the New Musicology, as part of a critique of the empirical bias of musicology. Its aim was to reconnect music with society, and it promised access to music's cultural meaning – that which Subotnik refers to as its 'humanistic sorts of truth'.[60] American musicology at this time 'drew on Adorno in order to open up new avenues of scholarly inquiry into music', he suggests, and 'not to remind itself that close analysis of musical structure remains a sine qua non for those who want to walk those new paths with some authority'.[61]

---

[59] Carl Dahlhaus, *Nineteenth-Century Music*, trans. J. Bradford Robinson (Berkeley, CA and London: University of California Press, 1989), 265–76.

[60] Steven Vande Moortele, 'The Philosopher as Theorist: Adorno's *material Formenlehre*', in *Formal Functions in Perspective: Essays on Musical Form from Haydn to Adorno*, ed. Steven Vande Moortele, Julie Pedneault-Deslauriers, and Nathan John Martin (Rochester, NY: University of Rochester Press, 2015), 411–33 (413). Vande Moortele is citing Rose Rosengard Subotnik, 'The Role of Ideology in the Study of Western Music', *Journal of Musicology* 2 (1983): 1–12 (9).

[61] Vande Moortele, 'The Philosopher as Theorist', 413. Vande Moortele is quick to add that 'this is not a critique of new musicology, nor is it a defense of Adorno against the new musicology'. Rather, it is an attempt to open up new ways of considering Adorno in relation to music that are based on his analytical insights into music, rather than his dialectical sociological thought in the abstract.

The work of those who employ 'musicology's Adorno' involves something of a move away from the close analysis of musical structure that the second persona, 'music theory's Adorno', espoused in essays such as 'On the Problem of Musical Analysis', where Adorno asserted that 'works need analysis for their "truth content" [*Wahrheitsgehalt*] to be revealed'.[62] Music theory's Adorno further cautions that 'criticism which is of any value is founded in analysis; to the extent that this is not the case, criticism remains stuck with disconnected impressions, and thus, if for no other reason than this, deserves to be regarded with the utmost suspicion'.[63] Vande Moortele makes a convincing and thoughtful case for reconnecting the 'humanistic sorts of truth'[64] that inhere in the writings of musicology's Adorno with the musical analysis that music theory's Adorno insists is an 'essential component of the cultural interpretation of music'.[65]

Whereas Julian Johnson posits that 'there is no "Adornian" analytical technique', there are, as Vande Moortele suggests, many aspects of Adorno's 'material theory of form' (*material Formenlehre*) that resonate with central concerns of the modern theory of formal functions.[66] The term '*material Formenlehre*' is intricately linked to Adorno's interpretation of Mahler, appearing for the first time in his Mahler book.[67] As Vande Moortele further asserts, Adorno promotes the interconnectedness of 'old' formal functions (traditional categories such as 'statement', 'continuation', 'contrast', 'dissolution', 'succession', 'elaboration', 'return', and 'modified return') with 'new' ones he associates with Mahler: Mahlerian categories such as '*Suspension, Durchbruch* (breakthrough) and its opposite *Weltlauf* (course of the world) and *Erfüllung* (fulfilment) along with its opposites *Zusammenbruch* (collapse) or *Katastrophe*'.[68] The philosopher made a point of emphasizing the ancestry of these terms in 'the formal vocabulary of classical and romantic music', and of highlighting their 'fundamental compatibility' with that vocabulary and repertoire. What the traditional and Mahlerian categories of form have in

---

[62] Theodor W. Adorno, 'Zum Problem der musikalischen Analyse', *Frankfurter Adorno-Blätter* 7 (2001): 73–90, translated by Max Paddison as ' On the Problem of Musical Analysis', *Music Analysis* 1 (1982): 169–87 (176).

[63] Adorno, 'On the Problem of Musical Analysis', 176.

[64] Subotnik, 'The Role of Ideology in the Study of Western Music', 9.

[65] Vande Moortele, 'The Philosopher as Theorist', 413.

[66] Julian Johnson, 'Analysis in Adorno's Aesthetics of Music', *Music Analysis* 14 (1995), 295–313 (300); Vande Moortele, 'The Philosopher as Theorist', 417 and 426.

[67] Adorno, *Mahler: A Musical Physiognomy*, 44.

[68] Vande Moortele, 'The Philosopher as Theorist', 417–18.

common, according to Adorno, 'is that both can be understood as functions, that is to say, in terms of the work that individual formal units do in relation to the form as a whole'.[69]

The analytical vignettes that follow, therefore, proceed from an awareness that Adorno showed a great appreciation for formal analysis – even if he did not actively practise it in his writings – and that he established connections between the treatment of form and social readings of music. For the social aspect of music, as Adorno understands it, resides in its generic form.

## 5.3  Three Analytical Vignettes

### 5.3.1  Sonata for Violin and Piano in G Major, Op. 78

The final movement of Brahms's Sonata for Violin and Piano in G Major, Op. 78, is a rondo. Anthony Newcomb describes this as 'the form of the conventional happy ending finale',[70] but Brahms's treatment of tonality and formal functions challenges such an interpretation of this form. Although its generic title declares this first Sonata for Violin and Piano to be in G major, too many instances of minor and diminished modalities intruding into the tonal space seem to pull the expressive trajectory of the sonata away from what the title explicitly stipulates. Indeed, the whole sonata seems poised to shift from tonic major to tonic minor as it unfolds.[71]

Even though the finale eventually re-establishes the major mode in reverse, first through E♭ major, before arriving at G major, it is continually thwarted in doing so (Table 5.2). With the music hovering on the dominant and lacking tonic support as the finale begins, the opening of this rondo form is a musical evocation of yearning, one that is achingly recalled in each refrain of this A–B–A–C–A form. The quotation from 'Regenlied', Op. 59 No. 3, that lies behind the whole piece, saturating the previous two movements and underpinning the entire finale, has an important dotted

---

[69] Vande Moortele, 'The Philosopher as Theorist', 419. See Adorno, *Mahler: A Musical Physiognomy*, 47.

[70] Newcomb, 'Narrative Archetypes and Mahler's Ninth Symphony', 126.

[71] For a more detailed reading of this entire sonata, see Dillon Parmer and Nicole Grimes, '"Come Rise to Higher Spheres!" Tradition Transcended in Brahms Violin Sonata No. 1 in G Major, Op. 78', *Ad Parnassum: A Journal of Eighteenth- and Nineteenth-Century Instrumental Music* 6/11 (April 2009): 129–52.

**Table 5.2** Formal outline of Brahms, Sonata for Violin and Piano No. 1 in G Major, Op. 78 IV. Allegro molto moderato, Rondo form

| Bars | 1–9 | 10–22.1 | 22–29 | 29–37.1 | 37–41.1 | 41–45.1 | 45–52.3 | 53–60 | 61–69 | 70–82.1 | 82–85 | 85–113.1 | 113–123 | 124–139 | 140–159.1 | 159–164 |
|---|---|---|---|---|---|---|---|---|---|---|---|---|---|---|---|---|
| Large-scale function | Refrain 1 | | | Episode 1 | | | | | Refrain 2 | | | Episode 2 | | Refrain 3 | | |
| Interthematic function | A | | | B | | | | | A | | | C | | A | | |
| Thematic material | A1 | A2 | TR (A2-based) | B1 | B2 | B1 | B2 | RT (A1-based) | A1 | A2 | TR (C1-based) | C1 | RT (A1 & A2-based) | A1 & A2 | | |
| Framing function | | | | | | | | | | | | | | | | Coda |
| Tonal plot | G minor | | | D minor | | | | | G minor | | | E♭ major | | G minor | → G major | G major |
| Structural cadence | → i:HC | ⇒ i: PAC | | ⇒ v: PAC | | | ⇒ v:PAC | | → i:HC | ⇒ i: PAC | ⇒ VI:PAC | ⇒ VI: PAC | | | ⇒ I:PAC | ⇒ I: PAC |
| Poetic allusion | 'Regenlied' | | | | | | | | | | Adagio | | | | | |

**Example 5.1** Brahms, Sonata for Violin and Piano No. 1 in G Major, Op. 78, I, bars 84–5

rhythm. The literary subject for the song – a nostalgic yearning for lost youth – provides a context for clarifying the expressive narrative of the sonata as a whole. The relationship that emerges between the movements of this sonata is bound up with theme, motif, and formal plot. The closing theme from the first movement, for instance, reappears in the next, expressively transformed into a funeral march.

This very theme is later conjured up in the finale in the transition from the second refrain to the second episode at bar 84 (Example 5.1). The arrival at the submediant of E♭ major, therefore, coincides with a recollection of the second movement Adagio and its portents of fate.[72] The music in the third movement does eventually shift to its apparent goal of the tonic major at bar 140, yet it is not until bar 159, six bars before the conclusion of the entire work, that tonal resolution is offered with a perfect authentic cadence in G major. The goal has been reached but, arriving in the coda, it is by definition post-structural, an afterthought that follows the formal conclusion of the work. For a finale that employs the minor-to-major progression, the character of this ending is far from jubilant or affirmative.

## 5.3.2 Sonata for Violin and Piano No. 2 in A Major, Op. 100

The finale of the Sonata for Violin and Piano No. 2 in A Major, Op. 100, widely celebrated for the 'lyrical' quality in Brahms's music that Adorno mentions in the Beethoven book, at first seems to be a less likely candidate for inclusion in a list of works that forego 'happy

---

[72] I recall here the suggestion made in Chapter 1 that E♭ major is a tonality to which Brahms repeatedly turned in works associated with loss and bereavement, with each of these works being decidedly wistful and melancholic in nature.

endings'. However, the Lieder intimately related to this sonata are bound up with memories and a sense of personal reckoning. The songs explicitly connected to this third movement are both from the *Fünf Lieder*, Op. 105,[73] composed during the chamber music summer at Thun. 'Immer leiser wird mein Schlummer' is concerned with the notion of a farewell to this world and its attendant grief. The poem 'Auf dem Kirchhofe' by Detlef von Liliencron is set in an abandoned graveyard 'blown by storm and heavy with rain'. Here, the protagonist explores head-on the issue of an afterlife, contemplating the metaphor found in the opposition between the terms 'gewesen' (departed) and 'genesen' (healed). As Eric Sams observes, 'no song ever came closer to the restrained, almost rationalist, melancholy of the *German Requiem*'.[74] The two poems run as follows:

### Immer leiser wird mein Schlummer

Immer leiser wird mein Schlummer,
Nur wie Schleier liegt mein Kummer
Zitternd über mir.
Oft im Traume hör' ich dich
Rufen drauß vor meiner Tür:
Niemand wacht und öffnet dir,
Ich erwach' und weine bitterlich.

Ja, ich werde sterben müssen,
Eine Andre wirst du küssen,
Wenn ich bleich und kalt.
Eh' die Maienlüfte wehn
Eh' die Drossel singt im Wald:
Willst du einmal noch mich
    sehn,
Komm, o komme bald!

Ever softer grows my slumber
Only like a veil lies my sorrow
Trembling over me.
In my dreams I often hear you
Calling outside my door,
No one wakes and lets you in
I awake and weep bitterly.

Yes, I shall have to die,
You will kiss another,
When I am pale and cold.
Ere the May breezes blow,
Ere the thrush sings in the
    wood:
Will you see me yet once more,
Come, oh come soon![75]

---

[73] Brahms, *Fünf Lieder für eine tiefere Singstimme mit Begleitung des Pianoforte* (1888).

[74] Eric Sams, *The Songs of Johannes Brahms* (New Haven, CT and London: Yale University Press, 2000), 304.

[75] This translation is taken from Yonatan Malin, 'Metric Displacement Dissonance and Romantic Longing in the German Lied', *Music Analysis* 25/3 (2006): 251–88 (268).

**Auf dem Kirchhofe**

| | |
|---|---|
| Der Tag ging regenschwer und sturmbewegt, | The day passed heavy with rain and blown by storm |
| Ich war an manch [vergessenem] Grab gewesen, | I had stood by many a forgotten grave, |
| Verwittert Stein und Kreuz, die Kränze alt, | Where stone and cross were weather-beaten, |
| Die Namen überwachsen, kaum zu lesen. | The names overgrown and hardly readable. |
| | |
| Der Tag ging sturmbewegt und regenschwer, | The day passed blown by storm and heavy with rain, |
| Auf allen Gräbern fror das Wort: Gewesen. | On all the graves froze the word: Departed. |
| Wie sturmestot die Särge schlummerten, | How still amid the storm the coffins slumbered. |
| Auf allen Gräbern taute still: Genesen. | On all the graves the word silently thawed into: Healed.[76] |

The narrative context of the poetry is interwoven into the musical fabric of this sonata form in a wonderfully apt manner. The rising thirds heard in bars 8, 10, 12, and 15–20, as numerous commentators since Kalbeck have noted, recall 'Immer leiser', so that, with the greatest poetic resonance, each return of the primary material beckons a renewed farewell (Table 5.3). With the primary zone fashioned as a rounded binary, the thematic material for P2 at bar 12 emerges from melody of the cadential gesture at the end of P1, just as the thematic material for P1 can be understood retrospectively to emerge from the rising thirds that end P2. From the outset of the movement, therefore, there is a preoccupation with that which emerges at the end of a process. The ascending diminished seventh arpeggios that initiate the secondary zone at bar 31 have a transitional quality not typical of a secondary theme. They recall the well-known trope of darkness to light of 'Auf dem Kirchhof', miniature versions of an *ad astra* plot archetype contained within a larger structure that vexes precisely that broader expressive trajectory.

The formal features of the development section further resonate with the narrative context that emerges from the relationship with these songs. The pre-core at bar 63 returns to the P1 material that recalls 'immer leiser'. Brahms here gives the impression of a rondo form. The core of the

---

[76] This translation is taken from Eric Sams, *The Songs of Johannes Brahms*, 304.

**Table 5.3** Formal outline of Brahms, Sonata for Violin and Piano No. 2 in A Major, Op. 100 III: Allegretto grazioso (quasi Andante)

| Bars | 1–12 | 12–19 | 20–31.1 | 31–59.1 | 59–62 | 63–74.1 | 74–89 | 90–112.1 | 112–123.1 | 123–136 | 137–147 | 146–158 |
|---|---|---|---|---|---|---|---|---|---|---|---|---|
| Large-scale function | Exposition | | | | | Development | | | Recapitulation | | | |
| Interthematic function | P | | | S | | Pre-core | Core | RT | P | S | | |
| Thematic material | P1 | P2 | P1 | TR-like | Post-cadential | P1 | P2 + extension | New lyrical theme | P1 | TR-like | P1 | |
| Framing function | | | | | | | | | | | Coda 1 | Coda 2 |
| Tonal plot | A major | | | Diminished 7th → E major | | A major | A major →V/ F♯ minor | On F♯ minor | On D major | On D minor | Tonic support delayed | |
| Structural cadence | I:PAC | | I:PAC | V:PAC | | I:PAC | | | | | Weak I:PAC at 141; I:PAC at 146 | I:PAC at 158 |
| Poetic allusions | 'Immer leiser wird mein Schlummer' | | | 'Auf dem Kirchhofe' | | | | | | | | |

development at bar 74 sees the tonality fall from the tonic A major down a minor third to F♯ minor, in which key a new lyrical theme emerges, one that seems to compensate for the transition-like character of the secondary zone.[77] The chain of falling thirds, a topic associated with death in Brahms's music and one more broadly considered to be a symbol of alienation and loss,[78] continues to D major at bar 112 at the onset of a typically Brahmsian smudged recapitulation on the subdominant. This truncated recapitulation sees the return in the primary zone only of the P1 material, with its evocative farewell. The diminished seventh theme, redolent of a sorrow-to-comfort progression, launches a move from the end of the secondary zone now in D minor to a coda rotation, but without having had an ESC. The P1 theme at bar 137 is heard over a dominant 6–4, the lack of tonic support once again heightening the intensity of the spiritual journey. Following a weak perfect authentic cadence at bar 141, a I:PAC is heard at bar 146. The transcendent A major melody voices the expressive apotheosis of the work, as one last I: PAC at the obligatory register closes the piece. Here again Brahms's spiritual struggle extends right to the end of the piece, the tonal resolution having the hallmarks of an afterthought that follows the conclusion of the sonata space proper.

### 5.3.3   Piano Trio No. 3 in C Minor, Op. 101

The Piano Trio in C Minor, the only ostensibly minor mode work and the only sonata-form movement on Adorno's list of ideal finales, epitomizes the 'art of economical fragmentation' that he extolled in his 1934 essay on Brahms and exemplifies the 'specific developmental technique' that he considered Brahms to have 'further constructed and increased' from the Beethovenian model.[79] Many musical commentators have noted an 'impression of concision' in Op. 101 which, as Ryan McClelland observes, 'is enhanced by the complete absence of exact repetition in any of the four movements, the placement of each [. . .] in either C minor or C major, and the work's motivic economy' (Table 5.4). [80]

---

[77]  Brahms's treatment of form in this movement is redolent of Mozart's treatment of form in the first movement of the 'Hunt' Quartet, K458, which also elicits a rounded binary primary zone and a new lyrical theme in the development section.

[78]  See Newcomb, 'Narrative Archetypes and Mahler's Ninth Symphony', 122.

[79]  See the Appendix.

[80]  Ryan McClelland, 'Metric Dissonance in Brahms's Piano Trio in C Minor, Op. 101', *Intégral* 20 (2006): 1–42 (2).

**Table 5.4** Formal outline of Brahms, Piano Trio No. 3 in C Minor, Op. 101/IV

| Bars | 1–12 | 12–31.1 | 31–59.1 | 59–62 | 63–74.1 | 74–89 | 90–112.1 | 112–123.1 | 123–136 | 137–147 | 146–158 |
|---|---|---|---|---|---|---|---|---|---|---|---|
| Large-scale function | Refrain 1 | | Episode 1 | | Refrain 2 | | Episode 2 | | | Refrain 3 | |
| Interthematic function | A | | B | | A | | C | | | A rhetoric | A |
| Thematic material | A1 | TR | B1 | RT | A1 | TR | C1 | A1 → TR | B1 | A1 → TR | A1 |
| Framing function | | | | | | | | | | | Coda |
| Tonal plot | A major → C♯ minor | A major | A major → E major → | | A major | A major → F♯ minor | F♯ minor | On D major | D minor | On A major (No tonic support) | A major |
| Structural cadence | ⇒ I:PAC | | ⇒ V:PAC | | ⇒ I:PAC | → III:HC | | | | ⇒ I:PAC at 147 | → I:PAC |
| Poetic allusions | | 'Immer leiser' | 'Auf dem Kirchhofe' | | | | | | | | |

Peter Smith also notes as significant the fact that 'both within and across movements [in Op. 101], Brahms allows C major itself to stand in opposition to C minor', pointing to the 'potential for solace in the real world of the home tonic'.[81] Although, as McClelland notes, 'the third movement functions expressively as a release after the shadowy second movement and a calm before the unsettled finale', it nonetheless 'sustains the [. . .] thread of metric complexity'[82] that runs throughout this composition. The finale, then, if it is to be understood as the expressive culmination of the Trio, perpetuates 'the varying stages of conflict and resolution' from earlier movements.[83] McClelland lucidly demonstrates how this is the case by relating metric dissonance to formal design with particular reference to the interrelatedness of metric processes across the construction of the entire work.

I further suggest that, as in Op. 78, the pronounced lack of resolution in this 'grimly energetic finale', as Tovey would have it,[84] is again intensified by Brahms's treatment of form. We can develop Adorno's aphoristic thought on (the failure of) this finale by adopting a view of sonata form that translates the *Formenlehre* sonata structure into a narrative plot archetype modelled on the work of James Hepokoski and Warren Darcy.[85] Here I use the following abbreviations for the sonata's cadential and interthematic functions: A (first subject/first-subject group); B (second-subject group); TR (transition); EEC (essential expositional closure); ESC (essential sonata closure): PAC (perfect authentic cadence); IAC (imperfect authentic cadence); MC (medial caesura).[86]

The elements of continuous exposition in this movement are even more pronounced than McClelland suggests. The tonality is never clearly established within the first-subject group, with C minor 'acting more as a tonic to be yearned for, rather than heard', to borrow a phrase

---

[81] Peter Smith, *Expressive Forms in Brahms's Instrumental Music: Structure and Meaning in His Werther Quartet* (Bloomington, IN: Indiana University Press, 2005), 252.

[82] McClelland, 'Metric Dissonance in Brahms's Piano Trio in C Minor, Op. 101', 38.

[83] McClelland, 'Metric Dissonance in Brahms's Piano Trio in C Minor, Op. 101', 3.

[84] Donald Francis Tovey, 'Brahms's Chamber Music', in *Essays and Lectures on Music* (Oxford: Oxford University Press, 1949), 220–71 (263).

[85] James Hepokoski and Warren Darcy, *Elements of Sonata Theory* (Oxford: Oxford University Press, 2006).

[86] For a clear explanation of the EEC (essential expositional closure) and ESC (essential structural closure), see James Hepokoski, 'Back and Forth from *Egmont*: Beethoven, Mozart, and the Non-Resolving Recapitulation', *19th-Century Music* 25/2–3 (2002): 127–54 (128–36). On the MC (medial caesura), see Hepokoski, 'The Medial Caesura and Its Role in the Eighteenth-Century Sonata Exposition', *Music Theory Spectrum* 19/2 (1997): 115–54. I use the cadential designations PAC and IAC after William Caplin, *Classical Form: A Theory of Formal Functions for the Instrumental Music of Haydn, Mozart, and Beethoven* (Oxford: Oxford University Press, 2000).

from Harper-Scott.[87] An absence of clear demarcation of formal functions sees the first-subject group elide with the transition. Following a medial caesura at bar 34, we enter the second-subject space. In his article 'Beyond the Sonata Principle', Hepokoski argues that second-subject material is 'the most generically critical' of the exposition.[88] Its function is to establish cadential confirmation in the secondary key by securing the cadence referred to as the EEC. Sonata Theory, as Seth Monahan further clarifies, 'regards the eighteenth-century exposition as having both determinative and referential functions. It is determinative in that it proposes how the recapitulation is likely to be effected.'[89] The failure of the EEC tends to have ramifications across the entire movement for it signals the potential failure of the ESC (the corresponding cadence in the recapitulation that secures the second-subject material in the 'home' key) and, therefore, indicates the failure of the sonata as a whole.

As we have seen in the compositions examined in earlier chapters, Brahms tends to use the rhetoric and gesture of classical form to critique that tradition and to imbue it with his own Brahmsian style, an integral part of the historically conscious nature of his music that has been widely commented upon.[90] Brinkmann considers this facet of Brahms's œuvre in relation to Harold Bloom's concept of the anxiety of influence, whereby a composer critiques an earlier model. In the C Minor Piano Trio, Brahms's critique is most clearly evident in the second-subject space. Rather than the expected EEC, the cadence marking the end of the second-subject group – which has played out a tonal conflict between the dominant G minor and its mediant, B♭ major – is an imperfect authentic cadence in the dominant at bar 66, the third scale degree in the violin at this point instilling the music with a sense of restlessness. Although Brahms presents the rhetoric of a closing section at bar 66, the absence of a satisfactory cadence means that we are still in the second-subject space (Example 5.2).[91]

Despite its closing-section rhetoric, we might read the material in bars 66–84 as a continuation of the second-subject group and therefore expect

---

[87] Harper-Scott, *Edward Elgar, Modernist*, 68.

[88] Hepokoski, 'Beyond the Sonata Principle', *Journal of the American Musicological Society* 55/1 (Spring 2002): 91–154 (134).

[89] Seth Monahan, '"Inescapable" Coherence and the Failure of the Novel-Symphony in the Finale of Mahler's Sixth', *19th-Century Music* 31/1 (2007): 53–95 (63).

[90] See, for instance, Mark Burford, '"The Real Idealism of History": Historical Consciousness, Commemoration, and Johannes Brahms's "Years of Study"', unpublished PhD dissertation, Columbia University (2005); and Peter J. Burkholder, 'Brahms and Twentieth-Century Classical Music', *19th-Century Music* 8/1 (1984): 75–83.

[91] Again, see Hepokoski and Darcy, *Elements of Sonata Theory*, 117.

**Example 5.2** Brahms, Piano Trio No. 3 in C Minor, Op. 101, IV, bars 65–6

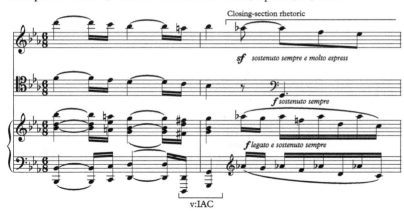

a deferred EEC at the end of this section. Yet, the first perfect authentic cadence heard in this movement is delayed across the bar line from bar 83 to 84 and is therefore elided with the development. This belated cadence creates the effect of carrying forward unresolved material as we are propelled into the development section. More fundamentally, the absence of a satisfactory cadence in the second-subject space indicates the 'failure' of the sonata form in this movement.[92] The development section, for its part, also reneges on its cadential promise. Although a perfect authentic cadence is sounded in the tonic at bar 120, its impact is not only diminished, but it is broken by the 'musical fabric' being 'severed', as McClelland evocatively puts it, by the silence that follows the expectant dominant (Example 5.3).[93]

This moment of severing marks what ought to be the moment of return, a critical point in sonata form from both theoretical and metaphysical points of view. Webster asserts that the simultaneous return of the key and the main theme in sonata form, the 'double return', as he calls it, is 'the central aesthetic event of the entire movement'. 'Without this return', Webster continues, 'the development has no point'.[94] Adorno is of a similar mind, arguing that the 'recapitulation was the crux of sonata form'.[95] But Adorno goes a step further than Webster, attributing a metaphysical significance to this point of return:

---

[92]  Hepokoski and Darcy make a fundamental distinction between sonata and non-sonata spaces. See Hepokoski and Darcy, *Elements of Sonata Theory*, 281ff.

[93]  McClelland, 'Metric Dissonance in Brahms's Piano Trio in C Minor, Op. 101', 34.

[94]  James Webster, 'Sonata Form', in *The New Grove Dictionary of Music and Musicians* (London: Macmillan, 1980), 497–8.

[95]  Further discussed in Steven Vande Moortele, *Two-Dimensional Sonata Form: Form and Cycle in Single-Movement Instrumental Works by Liszt, Strauss, Schoenberg, and Zemlinsky* (Leuven: Leuven University Press, 2009), 54.

**Example 5.3** Brahms, Piano Trio No. 3 in C Minor, Op. 101, IV, bars 117–24

Beethoven mastered [the recapitulation] by means of a tour de force that became a rule with him: at the fertile moment at the beginning of the recapitulation he presents the result of the dynamic, the evolution as the affirmation and justification of what has been, what was there in any case. That is his complicity with the guilt of the great idealistic systems, with the dialectician Hegel, for whom in the end the essential character of negations, and so of becoming, amounted to a theodicy of being.[96]

We recall, however, that because of Brahms's ongoing manipulative treatment of form and tonality, which continuously defers and destabilizes cadential structures, this recapitulation cannot demonstrate 'the theoretical affirmation and justification of what has been', for these events, although hinted at, never actually occurred in the exposition. To put that another way,

[96] Adorno, *Mahler: A Musical Physiognomy*, 94.

the 'structure of promise' (EEC) – which is a condition of the 'structure of accomplishment' (ESC) – was never actually established. Brahms, therefore, utterly frustrates the generic expectations outlined by Adorno in his dialectical account of Beethoven.[97] The wholeness of this sonata was never posited at its opening, and it therefore should not be hoped for at its close.

The point of recapitulation at bar 124 again vexes our expectation of a 'double return'. Once again, we are thrust forward without formal delineation from bar 124 to the second-subject space. The shadow cast by the failure of the EEC in the exposition here results in the absence of an ESC in the recapitulation, with the lack of the tonic in the upper voice of the cadence at bar 176. The fifth scale degree in the violin instead sounds forth an imperfect authentic cadence at this crucial point in the sonata form, thereby confirming the 'failure' of this sonata movement as a whole. The second subject's motivic material once more poses as that of a closing section, before the music shifts to the major modality as we enter the realm of the coda. Yet the promise of the eventual solace of C major even here is threatened, as this resolution is once again delayed across the bar line from 189 to 190, as it was in the exposition, thereby 'ending the recapitulation on a G-major question mark', as Smith astutely puts it, 'rather than a C-minor period' (Example 5.4).[98]

The music at this point persists in its unfulfilled state with an extended dominant preparation. Tonic-cadential closure is deferred until as late as bar 228 in the second coda, when Brahms finally delivers an emphatic tonal resolution in C major. The structural-rhetorical crisis of this Piano Trio, therefore, is even more pronounced than that in the 'Regenlied' Sonata. The term 'sonata failure', as Hepokoski uses it, 'is not intended as a criticism; rather it is a way of describing a crucial element of what appears to be the expressive or narrative intentions of the composer – of the

---

[97] Hepokoski, 'Back and Forth from *Egmont*'" 129. This sonata qualifies for Hepokoski's second category of 'failed' recapitulations, 'suppression of a perfect authentic cadence within secondary-theme space, or its equivalent, at the end of the exposition and recapulation'. See Hepokoski, 'Back and Forth from *Egmont*', 152. The blurring of articulation at the beginning of the recapitulation such as we witness in this movement is certainly not unusual for Brahms's recapitulatory techniques, as Peter H. Smith argues. In place of the double return, 'Brahms favors an extended and formally ambiguous overlap that continues the motivic and harmonic-contrapuntal process of the retransition, while simultaneously introducing elements of a gradually emerging, large-scale restatement'. Peter H. Smith, 'Formal Ambiguity and Large-Scale Tonal Structure in Brahms's Sonata-Form Recapitulations', unpublished PhD dissertation, Yale University (1992), 1–2. In this instance, as we will see, however, the ambiguity extends well into the recapitulation. It is unusual for him to extend this blurring of functions right to the end of the recapitulation.

[98] Smith, *Expressive Forms*, 254.

Example 5.4  Brahms, Piano Trio No. 3 in C Minor, Op. 101, IV, bars 188–90

I:PAC resolution to C major delayed across the barline

musical "story" that is unfolded in, around, and through the sonata'.[99] Any sense of resolution in this sonata form lies 'beyond rhetorical sonata space' in the 'functionally enhanced coda'.[100] This falls outside sonata space and therefore consigns this work, from a purely theoretical perspective, to the status of a bleak failure. All three of the works on Adorno's list of ideal finales, therefore, fail to reach an affirmative ending.

## 5.4   Brahms and the Aesthetics of Failure

In positioning Brahms's finales in relation to Mahler in the *Beethoven* book, Adorno invites an exploration of his writings on Mahler as they relate to Brahms and the aesthetic categories of endings and artistic failures. In contrast to 'the failure of the concluding movements of Mahler's Fifth and Seventh Symphonies',[101] Adorno considers the Finale of the Sixth to be preeminent in Mahler's oeuvre, because 'more monumentally composed than all the rest, it shatters the spell of affirmative illusion'.[102] The trouble with 'the hackneyed happy endings of earlier symphonies' and of Mahler's Fifth and Seventh, in Adorno's system, is that 'they cannot deliver what they postulate'. In this respect, he admonishes Mahler for making 'music as if joy were already in the world'. Mahler's 'successful final

---

[99]  Hepokoski, 'Elgar', in *The Nineteenth-Century Symphony*, ed. D. Kern-Holoman (New York, NY and London: Schirmer, 1997), 342, n. 11.

[100]  Hepokoski discusses the eventual resolution of non-resolving sonatas, usually in the coda, in Hepokoski, 'Back and Forth from *Egmont*', here at 134.

[101]  Adorno, *Beethoven*, 74.    [102]  Adorno, *Mahler: A Musical Physiognomy*, 135.

movements', he suggests, 'are those that ignore the radiant path *ad astra*'. The Sixth is extolled because it 'heightens its first movement and negates it', whereas the Ninth Symphony and *Das Lied von der Erde* look 'questioningly into uncertainty'.[103]

Although Adorno speaks of endings in music, art, philosophy, and politics, 'they are negative endings brought about through catastrophic decay, degeneration, and defeat'.[104] Endings for Adorno, as Lydia Goehr observes, 'are not metaphysical triumphs over history nor achievements or completions of movement. They are metaphysical expressions of historical loss.'[105] Such expressions form an integral part of Adorno's aesthetics of failure, which is divided into two broad categories that are centred around 'authenticity' and 'resignation'.

### 5.4.1   Authentic Failure

The notion of authenticity refers to a work of art that has a reconciliation in its sights, but, because of its faithfulness to the rupture that exists between objective form and subjective content, it cannot achieve this reconciliation. This relates to Adorno's thinking on 'the character of art as appearance' in connection with nature: 'It keeps hold of the image of reconciliation without the reconciliation really being achieved'.[106]

The notion of 'authenticity' can be further understood in relation to 'a modernist, fractured relationship between the individual and the social, the internal structure of the artwork and the external conditions within which it functions'.[107] 'Authentic works', Adorno writes, 'unfold their truth content, which transcends the scope of individual consciousness, in a temporal dimension through the law of their form'.[108] This is a central aspect of Adorno's advocacy of modernist art which, as Bowie suggests, 'depends precisely on the fact that it does not pretend to achieve such reconciliation'.[109] Max Paddison elucidates the relationship between

---

[103] All excerpts in this paragraph from Adorno, *Mahler: A Musical Physiognomy*, 136–8.

[104] Lydia Goehr, '*Doppelbewegung*: The Musical Movement of Philosophy and the Philosophical Movement of Music', in *Sound Figures of Modernity: German Music and Philosophy*, ed. Jost Hermand and Gerhard Richter (Madison, WI: University of Wisconsin Press, 2006), 19–63 (38–9).

[105] *Ibid.*, 38–9.

[106] Adorno, 'Ästetik', 6885, as cited in Bowie, *Adorno and the Ends of Philosophy*, 152.

[107] Max Paddison, 'Authenticity and Failure in Adorno's Aesthetics of Music', in *Cambridge Companion to Adorno*, ed. Tom Huhn (Cambridge: Cambridge University Press, 2004), 198–221 (199).

[108] Adorno, *Prisms*, 143.       [109] Bowie, *Adorno and the Ends of Philosophy*, 152.

authenticity and failure in Adorno's aesthetics. The notion of authenticity, he writes,

> whereby a work attempts to achieve consistency of form (which implies integration) through a critical relationship to the handed-down material (material which, since the period of the late Beethoven and Berlioz has tended increasingly toward fragmentation and disintegration), leads to failure, according to Adorno – a kind of failure which is not simply the result of technical inadequacy on the part of the composer but rather comes from the impossibility of succeeding in the task to be faced, a task which must be undertaken nevertheless.[110]

In Adorno's critical system, this category of failure constitutes failure at the highest artistic level.

### 5.4.2 Inauthentic Failure

The notion of 'resignation', on the other hand, is an entirely different form of failure, one that is related to the notion of 'inauthenticity' for Adorno. This refers to a work of art that achieves reconciliation when the material has not earned it; that is, it achieves reconciliation despite the interaction of the objective form and the subjective content. Such works comprise those that 'do not internalize this fractured relationship, which are not self-reflexive, and which remain content to comply with the traditional stereotypes – what Adorno calls "resigned art"'.[111] A consideration of Adorno's criticism of Wagner further clarifies this second category of failure. The third accusation that Adorno levelled at Wagner, in Alain Badiou's reading, is that Wagner's 'basic strategy is dialectical'. Badiou zones in on what Adorno considers objectionable in this scheme:

> Differences are nothing but the means for getting to the affirmative finale. It does indeed seem as though we are immersed in differences, dissonances, but the bottom line is that it is all really about reconciliation. That is what the affirmative finale epitomizes, and dissonance is explored not from the standpoint of its future development but rather from that of its ultimate elimination, even if the latter is delayed, slowed up, or particularly convoluted.[112]

The degree to which tonal formal functions are thwarted matter less to Adorno than the fact that a particular piece of music is composed within the tonal tradition. Adorno's review of Berg's *Wozzeck* provides a useful

---

[110] Paddison, 'Authenticity and Failure in Adorno's Aesthetics of Music', 216.    [111] *Ibid.,* 199.

[112] Alain Badiou, *Five Lessons on Wagner*, trans. Susan Spitzer, with an Afterword by Slavoj Žižek (London and New York, NY: Verso, 2010), 78.

counterexample: 'The operas of Berg propose the category of subjectivity in a thoroughly dialectical way, not as some nostalgic lament for the condition of an earlier age'.[113]

The distinction between authenticity and resignation, therefore, is determined by the degree to which an artwork has earned its failure or the degree to which that failure is integral to its material which, post-Beethoven, is the result of a rupture between the traditional (objective) form and the (subjective) content. Adorno synthesizes both categories of failure in art in the Beethoven manuscript:

Art works of the highest rank are distinguished from the others not through their success – for in what have they succeeded? – but through the manner of their failure. For the problems within them, both the immanent aesthetic problems and the social ones ... are so posed that the attempt to solve them must fail, whereas the failure of lesser works is accidental, a matter of mere subjective incapacity. A work of art is great when it registers a failed attempt to reconcile objective antinomies. That is its truth and its 'success': to have come up against its own limit. In these terms, any work of art which succeeds through not reaching this limit is a failure.[114]

For Adorno, then, Brahms's music qualifies not as an authentic but rather as an inauthentic failure. Although the philosopher recognizes melancholy and nostalgia in Brahms's music, he does not accord this any historical significance. In other words, whereas he registers Brahms's loss, he declines to dignify Brahms's failure.

## 5.5   The Future of Nostalgia

Each of Adorno's chosen Brahms finales has a probing or searching quality. As we have seen, unfulfilled expectations and unresolved tensions linger in these finales, often confronting issues from earlier movements, so that each is marked by a sense of grappling. Webster has for many years been interested in the expressive nature of

---

[113] Julian Johnson, 'Berg's Operas and the Politics of Subjectivity', in *Music, Theatre, and Politics in Germany: 1848 to the Third Reich*, ed. Nikolaus Bacht (Aldershot: Ashgate, 2006), 211–33 (229).

[114] Adorno, *Beethoven*, 99–100. The final correction to Chapter 46 of Thomas Mann, *Doktor Faustus*, is also pertinent in this regard, where Adorno considered Mann 'to have made the religious element of hope too positive'. Reinhold Brinkmann relates this to Adorno's 'act of preservation (of art, of the Absolute) through uncompromising negativity'. See Brinkmann, *Late Idyll*, 223–5.

Brahms's endings.[115] He draws attention to the underlying ambivalence the composer felt toward emphatic expressions of the *ad astra* archetype. From the *Alto Rhapsody* onward, Webster argues, 'Brahms abjured heaven-storming instrumental endings, and he never returned to them'.[116] His later uses of the minor-to-major progression achieve their outcome 'with a sense neither of undue strain nor of unearned triumph'.[117] More modest versions of this plot archetype, such as we find in Opp. 78, 100, and 101, were more in keeping with what Webster refers to as a 'heightened consciousness of one's humanity'.[118]

As Webster and others have noted, Brahms had long been preoccupied with the 'problem of how to end' a composition.[119] Christopher Reynolds, for instance, explores how the composer struggled with the question of 'how to write a satisfactory symphonic finale' for the work that was to become the Piano Concerto No. 1 in D Minor, Op. 15.[120] With regard to that special category of Brahms's works with a trajectory from C minor to C major, Webster notes that three of these – the String Quartet, Op. 51 No. 1, the Piano Quartet, Op. 60, and the Piano Trio, Op. 101 (to which we will return) – despite being finished in the first half of the 1870s had originated long before then.[121] This adds a further dimension to their sense of carrying forward unresolved issues.

This sense of resignation that is so integral to much of Brahms, and which is bound up with elements of recollection and nostalgia, is redolent of what Adorno describes as music's return to the land of childhood. We might well think of this in terms of a 'spiritual journey' in Brahms's music identified by Marjorie Hirsch whereby 'childhood's simplicity,

---

[115] This is a topic that James Webster has contemplated for over two decades as evidenced, for instance, in 'Brahms's *Tragic Overture*: The Form of Tragedy', in Robert Pascall, ed., *Brahms: Biographical, Documentary and Analytical Studies* (Cambridge: Cambridge University Press, 1983), 115; and ' The *Alto Rhapsody*: Psychology, Intertextuality, and Brahms's Artistic Development', in *Brahms Studies*, ed. David Brodbeck (Lincoln, NE: University of Nebraska Press, 2001), III, 19–45.

[116] Webster, 'The *Alto Rhapsody*', 44. Webster points to one anomaly in the post *Alto Rhapsody* C minor repertoire, suggesting that Brahms 'nevertheless felt compelled to complete the First Symphony along Beethovenian lines', the reason for which 'we can only speculate'.

[117] Webster, 'The *Alto Rhapsody*', 44.     [118] Webster, 'Brahms's *Tragic Overture*', 115.

[119] Webster, 'The *Alto Rhapsody*', 42. See also Mitchell Morris, 'Musical Virtues', in *Beyond Structural Listening*, ed. Andrew dell'Antonio (Berkeley, CA and London: University of California Press, 2004), 44–69.

[120] Christopher Reynolds, 'A Choral Symphony by Brahms?', *19th-Century Music* 9 (1985): 3–25 (17).

[121] Webster, 'The *Alto Rhapsody*', 42.

purity, and joy are recalled but never recovered'.[122] In Brahms's music, where childhood is recalled, yet not recovered, there is a gradual realization for composer and listener alike that joy resides in that very recollection. It is perhaps for this reason that Adorno refers to Brahms's 'splendid resignation'.

Svetlana Boym makes an incisive distinction between two types of nostalgia: restorative nostalgia and reflective nostalgia, both of which provide 'ways of giving shape and meaning to longing'.[123] Restorative nostalgia emphasizes *nostos*, that is, a return home. Reflective nostalgia dwells in *algia*, that is, longing and loss. Those in the first category, she asserts, 'do not think of themselves as nostalgic; they believe that their project is about truth'. They are concerned with the reconstruction of monuments of the past. Reflective nostalgia, on the other hand, has no such restorative aims. It belongs to the realm of contemplation, lingering imaginatively 'on ruins, the patina of time and history, in the dreams of another place and another time'.[124]

Whereas Adorno had no interest in reconstructing tonality, there is a decidedly restorative mentality to the manner in which he conceives of tonal music as a dead, fossilized historical artefact. The potential for this 'beauty as the reflection of past hope' to live is confined to a particular historical age beyond which it is frozen in time.[125] His preoccupation with the late age – the *Spätstil* – in which Brahms composed lends a bittersweet irony to his reception of this composer. The metaphor that he employs to describe the sense of loss in Brahms's music – '*as if* music were returning to the land of childhood' – is paradigmatic of Boym's reflective nostalgia. It exhibits the temporal to-and-fro of an imaginative return to a lost paradise that gives rise to a beautiful future, to an envisioning of the ideal. Yet Adorno's glimpse of reflective nostalgia is trapped in the terminus of Boym's other category, restorative nostalgia. Due to what Leppert describes as 'the regret and sorrow inhabiting Adorno's elegy', despite finding the perfect metaphor to describe Brahms's elegiac music, he could not permit himself the joy of participating in the spiritual journey of recollection.

---

[122] Hirsch, *Romantic Lieder and the Search for Lost Paradise*, 150. Yet, 'despite the despondency of the speaker in each poem', she writes, referring to Brahms's *Kunst-Kinderlieder* and the 'Heimweh' Lieder, 'the musical settings together convey a positive message'. Here at 148.

[123] Boym, *The Future of Nostalgia* (New York, NY: Perseus, 2001), 41.    [124] *Ibid.*, 41.

[125] Adorno, *Mahler: A Musical Physiognomy*, 154.

# Epilogue

This book has been concerned with two interrelated themes as they pertain to Brahms. The first is the manner in which the composer persistently addressed issues concerning the human condition in his fate-related works. The second is the question of how Brahms's music is intricately interwoven in the fabric of musical modernism. Each of the Brahms compositions explored in the preceding chapters espouses the poetics of loss in German culture. On each occasion, the expression of this loss gives rise to an artwork that provides a source of solace through spiritual edification. The two themes of the book, therefore, intersect in the realm of the human, that is both the sense of humanity and the aesthetic humanism which Brahms's elegiac output embraces.

It is only with the fullness of time that the splendid richness of Brahms's engagement with culture in his musical output and the multivalent nature of his compositions have come to be fully appreciated. A case in point is Adorno's reception of Brahms. The synthesis of compositional and social (read objective and subjective) conditions in which Brahms's compositions were created might well have rewarded deeper exploration on Adorno's part. For instance, he might have further explored the aesthetic affinities between Brahms and Mahler whereby so much of their music is coded by the hermeneutic content of their songs, as we discovered in Chapter 5 in relation to the 'Regenlied' Sonata and the Sonatas for Violin and Piano in A Major. Further examples include Brahms's proposed orchestral composition on the themes of the *Vier ernste Gesänge* explored in Chapter 4. The Andante of the Piano Concerto No. 2 in B♭ Major, Op. 83, is also pertinent here. Its first theme might be understood to relate to the opening of 'Immer leiser wird mein Schlummer', Op. 105 No. 2, and the *Più Adagio* reuses the second part of 'Todessehnen', Op. 86 No. 6.[1] These Lied-related compositions all fit into the late nineteenth-century category of works that, as Julian Horton puts it, 'impel a threefold model of comprehension, as

---

[1] On the relationship between 'Todessehnen' and the Second Piano Concerto, see Julian Horton, *Brahms's Piano Concerto No. 2, Op. 83* (Leuven: Peeters, 2017), 310–13.

instrumental forms, textual ciphers, and synthetic artworks ramifying form and textual meaning'.[2]

An understanding of how Brahms's Elegies absorb the German intellectual tradition offers renewed and enriched insight into artworks of *fin-de-siècle* Vienna. One such work is the *Brahmsphantasie (Brahms Fantasy)*, an exquisitely beautiful multimedia bound volume that Brahms's friend the artist Max Klinger (1857–1920) presented to him on 1 January 1894. It contains original etchings, engravings, and lithographs by Klinger interspersed amongst which are six musical scores by Brahms, five Lieder with the shared themes of love and loss, and the piano vocal score for *Schicksalslied*, Op. 54.[3] This extended meditation on human fate, the divine, love, and the nature of memory realizes the ideal unity of literature, the visual arts, and music that is integral to Brahms's aesthetic outlook, as evidenced in compositions such as *Nänie* and *Gesang der Parzen*. Klinger explained to Brahms that his basic idea for the song cycle found within the *Brahmsphantasie* was to capture something of how a 'tender, too tender reflection on what is past and what is lost' is overcome 'through powerful, energetic pulling together of oneself', a description that might well serve as an account of the aesthetic sensibility that pervades Brahms's Elegies.[4]

Folded into the embrace of Klinger's extraordinary work are a number of elements that are directly related to Brahms's elegiac output, the magnificence of his multimedia approach paying homage to the staggering degree of learning and intertextuality that is contained within Brahms's compositions. These include an image of Homer, a reading of the Prometheus myth, and the inclusion of Hölderlin's poem 'Schicksalslied', the very poem Brahms had set in his composition of the same name. In considering Klinger's remarkable visual composition, Kevin Karnes suggests that the

---

[2] Horton, *Brahms's Piano Concerto No. 2, Op. 83*, 309.

[3] Numerous scholars have given sustained attention to Klinger's *Brahmsphantasie*. See, for instance, Thomas K. Nelson, 'Klinger's Brahmsphantasie and the Cultural Politics of Absolute Music', *Art History* (1996): 26–43; Jan Brachmann, *'Ins Ungewisse hinauf': Johannes Brahms und Max Klinger im Zwiespalt von Kunst und Kommunikation* (Kassel: Bärenreiter, 1999); Walter Frisch, *German Modernism: Music and the Arts* (Berkeley, CA and London: University of California Press, 2005), 88–106; Kevin C. Karnes, *A Kingdom Not of This World: Wagner, the Arts, & Utopian Visions in Fin-de-Siècle Vienna* (Oxford: Oxford University Press, 2013), 37–56; and Yonatan Malin, '"Alte Liebe" and the Birds of Spring: Text, Music, and Image in Max Klinger's *Brahms Fantasy*', in *Expressive Intersections in Brahms: Essays in Analysis and Meaning*, ed. Heather Platt and Peter H. Smith (Bloomington, IN: Indiana University Press, 2012), 53–79. The Lieder Klinger included in the *Brahmsphantasie* are 'Alte Liebe', Op. 72 No. 1, 'Sehnsucht', Op. 49 No. 3, 'Am Sonntag Morgen', Op. 49 No. 1, 'Feldeinsamkeit', Op. 85 No. 2, and 'Kein Haus, keine Heimat', Op. 94 No. 5.

[4] Frisch, *German Modernism*, 99.

artist might have heard Brahms's *Schicksalslied* as a profound meditation on the human condition.[5] The presence of Prometheus unbound in the *Brahmsphantasie* captures the temporal nature of Brahms's *Schicksalslied* and its lengthy contemplation on the impassability of the cleft between the divine and human realms. Mirroring the structure of *Schicksalslied*, Klinger's work also espouses an aesthetic spiral.

It took literary critics more than a century to discover the structure of Hölderlin's *Hyperion*, 'since it is folded into the thematic and philosophical texture of the book'.[6] In his setting, Brahms intuited its complex poetic and philosophical meaning with an artistic sensitivity to Hölderlin that was not to be equalled until the late twentieth century.[7] What composers such as Wolfgang Rihm, Luigi Nono, and György Ligeti were undoubtedly drawn to in Hölderlin, as I argued in Chapter 1, was 'the literature of humanity'. This entails 'a belief in the possibility and significance of formation, "Bildung", which applies equally to the individual human life and to the individual work of art'.[8] By intricately interweaving compositional process in *Schisksalslied* with intellectual tradition and philosophical thought, Brahms bestowed upon posterity a musical manifestation of *Bildung* in the form of a quintessentially Brahmsian fabric. Through Brahms, Klinger then introduced the visual to this aesthetic spiral in a convergence of art forms.

Walter Frisch proposes that Klinger's *Brahmsphantasie* is 'a work of convergence'. This is not merely an instance of one art form responding to another, he avers. Rather, in 'a small but stunning moment of convergence, the artist has actually recreated in visual terms – with the "immanent" materials of his art – an essential aspect of the music'. Both Brahms and Klinger testify to such a convergence in an unusually forthright exchange between the artist and the composer, who was notoriously reticent in commenting on his artistic process. Klinger writes of 'attempting to capture moods that remain "unexpressed" in music alone, whilst Brahms notes that "all art speaks the same language"'.[9]

Klinger's idea of how one artwork can provide a completion or an extension (*Ergzänzung*) of another anticipates important aspects of late twentieth-century art and music that also pertain to Brahms. We have been

---

[5] Karnes, *A Kingdom Not of This World*, 55.    [6] Minden, *The German Bildungsroman*, 119.
[7] I refer to Hanns Eisler, *Ernste Gesänge* (1962), Heinz Holliger, *Scarandelli-Zyklus* (1978–91), Wolfgang Rihm, *Hölderlin-Fragmente* (1977), Luigi Nono, *Fragmente-Stille, an Diotima* (1979–80), György Ligeti, *Hölderlin Phantasien* (1982), Hans Werner Henze, Seventh Symphony (1983–4), and Benjamin Britten, *Hölderlin-Fragmente* (1958).
[8] Minden, *The German Bildungsroman*, 125.    [9] Frisch, *German Modernism*, 97.

concerned with the concept of aesthetic humanism, which can now be understood as a collective term for a series of artworks that manifest a sense of nostalgic teleology – that is, works that contain an element that both looks to the past and is taken up again in the future. This temporal process is closely related to the concept of *Bildung* (a spiritual journey that unfolds in time) and it resonates, reverberates, and is refracted through the music of composers from the late eighteenth century to the present, including Beethoven, Brahms, Schumann, Mahler, Rihm, Nono, and Ligeti, amongst others. Each of these chronologically disparate composers espouses the riches of an earlier (sometimes imaginary) culture by way of envisioning a more beautiful sense of the future, in at least one aspect of their output.[10] These works are characterized by a rich network of allusion and reference and a potent sense of interiority. Contributing to the increasing intensity of this nostalgic teleology is the incremental manner in which these cultural references accrue over time. This finds an artistic analogy in the paintings of Anselm Kiefer and Arnulf Rainer, whose concept of *Übermalung* literally paints over earlier, pre-existing images.[11] We can further understand this process in relation to Rihm's account of the manner in which 'music answers music'.[12] The case of his *Symphonie: Nähe fern*, a response to Brahms, will illustrate the point.[13]

In 2011, the director of the Luzerner Sinfonieorchester commissioned Rihm to write four orchestral pieces as pendants to the Brahms symphonies. Following the successive premieres of each of the four orchestral movements between June 2011 and June 2012, Rihm's *Symphonie 'Nähe fern'* was premiered in August 2012 as part of the Lucerne Festival. This five-movement

[10] I have in mind here compositions such as Beethoven, Symphony No. 9, Schumann, *Gesang der Frühe*, Mahler, Symphony No. 8, Nono, *Fragmente-Stille, an Diotima*, and Ligeti, *Lontano* and the *Horn Trio*.

[11] Laura Tunbridge discusses this concept in relation to the music of Schumann. See Laura Tunbridge, 'Deserted Chambers of the Mind (Schumann Memories)', in *Rethinking Schumann*, ed. Roe-Min Kok and Laura Tunbridge (Oxford: Oxford University Press, 2011), 395–410.

[12] Wolfgang Rihm, quotation from the composer in conversation with Tom Service, Rihm Composer in Focus Day, Wigmore Hall, London, 28 February 2015.

[13] *Symphonie 'Nähe fern'* is just one of a number of Rihm's compositions that respond directly to the music of Brahms, including the 1985 composition *Brahmsliebewalzer* (1983) which conjures up Brahms's *Sixteen Waltzes*, Op. 39, the *Ernster Gesang* (1996), which is the product of Rihm's prolonged immersion in Brahms's last published opus, the *Vier ernste Gesänge*, Op. 121 – a composition that was dedicated to Max Klinger – and *Das Lesen der Schrift* (2001/2), which comprises four pieces for orchestra intended to be incorporated between the movements of *Ein deutsches Requiem*. On Rihm's Brahms pieces, see Nicole Grimes, 'Brahms as a Vanishing Point in the Music of Wolfgang Rihm: Reflections on *Klavierstück Nr. 6*', in *Music Preferred: Essays in Musicology, Cultural History and Analysis in Honour of Harry White*, ed. Lorraine Byrne Bodley (Vienna: Holitzer, 2018), 523–49.

work comprises the four commissioned movements and an interpolated second movement, which orchestrates Rihm's 2004 setting of Goethe's poem 'Dämmerung senkte sich von oben' ('Twilight down from high has drifted', 1828). This poem sets in motion a series of responses that we may plot along a continuum from Goethe to Brahms's setting of this poem (Op. 59 No. 1, 1873), via Brahms's Four Symphonies (1871–85), through Rihm's rendering of Goethe's poem for voice and piano (2004), and finally to Rihm's 2012 symphonic work. Rihm speaks of this composition as 'shaping something of my own that took up the thread of a conversation and moved it on a stage further. So, no philology, but distant proximity – proximate distance [ferne Nähe – nähe Ferne]'.[14] *Symphonie 'Nähe fern'* might profitably be understood in relation to Husserl's late concept of 'genetic phenomenology', that is, the study of how something gains sense through time.[15]

The multifarious layers of allusion in *Symphonie 'Nähe fern'* betray a preoccupation with art and literature that Rihm shares with Brahms, evident in their diaries and notebooks containing excerpts of favourite passages, or recording their thoughts on artists and writers.[16] Both composers have a propensity toward philosophical reflection in their music, and both were largely preoccupied with the poetry of the New Humanists at the turn of the nineteenth century, that is, Goethe, Schiller, and Hölderlin. Rihm also composed a *Harzreise im Winter* in 2012 for baritone and piano as the most extended of his *Goethe Lieder*, along with an array of Lieder after Schiller and Hölderlin, the most extensive of these being the *Hölderlin-Fragmente.*[17]

---

[14] Rihm quoted in Mark Sattler, Sleeve Notes to Wolfgang Rihm. *Symphonie 'Nähe fern'.* Luzerner Sinfonieorchester & James Gaffigan. Paris: Harmonia Mundi, 2013. HMC902153.

[15] See Dermot Moran, *Husserl's Crisis of European Sciences and Transcendental Phenomenology: An Introduction* (Cambridge University Press, 2012).

[16] On Wolfgang Rihm's preoccupation with art, see Ulrich Mosch, 'Zur Rolle bildnerischer Vorstellungen im musikalischen Denken und Komponieren Wolfgang Rihms', in *Musikwissenschaft zwischen Kunst, Ästhetik und Experiment*, ed. Reinhard Kopiez (Würzburg: Königshausen & Neumann, 1998), 387–92; and Wolfgang Rihm, 'Vor Bildern', in *Intermedialität: Studien zur Wechselwirkung zwischen den Künsten*, ed. Günter Schnitzler and Edelgard Spaude (Freiburg im Bresigau: Rombach Verlag, 2004), 95–129, in which Ulrich Mosch has collated excerpts from Rihm's diaries concerning art and argues that art became more and more important for Rihm's output from 1980/1 onward. On Brahms's preoccupation with art, in addition to the preceding chapters in this book, see Reinhold Brinkmann, 'Johannes Brahms und die Maler Feuerbach, Böcklin, Klinger und Menzel', *Vom Pfeifen und von alten Dampfmaschine: Essays zur Musik von Beethoven bis Rihm* (Munich: Paul Szolnay Verlag, 2006), 108–39; and Leon Botstein, 'Brahms and Nineteenth-Century Painting', *19th-Century Music* 14/2 (Autumn 1990), 154–68.

[17] Relevant here is also the fact that Rihm has reflected in writing on the poetry of the new Humanists, most prominently in an essay that explicitly evokes Goethe's *Iphigenie*. See

On the basis of these works and his compositions that respond to Schumann and Mahler, Rihm can be identified as one of a number of composers whose music since the late twentieth century exhibits an increasing engagement with the past and an incremental intensification of nostalgic teleology as each composition accrues the cultural associations of its precursor.[18] From the perspective of the early twenty-first century, we see that the output of this generation of neo-Romantic composers is marked by increased historical reflection and a rich network of associations to the literary, philosophical, and musical output of Germany's recent past.

As was the case with Brahms's music during his lifetime and throughout the twentieth century, this nostalgic element has been met with critical and scholarly dissent, a critical stance that is bound up in no small measure with the terminology used to refer to this repertoire, namely either neo-Romantic or postmodern. Hermann Danuser, for instance, has repeatedly cast neo-Romanticism pejoratively as being anachronistic when considered in relation to the era of avant-gardism in German music, an era which relates to what Adorno referred to in *Minima Moralia* as 'the failure of culture' ('Mißlingen der Kultur').[19] Danuser's linear viewpoint acknowledges the nostalgia that is central to this repertoire but fails to recognize its nostalgic teleology. In other words, Danuser positions neo-Romanticism as looking only to the past and, at that, only to the immediate past. Such a perspective is not confined to musical commentators, moreover.[20]

Ligeti, for instance, was representing a wider point of view within the composers' community when he wrote in 1978 that 'I quite agree with the complete rejection of the last twenty years on the part of the young composers. [ . . . ] But they should do something genuinely new, instead of

Wolfgang Rihm, 'Verzweifelt human. Neue Musik und Humanismus?' in Rihm, *Offene Enden: Denkbewegung um und durch Musik*, ed. Ulrich Mosch. Munich: Hanser, 2002, 225–44.

[18] On Rihm and Schumann, see Alastair Williams, 'Swaying with Schumann: Subjectivity and Tradition in Wolfgang Rihm's "Fremde-Szenen" i–iii and Related Scores', *Music & Letters* 87/3 (2006), 379–97; and Laura Tunbridge, 'Deserted Chambers of the Mind (Schumann Memories)', *Rethinking Schumann* ed. Roe-Min Kok and Laura Tunbridge (Oxford: Oxford University Press, 2011), 395–410. On Rihm and Mahler, see Thomas Schäfer, 'anwesend/ abgekehrt: Notizen zu Wolfgang Rihm's Komponieren der 1970er Jahre mit Blick auf Gustav Mahler', in *Wolfgang Rihm*, ed. Ulrich Tadday (Munich: Richard Boorberg Verlag, 2004), 99–108.

[19] Adorno, *Negative Dialectics*, trans. E. B. Ashton (London: Routledge, 1990), 360.

[20] See Hermann Danuser, *Die Musik des 20. Jahrhunderts*. Neues Handbuch der Musikwissenschaft, Band vii. Laaber: Laaber Verlag, 1984; and Danuser, 'Postmodernes Musikdenken – Lösung oder Flucht?' In *Neue Musik im politischem Wandel*, Veröffentlichungen des Instituts für Neue Musik und Musikerziehung, ed. Hermann Danuser (Darmstadt. Schott, 1991).

returning to late-Romantic, pathos-filled music'.[21] Here we discern an echo of Adorno's categories of logic and tone as they relate to the music of Brahms as a representative of a late age, and a censure of nostalgia, pathos, and an autumnal character. Amy Bauer has underlined Ligeti's ambiguity in his attitude toward the nostalgic in music: he was at once highly critical of it, yet contrary to this critical stance, in many of his own pieces, he 'sought to evoke a vanished place or time', as Bauer elegantly frames it.[22] This is evident, for example, in the *Horn Trio*, an homage to Brahms, and the 1982 composition *Drei Phantasien nach Friedrich Hölderlin*. Ligeti's commentary on his own historically conscious output betrays an unconscious affinity with the concept of aesthetic humanism. His 1974 articles on Mahler's forms exemplify the point, for here he celebrates 'not only their sense of physical space, but [also] their sense for historical reflection'.[23] Drawing a connection with his own compositional process in *Lontano* Ligeti offers the following observation of Mahler:

We can grasp the work only within our tradition, within a certain musical education [by which he refers to Germanic music]. If one were not quite acquainted with the whole of late-Romanticism, the quality of being at a distance [. . .] would not be manifest in this work. For this reason, the piece is double-edged: it is in a sense traditional but not literally as with Stravinsky, it does not treat exact quotations from late romantic music, but certain types of later romantic music are just touched upon. [. . .] The forms can be heard from a distance and from long ago: almost, as it were, like the post horn from Mahler's Third Symphony.[24]

The nostalgic teleology that characterizes Ligeti's comment and his neo-Romantic compositions is of a piece with that of Brahms, Mahler, and Rihm, amongst others. For it is consistently coded by the quintessentially German characteristics of aesthetic humanism that have persisted in German arts and letters since the late eighteenth century. This, in turn, is intricately linked to the notion of *Bildung* and German Idealism. As Kristin Gjesdal reminds us, the 'nineteenth-century philosophy of *Bildung* is not a thing of the past, but a repertoire of philosophical tools and concepts that enables critical reflection'.[25] Brahms's modernism, I suggest, resides precisely in this philosophical sense of reflection, which places him along

---

[21] György Ligeti, *György Ligeti in Conversation with Péter Várnai, Josef Häusler, Claude Samuel, and Himself* (London: Eulenburg, 1983), 74. As cited in Amy Bauer, *Ligeti's Laments: Nostalgia, Exoticism, and the Absolute* (Aldershot: Ashgate, 2011).

[22] Bauer, *Ligeti's Laments*, 17.     [23] *Ibid.*, 104.

[24] Ligeti, *Ligeti in Conversation*, 93. As cited in Bauer, *Ligeti's Laments*, 105.

[25] Kristin Gjesdal, 'Bildung', in *The Oxford Handbook of German Philosophy in the Nineteenth Century*, ed. Michael N. Forster, and Kristin Gjesdal (Oxford: Oxford University Press, 2015).

a continuum of aesthetic humanism that runs from the writings of Schiller, Goethe, and Hölderlin right up to the present. This is an ongoing process in the German intellectual tradition, central to which is the capacity for reflection, with historical consciousness thereby becoming a fingerprint of modernism.

Karnes argues that 'a powerful current of optimism ran counter and parallel to the cultural pessimism' described in numerous accounts of *fin-de-siècle* Vienna.[26] This also found expression in Brahms, whose music, whilst grappling with issues central to the human condition, ennobles, edifies, and uplifts. Like Nietzsche, Brahms was sceptical of Schopenhauer's pessimism. Yet, unlike the Vienna Secessionists, he does not embrace a utopian vision. Brahms's kingdom is emphatically of this world, with the ideal content of his music being the product of a human spirit, not a transcendent one.[27] In this way, Brahms merges aesthetics and ethics. He attributes a privileged status to art, not just as a body of works to be revered, but through which we may intuit something greater than our (individual) selves.

---

[26] Karnes, *A Kingdom Not of This World*, 3.

[27] Mark Burford makes precisely this observation of Eduard Hanslick's writings. Mark Burford, 'Hanslick's Idealist Materialism', *19th-Century Music* 30/2 (Fall 2006): 166–81 (171).

# Appendix

## Translation of Theodor Adorno, 'Brahms aktuell' (1934)[1]

In the 'New Music Lexicon' of 1926,[2] which claims to set the standard for the modern epoch and for the production of the recent past, it was said of Brahms: 'For the "modern" he is certainly the least influential of all the masters, which does not in the least derogate his greatness, nor the fulfilment of his historical mission'. The logic of the sentence is apparent, which seems to be prompted by that merry alacrity to award innovation to that which in the long run is even more recent. After all what should the 'fulfilment of the historical mission' mean thirty-odd years after his [Brahms's] death, when at the same time it is said he has no more 'influence'? Nevertheless, it is worthwhile contradicting objectively, not for Brahms's sake, who does not require such defence, but for the sake of the legitimate new music, which is misconstrued and discredited through such theses and can better justify itself the further it is from such hasty attitudes, which are not only thankless but are proven to be more than superficial in the present day.

---

[1] All translations are my own. An earlier version of this translation appears in my 'The Sense of an Ending: Adorno, Brahms, and Music's Return to the Land of Childhood', in *Irish Musical Analysis*, ed. Julian Horton and Gareth Cox (Dublin: Four Courts Press, 2014), 123–6. Before then, this essay had never before been translated into English, however, fragments of it are translated in Margaret Notley, *Lateness and Brahms: Music and Culture in the Twilight of Viennese Liberalism* (Oxford: Oxford University Press, 2007), at 36, 71, and 78, and in Max Paddison, *Adorno's Aesthetics of Music* (Cambridge: Cambridge University Press, 1993), 254. I have consulted these fragments in the process of my own translation and in most cases slightly amended them.

[2] Adorno is likely referring to Alfred Einstein, trans., arr., and ed. A. Eaglefield-Hull, *Das Neue Musiklexikon: Nach dem Dictionary of Modern Music and Musicians* (Berlin, Hesses, 1926).

To begin with, even the *historical* review of the origin of new music cannot justify this thesis. Reger, whom the same journal generously guarantees is the actual historical link between the postclassical, postromantic, and the new music, is utterly unthinkable without Brahms. The revision [*Wiederaufnahme*] of absolute music in the context of the chamber music sonata, the controlled [*Griffen*] piano movement, but more fundamentally than that, however, the technique of the motivic fragmentation of themes, its conversion through the pervasive principle of development, and above all the style of *harmonic* polyphony is unthinkable without Brahms. Even the most radical of all Reger's achievements – making prose by virtue of easing up on metre – is as a result of Brahms's expansions and cuts. Just how much the young Schoenberg owes to [Brahms] can be recognized by a cursory glance at the Lied 'Am Wegrande' from Op. 6, which is already the evolutionary period. It is less well known that Hindemith's first chamber music compositions (up as far as Op. 10) often grapple with Brahms. That should suffice historically; nonetheless, historians could come to the conclusion that Brahms has been 'superseded'. What is the situation now?

Certainly, nobody still writes the burdensome sixths over syncopated triplets; fewer the faithful reprises, particularly in shorter piano pieces, and the Brahmsian 'tone' of laboriously released muteness, the heavy breathing of a more or less unremitting ageing of music, can be recognized as imitation, whenever one attempts it – because it is so profoundly associated with the Brahmsian source, and that also means that his procedure and his tone form such an inextricable union. [Works that attempt to imitate this] no longer appear to be by Brahms to the extent that, to use his own expression, 'any ass can hear'.

His [Brahms's] essence is not so easily recognized, but it is all the more effective as a secret. It can most likely be deduced by mediating on [his] source material. It was the Schumannesque, that melodious homophony, that for the sake of song and harmonic discovery had softened the seriousness of the grand Beethovenian sonata construction by means of subjective expression, and transformed its contrasts into lyrical *Liederspiel* and its tectonic repetitions into the gyrating, obsessive behaviour of the trapped self. After the Schumannian sacrifice, in Brahms the objective spirit of the sonata deliberates upon itself, as it were. Its whole greatness lies in how strictly such mediation commits itself to the place and the hour in which it takes place. The unmediated recourse to Beethoven is not possible in the name of Schumann's subjectivity and its altered musical material; the chromaticism of the New Germans and Chopin, which has still not found its great success in the theatre of the mature Wagner, seems, meanwhile – in the area of sonata form – to be a mere intensification of the Schumann situation. The dynamic way through is not that of Brahms, but also not, or only occasionally, to go backwards: much more it is one of immersion [*Versenkung*]. His [Brahms's] music examines its material – that of the high Romanticism of Schumann – profoundly in its self-motivation [*Selbstgegebenheit*] until it becomes objectified: objectification of the Subject. What is achieved in Wagner through a dynamic tempest is achieved in Brahms through stubborn insistence. His results, however, have a more lasting quality, a lasting quality precisely for the ensuing compositional practice: the less they stick to the exterior surface of the sound phenomenon, the less they are exposed to wear and tear as a kind of 'stimulus'.

[The] exact analysis [of Brahms's music] would be a significant art-theoretical matter; certainly no less so than Bruckner's. If we are to confine ourselves to catchwords: the harmonic discoveries of Schumann were dissolved from their expressive isolation, and the harmonic structure then determined anew according to them; they [the harmonic discoveries] form autonomous scale steps, which in turn make the meaningful, chordal, distribution of balance [*Gleichgewichtsverteilung*] capable of lengthy expansion and, nevertheless, keep that subjectively developed wealth of the 'classical' scheme of subdominant, dominant, and tonic.

Beethoven's symphonic terse style [*Lapidarstil*], with its sequencing of exactly maintained motives (the first movement of the fifth), is as little compatible with such harmonic awareness as is the Wagnerian chromatic sequence: instead, Beethoven's specific developmental technique is further constructed and increased to an art of variation [*Kunst der Variation*], which in the exposition and development sections creates something unremittingly new from the old or familiar, without permitting a 'free', constructively coincidental note.

This speaks to an art of economical fragmentation of themes into the smallest motives, which as a consequence of the sonata is developed similar to that of Wagner from the confines of the dramatic, terse characterization, without sacrificing the formative theme as material medium between motive and large-scale form. It is a magnificent, uncomfortable *absence of naïveté – a reflective posture* [Adorno's emphasis] of composition in today's heightened material consciousness that Brahms commands, in decided contrast to Bruckner, and whose particular musical *epistemological* character of a healing art is proved healthy only if the painful romantic drive for affect is dead.

The regeneration and reconstruction of the sonata remains to this day an idea that is still unresolved. In the incomparable first movement of Brahms's Fourth Symphony, it is formulated most precisely.

The situation with current music, however, and the problematic history of its best representatives, makes the resumption of Brahmsian intentions impossible to refuse. It follows that our dissonances do not appear to be a stimulus or the expression of a chaotic condition of the soul, but rather merely to be new musical *material*; after the resort to the neoclassical became too short and foreign to the material [*materialfremd*], those categories of musical consciousness that Brahms developed from the material, and which, undiscovered until today, even transcend it, are long overdue. The stages of Brahmsian thought provide the foundation for all legitimate composition in rows; its reserved, modifying dynamics are a corrective to the imitated stiffness; the economy of its art of variation forcefully teaches the economy of the procedure for the material involved; and the necessary reorganization of large form in Brahms's best works is – it must be emphasized – still to be carried out. It could easily come to pass that one will find the substance of the new music precisely in the fulfilment of those Brahmsian postulates – which could be related to certain theories of the late Hölderlin – while the disconcerting sounds will triumph as necessary, indeed, as mere accidents of their implicitness (matter-of-course).

Even if Brahms's tone is always without 'influence', what is this obvious influence in art? It has established *laws* whose obligatory exactitude competes with its waiting latency. The time will come when future Brahmsian performances that realize the laws (constructive principles), and not the academic heritage or the autumnal colours, will be uncovered, just as they have been so fruitful up to now.

# Bibliography

Abrams, M. H. *Natural Supernaturalism: Tradition and Revolution in Romantic Literature*. New York, NY and London: Norton, 1971.

'Rationality and Imagination in Cultural History: A Reply to Wayne Booth', *Critical Inquiry* 2/3 (1976): 447–64.

Adorno, Theodor W. *Beethoven: The Philosophy of Music*. Translated by Edmund Jephcott. Cambridge: Polity Press, 1998.

*Mahler: A Musical Physiognomy*. Translated by Edmund Jephcott. Chicago, IL and London: University of Chicago Press, 1992.

*Aesthetic Theory*. Translated by Robert Hullot-Kentor. London: Continuum, 1997.

*Gesammelte Schriften: Musikalische Schriften V*. Edited by Rolf Tiedemann and Klaus Schutz. Frankfurt am Main: Suhrkamp Verlag, 1984.

*Noten zur Literatur*. Frankfurt am Main: Suhrkamp, 1974.

*Notes to Literature*. Edited by Rolf Tiedemann. Translated by Shierry Weber Nicholsen. 2 vols. New York, NY: Columbia University Press, 1992.

*Philosophy of New Music*. Translated by Robert Hullot-Kentor. Minneapolis, MN and London: University of Minnesota Press, 2006.

*Prisms*. Translated by Samuel and Shierry Weber. Cambridge, MA: MIT Press, 1981.

'Zum Problem der musikalischen Analyse', *Frankfurter Adorno-Blätter* 7 (2001): 73–90.

Adorno, Theodor W. and Susan Gillespie. 'Music, Language, and Composition', *Musical Quarterly* 77/3 (1993): 401–14.

Adorno, Theodor W. and Max Paddison. 'On the Problem of Musical Analysis', *Music Analysis* 1/2 (1982): 169–87.

Agawu, Kofi. *Playing with Signs: A Semiotic Interpretation of Classical Music*. Princeton, NJ: Princeton University Press, 1991.

Allgeyer, Julius. 'Anselm Feuerbach', *Österreichische Wochenschrift für Wissenschaft und Kunst* (1872): 641–652.

*Anselm Feuerbach: Sein Leben und Kunst, mit Selbstbildnis des Künstlers*. Bamberg: Buchner, 1894. Rev. edn Berlin and Stuttgart: Neumann, 1904.

Anzengruber, Ludwig and Peter Rosegger. *Peter Rosegger/Ludwig Anzengruber Briefwechsel: 1871–1889*. Edited by Konstanze Fliedl and Karl Wagner. Vienna, Cologne, et al.: Bölhau, 1995.

Aschheim, Steven. *The Nietzsche Legacy in Germany, 1890–1990*. Berkeley, CA: University of California Press, 1994.

Babich, Babette. *Words in Blood, Like Flowers: Philosophy and Poetry, Music and Eros, in Hölderlin, Nietzsche, and Heidegger*. Albany, NY: State University of New York, 2006.

Bacht, Nikolaus, ed. *Music, Theatre, and Politics in Germany: 1848 to the Third Reich*. Aldershot: Ashgate, 2006.

Badiou, Alain. *Five Lessons on Wagner*. Translated by Susan Spitzer with an afterword by Slavoj Žižek. London and New York, NY: Verso, 2010.

Balfour, Ian. *The Rhetoric of Romantic Poetry*. Stanford, CA: Stanford University Press, 2002.

Barham, Jeremy. *The Cambridge Companion to Mahler*. Cambridge: Cambridge University Press, 2007.

Bauer, Amy. *Ligeti's Laments: Nostalgia, Exoticism, and the Absolute*. Aldershot: Ashgate, 2011.

Behler, Constantin. *Nostalgic Teleology: Friedrich Schiller and the Schemata of Aesthetic Humanism*. Bern and New York, NY: Peter Lang, 1995.

Beiser, Frederick C, ed. *The Cambridge Companion to Hegel and Nineteenth-Century Philosophy*. Cambridge: Cambridge University Press, 2008.

Beller-McKenna, Daniel. 'The Great Warum? Job, Christ, and Bach in a Brahms Motet', *19th-Century Music* 19/3 (1996): 231–51.

'How "deutsch" a Requiem? Absolute Music, Universality, and the Reception of Brahms's *Ein deutsches Requiem* Op. 45', *19th-Century Music* 22/1 (1998): 3–19.

'Reconsidering the Identity of an Orchestral Sketch by Brahms', *Journal of Musicology* 13/4 (1998): 508–37.

*Brahms and the German Spirit*. Cambridge, MA: Harvard University Press, 2004.

Billington, James. *The Icon and The Axe: An Interpretive History of Russian Culture*. London: Vintage, 1970.

Boyd, Malcolm. 'Brahms and the *Four Serious Songs*', *Musical Times* 108/1493 (1967): 593–95.

Bobéth, Marek. *Herman Goetz: Leben und Werk*. Winterthur: Amadeus Verlag, 1995.

Botstein, Leon. 'Brahms and Nineteenth-Century Painting', *19th-Century Music* 14/2 (1990): 154–68.

Bove, Cheryl K. *Understanding Iris Murdoch*. Columbia, SC: University of South Carolina Press, 1993.

Bowie, Andrew. *Aesthetics and Subjectivity from Kant to Nietzsche*. Manchester and New York, NY: Manchester University Press, 2003.

*Music, Philosophy and Modernity*. Cambridge: Cambridge University Press, 2007.

*Adorno and the Ends of Philosophy*. Cambridge: Polity Press, 2013.

Boym, Svetlana. *The Future of Nostalgia*. New York, NY: Basic Books, 2001.

Bozarth, George. 'Paths Not Taken: The "Lost" Works of Johannes Brahms', *Music Review* 50 (1989): 185–205.

Bozarth, George, ed. *Brahms Studies: Analytical and Historical Perspectives*. Oxford: Oxford University Press, 1989.

Brachmann, Jan. '*Ins Ungewisse hinauf*: *Johannes Brahms und Max Klinger im Zwiespalt von Kunst und Kommunikation*. Kassel: Bärenreiter, 1999.

*Kunst, Religion, Krise: Der Fall Brahms*. Kassel et al.: Bärenreiter, 2003.

Brahms, Johannes. *Johannes Brahms im Briefwechsel mit Heinrich und Elisabet von Herzogenberg*. Edited by Max Kalbeck. Berlin: Deutsche Brahms-Gesellschaft, 1908.

*Johannes Brahms: The Herzogenberg Correspondence*. Edited by Max Kalbeck. Translated by Hannah Byrant. London: Murray, 1909.

*Billroth und Brahms im Briefwechsel*. Edited by Otto Gottlieb-Billroth. Berlin and Vienna: Urban & Schwarzenberg, 1935.

*Johannes Brahms im Briefwechsel mit Hermann Levi, Friedrich Gernsheim, sowie den Familien Hecht und Fellinger*. Tutzing: Hans Schneider, 1974.

*Johannes Brahms im Briefwechsel mit Karl Reinthaler, Max Bruch, Hermann Deiters, Friedr. Heimsoeth, Karl Reinecke, Ernst Rudorff, Bernhard und Luise Scholz*. Edited by Wilhelm Altmann. Tutzing: Hans Schneider, 1974.

*Johannes Brahms Briefe an P. J. Simrock und Fritz Simrock*. 4 vols. Tutzing: Hans Schneider, 1974.

*Brahms & Billroth: Letters from a Musical Friendship*. Translated by Hans Barkan. New York, NY: Greenwood, 1977.

*Johannes Brahms: A Life in Letters*. Edited by Styra Avins. Translated by Josef Eisinger. Oxford: Oxford University Press, 2001.

*The Brahms Notebooks: The Little Treasure Chest of the Young Kreisler*. Edited by Carl Krebs. Translated by Agnes Eisenberger. Annotated by Siegmund Levarie. New York, NY: Pendragon, 2003.

Brinkmann, Reinhold. *Late Idyll: The Second Symphony of Johannes Brahms*. Translated by Peter Palmer. Cambridge, MA: Harvard University Press, 1995.

*Vom Pfeifen und von alten Dampfmaschine: Essays zur Musik von Beethoven bis Rihm*. Munich: Paul Szolnay Verlag, 2006.

Brodbeck, David. 'On Some Enigmas Surrounding a Canon by Brahms', *Journal of Musicology* 20/1 (2003): 73–103.

Brodbeck, David, ed. *Brahms Studies, Vol. i*. Lincoln, NE: University of Nebraska Press, 1994.

*Brahms Studies, Vol. ii*. Lincoln, NE: University of Nebraska Press, 2001.

Brown, Gregory W. 'Firm Footing in the Heavens and Faltering Steps on Earth: Harmonic Language and Structure as Word Painting in Johannes Brahms's *Gesang der Parzen*', *The Choral Scholar: The Online Journal of the National Collegiate Choral Organization* 2/1 (2010): 17–24.

Burckhardt, Jacob. *Die Cultur der Renaissance in Italien: Ein Versuch. 3rd edn.* Edited by Ludwig Geiger. Leipzig: E. A. Seemann, 1877/8.

Burckhardt, Sigurd, ed. *The Drama of Language: Essays on Goethe and Kleist.* Baltimore, MD and London: Johns Hopkins University Press, 1970.

Burford, Mark. "'The Real Idealism of History": Historical Consciousness, Commemoration, and Brahms's "Years of Study"'. Unpublished PhD dissertation, Columbia University (2005).

Burkholder, Peter J. 'Brahms and Twentieth-Century Classical Music', *19th-Century Music* 8/1 (1984): 75–83.

Burnham, Scott. 'Between *Schicksalslied* and Seligkeit: Morality as Music in Brahms'. Keynote lecture delivered at the conference 'Brahms in the New Century', 21–23 March 2012, Graduate Centre, City University, New York, NY.

Burnham, Scott and Michael Steinberg, eds. *Beethoven and His World.* Princeton, NJ: Princeton University Press, 2000.

Byrne, Lorraine, ed. *Goethe: Musical Poet, Musical Catalyst.* Dublin: Carysfort Press, 2004.

Carter, Tim and John Butt, eds. *The Cambridge History of Seventeenth-Century Music.* Cambridge: Cambridge University Press. 2005.

Chua, Daniel. 'Believing in Beethoven', *Music Analysis* 19/3 (2000): 409–21.

Clive, Peter. *Brahms and His World: A Biographical Dictionary.* New York, NY: Scarecrow Press, 2006.

Comini, Alessandra. *The Changing Image of Beethoven: A Study in Mythmaking.* Santa Fe, NM: Sunstone Press, 2008.

Cosgrove, Mary and Anna Richards, eds. *Sadness and Melancholy in German-Language Literature and Culture. Edinburgh German Yearbook.* Rochester, NY: Camden House, 2011.

Cross, Jonathan. *The Stravinsky Legacy.* Cambridge: Cambridge University Press, 2000.

Dahlhaus, Carl. *Between Romanticism and Modernism: Four Studies in the Music of the Later Nineteenth Century.* Translated by Mary Whittall and Arnold Whittall. Berkeley, CA and London: University of California Press, 1980.

*Nineteenth-Century Music.* Translated by J. Bradford Robinson. Berkeley, CA and London: University of California Press, 1989.

*Ludwig van Beethoven: Approaches to his Music.* Translated by Mary Whittall. Oxford: Clarendon Press, 1991.

Danuser, Hermann. *Die Musik des 20. Jahrhunderts. Neues Handbuch der Musikwissenschaft, Band VII.* Laaber: Laaber Verlag, 1984.

Danuser, Hermann, ed. *Neue Musik im politischem Wandel.* Veröffentlichungen des Instituts für Neue Musik und Musikerziehung. Darmstadt: Schott, 1991.

Daverio, John. 'The "Wechsel der Töne" in Brahms's *Schicksalslied*', *Journal of the American Musicological Society* 46/1 (1993): 84–113.

Dell'Antonio, Andrew, ed. *Beyond Structural Listening*. Berkeley, CA and London: University of California Press, 2004.

Deterding, Klaus, ed. *Wahrnehmungen im poetischen All: Festschrift für Alfred Behrmann*. Heidelberg: Winter, 1993.

Dietrich, Albert. *Erinnerungen an Johannes Brahms in Briefen besonders aus seiner Jugendzeit*. Leipzig: O. Wigand, 1898.

Dove, Patrick. *The Catastrophe of Modernity: Tragedy and the Nation in Latin American Literature*. Lewisburg, PA: Bucknell University Press, 2004.

Eldridge, Richard. *The Oxford Handbook of Philosophy and Literature*. Oxford: Oxford University Press, 2009.

Fehl, P. P. *Decorum and Wit: The Poetry of Venetian Painting: Essays in the History of the Classical Tradition*. Vienna: Irsa Verlag, 1992.

Fisk, Charles. *Returning Cycles: Contexts for the Interpretation of Schubert's Impromptus and Last Sonatas*. Berkeley, CA: University of California Press, 2001.

Floros, Constantin. *Johannes Brahms, 'Free but Alone': A Life for a Poetic Music*. Translated by Ernest Bernhardt-Kabisch. Frankfurt am Main: Peter Lang, 2010.

Forster, Leonard., ed. *Penguin Book of German Verse*. Reprinted and with revisions. Harmondsworth: Penguin Books, 1959.

Forster, Michael N. and Kristin Gjesdal, eds. *The Oxford Handbook of German Philosophy in the Nineteenth Century*. Oxford: Oxford University Press, 2015.

Foster, John Burt. 'Review of Svetlana Boym: The Future of Nostalgia', *Modern Language Quarterly*, 64/4 (2003): 513–17.

Frank, Mitchell B. 'Painterly Thought: Max Liebermann and the Idea of Art', *Racar* 37/2 (2012): 47–59.

Frisch, Walter. *Brahms and the Principle of Developing Variation*. Berkeley and Los Angeles, CA: University of California Press, 1984.

   '"You Must Remember This": Memory and Structure in Schubert's String Quartet in G Major, D. 887', *Musical Quarterly* 84/4 (Winter 2000): 582–603.

   *Brahms: The Four Symphonies*. New Haven, CT and London: Yale University Press, 2003.

   *German Modernism: Music and the Arts*. Berkeley and Los Angeles, CA: University of California Press, 2005.

Frisch, Walter and Kevin C. Karnes, eds. *Brahms and His World*. Princeton, NJ: Princeton University Press, 2007.

Fuchs, Ingrid, ed. *Intentionaler Brahms-Kongress Gmunden 1997: Kongreßbericht*. Tutzing: Hans Schneider, 2001.

Geiringer, Karl. *Johannes Brahms: Leben und Schaffen eines deutschen Meister*. Vienna: Rudolf M. R. Ohrer, 1935.

   *Brahms: His Life and Work*. 3rd edn. New York, NY: Da Capo, 1981.

   *On Brahms and His Circle*. Revised and enlarged by George Bozarth. Sterling Heights, MI: Sterling Heights Press, 2006.

Gillespie, Susan. 'Translating Adorno: Language, Music, and Performance', *Musical Quarterly* 79/1 (1995): 55–65.

Gilliam, Bryan, ed. *Richard Strauss: New Perspectives on the Composer and His Work*. Durham, NC and London: Duke University Press, 1992.

Goethe, Johann Wolfgang van. *Correspondence between Schiller and Goethe from 1794 to 1805*. Trans. George H. Calvert, 2 vols. New York, NY and London: Wiley and Putnam, 1845.

*Briefwechsel zwischen Schiller und Goethe in den Jahren 1794 bis 1805*. 2 vols. Stuttgart and Augsburg: J. G. Cotta'scher Verlag, 1856.

*Wilhelm Meister's Apprenticeship and Travels*. Translated by Thomas Carlyle. Boston, MA: Ticknor and Fields, 1865.

*Italian Journey [1786–1788]*. Translated by W. H. Auden and Elizabeth Mayer. London: Penguin, 1962.

*Iphigenie in Tauris: Ein Schauspiel/Iphigenie auf Tauris: A Play*. Translated by Anna Swanwick. Wolf Pup Books, n. d.

Goltz, Maren, Wolfgang Sandberger, and Christiane Wiesenfeldt, eds. *Spätphase(n)? Johannes Brahms's Werke in der 1880er und 1890er Jahre: Internationales Musikwissenschaftliches Symposium, Meiningen 2008*. Munich: Henle, 2010.

Griffith, Mark and Donald J. Mastronarde, ed. *Cabinet of the Muses: Essays on Classical and Comparative Literature in Honour of Thomas G. Rosenmeyer*. Atlanta, GA: Scholars Press, 1990.

Grimes, Nicole. 'The Schoenberg/Brahms Critical Tradition Reconsidered', *Music Analysis* 31/2 (2012).

Grimes, Nicole and Dillon Parmer. '"Come Rise to Higher Spheres!" Tradition Transcended in Brahms Violin Sonata No. 1 in G Major, Op. 78', *Ad Parnassum: A Journal of Eighteenth- and Nineteenth-Century Instrumental Music* 6/11 (2009): 129–52.

Grimes, Nicole, Siobhán Donovan, and Wolfgang Marx, eds. *Rethinking Hanslick: Music, Formalism, and Expression*. Rochester, NY: University of Rochester Press, 2013.

Hall, Edith. *Adventures with Iphigenia in Tauris: A Cultural History of Euripides' Black Sea Tragedy*. Oxford: Oxford University Press, 2013.

Hamilton, Katy and Natasha Loges, eds. *Brahms in the Home and the Concert Hall: Between Private and Public Performance*. Cambridge: Cambridge University Press, 2014.

Hancock, Virginia. *Brahms's Choral Compositions and His Library of Early Music*. Ann Arbor, MI: UMI Research Press, 1983.

Hanslick, Eduard. *Concerte, Componisten und Virtuosen der letzten fünfzehn Jahre, 1870–1885: Kritiken*. Berlin: Allgemeiner Verein für Deutsche Literatur, 1886.

*Aus meinem Leben*. 2 vols. Berlin: Allgemeiner Verein für Deutsche Litteratur, 1894.

*Sämtliche Schriften: historisch-kritische Ausgabe. Aufsätze und Rezensionen 1844–1848*. Edited by Dietmar Strauß, 7 vols. Vienna: Böhlau, 1993.

Harper-Scott, J. P. E. *Edward Elgar: Modernist*. Cambridge: Cambridge University Press, 2006.

———. *The Quilting Points of Musical Modernism: Revolution, Reaction, and William Walton*. Cambridge: Cambridge University Press, 2012.

Hegel, Georg Wilhelm Friedrich. *Phänomenologie des Geistes*. Edited by Johannes Hoffmeister. Hamburg: Meiner Felix Verlag, 1987.

———. *Werke*. Edited by Eva Moldenhauer and Karl Markus Michel, 3 vols. Frankfurt am Main: Suhrkamp, 1986.

Heidegger, Martin. *Erläuterungen zu Hölderlin's Dichtung*. Frankfurt am Main: V. Klostermann, 1951.

Heilmann, Christoph, ed. *'In uns selbst liegt Italien': Die Kunst der Deutsch-Römer*. Munich: Hirmer Verlag, 1987.

Heister, Hanns-Werner, ed. *Johannes Brahms oder die Relativierung der 'absoluten' Musik*. Hamburg: Von Bockel Verlag, 1997.

Heller, Erich. *The Disinherited Mind: Essays in Modern German Literature and Thought*. Harmondsworth: Penguin, 1961.

Henrich, Dieter. *The Course of Remembrance and Other Essays on Hölderlin*. Stanford, CA: Stanford University Press, 1997.

Hepokoski, James. *Sibelius, Symphony No. 5*. Cambridge: Cambridge University Press, 1993.

———. 'The Medial Caesura and Its Role in the Eighteenth-Century Sonata Exposition', *Music Theory Spectrum* 19/2 (1997): 115–54.

———. 'Beyond the Sonata Principle', *Journal of the American Musicological Society* 55/1 (2002): 91–154.

———. '"Back and Forth from Egmont: Beethoven, Mozart, and the Non-Resolving Recapitulation', *19th-Century Music* 25/2–3 (2002): 127–54.

Hepokoski, James and Warren Darcy. *Elements of Sonata Theory: Norms, Types, and Deformations in the Late-Eighteenth-Century Sonata*. Oxford and New York, NY: Oxford University Press, 2006.

Hermand, Jost and Gerhard Richter, eds. *Sound Figures of Modernity: German Music and Philosophy*. Madison, WI: University of Wisconsin Press, 2006.

Heuberger, Richard. *Erinnerungen an Johannes Brahms*. Edited by Kurt Hofmann. Tutzing: Hans Schneider, 1976.

Hilliard, K. F. '"Nänie": Critical Reflections on the Sentimental in Poetry', *Publications of the English Goethe Society* 75/1 (2006): 3–13.

Hirsch, Marjorie. *Romantic Lieder and the Search for Lost Paradise*. Cambridge: Cambridge University Press, 2007.

Hofmann, Kurt. *Die Bibliothek von Johannes Brahms*. Hamburg: Wagner, 1974.

Hölderlin, Friedrich. *Sämmtliche Werke*. Edited by Christoph Theodor Schwab, 2 vols. Stuttgart & Tübingen: J. G. Cotta'scher Verlag, 1846.

———. *Sämmtliche Werke*. Edited by Friedrich Beißner, 3 vols. Stuttgart: Kohlhammer, 1943–85.

*Hyperion or The Hermit in Greece*. Translated by Willard R. Trask. New York, NY: Frederick Ungar Publishing Co., 1965.

*Selected Poems and Fragments*. Translated by Michael Hamburger. Edited by Jeremy Adler. London: Penguin, 1998.

*Friedrich Hölderlin: Essays and Letters*. Edited, translated, and with an introduction by Jeremy Adler and Charlie Louth. London: Penguin, 2009.

Homer. *Homers Odysee*. Translated by Johann Heinrich Voß. Reprint of the first edition from 1781 with an introduction by Michael Bernays. Stuttgart: J. G. Cotta'schen Buchhandlung, 1881.

*The Odyssey*. Translated by Robert Fagles. Introduction and notes by Bernard Knox. London: Penguin, 1997.

Horkheimer, Max and Theodor W. Adorno. *Dialektik der Aufklärung: Philosophische Fragmente*. Frankfurt am Main: Fischer-Taschenbuch-Verlag, 1944.

*Dialectic of Enlightenment: Philosophical Fragment*. Translated by Edmund Jephcott. Stanford, CA: Stanford University Press, 2002.

Horstmann, *Untersuchungen zur Brahms-Rezeption der Jahre 1860–1880*. Berlin: Wagner, 1986.

Horton, Julian. 'Brahms, Bruckner and the Concept of Thematic Process', in *Irish Musical Analysis* (Dublin: Four Courts Press, 2014), 78–105.

*Brahms' Piano Concerto No. 2, Op. 83: Analytical and Contextual Studies*. Leuven: Peeters, 2017.

Huhn, Tom. *Cambridge Companion to Adorno*. Cambridge: Cambridge University Press, 2004.

Jackson, Timothy. 'The Tragic Reversed Recapitulation in the German Classical Tradition', *Journal of Music Theory* 40/1 (1996): 61–111.

Jacobsen, Christiane, ed. *Johannes Brahms: Leben und Werke*. Wiesbaden: Breitkopf & Härtel, 1983.

John, James A. 'Johannes Brahms's *Nänie*, Op. 82: A Study in Context and Content'. DMA Dissertation, Eastman School of Music (2001).

Johnson, Julian. 'Analysis in Adorno's Aesthetics of Music', *Music Analysis* 14 (1995): 295–313.

*Webern and the Transformation of Nature*. Cambridge: Cambridge University Press, 1999.

Judson, Pieter. *Exclusive Revolutionaries: Liberal Politics, Social Experience, and National Identity in the Austrian Empire, 1848–1914*. Ann Arbor, MI: University of Michigan Press, 1996.

Kaiser, Gerhard. *Vergötterung und Tod: Die thematische Einheit von Schillers Werk*. Stuttgart: J. B. Metzlersche Verlagsbuchhandlung, 1967.

Kalbeck, Max. *Johannes Brahms*. 4 vols. Berlin: Deutsche Brahms-Gesellschaft, 1909.

Kant, Immanuel. *Political Writings*. Edited by H. S. Reiss. Cambridge: Cambridge University Press, 1991.

Karnes, Kevin C. *A Kingdom Not of This World: Wagner, the Arts, and Utopian Visions in Fin-de-Siècle Vienna*. Oxford: Oxford University Press, 2013.

Kaufmann, Walter. *Nietzsche: Philosopher, Psychologist, Antichrist*. Princeton, NJ: Princeton University Press, 1974.

Kerman, Joseph. '*An die ferne Geliebte*', in Alan Tyson, ed. *Beethoven Studies*. New York, NY: Norton, 1973.

Kern-Holoman, D., ed. *The Nineteenth-Century Symphony*. New York, NY and London: Schirmer, 1997.

Kindermann, William and Harald Krebs, eds. *The Second Practice of Nineteenth-Century Tonality*. Lincoln, NE and London: University of Nebraska Press, 1996.

Kivy, Peter. *Introduction to a Philosophy of Music*. Oxford: Clarendon Press, 2002.
*Sounding Off: Eleven Essays in the Philosophy of Music*. Oxford: Oxford University Press, 2012.

Kohn, Ben and George Bozarth. 'New Evidence of the Genesis of Brahms's G Major Violin Sonata, Op. 78', *American Brahms Society Newsletter* 9/1 (1991): 5–6.

Kok, Roe-Min and Laura Tunbridge, eds. *Rethinking Schumann*. Oxford: Oxford University Press, 2011.

Kopiez, Reinhard. *Musikwissenschaft zwischen Kunst, Ästhetik und Experiment*. Würzburg: Königshausen & Neumann, 1998.

Korsyn, Kevin. 'Brahms Research and Aesthetic Ideology', *Music Analysis* 12/1 (1993): 89–103.

Krebs, Harald. 'Alternatives to Monotonality in Early Nineteenth-Century Music', *Journal of Music Theory* 25/1 (1981): 1–16.

Krell, David Farrell. *The Tragic Absolute: German Idealism and the Languishing of God*. Bloomington, IN: Indiana University Press, 2005.

Kretzschmar, Hermann. 'Neue Werke von J. Brahms', *Musikalisches Wochenblatt* 7 (1874): 95–7; 9 (1874): 107–11.

Kreuzhage, Eduard. *Hermann Goetz: Sein Leben und seine Werke*. Leipzig: Breitkopf & Härtel, 1916.

Kross, Siegfried. *Die Chorwerke von Johannes Brahms*. Berlin: Max Hesses Verlag, 1963.

Kuzniar, Alice A. *Delayed Endings: Nonclosure in Novalis and Hölderlin*. Athens, GA: University of Georgia Press, 2008.

Lewis, Charles. 'Hölderlin and the Möbius Strip: The One-Sided Surface and the "Wechsel der Töne"', *Oxford German Studies* 38/1 (2009): 45–60.

Litzmann, Berthold. *Clara Schumann–Johannes Brahms: Briefe aus den Jahren 1853–1896*. 2 vols. Leipzig, 1927.

Lockwood, Lewis. *Beethoven: The Music and the Life*. New York, NY: Norton, 2003.

Lockwood, Lewis and Mark Kroll, eds. *The Beethoven Violin Sonatas: History, Criticism, Performance*. Urbana and Chicago, IL: University of Illinois Press, 2004.

Lockwood, Lewis and James Webster, eds. *Beethoven Forum* ii. Lincoln, NE and London: University of Nebraska Press, 1993.

Loges, Natasha. 'Exoticism, Artifice and the Supernatural in the Brahmsian Lied', *Nineteenth-Century Music Review* 3/2 (2006): 137–68.

*Brahms and His Poets*. Rochester, NY: Boydell and Brewer, 2017.

Luft, David S. *Eros and Inwardness in Vienna: Weininger, Musil, Doderer*. Chicago, IL: University of Chicago Press, 2003.

MacDonald, Malcolm. *Brahms*. New York, NY: Schirmer, 1990.

Mak, Su Yin. 'Schubert as Schiller's Sentimental Poet', *Eighteenth-Century Music* 4/2 (2007): 251–63.

Malin, Yonatan. 'Metric Displacement, Dissonance and Romantic Longing in the German Lied', *Music Analysis* 25/3 (2006): 251–88.

Marsh, Roger. '"A Multicoloured Alphabet": Rediscovering Albert Giraud's *Pierrot Lunaire*', *Twentieth-Century Music* 4/1 (2007): 97–121.

Marston, Nicholas. *Schumann: Fantasie, Op. 17*. Cambridge: Cambridge University Press, 1992.

'Schubert's Homecoming', *Journal of the Royal Musical Association* 125/2 (2000): 248–70.

Martinson, Steven D., ed. *A Companion to the Works of Friedrich Schiller*. Rochester, NY: Camden House, 2005.

Mauro, Rosemarie P. 'The Gesang der Parzen of Goethe and Brahms: A Study in Synthesis and Interpretation'. Unpublished MA thesis, University of Washington, 1986.

McClelland, Ryan. 'Metric Dissonance in Brahms's Piano Trio in C Minor, Op. 101', *Intégral* 20 (2006): 1–42.

McCorkle, Margit. *Johannes Brahms: Thematisch-bibliographisches Werkverzeichnis*. Edited by Margit McCorkle and Donald McCorkle. Munich: Henle, 1984.

McGeary, Thomas. 'Schoenberg's Brahms Lecture', *Journal of the Arnold Schoenberg Institute* 15/2 (1992): 5–99.

McGrath, William J. *Dionysian Art and Populist Politics in Austria*. New Haven, CT: Yale University Press, 1974.

McManus, Laurie. 'The Rhetoric of Sexuality in the Age of Brahms and Wagner'. Unpublished PhD dissertation, University of North Carolina (2011).

McMullan, Gordon and Sam Smiles. *Late Style and Its Discontents: Essays in Art, Literature, and Music*. Oxford: Oxford University Press, 2016.

Meiner, Carsten and Kristin Veel, eds. *The Cultural Life of Catastrophes and Crisis*. Berlin: de Gruyter, 2012.

Miller, Elaine P. *The Vegetative Soul: From Philosophy of Nature to Subjectivity in the Feminine*. Albany, NY: State University of New York Press, 2002.

Minden, Michael. *The German Bildungsroman: Incest and Inheritance*. Cambridge: Cambridge University Press, 1997.

Minor, Ryan. *Choral Fantasies: Music, Festivities, and Nationhood in Nineteenth-Century Germany*. Cambridge and New York, NY: Cambridge University Press, 2012.

Mirka, Danuta, ed. *The Oxford Handbook of Topic Theory*. Oxford: Oxford University Press, 2014.

Monahan, Seth. '"Inescapable" Coherence and the Failure of the Novel-Symphony in the Finale of Mahler's Sixth', *19th-Century Music* 31/1 (2007): 53–95.

*Mahler's Symphonic Sonatas*. Oxford: Oxford University Press, 2015.

Moran, Dermot. *Husserl's Crisis of European Sciences and Transcendental Phenomenology: An Introduction*. Cambridge: Cambridge University Press, 2012.

Müller, Günther. *Morphologische Poetik: Gesammelte Aufsätze*. Edited by Elena Müller. Tübingen: Max Niemeier Verlag, 1968.

Musgrave, Michael. *The Music of Brahms*. Oxford: Clarendon Press, 1985.

'Review of Reinhold Brinkmann', *Late Idyll: The Second Symphony of Johannes Brahms*, in *Music and Letters* 80/3 (1999): 465–9.

Musgrave, Michael, ed. *The Cambridge Companion to Brahms*. Cambridge: Cambridge University Press, 1999.

Musgrave, Michael and Bernard D. Sherman, eds. *Performing Brahms: Early Evidence of Performance Style*. Cambridge: Cambridge University Press, 2003.

Muther, Richard. *The History of Modern Painting*. London: Henry & Co., 1896.

Nelson, Thomas K. 'Klinger's *Brahmsphantasie* and the Cultural Politics of Absolute Music', *Art History* 19/1 (1996): 26–43.

Niekerk, Carl. *Reading Mahler: German Culture and Jewish Identity in Fin-de Siècle Vienna*. Rochester, NY: University of Rochester Press, 2010.

Nielinger-Vakil, Carola. 'Quiet Revolutions: Hölderlin Fragments by Luigi Nono and Wolfgang Rihm', *Music and Letters* 81/2 (2000): 245–74.

Niemann, Walter. 'Brahms' *Gesang der Parzen*', *Zeitschrift für Musik* 89/7 (1922): 156–60.

*Brahms*. Translated by Catherine Alison Phillips. New York, NY: Tudor Publishing Company, 1937.

Nietzsche, Friedrich. *Der Fall Wagner. Götzen-Dämmerung. Nietzsche contra Wagner. Der Antichrist. Gedichte*. Leipzig: Druck und Verlag von C. G. Naumann, 1895.

*The Birth of Tragedy* and *The Case of Wagner*. Translated by Walter Kaufmann. New York, NY: Vintage, 1967.

*Twilight of the Idols and The Antichrist*. Translated by R. J. Hollingdale. London: Penguin, 1990.

*Basic Writings of Nietzsche*. New York, NY: Random House, 2000.

Nisbet, H. B., ed. *German Aesthetic and Literary Criticism: Winckelmann, Lessing, Hamann, Herder, Schiller, Goethe*. Cambridge: Cambridge University Press, 1985.

Notley, Margaret. 'Brahms's Chamber Music Summer of 1886: A Study of Opp. 99, 100, 101, and 108'. Unpublished PhD dissertation, Yale University (1992).

'Nineteenth-Century Chamber Music and the Cult of the Classical Adagio', *19th-Century Music* 23/1 (1999): 33–61.

'Plagal Harmony as Other: Asymmetrical Dualism and Instrumental Music by Brahms', *Journal of Musicology* 22/1 (2005): 90–130.

*Lateness and Brahms: Music and Culture in the Twilight of Viennese Liberalism.* Oxford: Oxford University Press, 2007.

Ophüls, Gustav. *Erinnerungen an Johannes Brahms.* Berlin: Verlag der Deutschen Brahms-Gesellschaft, 1921.

'Brahms-Erinnerungen', *Zeitschrift für Musik* 89/7 (1922): 156–60.

*Erinnerungen an Johannes Brahms. Ein Beitrag aus dem Kreis seiner rheinischen Freunde.* Munich: Langewiesche –Brandt, 1983.

Orel, Alfred. *Johannes Brahms und Julius Allgeyer: Ein Künstlerfreundschaft in Briefen.* Tutzing: Hans Schneider, 1964.

Osthoff, Wolfgang, Helen Geyer, and Astrid Stäber, eds. *Schiller und die Musik.* Vienna: Böhlau, 2007.

Paddison, Max. *Adorno's Aesthetics of Music.* Cambridge: Cambridge University Press, 1993.

Papanikolaou, Eftychia. 'Brahms, Böcklin, and the *Gesang der Parzen*', *Music in Art: International Journal for Music Iconography* 30/1–2 (2005): 155–65.

Pape, Walter, ed. *A View in the Rear Mirror: Romantic Aesthetics, Culture, and Science Seen from Today: Festschrift for Frederick Burwick on the Occasion of His Seventieth Birthday.* Trier: Wissenschaftlicher Verlag, 2006.

Parmer, Dillon R. 'Brahms: Song Quotation, and Secret Programs', *19th-Century Music* 19/2 (1995): 161–90.

'Musical Meaning for the Few: Instances of Private Reception in the Music of Brahms', *Current Musicology* 83 (2007): 109–30.

Pascall, Robert, ed. *Brahms: Biographical, Documentary and Analytical Studies.* Cambridge: Cambridge University Press, 1983.

Peattie, Thomas. *Gustav Mahler's Symphonic Landscapes.* Cambridge: Cambridge University Press, 2015.

Peters, Mark. 'Introduction to, and Catalogue of Brahms's Library'. Unpublished Master's Thesis, University of Pittsburgh (1999).

Petersen, Peter. 'Works for Chorus and Orchestra'. Liner Notes for Johannes Brahms, *Werke für Chor und Orchester.* Deutsche Grammophon 449 651-2.

Pippin, Robert R. 'Nietzsche and the Melancholy of Modernity', *Social Research* 66/2 (1999): 495–520.

Plantinga, Leon. *Schumann as Critic.* New Haven, CT: Yale University Press, 1967.

Platt, Heather and Peter H. Smith, eds. *Expressive Intersections in Brahms: Essays in Analysis and Meaning.* Bloomington, IN: Indiana University Press, 2012.

Prawer, S. S. ed. and trans. *The Penguin Book of Lieder.* London: Penguin, 1977.

Preißinger, Cornelia. *Die vier ernsten Gesänge Op. 121: Vokale und instrumentale Gestaltungsprinzipien im Werk von Johannes Brahms.* Frankfurt am Main et al.: Peter Lang, 1993.

Pugh, David. *Dialectic of Love: Platonism in Schiller's Aesthetics.* Montreal & Kingston: McGill-Queen's University Press, 1996.

Puttfarken, Thomas. *Titian and Tragic Painting: Aristotle's Poetics and the Rise of the Modern Artist.* New Haven, CT and London: Yale University Press, 2005.

Reynolds, Christopher. 'A Choral Symphony by Brahms?', *19th-Century Music* 9/1 (1985): 3–25.

'The Representational Impulse in Late Beethoven, I: *An die ferne Geliebte*', *Acta Musicologica* 60/1 (1988): 43–61.

'Brahms Rhapsodizing: The *Alto Rhapsody* and its Expressive Double', *Journal of Musicology* 29/2 (2012): 191–238.

Richter, Simon and Daniel Purdy, eds. *Goethe Yearbook* xv. Rochester, NY: Boydell and Brewer, 2008.

Rihm, Wolfgang. *Offene Enden: Denkbewegung um und durch Musik.* Edited by Ulrich Mosch. Munich: Hanser, 2002.

Rodgers, Stephen. *Form, Program, and Metaphor in the Music of Berlioz.* Cambridge: Cambridge University Press, 2009.

Rosegger, Peter. *Der Gottsucher.* Hamburg: Projekt Gutenberg, 2012.

Rosegger, Peter and Ludwig Anzengruber. *Peter Rosegger/Ludwig Anzengruber Briefwechsel: 1871–1889.* Edited by Konstanze Fliedl and Karl Wagner. Vienna, Cologne et al.: Bölhau, 1995.

Rosen, Charles. *Sonata Forms.* New York, NY and London: Norton, 1988.

*The Romantic Generation.* Cambridge, MA: Harvard University Press, 1995.

Rumph, Stephen. *Beethoven after Napoleon: Political Romanticism in the Late Works.* Berkeley, Los Angeles, CA, and London: University of California Press, 2004.

Russell, Peter. *Johannes Brahms and Klaus Groth: The Biography of a Friendship.* Aldershot: Ashgate, 2006.

Ryan, Lawrence. *Hölderlins 'Hyperion': Exzentrische Bahn und Dichterberuf.* Stuttgart: Kohlhammer, 1965.

*Hölderlins Lehre vom Wechsel der Töne.* Stuttgart: Kohlhammer, 1960.

Sams, Eric. *The Songs of Johannes Brahms.* New Haven, CT and London: Yale University Press, 2000.

Sandberger, Wolfgang, ed. *Ich will euch trösten:* Johannes Brahms, Ein Deutsches Requiem: *Symposium. Ausstellung. Katalog.* Lübeck: Brahms Institut, 2012.

Sattler, Mark. Sleeve Notes to Wolfgang Rihm. *Symphonie 'Nähe fern'.* Luzerner Sinfonieorchester and James Gaffigan. Paris: Harmonia Mundi HMC902153, 2013.

Savage, Robert. *Hölderlin After the Catastrophe: Heidegger–Adorno–Brecht.* London: Camden House, 2008.

Scheffler, Karl. *Deutsche Maler und Zeichner im Neunzehnten Jahrhundert*. Leipzig: Insel-Verlag, 1911.

Schelling, F. W. J. von. *System of Transcendental Idealism*. Translated by Peter Heath with an introduction by Michael Vater. Charlottesville, VA: University Press of Virginia, 1978.

Schelling, F. W. J. von. *Sämmtliche Werke*. Edited by K. F. A. Schelling. Stuttgart and Augsburg: J. G. Cotta'scher Verlag, 1856–64.

Schenker, Heinrich. *Beethoven's Ninth Symphony: A Portrayal of Its Musical Content, with Running Commentary on Performance and Literature As Well*. Translated by John Rothgeb. New Haven, CT: Yale University Press, 1992.

Scher, Peter, ed. *Music and Text: Critical Inquiries*. Cambridge: Cambridge University Press, 1992.

Schiller, Friedrich. *Sämmtliche Werke. Zwölf Bänden in sechs*. Stuttgart und Tübingen: J. G. Cotta'scher Verlag, 1847.

*On the Aesthetic Education of Man: In a Series of Letters*. Edited, translated, and with an introduction by Elizabeth M. Wilkinson and L. A. Willoughby. Oxford: Clarendon Press, 1967.

*Sämmtliche Werke, 7th edn*. Edited by Gerhard Fricke and Herbert G. Göpfert, 5 vols. Darmstadt: Wissenschaftliche Buchgesellschaft, 1984.

Schleiermacher, Friedrich. *Über die Religion: Reden an die Gebildeten unter ihren Verächtern*. Berlin: Unger Verlag, 1799.

*On Religion: Speeches to its Cultured Despisers*. Edited by Richard Crouter. Cambridge: Cambridge University Press, 1996.

Schmalfeldt, Janet. *In the Process of Becoming: Analytical and Philosophical Perspectives on Form in Early Nineteenth-Century Music*. Oxford: Oxford University Press, 2011.

Schmidt, Christian Martin. *Reclams Musikführer Johannes Brahms*. Stuttgart: Reclam, 1994.

Schneider, Helmut. ed. *Deutsche Idyllentheorien im 18. Jahrhundert*. Tübingen: Narr, 1988.

Schnitzler, Günter and Edelgard Spaude, eds. *Intermedialität: Studien zur Wechselwirkung zwischen den Künsten*. Freiburg im Bresigau: Rombach Verlag, 2004.

Schoenberg, Arnold. *Fundamentals of Musical Composition*. London: Faber, 1970.
*Style and Idea*. London: Faber, 1975.
*Structural Functions of Harmony*. London: Faber, 1983.

Schopenhauer, Arthur. *World as Will and Representation*. Translated by E. F. J. Payne, 2 vols. New York, NY: Dover, 1969.

Schorske, Carl E. *Fin-de-siècle Vienna: Politics and Culture*. New York, NY: Alfred Knopf, 1980.

Schubring, Adolf. 'Die Schumann'sche Schule: Schumann und Brahms: Brahms's vierhändige Variationen', *Allgemeine musikalische Zeitung* 3 (1868): 41–2 and 49–51.

Schumann, Robert. 'Neue Bahnen', *Neue Zeitschrift für Musik*, 28 October 1853, 185–6.

Selz, Peter. *German Expressionist Painting*. Berkeley, Los Angeles, CA, and London: University of California Press, 1957.

Sheehan, James J. *Museums in the German Art World: From the End of the Old Regime to the Rise of Modernism*. Oxford: Oxford University Press, 2000.

Silz, Walter. *Hölderlin's* Hyperion: *A Critical Reading*. Philadelphia, PA: University of Pennsylvania Press, 1969.

Smith, Peter. 'Formal Ambiguity and Large-Scale Tonal Structure in Brahms's Sonata-Form Recapitulations'. Unpublished PhD dissertation, Yale University (1992).

*Expressive Forms in Brahms's Instrumental Music: Structure and Meaning in His Werther Quartet*. Bloomington, IN and Indiana: Indiana University Press, 2005.

Sophokles. *Tragödien*. Translated by Gustav Wendt, 2 vols. Stuttgart: Verlag der J. G. Cotta'schen Buchhandlung, 1884.

Speidel, Ludwig. 'Schauspieler', in Ludwig Speidels Schriften. *Vol. IV*. Berlin: Meyer & Jessen, 1911.

Sponheuer, Bernd, Siegfried Oechsle, Friedhelm Krummacher, Helmut Well, eds. *Rezeption als Innovation: Untersuchungen zu einem Grundmodell der europäischen Kompositionsgeschichte–Festschrift für Friedhelm Krummacher zum 65. Geburtstag*. Kassel: Bärenreiter, 2001.

Steinberg, Michael. *Choral Masterworks: A Listener's Guide*. Oxford and New York, NY: Oxford University Press, 2005.

Stekel, Hanns Christian. *Sehnsucht und Distanz: Theologische Aspekte in den wortgebundenen religiösen Kompositionen von Johannes Brahms*. Frankfurt am Main, et al.: Peter Lang, 1997.

Stockhausen, Julia, ed. *Julius Stockhausen: Der Singer des Deutschen Liedes*. Frankfurt am Main: Englert und Schlosser, 1927.

Struck, Michael. 'Revisionsbedürftig: Zur gedruckten Korrespondenz von Johannes Brahms und Clara Schumann: Auswirkungen irrtümlicher oder lückenhafter Überlieferung auf werkgenetische Bestimmungen (mit einem unausgewerteten Brahms-Brief zur Violinsonate Op. 78)', *Die Musikforschung* 41/3 (1988): 235–41.

Subotnik, Rose Rosengard. 'Adorno's Diagnosis of Beethoven's Late Style: Early Symptom of a Fatal Condition', *Journal of the American Musicological Society* 29/2 (1976): 242–75.

'The Historical Structure: Adorno's "French" Model for the Criticism of Nineteenth-Century Music', *19th-Century Music* 2/1 (1978): 36–60.

'The Role of Ideology in the Study of Western Music', *Journal of Musicology* 2/1 (1983): 1–12.

Tadday, Ulrich, ed. *Wolfgang Rihm*. Munich: Richard Boorberg Verlag, 2004.

Taylor, Benedict. *Mendelssohn, Time and Memory: The Romantic Conception of Cyclic Form*. Cambridge: Cambridge University Press, 2011.

*The Melody of Time: Music and Temporality in the Romantic Era*. Oxford: Oxford University Press, 2015.

Thatcher, David. 'Nietzsche and Brahms: A Forgotten Relationship', *Music and Letters* 54/3 (1973): 261–80.

Tovey, Donald Francis. *Essays and Lectures on Music*. Oxford: Oxford University Press, 1949.

Tunbridge, Laura. *Schumann's Late Style*. Cambridge: Cambridge University Press, 2007.

Valdez, Damian. *German Philhellenism: The Pathos of the Historical Imagination from Winckelmann to Goethe*. New York, NY: Palgrave Macmillan, 2014.

Vande Moortele, Steven. *Two-Dimensional Sonata Form: Form and Cycle in Single-Movement Instrumental Works by Liszt, Strauss, Schoenberg, and Zemlinsky*. Leuven: Leuven University Press, 2009.

Vande Moortele, Steven, Julie Pedneault-Deslauriers, and Nathan John Martin, eds. *Formal Functions in Perspective: Essays on Musical Form from Haydn to Adorno*. Rochester, NY: University of Rochester Press, 2013.

Van Rij, Inge. *Brahms's Song Collections*. Cambridge: Cambridge University Press, 2006.

Wagner, Richard. *Richard Wagner's Prose Works*. 4 vols. London: Kegan Paul, 1892.

Webern, Anton. *The Path to the New Music*. Edited by Willi Reich. Translated by Leo Black. Bryn Mawr, PA: Universal Edition, 1975.

Weingartner, Felix. *The Symphony Since Beethoven*. Translated by Maude Barrows Dutton. Boston, MA: Oliver Ditson, 1904.

Widmann, Josef Viktor. 'Nietzsches gefährliches Buch', *Der Bund*, 16 September 1886, 256.

'Nietzsches *Abfall von Wagner*', *Der Bund*, 20–21 November 1888, 321–2.

*Jenseits von Gut und Böse: Schauspiel in drei Aufzügen*. Stuttgart: Cotta, 1893.

'Über Nietzsches "Antichrist"', *Der Bund*, 12 January 1895, 11.

*Recollections of Johannes Brahms*. Translated by Dora E. Hecht. London: Seeley & Co. Limited, 1899.

'Nietzsche's Dangerous Book', translated by Tim Hyde and Lysane Fauvel. *New Nietzsche Studies: The Journal of the Nietzsche Society* 4/1–2 (2000): 195–200.

Widmann, Max. *Josef Viktor Widmann. Ein Lebensbild. Zweite Lebenshälfte*. Leipzig: Hirzer, 1924.

Wilkinson, Elizabeth M. and L. A. Willoughby. *Models of Wholeness: Some Attitudes to Language, Art and Life in the Age of Goethe*. Edited by Jeremy Adler, Martin Swales, and Ann Weaver. Oxford and Bern, et al.: Peter Lang, 2002.

Williams, Alastair. 'Swaying with Schumann: Subjectivity and Tradition in Wolfgang Rihm's 'Fremde-Szenen' I–III and Related Scores', *Music & Letters* 87/3 (2006), 379–97.

Wolfgang, Erich and Morten Solvik, eds. *Mahler im Context: Contextualizing Mahler*. Vienna: Böhlau, 2011.

Yates, W. E. *Theatre in Vienna: A Critical History, 1776–1995*. Cambridge: Cambridge University Press, 2005.

# Index

271